Anne Baker trained as a nurse at Birkenhead General Hospital, but after her marriage went to live in Libya and then in Nigeria. She eventually returned to her native Birkenhead where she worked as a Health Visitor for over ten years. She now lives with her husband on a ninety-acre sheep farm in North Wales. Her previous novels, *Like Father, Like Daughter* and *Paradise Parade*, are also available from Headline.

D0877944

Legacy of Sins

Anne Baker

HEADLINE

First published in 1993
by HEADLINE BOOK PUBLISHING

First published in paperback in 1993
by HEADLINE BOOK PUBLISHING

10

ISBN 0 7472 4219 4

Typeset by Letterpart Limited, Reigate, Surrey
Printed and bound in Great Britain by
Clays Ltd, St Ives plc

HEADLINE BOOK PUBLISHING
A division of Hodder Headline PLC
338 Euston Road
London NW1 3BH

CHAPTER ONE

6 March 1937

'Rose Evadne Quest, Born 6 March 1916.'

The elegant copperplate handwriting came leaping off her birth certificate. She felt her mouth sag open in disbelief.

'Place of birth: St Catherine's Workhouse, Birkenhead.' Rosie was choking for air, awash with sudden horror. She'd been born in the workhouse!

This was the first time she'd had so much as a hint of it. Her fingers were icy and shaking as she pushed her plate of scrambled eggs away. She felt sick and couldn't touch another mouthful. Neither could she stop her cousin Phyllis's fingers edging the certificate round. Irritated, she snatched it back, but not before Phyllis had read it.

'Born in the workhouse! Oh my God!' The shocked horror on Phyllis's face opened the wound further. 'And just look at this.' Her finger was stabbing at the column that should have shown Rosie's father's name. With a gasp, Rosie saw a line had been ruled straight through it.

'You don't even know who he is,' Phyllis said

spitefully, dragging her chair farther away. 'But you must look like him. All that frizzy gingery hair.'

Rosie lifted her eyes from her birth certificate to the mirror near the back door, with a clothes brush hanging on one side and shoe horn on the other. Her coppery curls were reflected back at her.

'It's pretty hair, Rosie,' her Uncle Will said, and she looked again. Her shocked green eyes burned in a heart-shaped face that was paler than usual. Only the line of her chin showed she'd any fight left in her. Uncle Will's work-worn hand rested for a moment on her arm in a gesture of comfort.

No other member of the Quest family had red hair. Her eyes surveyed them in turn while they sat at table. Uncle Will's hair was white and wispy, but his original colouring showed in his wild eyebrows, bushy entanglements of dark wiry hair. Aunt Maud had iron-grey hair, scraped into a severe bun, and the vestiges of a black moustache. She also had great furrows of discontent running from her nose to her mouth, dragging her thin lips down at the corners. Phyllis their daughter was a glossy brunette. Nobody else had curls. Quest hair was uncompromisingly straight. Her cousin was right: Rosie flaunted her unknown paternity.

From her seat she could see Phyllis in the mirror too, with her taller willowy figure and smooth pageboy hair that needed a row of curling pins every night to turn it neatly under. It was always Phyllis who attracted attention when they were together. She was usually smartly dressed because she worked in the office, and had no need to wear old clothes or an overall to go to work.

'Wasn't Rosie's mother your sister, Dad?'

'Yes – our Grace. The youngest in our family and the only girl.'

Rosie stared down at the certificate again, tears distorting her vision. It gave her mother's name as Grace Mary Quest. She'd asked Uncle Will years ago why her name was Quest too. He'd fobbed her off by saying he'd adopted her and wanted her to have the family name.

Aunt Maud turned on her viciously. 'Your mother was a naughty girl. She sinned.' Rosie saw her narrow face damning what Grace had done.

She couldn't picture her mother in her mind's eye. It was the still set features in the sepia photograph on her dressing-table she saw. But she could remember some things: her laughter and the fierce loving hugs she used to give her. Rosie knew she'd been happy with Grace. She swallowed, her mouth felt dry. 'I hardly know anything about her.'

'When she was laid to rest, we vowed we'd never speak of her again. Didn't we, Will?'

'If you don't tell me I'll never know,' Rosie said fiercely. 'She was my mother, I've a right. I'm of age.' Uncle Will had his head in his hands.

The kettle started to sing again, suspended on its chain over orange flames sparking up in the black-leaded range. Open beams, black with age, ran the length of the kitchen ceiling.

'It's best forgotten.' Maud got up to clear the breakfast table as though to put an end to the matter.

'No,' Rosie protested. 'I want to know.' Her heart

3

was breaking for what her mother must have gone through.

'She was a kept woman,' her aunt said bitterly.

'You can't call her kept if she was in the workhouse!' Rosie was vehement.

'He got her out.'

'My father, you mean?' She felt buffeted by the emotional turmoil.

'Yes.'

'Who was he?'

'She never told us. We don't know.' Will raised his balding head to look at her. His eyes were dark with sorrow.

'Nor want to,' his wife added with a sniff.

'Uncle Will . . .' Rosie tried to think. 'My mother has been dead for eighteen years. Surely what she did can be forgiven and forgotten now?'

'Some things can never be forgiven.' Maud's lips were at their tightest. 'She brought disgrace on her family.'

'She didn't break the law. She wasn't a criminal.'

Aunt Maud's arctic grey eyes stared into Rosie's. 'She was a kept woman. She bore you outside marriage. She broke God's law. Her sin tainted us all, it taints you now. "Unto the seventh generation", that's the teaching. God's word.'

Rosie shivered, cold fingers twisting her gut.

'Your birth certificate tells the world what she did, and that's her fault.'

Rosie gasped with renewed horror as she remembered why she'd asked for it.

'You've got to take it to work if you want to join the

pension scheme,' Phyllis said. 'To verify your age.'

'It might be better if she didn't,' Maud retorted nastily. Uncle Will put his knife and fork down, his breakfast only half eaten.

'Last week, you were very insistent I should.' Rosie stirred her tea desperately. 'You said it would be a good thing to save some of my wages.'

Lines of worry deepened on Uncle Will's forehead.

'You've come of age, it's your problem not ours. You'd have had to find out one day,' her aunt dismissed her.

Rosie took a deep shuddering breath. To be born in the workhouse put her at the bottom of the heap. Nobody could sink lower. Her mother had given birth to her while living on public charity, despised by everyone; one of those hapless, helpless incompetents from the workhouse. What must she have gone through?

Maud turned back to her. 'It'll reflect on our Phyllis too, ruin her good name. I wish she'd never gone to work for Shearing's.'

'She couldn't get a job anywhere else,' Will burst out angrily. 'She tried, didn't she, when she came out of college? I had to ask Edwin Shearing.'

Rosie ran her tongue over dry lips. Uncle Will's face was grey. Pity and regret didn't touch Aunt Maud; her only concern was how this would affect Phyllis.

'Grace put herself outside our care,' she sniffed. 'We won't speak of her again.'

'But there's so much I want to know. When did we leave the workhouse?'

'You were about a year old.'

5

'What made my father get us out? I mean, if he let my mother go in . . . And what was his name?'

'We've told you, we don't know,' said Maud.

'You must! You must have seen him.'

'No,' Will said. 'She wouldn't speak of him.'

'But why did she have to die?' Rosie wailed in agony.

Her uncle said: 'She had appendicitis.'

That came as another shock. 'What? But that can be cured. An operation – they've been doing it for years. The old King had it, Edward VII.'

'And made it fashionable,' Will agreed.

'Then why didn't they operate on my mother?'

'They did, but it was too late. You see, there was only you and her. The man didn't live with her.'

'He was away – fighting in the war? There was a war on.'

'The war was over when she died. He was married to someone else. Grace lived alone with you. She was very ill. By the time he came to see her, her appendix had burst and the infection spread all through her body. Septicaemia they put on her death certificate. See for yourself.' Maud pulled the other certificate out from the same envelope.

Rosie's heart turned over as she read: 'Grace Mary Quest, aged twenty-three years.'

'He let her die,' she breathed. 'It was his fault.' She was overcome with pity for poor Grace lying ill alone.

'It was her own fault,' Maud said severely. 'The life she lived. It cut her off from family and friends. She chose it. God took his revenge.'

Another thought hammered in Rosie's mind. 'But I was with her.'

'It's no good dwelling on it, lass. You've got to put it behind you.' Will was openly showing his sympathy. The gulf between him and Maud seemed to be widening by the minute.

'It haunts me to think of her being so ill, left alone. I couldn't help her, could I?' She was searching through dim and hazy memories, willing her mind to bring them into focus. She didn't know now whether she truly remembered or whether her mind simply conjured up the frightening images. Her mother lying on the bed, hot and sweating and groaning; Rosie herself unable to rouse her.

'The woman next-door said you'd gone to them with some garbled story they couldn't understand. You were only three and they didn't want to get involved, not with a woman like your mother. The neighbour took you back, pushed you into the kitchen and closed the back door on you.' Rosie felt the vomit rising in her throat.

'You were so young,' Will said.

Rosie closed her eyes. She had to shut that picture out of her mind. 'I'll be late. I've got to go to work.' She scrambled to her feet, turned for the stairs to get her coat.

'Aren't you taking this with you?' Aunt Maud pushed the two certificates back in the envelope and brandished it at her. 'Wasn't that why you wanted it?'

Rosie snatched the envelope and ran for the stairs. She quailed at the thought of telling anybody she'd been born in the workhouse. She zipped the envelope hurriedly in an inner pocket of her handbag. The facts had come upon her from nowhere. She'd never suspected a secret like this.

She was shivering. She'd told Mrs Shearing she'd bring her birth certificate in today! She would despise her for this, and what would Ben Shearing think? She didn't know whether she could show it to them. She wished there was no such thing as the pension scheme. She couldn't think straight any more. Her twenty-first birthday looked like being one of the worst days of her life.

Will Quest slid the last four empty milk bottles into the crate and signalled his horse with a click of his tongue. Then, with a heavy sigh and a lot of effort, he climbed up on the seat in front of the cart. Without waiting for him to pick up the reins, Flash slowly set the wheels in motion.

Poor Flash, he thought. She walks with her nose a few inches from the road, resigned to the indignity of pulling a milk float, and looking as though the job's too much for her. He could see her haunches moving more stiffly than his own, and her grey coat was dull and threadbare. She'd got her name from the white flash on her face, but now everybody laughed, thinking it an ironic reference to her ponderous movements.

It pained him to remember that Flash had once been a high-stepping mare bought for Maud to put between the shafts of the trap. He'd saddled her too, and she'd had enough verve to give a good ride.

He felt a pang of guilt. The horse was getting too old to work. When he opened her stable door these mornings, he was half fearful he'd find her dead in her stall. But today Flash just added to his burden of guilt. He couldn't believe he'd forgotten to wish Rosie a happy birthday.

'You're looking very pretty this morning,' he'd said at breakfast. 'You're not going to wear your best frock to work?'

'It's my birthday, Uncle Will.' She'd laughed, but it was a forlorn little sound because he'd forgotten; they'd all forgotten.

'Rosie! Many happy returns.' He'd pulled her to her feet and made a big show of congratulatory kisses, but he'd felt bad. He decided to do something later to mark her birthday, but to say so now would not help.

The awful trouble had come when she'd asked for her birth certificate. He'd kept that hidden from her all these years. Maud had seemed almost triumphant as she'd pushed it against her niece's plate. When Rosie had left for work, he'd said to her: 'I'm sorry about . . .'

'Don't worry, Uncle Will. It's not your fault.' Her tight little smile had made him ache for her, filled with regret. He'd done so little to make her happy. He'd meant to be a father to her but somehow he'd not succeeded, just as he'd not succeeded at most things in life.

Rosie had been a sweet little girl. She had clung to him rather than Maud. By the time she was four years of age her aunt had complained it was impossible to keep her in the house. She wanted to be out following him and Tom about the farm, helping with jobs they were doing. She'd been more of a hindrance at first, but it had taken only a few short years before she'd learned to make herself useful. She'd always been particularly good with the animals.

She'd been a solitary little girl, never wanting the company of other people, not even children. Tom had tried to take her home to his cottage and leave her with his wife, but though she spent more time there than with Maud, Rosie had made herself a series of little hideaways about the farm, where she spent time by herself.

All her childhood she'd had a bolt hole in the loft above Flash's stable, and another on top of the hay in the dutch barn. Will recognised the signs when he came across a new place. Tin boxes containing crayons, or a paintbox placed on the beams. Some of her own paintings put up with drawing pins. Her story books, sometimes an old cardigan or a few sweets in a jar. Her books, and a collection of brown apple cores.

Every spring she kept on asking him if the grass was beginning to grow. He knew she wanted that to happen before he had to feed the last of the hay to the cattle. Her den was always in the last bay to be used. She persuaded him and Tom to cut the hay into steps so she could lure the dog up there too. They did it to make it safer for her, afraid she might fall from the steep ladder with her hands full of cats or books. Rosie used to spend more time alone than he thought a child should. Grace had never been like that.

But she was like his sister in other ways. Every time Rosie laughed out loud, he heard Grace's laugh. She'd inherited his sister's talent for drawing and painting too. From a very young age, Rosie occupied herself for hours with paints and paper – though Grace had been able to catch a good likeness with a pencil, and Rosie seemed more interested in patterns and designs.

'We ought to try to send her to Art School,' he'd said to Maud when Rosie had been coming up for her fourteenth birthday. 'After all, her mother went.'

'Fat lot of good it did your Grace,' Maud had sneered. 'Better for Rosie to be put to a trade.'

Will sighed. He ached for Grace too. Even now he couldn't think calmly of her, or the manner of her death. The fact that it was Rosie's birthday made him remember how he'd brought Grace's belongings home. Remember too the large diamond brooch flashing on the bed of black velvet in the leather box, and the double strand of real pearls.

He'd shown them to Maud, and she'd snapped the boxes shut after one sour glance. 'These prove she had a rich lover. Jewellery only a rich man could afford to give his mistress,' she'd said. 'I don't want any of her things in my house. She was a fallen woman.'

Will had hidden the two leather cases under his socks, pushing them to the back of the drawer eighteen years ago, and had never opened them since. Occasionally he'd felt the boxes as he'd searched for clean socks. Like Maud, he hadn't wanted to see them again; they brought back painful memories. He'd been keeping them for Rosie, until she was old enough to appreciate their value.

But she was twenty-one today, and he'd forgotten it was her birthday.

Flash was turning in at the farm gate, moving a little faster now she was within sight of her stable. Will helped old Tom unload the crates of empty bottles. Tom Moffat was like Flash, getting long in the tooth. They all were.

Tom had come to Ivy Farm straight from school at the age of twelve. Will's father had been alive then and the farm prosperous. He'd worked for them all his life and now he was seventy. There was nothing he didn't know about cows. Once Ivy Farm had employed four men; now there was only Tom.

'It's a bright morning, Master,' he said. Tom's face had weathered from being always in the open air into a crazy network of fine wrinkles around healthy red cheeks.

Will unharnessed Flash and turned her into the paddock before going into the house. The kitchen was warm and savoury with the scent of roasting mutton. He hung the khaki drill coat he wore for the milk round behind the door, hooked his hat on the same peg, and smoothed out his wispy hair to cover more of his pink scalp.

Maud had the fire blazing up in the old-fashioned grate. Several saucepans simmered on trivets.

'You're late today.' There was an undercurrent of resentment in her voice as she turned from the hearth. Her face was sour with discontent.

'Sorry,' he said. 'I won't be a minute.'

'You might have called Tom in,' she complained. 'Instead of leaving me to do it.'

He went upstairs, memories of Grace laughing up at him shutting out Maud's ill humour. He opened the drawer and felt under his socks, fingers ready to close on the two small leather cases. The drawer was

12

lined with left-over wall paper, his fingers felt the
raised design as they searched right to the back. He
found a leather belt he'd forgotten was there, some
foreign coins a customer had slipped him without his
noticing, and a yellowing envelope.

Even after eighteen years he could remember the
exact wording of the letter, but he couldn't stop
himself taking it out and reading it again.

> Dear Will,
> I have to ask a great favour of you for there is no
> one else. Please look after my baby. Love her as I
> do. I know I did wrong. I'm sorry.
>
> Grace

His face was reflected back at him from the mirror,
plump cheeks hanging in despair and worry lines biting
into the flesh of his forehead. His yellowing eyes were
glazed with the shock and horror of it even after all this
time.

Suddenly he was scooping all his socks out on the
floor. Thick grey wool ones knitted by Maud to wear
about the farm in winter. Finer wool to wear with
shoes to go to church on Sundays. A cravat he never
wore. He was shaking with worry. Grace's jewellery
was not where he'd left it.

He went storming downstairs to the kitchen.
Maud was opening the oven to take out a roasting
pan. The shoulder of mutton had browned nicely,
surrounded by roast potatoes. Above it simmered an
enamel bowl of rice pudding with a thick brown skin
on top.

'What have you done with Grace's jewellery?' He could feel his anger rising.

'What jewellery?' she asked, but he didn't miss the nervous jerk of her hands. He watched her slide the mutton from the oven, spear it on to a serving dish, and put it on the table.

'You've taken them, haven't you? The brooch and the pearls?'

Maud picked up the carving knife and fork without answering.

Will wrenched them from her hand. 'Don't pretend you don't know what I'm talking about,' he shouted. 'Where have you put them?'

'I didn't want her things in my house.' She was tight-lipped, but Will saw apprehension flicker across her face.

'Where have you put them, woman? They're worth money. It's only right Rosie should have them now.'

'Well, she can't!' There was no mistaking the fear in her steel-grey eyes.

'Have you put them out in the stable or something? That was silly, they're valuable. It's only right we should keep them safe for Rosie.'

'I sold them.' She tucked a strand of iron-grey hair back into her bun.

He was aghast. 'What did you do that for?'

'To get money for Phyllis's school fees. You weren't earning enough.'

'Maud! That was Rosie's money not yours. You told me your egg money paid Phyllis's fees.'

'I've had to feed Rosie all her life, haven't I? If she

14

hadn't been here, I'd have had enough egg money for Phyllis's school.'

'Oh God!' Will covered his face with his hands. 'Phyllis didn't have to go to the Convent. I wasn't keen on her going. It isn't as if we are Catholics. I never could understand why you wanted that.'

'She's got a decent job, hasn't she? I didn't want her working in a factory.'

'But it doesn't matter that Rosie has to? Or that she went to the Council school and had to leave at fourteen?'

'You asked Edwin Shearing to take her on as an apprentice. She's got a trade.'

'I could have asked him to do the same for Phyllis.'

'I wanted her to be brought up nicely, to have a decent chance in life. She's your daughter too. Surely you want that?'

'Not on Rosie's money,' he said. 'She's had little enough.'

'If you'd been able to earn a decent living, I wouldn't have had to sell anything. I sold my mother's rings too, you know.' Maud's eyes shone with spite.

The back door scraped open. Will saw old Tom on the step taking off his hat. He always had his dinner with them; it had been part of his wages since his wife died nine years ago. Maud had never ceased to complain about the extra work it involved. Now she returned angrily to her cooking, draining the cabbage water into the gravy, flailing a knife in the cabbage pan with savage intensity.

'Come in, Tom,' Will said. 'Come and sit your-self down.' Tom had a permanent stoop and was rheumaticky from working about the yard or fields in the rain. The only protection he ever had was a sack across his shoulders, one that had held cattle food or hen meal.

Will scraped back his own chair and sat down heavily, aware that the atmosphere sparked with tension. Normally he'd have carved the meat. He sat and waited for Maud to do it.

'Good dinner today, Missis.' Tom was smiling from one to the other. It gave Will a pang to see him trying to defuse the hostility between them. Maud sniffed deprecatingly. He knew she didn't like being called Missis.

'What are we having for supper tonight?' Will asked.

'There'll be plenty of cold meat left.'

He helped himself from the dish of potatoes boiled in their skins and added them to the roast potatoes on his plate. 'And these reheated, I suppose?'

'Yes.'

'Couldn't we have something a bit more exciting? Something special for Rosie's birthday?'

'Is it Rosie's birthday?' Tom asked with his mouth full.

'Yes, she's twenty-one.'

'Come of age,' he said. 'A fine lass. A credit to your bringing up, Missis.'

'Have you made her a cake?'

'No.' Maud was vexed. Her mouth drooped more than usual.

'I think you should.'

'I was going into town this afternoon.'

'To get her a present?' He saw her lips tighten and

16

knew that hadn't been in her mind. 'You've got to make some effort. Coming of age is a big milestone. We can't just ignore it.'

'You'd forgotten till she reminded you this morning. Why take it out on me because I'd forgotten too?'

'We've both been reminded now,' Will said.

When he and Tom had finished their helpings of rice pudding and stood up to leave, he saw Maud, with a face like thunder, reaching for the flour in the cupboard near the fire.

CHAPTER TWO

Later that morning, after three hours of routine work, Rosie began to feel a little better. She hoped the rest of her day would be peaceful. She was guiding the bobbing foot of her machine round a shirt collar when she heard the door of the sewing room crash back and Mrs Shearing's heels beating an urgent tattoo across the bare boards.

Every machine whirred into action. Instinct made her fellow workers show greater devotion to their work, though Rosie knew they were paid on piece rates like herself.

Without looking up, she knew Beatrice Shearing, strong chin jutting forward, was coming up the room like a bow wave. Rosie shivered with foreboding. She was snipping off threads when she realised the footsteps had stopped in front of her machine.

'Rose, those samples, the new soft collars I gave you to make up . . .' Beatrice's hands began sorting through the contents of Rosie's work tray as she spoke. Her voice was aggressive and carried up the long room. 'I told you I wanted them this afternoon. Have you done them?'

'Yes, Mrs Shearing.' Every seamstress had reason to dread her visits to the sewing room. She had an impatient manner and sharp tongue, but from the day she'd started work Rosie felt she'd been singled out to bear the brunt of it. 'You told me to put them on your desk.' She moved her hands to where they couldn't be seen. She could feel them trembling.

'Telling you is one thing. Getting you to do it is another.' Beatrice Shearing's dark brown eyes held a sharpness that missed nothing.

'I did put them on your desk.'

'What's this?' Accusing fingers were jerking a twisted collar out of the tray and holding it aloft. The jagged line of stitching was only too obvious. Rosie was aware of the other machinists slowing to listen.

'I'm surprised at you, Rose Quest, a girl of your experience!' Rosie heard a half-suppressed sob from the newest apprentice who was sitting behind her, and couldn't believe anyone else in the room would miss it.

'You'll have to do it over. We can't have work of this standard on Shearing's shirts.'

Rosie flinched. For years she'd been struggling to find the best way of coping with Mrs Shearing's outbursts. Politeness was essential, she knew that. Only last week a woman had been given her cards for showing insolence in her manner, and they all knew how hard it was to find another job. She took a deep breath and stole an upward glance as she said steadily: 'I'm doing them over, Mrs Shearing.'

She noticed then that Ben, the second Shearing son, was following his mother. The other members of the

Shearing family were more popular with their workers. Ben had his mother's straight thick brown hair. His mouth was wide with a half smile always pulling at one corner, and his face could light up with enthusiasm. Though he'd only started work here two weeks ago, the whole sewing room agreed he did not have his mother's temperament. He was always friendly and good-humoured.

'You must keep your mind on your work,' Mrs Shearing stormed. Rosie knew she shouldn't let her employer reduce her to a nervous pulp. 'You girls! I daren't take my eyes off any of you, not for a moment.'

With another sob, the apprentice flung the collar she'd been unpicking on to Rosie's machine, and fled in the direction of the cloakroom.

'It's not your work, is it?' Ben said, and Rosie found the sympathy in his dark eyes equally difficult to cope with.

'Not your work?' his mother barked, dropping the collars back in the tray. 'Why didn't you say so?'

Rosie felt a scarlet tide rush into her cheeks but was given no time to say anything as Mrs Shearing steam-rollered on: 'I've talked to you about pensions, haven't I? Have you decided to join our scheme? Ben, have you given her details? Two shillings a week deducted from your wages and saved with a very reputable insurance company. A pension, or a lump sum if you leave before retirement age.'

'Yes, Mrs Shearing.'

'Have you filled in the application form?'

Rosie took a deep breath. 'Ye-es.' She should have

said she was thinking about it. What was the matter with her?

'It's in your own best interests. When will you be twenty-one?'

Rosie swallowed. 'Today,' she managed.

'Oh!' Beatrice Shearing's eyebrows rose. It didn't surprise Rosie. By now, she ought to have developed more poise and confidence.

'So that's why you're all dressed up? A bit over-dressed. Hardly suitable for the workroom!'

'Many happy returns,' Ben said quietly, then dropped his voice even lower. 'Your dress is very pretty. I'm sure it doesn't interfere with your sewing.' Rose felt her cheeks flame again; self-consciously she smoothed down the green wool.

She'd worn it today because it was her birthday, and she'd had to do something to mark it as a special day. She'd chosen the colour because it exactly matched her eyes, and she'd known Ben Shearing would see it and perhaps like what he saw.

'I made it,' she said. It had the fashionable shawl collar and a longer flowing skirt.

'Rose, how many times have you been told to keep your hair tied back?' Beatrice Shearing's own was restrained in an attractive chignon. 'It isn't safe here, flying loose. Not with our new band-driven machines.'

Rosie lifted her hands to her springy red hair. It had too much curl and was hard to control, but for once it all seemed securely anchored in the matching green ribbon at the nape of her neck.

'The bow has come undone.' Ben was smiling at her, and as her fingers grappled with the unseen ends, added: 'Here, let me.' Feeling very daring she turned her back to him. His fingers felt cool against her neck and sent frissons of excitement down her spine. 'Not a very good bow, I'm afraid.'

'Ben!' There was outrage in his mother's voice. 'I'm sure we've all got better things to do.'

Rosie sat slumped in her chair, watching them go up the room, knowing Mrs Shearing had seen her respond to Ben's touch. She felt worse when she heard Beatrice add: 'Really, Ben, you shouldn't encourage the girls like that. You'll give them ideas above their station.'

Every machine was still, every seamstress seemed to be holding her breath. At the door, Mrs Shearing spun on her heel to face them with the ferocity of a tigress.

'Girls, get on with your work! You do waste time, all of you. No wonder the orders are always late!'

Agonised, Rosie felt for another collar, dragging it under her needle. Around her, she heard other machines spin into action. She tried to concentrate on her work, relieved she was no longer the centre of attention, but machining was second nature to her. It all came too easily after the long years of apprenticeship.

Thoughts of Ben Shearing filled her mind. She liked the way his dark eyes followed her; the way his hair flopped across his eyes. She envied the assurance she saw in the way he held himself. Ben Shearing had every reason to be confident. He'd qualified as a chartered accountant before coming to take over the accounts and help manage the family firm.

Rosie had been struggling to keep him out of her thoughts since he'd started work here at the beginning of the month. She'd sensed immediately that his mother did not want him to be on familiar terms with the workforce, and especially with her. Since then, Rosie felt she was attracting more of her employer's attention, and that her tongue was developing a more venomous edge. She knew it was silly to risk rousing Beatrice Shearing's dislike further, but couldn't stop the trickle of hope that perhaps Ben liked her . . .?

Suddenly the sewing room door banged back on its hinges again, and Beatrice Shearing's slim figure in its neat brown dress burst in.

'Rose Quest,' her abrasive voice rose above the purr of the sewing machines, 'the samples I asked you to run up are not on my desk!'

Rosie jerked to her feet in alarm, her heart pounding.

'I put them there. On the corner. I did them as soon as you asked me.'

'Come and find them. I can't.'

Rosie swallowed, her legs felt like lead. Beatrice Shearing's hard gaze never left her face as she went to the door.

She passed Ben in the decaying grandeur of the reception hall, with its ornate plasterwork ceiling and floor of cracked black and white tiles. Shearing's Shirts were manufactured in what had once been the Albert Hotel. Ben was talking to her cousin Phyllis, whose desk was placed opposite the front door. She was employed as receptionist and assistant to Mrs Shearing's secretary, and provided a secretarial service to anyone else needing it.

Rosie caught sight of herself in one of the tarnished mirrors that still hung on the walls: a small slight figure, tight with tension. She looked awkward. There was no sign of the maturity which should have been hers at twenty-one. Beatrice Shearing's office was a cubicle walled off round a window. One glance told Rosie the collars had gone. It added to her embarrassment that she should seem inadequate in front of Ben.

'I put them there.' She pointed to the exact spot.

'But they aren't there now.' Beatrice had followed her to the door, dark eyes blazing with impatience. 'What have you done with them?'

'Somebody must have moved them.'

'Don't start blaming others for your inefficiency. Really, the time that's wasted looking for things!' Rosie cringed. This was tearing the last of her self-assurance to shreds.

'I'll go and see if Dad . . .' Ben had come in behind them. 'I think I saw him looking at collars.' He went off in a hurry to return with his father a few moments later. Edwin Shearing had the collars they were looking for in his hand.

'It's all right, Rosie. Not your fault.' He was as gentle as his wife was abrasive. 'I took them, Beatrice. Sorry, my dear.' His eyes met Rosie's, full of apology.

'Well, Rose, perhaps we'll let you join our pension scheme after all.' Beatrice was tight-lipped. 'Though you'll have to bring in your birth certificate before we can start you. You said you'd bring it today. I suppose you forgot?'

'Yes,' she gulped. 'I'm sorry.'

'You've filled in the form?' Ben asked.

'Yes,' she whispered. Mrs Shearing's simultaneous 'Yes' drowned hers out.

'I've seen to all that, Ben,' his mother added crossly.

Rosie was edging out of the cubicle, feeling as though she'd been mangled.

'Don't let Mother upset you,' Ben whispered, following her out. 'It's just her manner.'

She went back to her machine and stitched away as hard as she could. The apprentice returned to finish unpicking the collars that were not satisfactory; she had already damped and ironed them. Rosie re-stitched them with expert precision.

She found the familiar sounds of the sewing room soothing, and gradually felt herself unwind. She told herself she was a fool to let her mind dwell on Ben Shearing. It was making matters worse. She was making life harder for herself than it need be.

At the end of the working day, she was putting on her coat in the crowded cloakroom when she remembered the application form she'd filled in to join the pension scheme. She'd already given it to Phyllis. Now she decided she wanted it back before it went through the processing channels.

She headed towards the reception hall to see if Phyllis was still at her desk. An instant later, she wished she had not. Ben Shearing was talking to her again. Rosie felt unable to avoid him today. She saw her cousin's eyebrows lift, signalling that Rosie had no business to intrude on a private conversation.

She paused uncertainly. 'Are you ready to come home?' The typewriter was not yet covered. Phyllis

looked the perfect secretary/receptionist, with lipstick
and powder re-applied in the cloakroom every two
hours. Today she was dramatically dressed in a scarlet
dress that showed off her tall slim figure and smooth
brown hair.

'I hadn't realised.' Ben was looking from her to
Phyllis. 'You aren't much alike. You're sisters?'

'Cousins.' Phyllis's voice was cold. The look of
disdain on her face told Rosie she'd prefer not to be
related to her at all. 'But she lives with us. My parents
had to bring her up because she was orphaned as a
child.'

'I'll go on then,' Rosie said.

As she turned away, she heard Ben say: 'I'm sorry,
I'm keeping you and it's time to go home.'

'It doesn't matter. We usually walk home separ-
ately, I prefer to. We aren't close.'

Rosie let the door swing to behind her and went
down the cracked marble steps, taking great gulps of
air. Phyllis's tone cut her as much as her words. The
message she was giving Ben was unmistakable. 'Rosie
isn't worth bothering about.' She found it hurtful, but
then everything about Phyllis was hurtful. They had
lived in a state of armed neutrality for as long as she
could remember. Open warfare still broke out from
time to time.

She hardly noticed the traffic as she crossed the
main road into Birkenhead and went on in the direction of Ivy Farm, up what had once been the smart
residential roads of Rock Ferry.

'A farm?' everybody asked in amazement when she
gave her address.

'Yes, it's been there for the last two hundred years,' she would reply, smiling. Rosie walked along pavements bordered by houses, many of them recently built semi-detacheds. Slowly at first, and more quickly since the turn of the century, the town had begun to encroach on their fields.

Once the lane had run down the side of the house at Ivy Farm. In 1882 it had been widened and pavements had been constructed, along with seven pairs of tall and sombre houses with great bay windows under Gothic gables. It had been re-christened Gordon Drive, and the houses there had grand-sized room compared to those at the farm. She knew it was a big worry to Uncle Will that as the town expanded, his acreage shrank.

She let herself into the stone-flagged farm kitchen; it was the hub of the house, unchanging over the years, and their biggest room. A fire roared in a blackleaded range with its polished brass knobs. She went through to the hall and then up the creaking stairs to the bedroom she shared with Phyllis.

The ceiling was low and the old walls bulged. There were two single beds, Phyllis's nearer the small window. Rosie took off her best green dress and matching ribbon, reflecting that it would have been better if she'd not worn them to work after all. Or else covered up her finery with an overall as the older machinists did.

Hastily she pulled on the old skirt and jumper she wore about the farm. She always went out to help with the evening milking. At the back door she met Phyllis coming in.

'I do wish you wouldn't barge in when I'm talking to people in the office, Rosie. You've no manners. Ben Shearing wanted to talk to me.'

'I wanted my application form back. I've decided not to join their pension scheme.'

Her cousin smirked spitefully. 'You're too late, I handed it to Ben. You'll have to ask him if you want it back.'

'I heard it was your birthday,' Tom said, meeting Rosie at the door of the cow shed.

'Twenty-one today,' she agreed with forced brightness.

'I've bought a present for you.' He was pushing a paper bag into her hands which half covered a chocolate box with a picture of kittens on the lid. She pulled it out. A large two-shilling price sticker was still in place. 'Wish I was twenty-one again. Many happy returns.'

'Oh, Tom! Thank you.' She reached up and planted a kiss on his ruddy cheek. 'How kind to think of me.'

'You think of me often enough.'

'Shall we try one?' Rosie's fingers were pulling at the cellophane.

'No, lass, they're for you.' He was patting the back of her hand awkwardly. 'You've come to help us milk, even on your birthday?'

'Why not?' She smiled. 'You know I like it.' She helped at every milking, morning and evening, before she went to work and after she came home. Uncle Will told her often enough how grateful he was for her help, but for Rosie, working with animals brought its own reward. It had always given her pleasure and a sort of stability.

She hadn't liked hearing Uncle Will talk of getting milking machines, but she knew now he never would. They cost too much, and both he and Tom were past coping with what they called newfangled things. Yet hand milking a herd of nineteen was no easy task for two elderly men.

Rosie collected her bucket and stool and headed up the line of cows to Tinkerbell's stall. Tinkerbell was her favourite, a chestnut and white shorthorn with gentle brown eyes and long curling lashes. The agony of the day faded as she sat with her forehead resting against Tinkerbell's flank, rhythmically spurting milk into the pail between her knees, and with the scent of it warm in her nostrils.

The farm cat, an ancient tabby, came to rub herself against her leg. Rosie reached behind her for the old sardine tin, squirted one teat until she'd filled it, then set it back on the ground. The cat was purring as he rushed to lap it up.

'Don't spoil that cat!' Will's plump worry of a face was smiling as he clanked past with a brimming pail in each hand. 'It won't catch mice if you give it milk like that.'

Rosie smiled. This was what she enjoyed most in her day. Around her the sounds of milking went on. A slap on a flank as Tom told a cow to move over to make room for his stool. The soft rattle of a neck halter as a head went down to the trough. The occasional snort, a ponderous movement as a cow shifted its weight from one hoof to another – and all the time the rhythmic spurting of milk into buckets.

Rosie moved steadily from cow to cow as the milking proceeded, tipping bucketfuls of milk into churns. Marigold was always left till last. They were all guilty of hurrying or delaying their pace to avoid milking her.

'I'll do Marigold tonight,' she volunteered as Tom was finishing Hyacinth.

Marigold had a sharp streak in her nature. She was the cow they left till last in the hope somebody else would milk her. If Marigold was out of humour, she was not above kicking the pail or any human limb within reach.

Her reddish-brown tail should have ended in a cascade of white curls. Marigold seemed to keep it encrusted with dried excreta as a matter of policy, turning it a khaki colour. While she was being milked she flicked it threateningly, so that it clattered like a bead curtain. They had all felt the sting of it on their cheeks from time to time.

Marigold had a huge low udder that swung in the way of her legs when she walked, and was inclined to hold up her milk, so that fingers had to work twice as hard to get it frothing into the pail. When she did let it down, she could provide one and a half times as much as any other cow in the herd, which was why Uncle Will kept her on.

'No, you won't, Rosie, not tonight. You get in to your supper.'

When she went back to the house, the big kitchen table had been covered with a white cloth. In the centre was a large sponge cake oozing jam from between its layers. Uneven white letters trailed across deep pink icing to spell her name. Below that the number 21 stood out solidly.

'Thank you, Aunt Maud, it's lovely.' She felt a little spiral of excitement and laughed. She should have known they wouldn't let her twenty-first pass without some celebration.

'I don't hold with candles,' Aunt Maud said with her usual severity. 'Wax dripping on food. No sense in that.' A parcel wrapped in businesslike brown paper occupied the chair by her place at the table. It drew Rosie's attention like a magnet.

'You're of age now,' Phyllis said enviously, her scarlet office dress making her look exotically out of place in the old kitchen.

'Your turn will come,' her mother retorted. 'No point in wishing your life away.'

'Happy Birthday.' Phyllis offered a small package wrapped in red crêpe paper. 'A present for you, Rosie.'

'Lovely! You're both very kind.' She explored the present's shape through its covering, and with a jolt of pleasure decided it could be perfume. She kissed them both before unwrapping it.

'It is perfume, I thought it was,' she said excitedly, and then paused. She recognised the bottle that had stood on Phyllis's dressing-table for some months. Her boyfriend, an officer in the Merchant Navy, had brought it home from abroad, and Phyllis had said she didn't care for it.

Her cousin's dark eyes were watching her now. 'You said you liked it,' she said defensively. Rosie unscrewed the top and sniffed.

'I do,' she asserted. 'Thank you.'

'Set the table, Rosie,' Aunt Maud ordered.

She prodded the brown paper parcel. 'Is this for me too, Aunt Maud?'

'Wait till your uncle comes in. He said we ought to give you something to mark the occasion.'

'I can't wait!' Rosie laughed. 'It's exciting, all this fuss.' There had been precious few presents on earlier birthdays.

'You're grown up. Off our hands now.' Maud straightened up from the shoulder of cold mutton she'd been carving. Rosie was brought up short. Her aunt seemed to be implying Rosie would be leaving now, but she had nowhere else to go.

'I never thought I'd see this day.' Maud's sigh was almost one of satisfaction. 'It's been a long time coming.'

Rosie tried to shake off her foreboding. She'd known for a long time Aunt Maud had derived little pleasure from bringing her up; that she'd only done it because Uncle Will said it was their duty. The back door opened again and he came in.

'Our Phyllis has given Rosie a nice bottle of scent,' Maud hurried to tell him. 'You can open your big parcel now, dear.'

Rosie untied the string, trying to recapture the fizz of excitement she'd felt earlier. She hoped it would be a dress length.

A few weeks ago, when she'd been making a dress for Aunt Maud, they'd both gone shopping for the material and Rosie had admired a fine wood worsted in deep blue. She'd also seen a pattern she'd like to make up for herself. But the parcel was bulky; there must be more than one dress length here.

Carefully she peeled back the last corner of paper, hoping to see blue worsted. It was plain white cotton. She felt a sinking sense of disappointment that she had to hide. 'Thank you, Aunt. Very kind of you.'

'A practical present, Rose. For your bottom drawer.'

'Sheets.' She tried to smile. She'd seen her aunt hemming them on her sewing machine last month. She still did household sewing, though Rosie made most of their frocks now.

'A pair of double sheets, with two pillow cases and a bolster case. You'll need them one day.'

'Yes, of course,' she said, but since she'd never even had a boyfriend, a wedding seemed too far in the future to think about. 'One day.'

'Let's hope it isn't too long coming,' Maud said, making Rosie think again she couldn't wait to see her gone.

'Well now, Rosie, it's my turn.' Uncle Will was pushing a small gift-wrapped package towards her. 'Happy Birthday, love.'

With a gasp of delight she pulled at the gold ribbon and the sparkling paper fell away from a small leather box. 'Uncle Will!' she whooped.

The next instant she was aware that Phyllis and Maud had crowded closer and that her aunt was bristling with indignation. Slowly she opened the box. On a bed of black velvet three small gold flowers on curving stems sparkled up at her.

'A brooch. How lovely! Thank you, Uncle Will.'

'It's eighteen carat,' he said.

'It's beautiful,' Phyllis breathed. 'Really beautiful.'

'Really, Will!' Maud snorted indignantly. 'It's very extravagant of you when I'm finding it hard to make ends meet.'

Rosie heard him answer quietly, 'Had to make it up to her. You know why.'

'You're very generous.' Rosie was pinning her brooch on her old jumper when she felt the atmosphere suddenly turn chilly. Maud was savagely banging plates of meat on the table.

'Come on, it's ready and waiting.' They ate their cold mutton in silence. Afterwards Will tried to infuse more gaiety into the occasion.

'Come on, Phyllis, clear these plates. Then we'll sing "Happy Birthday" while Rosie cuts her cake.' She found the cake in front of her, the knife pushed in her hand, then Will's baritone was drowning out the other voices.

'You should have had candles to blow out,' Phyllis laughed.

Rosie had cut four careful slices, and eaten half hers when she said: 'I've been wondering if you have anything left that belonged to my mother? What happened to her things? Her clothes, for instance?'

'There were some trunks.' Will looked suddenly much older. 'Yes, two, I think.'

'It would have been better to have given all her stuff to St Vincent de Paul or the Salvation Army.' Maud's face was cold with anger again.

'In the attic?' Rosie asked hopefully. 'Can I look?'

Already she was on her feet, wanting to bound upstairs.

'I didn't want her things in my house,' Maud said.

'Where then?'

'Out in the stable,' her uncle admitted. Rosie was on the doormat pulling on her boots. 'Wait a minute, you won't be able to reach them and it's getting dark now. They're up in the hayloft. I nailed the door up after Tom put his foot through the floorboards. Tomorrow, Rosie, we'll open it.'

'Tomorrow then,' she said. She was finding it hard to be patient, but what was one more day when she'd waited eighteen years? She was starting to clear the table when another thought came to her.

'How did you get her things, Uncle Will? If you couldn't help when she was ill and you didn't know where we lived?'

'I knew, at the end.'

'But how?'

'She wrote to me, asking me to look after you.'

Rosie felt compassion knifing through her. 'She must have known then, that she was going to die?'

'Yes, I think she did.'

'Will! What did you do?'

'I went round to see her. Got the doctor to her. He sent her off to hospital. You know the rest.'

Rosie felt sick again. 'You brought me here?'

'Yes, love.'

'Was she very ill?'

'Yes, very ill indeed.'

'She died in hospital?'

'Yes.'

'What about the funeral?'

'I saw to that.'

'It cost more than we could afford,' Maud said bitterly. 'But somebody had to pay.'

'I meant,' Rosie said, 'did anyone else come? My father?'

'No lass, just Maud and me, and a few who remembered her – Tom and his wife.'

Aunt Maud was restive. She got up and looked in the pantry to see if the washing-up had been done to her satisfaction.

'Rosie,' she said, 'don't forget to take the presents we've given you up to your room.' Knowing how much her aunt hated any personal possessions to be left about, she scooped them up and headed for the bedroom she shared with Phyllis.

She hid the sheets in the bottom of her wardrobe and sank down on the edge of her bed, studying her mother's photograph on her dressing-table. In its heavy oak frame, behind glass, Grace's face smiled at her.

She was a slip of a girl, pretty, with soft straight hair and big dark eyes. Rosie ached with sympathy. Twenty-three years old when she died. Only two years older than she was herself now. There was a lump in her throat that wouldn't go away. She couldn't swallow. She was in the picture too, a three-year-old caught in her mother's arms. The sun was shining, they both looked happy.

She tried to remember more about those days. No clear recollections would come, but she knew it had been a time of happiness. She could remember her first days here at the farm. The strangeness, the feeling of loss, of being unwanted. Suddenly she grabbed the photograph. Her fingers were dismantling the frame as she remembered another picture she'd placed behind it years ago.

It slid out. Her fingers were shaking as she picked it up. It was as she thought: a picture of her mother with a man, his arm linked through hers. Years ago she'd asked Aunt Maud who he was and she'd said, 'Your father.' She studied him now, thin-faced, thick dark hair and a moustache.

She leapt up from her bed and tore back to the kitchen, her feet thudding on the stairs. Maud and Phyllis were sitting close to the fire on the oak settles which faced each other inside what had once been an open hearth. Uncle Will was poring over the evening paper at the table. The atmosphere seemed strained to breaking point.

'There was no need . . .' her aunt was insisting.

'This is my father,' Rosie choked, holding the sepia-toned photograph in one hand and jabbing her finger at the likeness of the man with the other.

'No,' Aunt Maud said grimly.

'Yes. You told me it was,' she insisted. 'I remember you told me it was.'

'I told you that when you were ten.' Maud's voice was weary. 'I had to, to satisfy you. You never stopped asking question after question.' Rosie recoiled in disbelief.

'I had to protect you. Protect us all from shame.' Her aunt got up to poke the fire, which didn't need it. 'A child must be shielded. I couldn't have you blathering it out all round the neighbourhood, could I? The Quests are a respectable family.'

'We've farmed here for three generations,' Phyllis added, examining her painted finger nails.

'We couldn't have you blurting out the truth unknowingly.' Maud looked stricken at last. 'It would have made folks look down on you. Look down on us all.'

'Who is he then?' Rosie asked, feeling icy inside.

'My brother George,' Will said. 'One of the three killed in the war.'

'You told me lies!' Rosie turned on Maud with rising fury. 'Isn't that a sin?'

'There are big sins and little sins. Some are merely white lies to ease a difficult situation.' Her aunt's face twisted with spite. 'You'll have to face what life sends. You're of age, a woman now. We all have our troubles, Rosie.'

CHAPTER THREE

Ben Shearing looked round his new office feeling a glimmer of triumph. It had been a little used store for years, still smelled musty, and he'd had to fight to get it. The only desk he could commandeer had been designed for a typist, and the new filing cabinet was still empty. Apart from that, all he had was a couple of chairs and a bentwood coat stand. Nevertheless he'd won and could hardly believe it. The confrontation left him feeling spent and unable to concentrate for the rest of the afternoon.

He'd come to the office on his first morning to find that his mother had had another portion of the entrance hall partitioned off to make an office for him. Not only was it adjacent to hers, she'd also had a communicating door put in.

'You'll need help to start with, Ben. I'll be able to give you a hand.'

'No doubt, but I'd like to be somewhere quieter.'

'You'll know what's going on in the business if you're down here in the middle of it.' He didn't doubt the truth of that, but it would keep him under her nose too.

His father and brothers Oliver and Stephen each used a room on the first floor, and Ben wanted to do the same. They had originally been bedrooms, high and roomy and a little cold in winter, but they were well away from Mother and noise of the workrooms.

He felt the weight of her surveillance even in his new room, but at least she couldn't hear him speaking on the phone or talking to staff. He could do some things without her knowing. Abruptly he scraped back his chair and strode to the window. It needed cleaning. For years he'd been looking forward to joining the family firm, everything he'd done in his life had been designed to prepare him for it. Now he was having misgivings.

Things were not as he'd imagined. His father might be owner and managing director on paper, but it had taken Ben one short week to realise his mother was in control here, just as she was at home.

He had supposed her sphere of responsibility to be solely the corset-making department. She had been trained as a corsetière as a girl, and before her marriage, she and her mother had set up a small business to make corsets. Years ago both businesses had been brought under the same roof, and as far as he could see now, Beatrice had run both ever since.

He had his own reservations about women's corsets, and could understand why the men of the family left them to her. Shirts were Shearing's main business; they'd been involved with them for generations. He could not understand how his father had allowed her to control them too.

Ben tossed his hair out of his eyes. It was a habit

he had when he felt restless or uneasy. He had always known the dynamics in his family were unusual. His mother held very strong opinions about everything, and wanted her own way. He knew she manipulated every detail of home and family to suit herself. To say she had a will of iron was an understatement. She could break iron as others broke biscuits. He should have foreseen she'd be running the business too, but first school then being articled had given him freedom, taken him out of her orbit. Even at home, his brothers had received more of her attention. Now, suddenly, he was feeling the full brunt of it.

On his first day here, he'd asked her about her corset making, believing it would be his responsibility to keep the accounts for that part of the business too. She'd soon set him right about that.

'I take care of the accounting as well as every other aspect of the corset company myself, but it won't hurt you to have some understanding, I suppose. Who knows? One day I may need your help.'

So she'd taken him on a tour of the rooms where her corsets were being made. Until that moment, he'd thought there was more glamour in ladies' underwear than men's shirts, and had been interested to see. He'd been deafened and bewildered by the rows of heavy industrial sewing machines, seaming up strong twill in sugar pink or flesh fawn.

In Beatrice's opinion, her corsets were supreme, her gift to womankind. She claimed she wore them herself and found them extremely comfortable. Ben doubted if they could be. He lifted a partly finished garment from a tray. It looked more a construction job than one of mere sewing.

'This will go on to be strengthened with twisted wire stays.' His mother smiled as she handed him one. 'These have now replaced whale bone. This model is reinforced with crossed panels to flatten a bulging abdomen.' She led him a few yards further and proudly held up another specimen. The buckles seemed strong enough to use on horse harness.

She halted him again by the machine that hammered in metal eyelet holes. At the end of the line a young girl with flying fingers was threading in long pink laces designed to criss-cross up the back so they could be adjusted to fit all figures. Ben tested a lace between his fingers. It was stronger than a bootlace.

'They allow the corset to be tightened for special occasions or to allow a woman to wear a dress grown too tight.' His mother's face shone with enthusiasm. 'They shape a woman's figure, Ben.'

He thought them horrendous contraptions, and afterwards had marvelled with his brother Stephen that women could be persuaded to wear them at all.

'They slim the waist,' his mother went on. 'Smooth the abdomen and lift the bust. Every woman can have exactly the figure she wants.'

'At a price,' he'd said, pulling a face.

'They retail from three shillings and sixpence.'

'I meant at the cost of comfort, the loss of freedom. They may improve the look of a woman, but they certainly won't improve the feel of her.'

'Ben, I'm surprised at you,' Beatrice said prudishly. 'I hope you don't go round feeling young ladies?'

In his time he'd hugged a few and cuddled others, and he'd swear none had been wearing contraptions like these.

'Mother,' he said, 'it's obvious that a woman wearing your corsets will feel as though she's encased in metal.'

'No,' she retorted. 'They're very comfortable. Extremely comfortable. I should know, I wear them.'

'Why bother?' He eyed her straight figure, unusually youthful for a woman of her age, and almost boyish. She was narrow-hipped, slim-waisted, and flat-chested. She had no flesh to re-shape. A decade ago she would have been a very fashionable shape.

'All women wear them, dear.' Her tone told him she thought it a foolish question. 'How would we hold up our stockings otherwise?' Ben turned over a finished corset with four robust suspenders of rubber, elastic and metal, and thanked God he'd been born a man.

'All they do for you is make you rigid.' But he knew as soon as he'd said it he was wrong about that too. Mother would be rigid whether she wore corsets or not.

'You men can't be expected to understand ladies' underwear, dear.' She gave her tinkling laugh. 'I try to explain because the time may come when I need you to help run the business.'

'Not for donkeys' years.'

'Perhaps not, but then you will see these garments listed in our books.'

He smiled. 'They won't be worn for much longer. It has to be a declining market.' He nearly added that only old women wore them now, but nobody could describe his mother as old; she had all the bounce and vigour of youth.

'The young won't be confined in these. Only women who have worn them for years. It's 1937, Mother. Haven't you heard of the Health and Beauty Movement? Women are being told to let the sun and air get to their bodies. They want to be a natural shape, and above all want to feel comfortable. A woman's figure is not a bolster to be moulded.'

'Our corsets are comfortable, dear.'

Ben decided that if she really found them comfortable, it must be a question of mind over matter. Mother had that sort of mind. He asked what the difference was between a corset and a corselet. She held up an example of each.

'A corselet is cut higher to support the bust.'

Ben shuddered. He ought to be used by now to Mother's euphemisms for the female figure: bust for breasts and hips for bottom. 'It's got the brassiere attached, all in one?'

'That's right, our separate brassieres are made in the next room.' He followed her through. 'You can't say these are old-fashioned.' She picked one up to show him. 'This is very latest thing, and we sell more of them than anything else.'

'Quite an invention.' Ben pulled at it. It was made of the same strong twill. 'Haven't you always made them?'

'No. Once it was fashionable for dressmakers to bone the bodices of frocks to support the bust. Dressmakers made tightly boned underbodices too, but of course in the twenties ladies wanted to flatten themselves. It was only after the bust had been flattened for a decade, that it suddenly became the height of fashion to have uplift.'

Ben threw the garment back on the pile. 'Who invented this then?'

'An American lady. It's said she was going to a ball in Paris when, with the help of her French maid, she stitched together two handkerchiefs and some pink ribbon. She called it a backless brassiere and sold the patent to the Warner Brothers Corset Company for $15,000. It came on the market as the Kestos Brassiere, but soon every corset maker was copying it. Ours have always sold well.'

'Did you copy it?'

'Yes. I tried to improve on it, but basically it was the same.'

'Couldn't you make them prettier? Lace and satin and stuff?' he asked.

'They are worn to provide support, dear.'

'Why don't you ask Lydia what the young wear? What they'd *like* to wear?'

'It might embarrass her.'

He stifled a smile. 'Ask Oliver then, he could find out.' She laughed, and he knew she thought he was joking. Mother only spoke about corsets in the factory. She'd told them all years ago that in mixed company, even at home, they were quite unmentionable.

He was still thinking of his first day here. 'I'm forty-eight,' Dad had said over a cup of tea in his office. 'I don't intend to die at my desk. I want you to learn how to manage the business.'

'What about Oliver?' He was Ben's elder brother, married now to the daughter of a margarine manufacturer, and no longer living at home.

'We don't know if Oliver wants to continue here, but if so I hope we can make the business support you both.' Oliver's future had been discussed at several family meals. He'd announced that his in-laws were trying to attract him into their business. 'Stephen, too, if he proves up to it.'

It had shocked Ben a little to hear it put so bluntly. All the family were writing off Stephen, the youngest. He hadn't done as well at school, showed no interest in further education, and met all his mother's wishes with head-on refusal. Ben had tried to tell him this was foolish. Now he knew it was suicidal. That Stephen had survived so far showed he had his own strengths.

Because he'd qualified as an accountant in order to take over the company accounts, Ben considered his duties and responsibilities to be clearly defined. He had thought it was just a question of coping with them in his own way, of getting a little practice and then learning to contribute more to the running of the business.

Now he found his mother was always behind him, pointing out the next move, as she was with other members of the family. They were all puppets doing her bidding, drawing their energy and impetus from her.

She was never going to give him a free hand, and he couldn't imagine she'd ever retire, let alone go within the next five years like Dad. Mother was threatening to sweep him along like a twig in the river. He knew he'd have to do the job his way to feel any self-respect. At twenty-four, he felt entitled to consider himself a man and be independent of her apron strings.

The factory closed at five-thirty, and the sound of raised voices, drumming footsteps and slamming doors carried upstairs. As it died away, Ben stood and stretched and began locking the drawers of his desk. It was considered family duty to stay five minutes longer and make sure everything was safely secured for the night.

His mother drove them home in the family car, with Father slumped in the front seat beside her, and Stephen and Ben in the back. The journey took only five minutes.

Ben loved the quiet of Rock Park, the high hedges and mature trees and the aura of settled family life that the old house possessed. Rock Park was an estate of houses designed for the wealthy merchants of Liverpool in the middle of the last century. In those days, they could reach it more easily than the suburbs of their own city, and travel in greater comfort on the frequent ferries.

Most houses were four stories high to take advantage of the spectacular views up and down the Mersey, and the kitchens and servants' quarters were on the ground floor. They were built in varying styles – some semi-detached with massive bay windows, others with mock Regency wrought-iron balconies.

Once home, his father liked to unwind over a drink. Grandmother was just coming downstairs to join him as they went in. Old but still beautiful, she'd worn black since their grandfather died forty years ago. It was all part of the family routine.

Ben had been told many times that the house had been bought for Grandma by Grandfather when she married him in 1880. She thought it the best in Rock Park. Shearing's Shirts had been very profitable in those years, and had provided the money to buy a comfortable house of six family bedrooms and three servants' rooms in the basement.

It had been built in 1841 when Rock Ferry had been at the height of its popularity, and in the gracious style of an earlier period. On the first floor, long sash windows with a gothic arch on top stretched from floor to picture rail. The house was solid and unchanging, suiting the family that had lived here and carried on business for several generations. Ben loved being part of it.

Oliver was always telling Mother it was high time they moved. He thought Rock Ferry was no longer a desirable residential area, and said it was becoming socially unacceptable to live there. Everybody who could was moving further out of town. In the depression, big houses were turned into flats or even rented by the room. Rock Park retained a certain decaying respectability, but the neighbouring areas were being eaten up by Merseyside's urban sprawl.

Ben bathed and changed, feeling the need to be quick. Dinner was served on week nights at the unfashionably early hour of six-fifteen.

'By the time we've worked all day we need a meal,' his mother said. 'We can't sit about till eight waiting for our dinner. That would waste the evening.'

'It's much too early,' he'd heard his grandmother

protest many times. 'I always had dinner served at
eight. I'm not hungry at six and it's quite improper to
drink before the sun goes down.' But they all knew it
didn't stop her having her pre-dinner sherry.

'It might suit gentlemen who have idled all day,'
Beatrice always allowed. 'And those who've eaten a
filling lunch with wine.' But she never gave an inch.
Guests were only ever invited at weekends when she
could see her way to eating a later meal.

Ben was always ready for his early dinner. Tonight
he had a few minutes in hand, and the view from the
window never failed to draw his attention. He could
see the gardens sloping down to the river, hedged with
lilac trees. There was a gate in the fence leading on to
the Esplanade.

The Mersey tide was full in and sparkling in the last
of the evening sun. The evenings were lengthening
now as spring approached. Ben lifted the binoculars he
kept ready on the sill. He loved to see the teeming
river life.

Riding at their permanent moorings were the *S.V.
Conway*, a black and white ship from Napoleon's war,
now a training ship for Merchant Naval Officers; and
the yellow-funnelled, grey-hulled *Indefatigable*, a Victorian iron ship, now a sea school for orphans of
seamen. The ferry boat *Royal Daffodil* was tied up at
Rock Ferry, and her passengers were streaming up the
pier. A coaster belched black smoke as it chugged up
to Runcorn.

The river, the business, and the old house gave Ben
a feeling of continuity, a sense of his place in life. He
wanted to follow in the footsteps of his forebears, live

out his time making shirts as well as, if not better than, they had. He didn't think of himself as ambitious, he didn't want to be of service to others like a doctor or fight battles to keep his country safe. He wanted to be like the rest of his family: law-abiding, upright, ordinary. Not rich, but not poor either.

It gave him pleasure to see the shirts his family made displayed in shop windows, proud to see advertisements on placards and in newspapers. 'Shearing's Shirts, made to suit gentlemen.'

Shearing's was just one of many garment-making factories in Birkenhead; he didn't believe any of them were ever going to make a fortune. What Ben wanted was to keep the company on a sound financial footing and earn a comfortable living for himself and his family. He wanted to marry and have sons to carry on the tradition. It gave him a feeling of warmth and comfort to belong to a family that others respected. He was proud of being a Shearing.

The gong for dinner boomed up the stairway, and he headed downstairs. His mother whisked past him on her way to the kitchen, her feet moving at twice the speed of his, chin jutting forward in deadly determination.

She had bathed and changed into a floor-length bronze skirt, and re-done her rich brown hair into its elegant chignon. She had never had help from a hairdresser, considering them a waste of time. Ben marvelled that at fifty years of age, there was no sign of grey in her hair. She looked decades younger than she was.

Seconds later she was with him in the dining room,

checking the table and that all possible preparations had been made on the sideboard. There was nothing in her busy manner to show she'd been a driving force at the factory all day.

Ben had hardly reached his chair before Grandma was being ushered in by Dad. She'd always seemed an austere lady, very correct, a stickler for convention, and it was felt in the family that she set a high moral tone for them all. He felt the continual undercurrent between her and his mother because Grandma had had to relinquish the running of the household, and Beatrice had her own very definite ideas about how things should be done.

At the last moment, his mother turned to the table, composing her face for the grace as she sank into her seat.

'Dear Lord . . .' Grandma's voice had developed a slight quaver. As he listened, Ben watched his mother's head bent in apparent supplication. It seemed out of character. Truly his mother bent her head to no one. She seemed to consider herself God's equal when it came to directing their daily affairs.

Her dark eyes snapped open and her hand whipped the cover off the soup tureen to coincide exactly with Grandma's last word. The ladle flashed in. A brimming soup plate came in his direction to pass up to Grandma at the head of the table. Mussel shells clinked in a creamy broth. Ben felt saliva fill his mouth. The smell was delicious.

'I have invited the Michelsons to dinner on Saturday evening.' His mother's dark eyes challenged him. 'They're bringing Sarah.' He felt a sudden rush of resentment, and halted the spoon halfway to his mouth. 'I expect you to be here, Ben.'

'Mother!' Fury was engulfing him. 'I am not going to marry Sarah Michelson. Whether I'm here or not will not further your plans.' The meal he'd looked forward to tasted like ashes. His appetite was gone.

'Sarah is a lovely girl.' His mother's eyes held the conviction that she knew best. Ben recognised the look, he'd seen it hundreds of times before.

'I know, Mother.'

'She'd make a suitable wife for you.'

He took a deep breath. He'd been through this a dozen times already. 'What makes you think you can choose a wife for me? I'll have to live with her, not you.'

Beatrice's laugh held all the energy and freshness of youth. He thought how ill it suited her. He was not disarmed as he was meant to be.

'Of course I don't expect to choose your wife, Ben.' Again the laugh. 'It's a very personal relationship. But I want you to marry well, and all I want to do, is to help you meet girls of the right calibre.'

'I don't need your help, Mother.' He heard the mulish note in his own voice and knew it would only fire her determination, but in this he was determined she would not have her way.

He looked to his father for support, but Edwin was avoiding eye contact with either of them. Stephen's head was bent low over his plate. Ben understood neither intended to take sides. For them, it was safer to remain neutral.

'You must meet nice girls, dear,' Beatrice was

saying with false gentleness. 'Give yourself a chance. All you see are the factory girls. One of them would be a liability, hold you back.'

One of them! He knew she meant Rosie Quest. He saw her again as she had been this morning, trying to stand up to his mother's needling. Rosie had tied the front strands of her hair back behind her head, and though the ends of her satin ribbon streamed down across her red-gold curls in an almost bridal style, it had still been tied firmly. He could see her now, her fingers feeling for the streamers, her cheeks scarlet with embarrassment.

'Let me,' he'd said, taking up the ribbons and trying to fashion them back into a bow. Her hair felt springy against his fingers, and at the nape of her slender neck the curls had been tighter. He'd had to fight the urge to push his fingers into them. He'd wanted to pull her round and kiss her curving mouth. It had been a struggle to keep his fingers fumbling on the ribbon.

Rosie had always fascinated him. She assaulted his senses, made his blood run with heat. He'd noticed her years ago when he used to go to the factory in his school holidays. She'd been an apprentice of fifteen then. His father said she was shy.

In his mind, he likened her to a forest deer unused to the ways of man, tempted closer by hunger in the depths of winter. Ben felt he'd need to lure her forward, one tentative step at a time, until he'd gained her confidence. Yet he sensed her interest in him; as though she wanted to creep closer but didn't quite dare.

Her small slight figure seemed poised for flight at

the first scent of danger. She had stylishly slim ankles to give her a turn of speed should he move too fast and frighten her off. Her deep green eyes held the wary look of one who assessed every risk before she made a move.

In the sewing room where harsh voices were continually raised above the noise of the machines, she was soft spoken and gentle in manner. He knew he'd have to gain her trust before she'd give anything of herself.

He knew the other girls thought her standoffish and reserved, but thought that really she wanted to join in their camaraderie. She was the sort of girl who shied away when he spoke to her, even if it was only to pass on some message from his mother.

'It's time you settled down, Ben, got married,' Beatrice said. 'Twenty-four is old enough. Surely you feel that? You'd like a wife and a home of your own, wouldn't you?'

He felt another surge of anger, wanting to deny it, but of course he wanted to marry. Wasn't it human nature to give and receive love?

He thought he'd found someone once or twice. He'd felt this blinding attraction to other girls, but always it had fizzled out or gone sour. In theory he wanted to marry, but had nobody in his life who would suit the part. It was a personal dissatisfaction that he hadn't established such a relationship. A rather painful area that he didn't want to discuss. He knew he would have to dismiss out of hand anybody his mother introduced as suitable. That was the effect her overbearing ways had on him.

'Sarah Michelson might suit Stephen,' he said

abruptly, and was rewarded by a searing glare from his
younger brother. Stephen had the typical Shearing
sandy curls and broad shoulders; he was a younger
version of Oliver without the moustache. He was
twenty-one, but his face was that of a teenager:
innocent, naive and vulnerable.

'She would not!' Stephen sounded aggressive.

Only Grandma was still forking her mussels, but her
ice blue eyes darted round the table. Ben felt she
should have reached tranquillity with old age, but
Grandma was never tranquil.

'You'll get into less trouble if you marry,' Beatrice
said, and that made him smoulder again. He knew
she'd seen and recognised all he'd felt when he'd tied
Rosie Quest's ribbon. 'You mustn't flirt with the girls
at work.'

'I wasn't flirting,' he ground out from between his
teeth.

'Come on, Ben.' She laughed again. 'You aren't
telling me you're serious about a working girl like
her?'

He felt overcome with confusion. He didn't want to
tell his mother anything. 'There's nothing to tell,' he
said. There wasn't, it was much too soon. He hardly
knew Rosie.

'You'd both better stay in on Saturday to entertain
this young lady.' His father looked up at last. 'No harm
in seeing her, is there?'

'I'd rather eat out,' Ben said.

'So would I,' Stephen supported him.

'Why?'

Ben bit into some bread to give himself time.

'Because Mother wants to marry me off to some girl I don't know.'

'You'll get to know her if you're here on Saturday.' Dad was glowering at him.

'I don't *want* to know her.'

'But you want to get married,' his mother put in. 'You've just said so.'

'I'm in no hurry.'

'Of course not, dear. It's not something that can be hurried. I have your interests at heart, believe me. I want you both to have happy marriages, like your father and I.'

Ben applied himself to the next course, speculating about his parents' relationship, somehow a little surprised to hear her describe it as happy. Dad seemed to arouse her impatience just as much as he and Stephen did. And as for Dad, if the rumours he'd heard . . .

'We've had a perfect partnership,' Beatrice went on, making Ben wonder if she was reading his thoughts. 'Marry the right person and you'll be set up for life. Marry within your class, that's paramount. Your father has been a model husband.'

The beef was a little on the tough side. Dad was chewing as though it was the most important thing in his life.

Ben could feel himself being swept headlong towards a showdown with his mother. Sooner or later they'd have an earthquake of a row. He shivered. It could be a fight to the finish, and he'd be very lucky indeed if he was the one to survive.

Dad straightened up in his chair and looked him in the eye at last. 'I would look upon it as a personal favour if both you boys would eat dinner here on Saturday. At least make yourselves pleasant to this girl. What happens after that is up to you.'

'All right,' Ben agreed, knowing now whose side Dad was on.

CHAPTER FOUR

'We've opened up the loft for you,' Will told Rosie as soon as she went to the cow shed the next evening. 'Tom has put some planks across the floor so you won't fall through, but be careful. Are you going to help us milk first?'

'Of course.' She felt a surge of anticipation at the thought of seeing her mother's belongings. She rushed to milk Marigold to get the job finished as soon as possible, and for once the cow gave no trouble.

Afterwards, when she and Tom were turning the herd out to pasture, watching them slither on the wet cobbles as they crossed the yard, she said: 'You must remember my mother?' She didn't miss the wary look he gave her from faded eyes.

'Aye, I remember her. Pretty little girl she was, always laughing.'

'I'm not like her, am I? To look at, I mean.'

'Not in any way, Rosie.'

'Tell me about her.'

'There's not a lot I remember,' he said awkwardly, no longer able to look her in the eye. 'It's a long time ago, and she left home when she was very young.'

'How old was she?'

'About your age, I suppose, or even younger.'

'Yes.' Rosie had already worked out that Grace was barely twenty when she'd been born. How could Maud be so damning about the sin she'd committed? Grace had hardly been old enough to know what sin was.

'You'll be wanting a light soon,' said Tom, reaching the storm lantern down from its hook. He lit it, took it up to the loft and hung it over the door. He'd already dragged the trunks as close to the doorway as he could get them. 'Floor's safer here, lass.'

Rosie hovered impatiently, feeling tantalised. At last he let her go inside the musty loft. There were two trunks and a suitcase. The last remnants of ten-year-old hay had turned to dust and covered everything. Huge cobwebs were festooned across half-seen rafters.

'Can you open them all right?' Tom asked from the ladder.

Rosie wanted to be alone to savour all she found, but she recognised the kindness that prompted him to ask. She bent to a battered tin trunk. The lid wouldn't budge. 'No.'

'I'll find a chisel to prise it open.' Rosie tried the steamer trunk and that opened easily, as did the suitcase. She let the lids fall back, not wanting even Tom's eyes to see her mother's things before she did. Below her in the stable she could see Flash through the rotting floorboards, sucking up her evening oats.

Tom came back, breathing heavily, to force the lid. 'Not been opened for donkeys' years. Didn't want to touch them till you were here. There you are, lass.' The lid of the tin trunk creaked open on rusting hinges. There was a strong smell of moth balls.

Rosie waited till he'd gone, then knelt in the dust. Inside were neatly folded clothes. An afternoon dress in midnight blue, with the bodice tucked and pleated in a long forgotten style. A smart coat in the same colour. They evoked no memories, she'd never seen them before, but they had belonged to her mother. Another more summery dress in deep red linen . . . the clothes were conjuring up the image of a young girl. Slim she must have been to fit inside the red linen. In her mind's eye, Rosie saw her wearing it, and wondered what sort of occasion it had been. There were high-heeled shoes and a fur stole.

Rosie sat back on her heels and tried to think. These clothes must have been expensive, yet her mother had been penniless before she was born, otherwise why go to the workhouse?

Clearly her fortunes had changed. Will had said her father had taken them out of the workhouse. It seemed odd he'd let her go there in the first place, unless his fortunes had somehow changed too? Or maybe she'd gone there and he hadn't known? Or again, terrible thought, had her mother lived with more than one man?

If there was a clue to his identity anywhere, it had to be here among Grace's possessions. Who was this man whose way of life had killed her poor mother? Rosie delved into the steamer trunk. There were ornaments, small pieces of porcelain and pottery. A table cloth half covered with delicate embroidered flowers, the frame still attached to it, and a threaded but rusting needle stuck in the hem.

She found books, half a dozen of them, and decided she'd take one or two over to her room to read. Poetry, and novels by E.M. Forster and Joseph Conrad. She flicked open their damp-speckled fly leaves. There were no messages written on them to give clues about other people in her mother's life.

Excitedly Rosie burrowed deeper, hoping for something she'd remember, but wanting to see everything.

There were more clothes, things Grace would have worn regularly. There was even a hobble skirt. All seemed very long, very formal, and belonged to a different era, but for the first time her mother seemed close enough to touch. She'd been a living, breathing, real person. She'd had smart clothes, more elegant than anything Rosie possessed, but no party clothes or evening dresses. Her mother had not had a social life either.

She found pencils and paints, crayons and charcoal, all dried up and brittle with age. The personal possessions Grace had used and worn were a wonderful birthday gift.

About half of one trunk was taken up by sketch books of drawings, water colours, patterns and designs. Rosie pored over them in delight, but she needed full daylight to appreciate this find. There were dozens of portraits of a curly-headed toddler. Rosie was in no doubt they were pictures of her in babyhood. She knew her mother had loved her dearly, it showed in every line and brush stroke, in the care and attention lavished on detail. Even in the light from the storm lantern, she could see her mother had had a rare talent.

Right at the bottom beneath them all, her fingers closed on a hard-backed notebook. Was this what she wanted most, a diary in which her mother had written down her thoughts and feelings and something about the life they'd lived? She was quivering with such hope and anticipation she could hardly bring herself to open it. When she did, she found the pages were ruled in columns and squares. Figures in faded ink trailed down the pages. It was an account book of some sort. Rosie's disappointment was searing. She put it on one side to study later.

There were still treasures to unearth. She pulled out a brown lizard-skin handbag. The gilt catch had not tarnished. She snapped it open. The lining was of soft kid, and showed the Mappin & Webb label on the inside pocket. She was delighted to find a comb and mirror. Her mother would have used them, and now she could too. They would narrow the distance, make her feel even closer. She found a lawn handkerchief with a threadworked border, a purse with notes and coins still in it. She turned them over with careful wonder.

She came across a receipted bill for coal and some bus tickets. In another inside pocket she felt a book. She thought at first it was a small notebook, but when she drew it out, found it was a bank deposit book in the name of Miss Grace Mary Quest. Rosie was suddenly tingling again. There was a credit balance of two hundred and forty-six pounds. That would have bought a lot in 1919. Even today . . .

Rosie sat back to ponder again. She could understand now why she'd felt a social misfit. She'd never been consciously aware of her early history but it had left its mark.

Years ago Uncle Will had urged her to bring her friends home as Phyllis did. It had revealed the fact that she had none. Well, none close enough to ask here. She couldn't give to people, couldn't unbend and be herself. Too many people resented her presence, like Aunt Maud, and Phyllis, and all Phyllis's friends. They seemed to look down on her. Beatrice Shearing was of the same mind.

Rosie sighed. It was not that her childhood had been unhappy; here on the farm she'd had so much she enjoyed. Space to play in the byre and the stable, the apple loft and barns. Nobody could feel out of sorts amongst animals, and she'd loved them all. The cows would come down the field to greet her if she went inside the gate. The dog followed her everywhere, nudging her to stroke his head. She'd ridden and groomed and fed Flash. She'd milked cows since she was seven years old, and fed hens and collected eggs.

Uncle Will and old Tom had been glad of her company and her help with haymaking and corn harvest, with potato lifting and milk bottle washing. This had always been her world. It had been Grace's world during her childhood too, but she'd been the much loved only daughter. According to Will, they had all made much of her.

'Rosie?' She heard his voice below. 'Come on in for supper, it's on the table.'

'Coming,' she called, pushing back the contents of the trunks, dropping their lids, and dimming the storm lantern. As she turned to go she saw she'd left out two of the books and tucked them under her coat. On the pretext of washing her hands in the bathroom, she took them up to her bedroom. She had a few books on a shelf, and added her mother's to them. Phyllis would be unlikely to notice, she didn't read much.

Rosie felt too excited to eat as she took her place at the table. She hardly tasted the cottage pie, and the sight of the half-eaten birthday sponge only reminded her of the trauma she'd been catapulted into last night.

Her mind was on her mother, she was hungry for facts about her. She remembered, years ago, asking Will: 'Where did Grace sleep? Which was her bedroom when you were children?' She'd been flushed with eagerness to ask if she might move her things and sleep where her mother had as a child.

There were two more bedrooms on the same floor and three larger attic bedrooms above them, but they hadn't been used for over twenty years. Rosie saw herself cleaning out the dust and spider's webs. Perhaps persuading Will to do something about the flaking plaster and the large patches of damp. A room of her own would be lovely. Surely Phyllis would help her achieve that?

'She had the little back bedroom,' he had said. 'As the only girl she got a room to herself.'

'Which is that?'

'Where the bathroom is now. I had it put in for Maud. There was no bathroom here when we were children.'

Rosie could still feel the disappointment as she'd bitten back her request. She understood now what a loss her mother's death had been. She felt full of love and sympathy for the hardships Grace must have endured.

'I've asked you twice,' – Phyllis was pushing her face close to hers – 'what have you found?'

Rosie didn't want to talk about it. 'Just her personal things: clothes, shoes, hats.'

'A lot of good they'll be after all this time. I didn't think there'd be anything of value.'

Rosie smiled, wanting above everything to get back to the loft, but because Phyllis helped Maud get the supper on the table, it was considered Rosie's job to wash up afterwards.

She hurried the dishes to the scullery as soon as she could. It opened off the kitchen and was tiny, more a walk-in pantry with a deep sink and draining board. The shelves all round were piled with dishes, pans and food. There was only enough room for one person at a time, and usually Rosie washed up, then Phyllis came to dry.

She pulled out the plug and because Phyllis was no longer in the kitchen, took up the tea towel and finished the job. Maud hated to see anything half done, and Rosie didn't want to upset her again tonight.

She was putting on her coat to go out to the stable loft again when the back door flew open. Phyllis, her handsome face flushed with triumph, came in.

'Dad, just look what I've found!' Grace's bank book went spinning up the long table to where Will was still sitting. 'I thought you said there was nothing of value, Rosie?'

She was suffused with indignation. 'You've been

rooting through her things!'

'Just as well I did. I don't suppose you would have mentioned this.' Rosie tried to snatch it back but Maud's hand was quicker.

'Two hundred and forty-six pounds,' she breathed in amazement. 'And we've had to scrimp and save all these years.'

'It's mine,' Rosie said. 'Give it to me.'

'Mother ought to be recompensed for all the money she's spent bringing you up,' Phyllis spat.

'I pay for my keep,' Rosie said. Maud had insisted she handed over her wage packet when she'd started as an apprentice at fourteen. She still gave it to her, and Maud handed back five shillings pocket money each week.

'She fed and clothed you for the first fourteen years,' Phyllis's face twisted greedily. 'Why should you have all this? It isn't fair.'

'Give it to me,' Will ordered, and reluctantly Maud handed it over. 'This belonged to our Grace. She didn't leave a will, but she'd want Rosie to have it.'

'Why should she have it all?' Phyllis repeated. 'It's a lot of money. Gerry and I could get married on that.' In the silence that followed, they all heard the coals settle in the range and the flames roar up.

'I wonder where she got it from?' Maud said.

'She was a whore, Rosie,' Phyllis taunted. 'It's tainted money. I don't think I want it after all.'

'Be quiet!' Will thundered. 'Grace was your aunt, and my sister. I think you should show more respect for the dead.'

'I was wondering,' Rosie faltered, 'will it still be

there? It's eighteen years after all.'

'The bank's still there at Charing Cross, why don't you take the book in and ask them?'

Rosie pushed her red curls off her forehead. 'I suppose I could go on the bus in my dinner hour.'

Will's forehead creased in thought. 'That won't give you much time. Would you like me to go?'

'Yes, please, and can we take the money out?'

'I'll ask them that at the same time,' he promised.

'Thank you,' she buttoned up her coat. 'I want to go and see if there's anything else.'

'The rest is a load of old rubbish,' Phyllis said spitefully. 'Just junk. She daubed a lot of paint on paper like you do. The whole lot needs throwing out.'

'See you do,' Maud said in her severe fashion. 'I don't want you bringing any of it in here.'

Rosie surreptitiously wiped her eyes. She wasn't going to let them see she was upset.

Out in the loft it seemed colder now. In her stall below, Flash was lying down, settled for the night, wheezing and snuffling. Rosie turned up the storm lantern and sat for a long time surrounded by her mother's things, listening to the scurrying of mice in the dusty hay.

Then she took out the account book and began to study it. The first page jerked her out of her apathy. It seemed to be a record of monies paid to Grace. The first date entered was June 1917, and the payment appeared to be from a magazine for an embroidery design. Why had she not looked in this notebook straight away? It was a wonderful find. It meant Maud was wrong. Grace had not been a kept woman. She'd been earning a living for them.

This was a record of what her mother had earned, but it also listed what she had sold. Rosie understood now why there had been so many half-worked designs in the sketch books. She'd been sketching out ideas. Those that hadn't worked out to her satisfaction, she'd abandoned.

She dug into the collection of sketch books and papers again, and her hand closed on what she sought: a file containing Grace's patterns that had been commercially printed. Thrilled, Rosie matched them up with illustrations of the finished cushion covers and tray cloths, blouses and baby clothes. Grace seemed to have specialised in baby dresses. Most had instructions attached as to what stitch should be used, and what colour thread.

Rosie turned back to the account book. Grace had been selling her paintings too. Even received commissions for some. That explained the two or three expensive outfits. Of course, she'd have had occasions when she'd need to be well turned out, look professional and prosperous.

Aunt Maud might despise her, but Grace had been successful. Her work must have brought her a sense of achievement. Rosie frowned. By comparison she was not achieving much, sewing shirts for Shearing's.

She was afraid Phyllis might come in again or her aunt tomorrow while she was at work. She couldn't bear to think of Maud's hands sorting through Grace's things, and was sure that if she left them here, she would. Her aunt's touch would defile them.

Suddenly she made up her mind – she would hide

them. But where? In the apple loft? On top of the hay in the barn? Yes, that was it, on top of the hay. She was the only person who ever went up there.

She had almost to empty the trunks to move them at all, and it was hard work getting them down from the loft, and even harder to haul them up the ladder when she'd got them to the barn. Will would have helped her if she'd asked, or Tom, but then they would have known where Grace's things were. Better this way. It took countless journeys. Flash was on her feet again before Rosie had finished.

She was no longer cold by the time she had moved everything and buried it in the hay. It was like burying the dead, she thought. Now Grace could rest. She was proud of her mother, proud of what she'd managed to do.

She strode back to the house, her mind dwelling on what Grace had achieved. The kitchen felt over-warm as she went in. Phyllis and Maud sat either side the fire, listening to the wireless. With a high handedness she'd never used before, Rosie snapped it off. Even Will looked up from his newspaper in surprise.

'I don't know how you dare say my mother was a kept woman,' she flared at Maud. 'You jump to all the wrong conclusions. Believing the worst of her, saying things that aren't true, when you knew nothing of her circumstances.'

'Of course she was.' She could see her aunt bristling to justify what she'd said.

'She earned her own living. Here's proof of it. Aren't I right, Uncle Will?' Rosie banged the account book down on the table for him to see.

'She was earning money from June 1917 onwards.'

'Nonsense, she'd just come out of the workhouse!'

'All the more credit to her then, that she could pull herself together and start selling her paintings and designs so quickly.'

'Somebody must have got her out. Guaranteed her living expenses.' Spite and suspicion were making Maud's cheeks red. 'Otherwise she'd have to stay where she was. They kept women like her till the child reached the age of fourteen and could support itself. Isn't that so, Will?'

'My mother was clever and talented. She didn't need to rely on hens to earn money like you do. She could paint and draw.'

Phyllis had her head craned over the account book. 'She didn't earn all that much,' she sniffed disdainfully. 'No great fortune.'

'Money went a long way in those days,' Rosie said defensively.

'Let me see,' Maud's fingers dragged the book up the table. 'I can quite understand your feelings, Rosie, but I think you owe me an apology.'

'Why?'

'You've been very hasty. Your mother may have earned some money, but she had income from somewhere else. She left almost as much in her bank account as she earned, according to this. Of course she was clever, Rosie. I never disputed that. But she was a kept woman. This certainly doesn't prove anything different. I was right about that.'

Ben Shearing stared at the figures his Comptometer

produced and felt like banging his head against the wall. It was so silly. He hadn't expected to have the slightest difficulty in producing last year's accounts for Shearing's Shirts.

He was surrounded by records in which a dozen or so employees detailed the materials they'd used and the garments they'd made. He had countless forms which listed everything from services received to wages paid. He had piles of invoices, settled and outstanding – and he had worked with growing frustration for three solid weeks.

On the first day he had been exhilarated at the thought of condensing all these figures to show exactly how much profit they had made for the year. Now he was finding the figures he turned out were not at all in line with what he'd expected.

The whole family were waiting to hear how much better they'd done last year. Mother had gone on and on about their increased turnover, Dad had said he'd improved efficiency and honed prices to the bone. They'd set higher sales targets, and Stephen had said he'd met them.

Ben had copies of the annual accounts for 1935, 1934 and 1933 on his desk, all neatly typed and signed by the auditors. Along with many other companies, they'd made only modest profits over the last decade because the country had been in the grip of a severe depression. But now business was improving for everybody, and Shearing's in particular were expecting a bumper year.

He'd studied their annual accounts avidly during the years he'd been articled, and thought he knew exactly how to do the same for 1936. Now, suddenly, he was awash in a sea of meaningless figures. They weren't adding up right.

Ben shivered. His feet were cold, and he wondered again whether he had been right to insist on using this room as an office. Mother had warned him about the lack of heating upstairs. He'd brought a portable electric fire from home, but it wasn't much help. The room he'd chosen had been designed as a hotel bedroom in 1870, and was provided with an open grate for a fire. On the spur of the moment he crumpled up the morning's copy of the *Telegraph* and pushed it up the chimney out of sight. That should stop the draught. When he withdrew his hand, his shirt cuff was black with ancient soot, and rubbing it with blotting paper didn't help.

He went restlessly to the window, feeling dissatisfied with the whole set up. He'd spent some months after qualifying studying the management of successful local businesses. Everything seemed so much less professional here. He was telling himself he needed more time to settle in when he heard a fist crash against the heavy panelling of his door. It was thrown open immediately.

'Ben, can I borrow your newspaper?' his brother Oliver asked. 'You get the *Telegraph*, don't you?'

'Not this morning,' he said coldly, feeling irked that Oliver had time to read two newspapers when he had barely looked at one. More so because his brother had collated some of the returns he was trying to work with. He'd described this as putting them into a 'more manageable form'.

'You did the accounts last year, didn't you, Oliver?' he asked.

He watched his brother straighten to his full six foot, looking concerned. He was taller than either Stephen or Ben, had broader shoulders and the sandy hair typical of the Shearings.

Ben had not seen so much of him over the last two years, and had not been sorry. Oliver had not lived in the family home since his marriage to Lydia Feltham.

'Yes, you know I did. As much as Mother allowed me to do. She kept issuing instructions, and checking I'd carried them out in accordance with her wishes. What's the problem?'

Ben couldn't look at him without all the old antagonism welling up. Brothers were supposed to love each other, but there had never been much love lost between him and Oliver. Two years older, he'd attracted love from everyone else. Certainly their mother favoured him in everything. Ben had long since accepted Oliver was higher in the family pecking order, and knew he'd been jealous of his brother all his life.

'The sales figures seem low. Stephen thinks they should be up on last year's.'

'Oh, Stephen!' said Oliver disparagingly. He had been educated at an expensive boarding school. It had given him a polish that neither Ben nor Stephen possessed.

'Business went down,' his father had explained apologetically years ago. 'Couldn't afford school fees like that for three of you.'

Ben and Stephen had gone to Birkenhead School.

Not that he was decrying the education he'd received there. Standards had been more than adequate, Stephen had found them too academic. It was the favouritism that Ben objected to.

'Are you sure you've added up the invoices properly?' he asked.

'Damn it, of course I'm sure!' Oliver exploded arrogantly, his dark eyes flashing fire.

'Can I see them? I'd like to check back. All I have are your returns.'

'Ben, I've drawn up the annual accounts for the last three years. You've only been given the job because you've trained as an accountant. It's no big deal. Mother will help you if you're stuck.'

'I'm not stuck exactly.' He could feel his hackles rising. 'But I would like . . .'

'Mother has them in her office. She's checked them as she checks everything. Why don't you ask her?'

As the door slammed shut behind him, Ben swore and sank back in his chair. The last thing he wanted to do was to consult Mother.

He looked again at his figures, pondering that if sales had been this low, then the balance of shirts made must still be held in stock. An inventory had been taken a couple of weeks ago, perhaps that was wrong? He recognised the signature of the storeman, a man who'd worked for them for all the years Ben could remember. He'd done the inventory in previous years.

Ben got to his feet. He would go along the corridor and look for himself. Garments completed and ready for despatch were stored in rooms on this floor. He couldn't count them again, of course. He knew it took three men a couple of days, and the count wouldn't be exactly the same anyway, since more shirts would have been made and others despatched. He went from room to room and concluded there was no great backlog of stock. The indications were that the inventory was correct.

As he passed his father's office, the door opened and Mrs Pratt from the kitchen came out with the tray of mid-morning tea and biscuits. She was rotund with an impressive circumference round the hips and abdomen. She wore tennis shoes on tiny feet, and had legs that looked thin below the massive overhang of stiffly starched white overall.

'Where will you have yours, Mr Ben?' she asked.

'Bring it in here,' his father called. 'Come and keep me company, Ben.' Phyllis Quest was just leaving with her notebook and a pile of files under her arm. She gave him a coquettish smile.

He slid into the chair she'd vacated, put his cup on the desk and asked : 'What possessed you to buy this decaying hotel, Dad? It doesn't make ideal factory premises.'

'The price.' His father smiled. 'The owners had gone bankrupt so it was cheap. Once there were many fine hotels in Rock Ferry. It was a resort visited by Royalty and the aristocracy.'

'Royalty? Who might that be?'

His father wore suits of loosely woven pepper-and-salt tweed. Ben had heard Mother threaten to send them to the Salvation Army, and not without cause. Dad wore them till the elbows began to give, then he

78

got Flora Pope in the sewing room to patch them with leather. He liked his suits to be comfortable, and by that he meant he liked them to have developed bulges to accommodate his knees. Pockets must sag under the weight of his pipe and tobacco pouch, and the collar must have settled into a thin tight roll across his rounded shoulders.

'George III. He stayed at the Rock Hotel, and ever after it was known as the Royal Rock.'

'That's going back a bit. I bet Royalty wouldn't come now. It's gone down in the world since then.' Ben met his father's benign and gentle gaze. He had the look of a man gone to seed, with a moth-eaten gingery moustache and thinning hair that had been sandy in his youth but was now dun-coloured.

'The Albert Hotel came complete with gardens and shrubberies. We managed to sell off a couple of acres with road frontage – where the shops are now.'

'I never knew that.' Ben was full of interest. 'It must have been a real bargain.'

'The bargain of all time, son. It was your mother's idea. We've been here nearly twenty years now.'

He was fascinated. 'Where were you before?'

'The original Shearing factory was in Tidal Way, an old building and much too small. We'd outgrown it. Do you know Dyson's – they make interlock vests in George Street?'

'Yes, was that ours? But that's a purpose-built factory, far superior to this.'

'We overstretched ourselves, lad. Got into debt. Your mother was making her corsets in a wooden shed at that time. The corset girls thought this place was luxury when they came here, I can tell you.'

'And you were both able to sell your old premises,' Ben mused. 'How much did the move save us, I wonder?' He laughed. 'It's the accountant in me that's asking.'

'Look in the old accounts if you want to know.' Ben followed the direction of his father's hand. He'd had cupboards built along one wall, some of which were glass-fronted. Ben took the key he was offered and unlocked them. They were packed with files and account books.

'Records go back to the start of the business. The whole story is there: annual accounts supported with payslips, and bills for materials, sales figures, everything. Shearing's Shirts from the very beginning to the present day. You ought to study them, Ben, you'd learn a lot.'

Enthralled, he ran his hands over the books, and took one out. It was heavy, elegantly bound with Florentine end papers. The figures were hand written in ink that was fading on pages yellowed with age.

'I'll start at the beginning, 1865, and work through. It'll be a labour of love.'

'They make fascinating reading. The story of our family too. Take care of them, Ben, I wouldn't like any to get lost.'

'Of course I will. I'll take them a year or two at a time. I can't wait to get started.'

He came back to the desk to finish his tea. 'I want to build this business up. I want it to be the success it was in Grandfather's day. And I'd like to knock down this old place and build a real factory again. Customers get the wrong impression when they come here.'

His father's eyebrows rose. 'It's our shirts they're buying. Why should they care where they're made? Re-building is damned expensive and would cause a dreadful upheaval.'

Ben smiled. He and Stephen had always seen Dad as a soothing influence on the family. No internal dynamo drove him, he moved along at his own comfortable pace.

'It's what I'd like to see, all the same.'

At the moment, shirts were being cut out in what had originally been the bar. It wasn't his imagination: there was still a faint smell of cigars and alcohol in the atmosphere.

Ben pondered his father's strategy for side-stepping Mother's managerial ways. He always agreed to go along with whatever she decided, but if he was not of like mind, somehow it went no further. Eventually, Dad got his own way where he thought it important. Ben had never known them fight about anything. Nobody, he reflected, liked arguments they couldn't win.

'You'll have to make more profit before we can afford a new building. Not only does it have to support your mother and me, but now it has to provide a living for you three boys.'

Ben bit into his biscuit. Three weeks ago he would have said cheerily: 'We can make it do that.' His one ambition in life had always been to improve the business and he'd seen no reason why he should fail. Now, with the latest figures unbelievably bad, it no longer seemed so easy.

The question he dreaded came. 'How did we do last year?'

Ben stifled a shudder as he met his father's gaze. There was something wrong. There must be some fault in the figures he was feeding in.

'Hard to say yet. Need a bit more time to work it out.' He stood up, wanting to get away before Father probed further.

Back in his own office, he got out his figures again and spread them across his desk. Step by step, he thought them through from the beginning.

Shearing's had made many more shirts last year than in previous years, an undisputed fact. The shirts were not being held in the stockrooms, and there were only sales receipts for about two-thirds of them. There was no paperwork to account for the rest. The problem was, where had they gone?

The thought hit him in the solar plexus leaving him gasping. Was he looking at deliberate fraud?

CHAPTER FIVE

Waiting at the bus stop, Will Quest pushed his hands deeper into the pockets of his mac. He shivered, as much from the feel of Grace's bank book as from the dank drizzle. Rosie's birthday had re-opened the raw wound of his sister's death. He'd been torn between anger and pity, and it had set the whole family at each other's throats. He hadn't expected it to leave him feeling balanced on a knife edge.

He ought to feel better now he'd been to the bank. Grace's account was still there, and the money in it. Even better, being a deposit account it had accrued interest over the last eighteen years. The book had been made up for him, and now the credit stood at four hundred and nine pounds, a nice nest egg for Rosie. It pleased him to think she'd have that behind her. She had little enough of anything else.

The bad news was they had advised him to see a solicitor about proving her legal right to it. Will sighed, and wished he knew more about such matters. Edwin Shearing would know, he ought to have a word with him. No point in wasting Rosie's capital on solicitor's fees if there was a way round it. Falling profits had taught him that much. Perhaps Rosie would talk to Edwin herself? After all, she saw him every day.

He saw the bus coming. Habit made him pull himself up the steep stairs, slide on to a damp seat, and polish the condensation from the window so he could see the endless terraces of houses, blue slate roofs shining in the rain, bricks blackened by smoke.

He took off his hat and shook the beads of moisture on to the floor, ran his fingers through his wispy grey hair.

The houses gave way to the bleak wasteland of industrial Birkenhead, the cranes of the shipyard rising like black monsters against the grey sky, half veiled in smoke and rain. Every inch was familiar, and who but a fool would be farming in such a place?

The town had grown in the middle of the last century; docks, shipyards, warehouses and dwellings for the workers had spread up the banks of the Mersey. Away from the river, little had changed until after the Great War when progress began eating away at his acres. Not town exactly, but suburbs, insidiously, a road at a time.

Four generations of Quests had rented Ivy Farm. He'd been brought up there, together with his three brothers. Odd that he, the eldest, should be the only one left. All his forebears had made sufficient income to live well. Hadn't he gone to school with the likes of the Shearings and counted them amongst his friends?

It added to his pain that he had failed where others of his family had succeeded. He blamed the depression, and the ever-encroaching town.

Lord Leverhulme owned most of the land about

here and, although a fair landlord, his agent had explained the need for land to build houses on. His lordship's own and other businesses had burgeoned in the Great War and needed more workers, and because the acres Will rented were near the town, it was his land that was being squeezed. Other farmers in the same position had given up.

Once his family had rented ninety good level acres in a ring fence. Of those, Will had only forty-two left. He'd been offered a further eleven acres of pasture beyond Lever Causeway in 1920 and had had to take them. It was good land for haymaking but at a distance from the farm, and when he wanted to graze it, the cows had to be walked there and back. The farmland was no longer in a ring fence and it took more time and energy to run.

The bus jerked forward again. Close proximity to the town had brought other problems. The shiftless, those who wouldn't or couldn't get work, fed their families at the expense of his. They dug up his potatoes before they were ready, took his apples before they were ripe. Old Tom had been telling him for years that eggs were being stolen from the henhouses. When the hens themselves began disappearing under cover of darkness, Will had sold them all off. It no longer made sense to keep anything but the milking herd.

Maud held it against him that their income had fallen year by year. He'd tried hard to remedy it by going into pigs, and lost money. He grew potatoes and carrots with a few other vegetables in season, and sold them from his milk float during his round. By cutting out the middle man he could just survive, but his turnover was too small.

The bus jerked forward again. Will felt so churned up he had a sour taste in his mouth, as though his body was out of kilter was well as his mind. The last few days had opened up a hornet's nest of trouble.

Grace had dealt him some body blows in her time. He'd been shocked when she ran away from home. Horrified to find she was having a child. She'd been defensive when he tried to talk to her, said she was all right and had no need of money. He'd said the only thing possible: 'If there's anything I can ever do, anything you ever need, let me know.' She never had.

Years later he'd met her in the street by accident, and she'd hardly deigned to speak to him. She'd had Rosie in a push chair then.

Her death had come as another numbing shock. He hadn't known she'd given birth in the workhouse till then, or that she was living so close. It couldn't have come at a worse time for him and Maud. It had swept them into another family crisis.

'You can't shackle me with her child,' his wife had wailed, and how could he blame her when she had twins of six months to look after already? They had always wanted a son, but Phyllis had weighed six pounds at birth and gained weight rapidly while Paul had been half her size, a frail and sickly infant hanging to life by a thread.

Phyllis had been a demanding baby who wanted her feed every three hours. Maud was devoting the rest of her time to the boy twin, and barely coping, when Rosie was thrust on her. The last thing she'd wanted was an energetic three-year-old to look after too.

They had both anguished over baby Paul, and had not been prepared for his death at ten months. That had come as another shock. In those days Will had been able to afford a girl living in to help Maud, but even so the children had exhausted her.

Will shuddered as he watched the rain come down more heavily, bouncing up from the pavements. The way Maud had treated Rosie on her birthday, the way she'd sold off Grace's jewellery without a word, had not only enraged him but brought an over-whelming sense of guilt that he'd allowed such things to happen.

Last night he'd seen her clearly for the first time in years, her grey hair screwed severely into a mean bun, her arctic eyes. Why had he not noticed before how thin and bony she'd become? She looked an embittered woman.

He'd been a disappointment to her, she made no secret of that. Nothing he ever did came up to her expectations. She always felt she was getting a raw deal. If she got her fair share of anything it was work or trouble, and after twenty years of marriage he had to ask himself how much of this was his fault.

Will sighed. He had to decide what to do about the farm lease. Last October, when he'd taken it for another year, he'd wondered if it was wise. He had to make up his mind what he would do next October. If he signed for another year, then he would have to make hay for next winter. It was no good just worrying about it.

Maud didn't want him to give up until it was

absolutely necessary. 'You're only fifty-five,' she'd told him indignantly last week. 'Other men retire at sixty-five, surely you can go on till then? We don't want to starve in our old age.' Maud was nine years younger than he was.

But already he'd left it too late. He'd closed up pastures in case he needed hay, and the grass was already eight inches high. If he was going to give up the lease, he ought to be making plans to sell the herd. He'd deliberated far too long about it. Perhaps it was just as well he had no son to follow him.

Will jerked upright, suddenly realising he'd gone past his stop. He went clattering down the iron stairs to swing impatiently on the open platform as the bus carried him further. What an old fool he was.

He had to tramp a quarter of a mile back in the rain. It gave him plenty of time to reflect. He remembered Phyllis's pretty face distorted with greed and envy as she'd demanded a share of Rosie's money last night. Already she had the same dissatisfied droop to her mouth as her mother. He'd hoped the two girls would grow up good friends.

Rosie had brought him compensations, but Maud had never accepted her, and Phyllis had taken her cue from her mother.

Poor Rosie. He could understand the shock she must have felt at the first sight of that birth certificate. He'd felt his own stomach muscles contract in sympathy.

'Why did you let it happen to her? Why didn't you help her?' Rosie had cried in her agony. He'd never understood why Grace hadn't asked for help then.

He would have done anything to stop her dying so miserably.

Will felt hatred rising in his throat for the man who had got his sister into trouble and abandoned her. She'd been loyal to him, never opened her mouth or hinted at who he might be.

He'd sworn revenge if ever he found out. Rosie's questions had revived the vengeful fury he'd felt eighteen years ago, brought back the itch to his fingers, made him want to close them round his throat and strangle the life out of her betrayer. Nothing was too bad for him.

Going up Gordon Drive he told himself he was an old fool. It was all too long ago. Eighteen years in her grave. What was the point of fire and brimstone after all this time? Rosie had said as much, and she was right.

Ben let his eyes assess the members of his family sitting round Dad's desk. Every month they had what his mother called a Board Meeting. She said it was necessary to discuss progress and future plans for the business. Ben suspected they were brought together to hear what had been decided for them, and what she expected them to do in the following weeks. How much more comfortable they would have been round the dining table at home.

Except, of course, that Oliver no longer lived with them. He looked at his brother now, noticing the knuckles of his fingers showed white as they gripped his fountain pen. He'd made no mark on the paper in front of him. Tension showed in the line of his shoulders and the set of his jaw. Usually Oliver looked relaxed. Mother held him up as an example of all that was poised and competent.

'If you do as well as your brother Oliver,' she would say. 'If you manage to make as good a marriage as your brother Oliver.'

Ben had spent several weeks worrying about their profit for 1936. He'd taken the figures apart and put them together again. Fraud was the only answer, Oliver was his prime suspect, but he hadn't dared say so to anyone.

Oliver shouldn't need money. He'd married Lydia Feltham, and her father had given them a house as a wedding present. Ben had heard Lydia had a handsome allowance too, Oliver spoke of it as her dowry. But his brother had a fine new car, and he hadn't said who had paid for that.

Ben sighed. Being the elder son by two years seemed to give Oliver untold advantages. He'd always been held superior to Ben and Stephen. Throughout childhood, they had known it was hopeless to try to earn Mother's affection. Oliver had it all. He could do no wrong in her eyes.

Ben found it hard to believe Oliver had deliberately bled money out of the business for his own use. Surely he wouldn't take from his own family? But he was becoming miserably aware that nobody else had the opportunity to do it.

If he were to go to Mother with his suspicions, he doubted she'd believe him. Tell Father then? But Dad was a neutral figure hovering on the sidelines. He'd long ago abdicated responsibility to Mother, and had very high principles when it came to honesty in business. He wouldn't believe that Oliver had not.

He watched his mother's pen flying across a notepad. She held it loosely as she took notes. 'Why don't you get Miss Gibbons to take the minutes?' he'd asked.

'We don't want the office staff in with us. She's not family.'

'Who types them?' Ben asked.

'She does, of course, but she types what I tell her to type.'

Ben shrugged: 'She'll know what goes on in these meetings then.' His mother never seemed to mind how much unnecessary work she gave herself, so long as every detail was as she planned it.

Mother had been on his back every day, wanting to see the figures for last year's profit. He didn't dare produce them. Seeing what he'd worked out in black and white would catapult the whole family into a crisis and start a lengthy post-mortem. He's said it was far too early to discuss the figures, he hadn't finalised them. That satisfied no one. Mother had driven him on to talk about the results in general terms. He'd said he was afraid the profit would be lower than they were all expecting. He was still hoping against the odds that it was just some stupid mistake he'd made.

'I really thought,' his father said, 'that last year would have been a better one. We all seemed to work harder and produce more. Very disappointing.'

'Overheads were higher.' Oliver's voice was tightly controlled. Ben noticed he didn't lift his eyes from his blank pad.

'Of course they were higher – we took on three new machinists.'

This year there'll be my salary too, Ben thought.

'Sales are the problem.' His mother's dark eyes flashed round them all. 'That's where the trouble lies.' Beside him, Ben felt Stephen bristle. Sales were his responsibility.

'I've increased them,' he insisted. 'I got more orders. New orders. I know I did.'

Ben's eyes went down the page to the figure he'd pencilled in for annual sales. Sales for shirts were down on the year before.

'Sales for corsets have increased marginally,' he said. 'Is that what you mean?'

'No.' Stephen screwed up his youthful features in agony. 'I got new orders for shirts. I was well up on the year before.'

Although Mother liked to keep her corset business separate for accounting purposes, in practice she said it would be wasteful to have separate salesmen going round in separate circles. Stephen worked at both businesses simultaneously.

'I think I ought to come out with you, Stephen,' his mother said. 'To visit some of our larger accounts. If you watch and listen, you'll see how it should be done.'

'Mother, you will not!' Stephen raised his voice by an octave. 'If I'm the Sales Manager, then I'll do the selling. What would the customers think? My mother leading me in by the hand, showing me how to do my job?'

'But we'll sell more,' she said coldly. 'We need to sell more.'

Ben doodled on his pad. He could well believe his mother would sell more. She was a *force majeure*. He could see customers agreeing to give large orders just to get her off their premises.

'I tell you,' Stephen was almost shouting, 'I increased sales last year.'

'The figures don't show that, Steve,' Oliver said shortly.

'They did!' he shouted. 'Do you think I didn't compare them month by month? I wanted to know how I was doing, and I was up each month.'

'You thought you were, dear.' His mother's voice held an unusual note of weariness. For once, she looked tired. 'Ben, you can see the problem?'

He shook his head. He and Stephen had always been allies. He wasn't planning on saying anything Stephen would resent. The truth was, something was very wrong and he wasn't sure what.

'We simply have to increase our sales.' Beatrice's chin jutted forward, her eyes blazing with fervour. 'Stephen, you must work harder, try harder. Our quality is up, our shirts are more fashion conscious.' She smiled at Oliver who had pressed for the longer pointed collars fashionable at the moment, and for a less formal look.

'Quantity is up. It's just a question of selling more. That's where we must do better now.' Beside him, Ben felt Stephen squirm in his chair.

'Why don't we all think carefully over the next few days?' Mother beamed at them all. 'And see if we can come up with some ideas on how this can be done. To help Stephen.'

There was dead silence. Ben doodled some more. He had the feeling it was his turn now.

'Ben, we ought to look into the overheads together,' she went on. 'There must be some way we can cut them.'

'Mother, you've appointed me the accountant. Let me deal with that.'

'We can't afford to waste money . . .'

'I'll save every possible halfpenny,' he said belligerently. If he were not aggressive, she'd walk all over him.

'See you do,' she snapped.

He meant to have the last word. 'You've given me the job. Give me time to do it.'

Beatrice pulled on her grey serge dress and sank to the stool in front of her dressing-table. In the mirror she watched her fingers flying up the row of buttons on the bodice. Without a pause, she reached for her comb and swept her abundant brown hair into a chignon, pinning it in place. Behind her she could see Edwin's bulk, still in striped pyjamas, sitting on the edge of the bed.

'Get a move on, Edwin,' she said, working vanishing cream into her cheeks. She watched him stir, lift the cup of early morning tea to his lips. It would have gone cold long since. 'Breakfast in ten minutes.' She tried to suppress the irritation it caused her to see him mooning about as though they had all day.

Before she went down to the kitchen to make sure Mrs Roper was getting on with breakfast, she ran up to the floor above to knock on another bedroom door. 'Ben, are you up?'

She paused just long enough to catch his reply before knocking again on the next door.

'Stephen, are you up?' There was no response. 'Breakfast in five minutes,' she added. There was still no response. Throwing open the door she found him curled up asleep, his morning tea untouched.

'Stephen, wake up!' Her impatience spilled over into anger. She saw his eyes open and blink up at her uncomprehendingly. 'You've overslept again.'

He sat up with a jerk. 'Sorry, Mother.'

'You stay out too late. How do you expect to do a day's work? Come on now, hurry up.'

Anger swept her downstairs as she wondered for the umpteenth time what the Shearing men would do without her to keep them functioning? They seemed to have been born without the urge to get out and do a day's work.

She could understand it in Edwin, but not in her sons. They were her own flesh and blood and should have inherited her sense of purpose and distaste for wasting time.

She had to hustle them again, to get them away from the breakfast table. Stephen had not finished his eggs and bacon. It annoyed her more to see him pick up the plate and bring it with him to the car. As they travelled along almost deserted streets of Victorian houses with their tightly curtained windows, the chink of his knife against the plate drove her to distraction.

She had to hold her temper in check by concentrating on Edwin's hands moving upon the steering wheel.

Usually, she used the travelling time to make a mental list of the jobs she had to attend to and work out their relative priority. Time was very important, and none of the Shearing men seemed to understand that.

She hadn't slept as well as usual. Over the last weeks she'd had niggling doubts about the results for last year. The figures weren't as high as they'd hoped. She'd tried to talk to Edwin about them several times.

'Let Ben collate the figures,' he'd said easily. 'He'll manage.' Beatrice had felt a quivering impatience; she could have done all Ben was doing in half the time. They needed to know where they were.

'He must do it, Beatrice. The children won't learn if you don't let them try. It's no good you doing their work for them.'

She had seen the sense of that and said nothing to Ben, but last week impatience had made her look in his desk to see how the accounts were coming out. What she saw made her more fearful. Sales were well down.

'Impossible to tell until everything is added up,' her husband had scoffed when she'd told him. 'We must look as though we trust Ben to do it. Anyway, we made more shirts than ever, and if we aren't carrying a lot of stock, they must have been sold.' But nothing he could say would stop the niggling doubts.

When she reached her office, Beatrice found it impossible to settle into her usual morning routine. Edwin was always telling her to relax.

She heard again her mother's voice: 'If you want a job done properly, you have to do it yourself.' She was constantly aware of the fire within her, making her strive for greater efficiency.

Not like Edwin who sat over his newspaper for an hour every morning, and what good did it do him? Far better if he got on with his work while his mind was clear and his body refreshed by sleep. 'An hour in the morning is worth two in the afternoon,' was another of her mother's sayings.

'Relax, Beatrice,' Edwin had laughed at first. 'Take it easy.' But he never hindered her now. He relied upon her to achieve what he could not. She would take the opportunity later, when Ben was not in his office, to look again at his figures. No harm in that, and she had to make sure he was going about the job properly.

As she walked round to the back door of the factory that machinists were told to use, Rosie clutched her handbag close against her body. Grace's bank book was in it. It was an unpleasant surprise to see the Shearings' green Rover already parked outside. She had meant to arrive before them this morning.

She had worked out in her mind that the start of the day was the best moment to catch Mr Shearing alone, and was cross with herself that this morning she had not been waiting for him as he'd come in. She hated asking favours of anyone, but neither could she have Uncle Will coming in to speak to him on her behalf. Already a feeling of dread was building up in her chest.

Of course, he did come to the sewing room several times a day, but she couldn't discuss her business there. All the girls would have their ears flapping, it would be far too public.

The back door slammed. She entered the bare passage and started to unbutton her coat. As she passed the open kitchen door, she caught a glimpse of pepper-and-salt tweeds. Her heart was racing but she made herself alter course and push the door wider. 'Mr Shearing?'

'Morning, Rosie.' He was rubbing his hands together affably while a cook, wearing white overall and cap, poured him a cup of tea.

The kitchen was made light and airy by a row of windows, but they were set high enough to prevent the kitchen maids of yore being distracted by what went on outside, and had to be opened and closed with a hook on the end of a pole.

'Could I have a word with you, please? Could you spare a moment?'

'What about? Thanks, Mrs Pratt, that's lovely.' He was coming towards her holding his cup.

'Well . . .' Rosie felt tongue tied with reluctance. She didn't want to talk of it in front of the kitchen staff either, or her business would be all over the factory by this afternoon. 'It's personal.'

'Oh! Well, in that case you'd better come up to my office. Will you have a cup of tea?'

Rosie felt the blood rush to her face. Tea first thing in the morning was enjoyed only by the family and senior staff. It was not served to machinists. 'I . . .'

'Another cup, Mrs Pratt, please.' He was pushing his own into her hand. Rosie caught Mrs Pratt's glance; it told her she was over-stepping the limits.

Every employee agreed that Edwin Shearing was a kindly and considerate boss, the very opposite of his wife. Rosie followed him into the main entrance hall.

They paused at Phyllis's desk and Rosie saw her eyebrows raised too though she knew well enough what Rosie was trying to do since Uncle Will had discussed it at supper last night.

'My paper please, Miss Quest.' Phyllis handed it to him while Rosie cringed with embarrassment. 'Of course, you two are cousins, aren't you?' His kindly eyes smiled into Rosie's.

Phyllis's agreement was frosty. She was looking down her handsome nose. Rosie then had to get the brimming cup upstairs without slopping its contents. She felt a dozen pairs of eyes watching her progress.

'Well, Rosie?' Edwin Shearing pushed open the door to his office, placed his tea on his desk and slid into his chair. 'Have a seat and tell me what I can do for you.' Her mouth felt dry. She took a sip of tea.

'My Uncle Will suggested I come to you, I hope you don't mind?'

'Of course not.' She watched him open his newspaper to glance at the headlines while her fingers fumbled in her bag for Grace's bank book. She pushed it across the desk for him to see.

'It belonged to my mother, but I can't get at the money. Nobody can until . . .'

Suddenly Edwin Shearing was straightening up in his chair, his smile fading. For a long moment he stared at the book, frowning and tense. Slowly he put out his hand and picked it up. The colour had drained from his cheeks, leaving them grey.

'It's years since she died, you see,' Rosie went on desperately, shocked at the effect she was having on him. She wondered why. 'Nobody knew it existed, till Uncle Will told me about her things. I found it in a handbag.'

'Grace Mary Quest,' he said, and she saw his eyes clouding. Suddenly the back of her neck was prickling with foreboding.

'Did you know her?' she asked hoarsely.

He looked up, his blue eyes benign again. 'Your Uncle Will was a great friend of my brother Harry.' He sighed. 'They were both much older. I can remember them taking me to your farm as a treat. Will let me feed the hens and collect the eggs. Yes, I remember Grace, though she was younger still.' Rosie gulped her tea in silence.

'Oliver is the person to handle this.' He went to the door to call him from the next office. Oliver took his time coming, his face stiff with reluctance when he did. Rosie found it hard to believe he was Ben's brother. There was a polish about him that the younger man did not have. An arrogance in the way he held his head. Oliver was physically more like his father, with sandy hair that curled and a military moustache.

'Oliver read law at college. He'll know exactly what to do.'

He stood aloof and lordly as his father explained, then his haughty gaze went to Rosie. 'Did she die intestate?'

'She died in hospital,' Rosie answered, and saw the disdainful look come over his face.

'Did she leave a will?'

'No.'

'That complicates matters. Other people may have a

claim on this money. Her husband . . .'

'No,' Rosie said stiffly. 'He's . . . no longer with us.'

'Oh. And you're the only child?' She gulped and nodded.

'You'll have to apply for letters of administration, and swear a statement,' he said.

'How do I do that?'

'Send off for forms to the Law Society, then fill them in.'

'Do it for her, Oliver, will you?'

He did not immediately agree. 'There's a charge for the form.'

'How much?' Rosie's spirits were ebbing. The notes she'd found in her mother's purse were all she had.

'I don't know exactly.' He shrugged his broad shoulders.

'Take it from company funds,' Edwin said. 'Rosie can pay our out-of-pocket expenses when she can get her hands on this.' He tapped the bank book.

'Exactly which account should I debit?' Oliver asked sarcastically.

Edwin sighed. 'Petty cash?'

Oliver's eyes rolled ceilingwards.

'It won't cost much,' Edwin said. 'Look, I'll pay the expenses.'

'Thank you.' Rosie felt relief and gratitude for his willing help, but a gnawing doubt too as to why he should be so generous.

'I'll need your mother's death certificate,' Oliver said briskly. 'Do you have it with you?'

'Yes.' Her fingers unzipped the inner pocket of her bag. She kept the envelope concealed below the desk, carefully withdrawing the death certificate and pushing back her birth certificate, though she knew she ought to show that to Edwin too and get it over with.

'Oh,' Oliver said, 'I'll need your father's death certificate too.'

Embarrassment was curling her toes, and making the blood rush to her cheeks. 'Why?'

'The rules of intestacy are laid down by law.' His nose lifted higher, Oliver was at his most pompous. 'The spouse inherits. Only if your father is deceased will you have clear entitlement to this.'

Rosie cast round desperately for the best way to make the next move. There was no best way. 'My mother never married.'

Oliver's smile was more than disdainful. 'That alters everything. The law does not recognise illegitimate children. You have no legal right to her money.'

Rosie wanted to die. She'd admitted all this, gone through this grilling for nothing. 'Somebody's entitled to it,' she said brusquely. 'The money is there.'

'If she'd only made a will,' he said in tones of lament.

'She was twenty-three.' Rosie was more than brusque. 'She wasn't planning to die. Who is entitled?'

'Her parents.'

'Both dead already.'

'Does she have brothers and sisters?'

'One brother.'

'Him then.'

Rosie sat stunned. The law would see that Maud got her share. Phyllis had been right to demand it.

'What about her things – clothes, personal possessions?' Her mouth was dry.

'The same applies.' Rosie couldn't believe she had no right to Grace's clothes, books, anything. She'd gloried in possessing them.

'I don't make the laws. I'm just explaining them.'

'Yes, thank you.'

'Do you still want me to go ahead?'

Rosie tried to think. 'Yes.' The money had lain idle and been no good to anyone all these years. 'Yes, Uncle Will has need of it. Better somebody uses it. He did say he wanted me to have it.'

'Isn't there something called a deed of variation, so that Will can hand it to Rosie?' Edwin asked slowly.

Oliver's well-groomed head nodded. 'That would add to the cost, the complication and the delay. If her uncle wants her to have it, there's nothing to stop him drawing the money out and handing it over.'

'Go ahead.' Edwin was frowning. 'That's what you want, isn't it, Rosie?' She nodded, feeling raw and exposed and somehow exploited. The law didn't re-cognise her right to anything.

'Right,' Oliver said briskly. 'I'll write off today.' He was scribbling a note of Grace's account number. 'You'd better look after this.' The bankbook came back across the desk. Rosie felt she was being dis-missed. She felt spent, could not prolong this terrible inquisition by bringing out her birth certificate though all the facts had now been laid bare. Oliver's proud Shearing eyes had shown how he regarded her.

She stood up, leaving her tea unfinished. 'Thank you.'

As she pulled the door closed behind her, she was

shivering. It had been a horrible experience that had left her shaking. One of the worst moments had been when she'd seen Edwin Shearing go pale at the sight of her mother's name on the bank book, and the explanation he'd given when she'd asked if he knew Grace did not ring true.

She remembered Will telling her that he and Harry had brought Edwin to the farm as a treat when he was young enough to enjoy collecting eggs and feeding hens, so that was true enough, but would Grace have been born at that time?

Will was fifteen years older than Grace, the eldest child in a large family of which she had been the youngest. He referred to her as his little sister, and felt responsible for her. That was why he'd been so guilt-ridden that she'd given birth in the workhouse.

At a guess, her mother would have been about seven years younger than Edwin. Rosie didn't think it possible that he could have known her then. At best, she would have been a baby and unlikely to have been out feeding hens with them. Even if she had, would an acquaintanceship as slight as that make him turn pale at the sight of her bank book nearly forty years later?

Edwin knew Grace better than that. There must have been another connection, and he'd avoided telling her what it was.

Surely he could not be her father? She went hot and cold at the thought, and then dismissed it out of hand. Of course not. He was far too gentle a person to allow anyone to go to the workhouse. Far too mindful of his responsibilities. She went slowly to the head of the stairs, pondering on this, when she realised Ben was coming up.

'Hello, Rosie.' His voice was friendly and teasing. A smile tugged at the corners of his mouth. 'What a memory you have. You said you'd bring in your birth certificate last week, and you've forgotten again.' He tossed his hair back from his eyes while she froze in renewed horror.

CHAPTER SIX

Ben felt like kicking himself. He saw immediately his words had made her pull away in alarm.

'Come in here,' he said, ushering her into his room and closing the door. Feeling she needed time to recover, he went to his desk and sat down.

'What do you think of my new office then?' When he looked up, she was biting her lip, her eyes anxious. 'What is it, Rosie?' he asked gently.

Slowly she opened her handbag, every line of her body tight with tension as she took out an envelope. He could see her fingers shaking as she handed it to him. 'I didn't know. It came as a shock.'

'What did?' She pushed the envelope closer. He didn't take his eyes from hers. They were dark green pools of agony.

'I was born in the workhouse.' Her voice was strangled. It took a moment to sink in, then he jerked out of his chair and pulled her into his arms. Her body felt soft and yielding. She was not encased in corsets.

'Rosie! What difference does that make? You can't help where you're born.' She half stifled a sob against his lapel. 'Hey, come on. What does it matter, you've got a good home now.'

Holding her close like this, Ben felt on fire, intoxicated. He had to pull her closer, allow his lips to touch her forehead then her cheek. Her hair felt springy against his neck.

'It matters.' Her voice was thick. 'Of course it matters. What will your mother think? She'll be horrified. She'd never have let me come here as an apprentice if she'd known.'

'Rubbish,' he said. 'Anyway, we don't have to tell her. I can confirm your birth date is correct. That's all we wanted it for, Rosie. Where you were born is none of our business.' He couldn't stop himself tightening his arms round her. He wanted to give her comfort, hating to see her upset.

'Can you?' She was struggling to free herself, fluttering in his arms like a bird. He let her go. Her green eyes had taken comfort from his words rather than his touch. She didn't seem aware of him as a man.

'Yes, nobody need know but me. It's not important where you were twenty years ago.'

'Twenty-one.' She smiled tremulously. 'Different for you. You come from a family with a good reputation. Shearings have been rich and successful for generations.'

'Hardly rich.'

'Compared with everyone else.'

Ben had been half aware of a commotion downstairs for some moments. Now they both heard running footsteps and somebody calling his name. A fist thumped on his door.

'Come in,' he said, but already the door had opened. Kitty Harmon from the sewing room could hardly get the words out. Her false teeth were clicking with agitation.

'Come quick, Mr Ben! Mary Green's burned herself!'

Ben felt a rush of dismay. Another accident! Mary Green was their newest apprentice. Rosie had already gone to the door. He wrenched open the top drawer of his desk, pushed her birth certificate under some papers and rammed it shut again. The next minute he was flying downstairs after her.

Accidents were the one facet of the business his mother said she was happy to leave to him. In her opinion, carelessness caused all accidents and gave the rest of the workforce an excuse to ogle, gossip and waste time. She said he had more patience for coping with the sick and injured.

All the girls were crowding to one end of the room, where the ironing board was always set up alongside a series of shelves.

Flora Pope the forewoman shouted: 'Sit down, girls, let him get through.'

The girl was flat out on the floor, her face grey and sweating, the ironing board turned over beside her. There was a strong smell of singeing wool.

'Switch the iron off, Flora,' he said.

'I already have.' Flora was a plump spinster of close on forty who wore spectacles of thick bottle glass. Usually she was a jolly person. He hadn't seen her like this before, jittery with anxiety. 'I think she's fainted.'

'What's happened now?' he heard his mother ask as

she came up the room. 'What is it this time?'

'Mary Green has fainted and burned herself.' He might have known Mother would come! She couldn't bear to miss anything.

'Burned a good shirt too,' Beatrice retorted, picking up the garment Mary had been ironing. There was a deep brown iron-shaped burn on the front. 'Our most expensive wool flannel too!' She was ripping off the two loose matching collars that were pinned to it. 'What a waste. These can be used for another shirt.'

Mary Green opened her eyes and tried to sit up. 'Take your time,' Ben said, lifting her hand. There was a minor burn on the side of her palm.

'She's dropped the iron too,' his mother said, picking it up and righting the ironing board. 'It's probably broken.'

'Pulled it on top of her,' Flora said. 'She couldn't help it. We've got a spare if it is. I'll see to it.' Even at that moment, Ben was aware of the frigid atmosphere between his mother and the forewoman.

'And I'll see to Mary, Mother. You don't want to waste your time on minor accidents.'

'It would be better if you didn't have to either,' she said, but turned to stride quickly up the room. Simultaneously, half the sewing machines started to whirr.

'Come on, Mary,' he said, helping her to her feet, finding it impossible not to feel pity for her washed-out appearance and mouse brown hair. 'Come to the kitchen, and have a cup of tea.'

The kitchen was a vast echoing cavern with long runs of brass pipework along the ceiling. It had several huge ovens along one wall, all of which needed blackleading. Above them were gantries that had once been laden with pans but now collected dust nobody could see. Once, luxurious multi-course meals for the one hundred and twenty-five guests of the Albert Hotel had been prepared here.

Now the many shelves were bare apart from a collection of large fish kettles and leaning towers of soup bowls. A motley collection of extra tables, benches and whitewood chairs had been brought here, and the room was used as a staff dining room as well as a kitchen now. Mary still seemed shaky, fourteen years old and as thin as a rake.

'Did you have any breakfast?' She shook her head, her face still grey and sweating.

'What about last night?'

'I had my tea.'

'And what was that? What did you eat?'

She couldn't look at him. 'Bread and jam.'

'You need to eat more. I think that's why you fainted. Make her a sandwich with that tea, Mrs Pratt, could you?'

'Me dad's out of work, you see.' The girl was drying her eyes. 'And I've got five brothers and sisters all at school.'

'It's not enough, Mary. You can't work all day on bread and jam.'

'I have my dinner here.' Ben sighed. He knew that for the last few years his mother had arranged for Mrs Pratt to make soup in big fish kettles every day. Bones were ordered from the butcher and fresh vegetables, beans and peas, lentils and barley, added to make a variety of thick broths. They were sold at a halfpenny a bowlful to the workers so that they had something hot in their stomachs at midday.

'It's the only way to get any work out of them in the afternoon,' his mother had said. 'If they don't eat, they slow down. Women feed their families but often go short themselves.'

'We could give it them for nothing,' his father had suggested.

'No, they only appreciate what they pay for,' Mother insisted. 'And at a halfpenny, it's a bargain they can't resist. Besides, it covers the cost to us.'

Ben knew it was good soup, he had it too. Mrs Pratt made sandwiches of hard-boiled egg or cooked ham for members of the family to eat with it. These days, Ben sat at the scrubbed tables with the sewing girls and noticed many of them brought only dry bread to eat with theirs, protesting that it was more than enough for them.

Mrs Pratt brought a ham sandwich and a cup of tea for the girl. 'There, you'll feel better after that,' he told her. 'Stay here, Mary, till you do. Do you want to go home then? Have the rest of the day off?'

The girl sniffed and shook her head. 'I'll be all right, thanks.'

'How's your hand?'

'Throbbing a bit.' Ben looked at her doubtfully, wishing he knew more about first aid.

'Shall I find her a bit of bicarbonate of soda?' Mrs Pratt asked. 'That's good for burns, isn't it?'

'Yes, please,' he said, hoping she was right. 'Keep her here for half an hour. Till she feels better.'

112

Beatrice Shearing felt irritable and out of sorts. It had annoyed her when Edwin had taken on Mary Green as an apprentice. She had asked him years ago to leave the choice of girls to her, but he couldn't say no if an employee asked him to start a relative. This girl was wasting cloth because she had no aptitude for sewing, and wasting other people's time by having careless accidents.

Beatrice let the sewing room door slam shut with disgust. She was heading back to her desk when suddenly she changed direction and went running upstairs. Ben would be occupied with the girl for the next few minutes; this was a good opportunity to see what he was doing with those figures.

It was high time he'd finished. Why was everybody so slow, so lackadaisical? Nobody seemed to care whether the work was done or not. Edwin had no energy and the whole factory took its cue from him. Piecework helped to keep the production workers at it, but as for the van drivers and cleaners, typists and kitchen staff, they would do nothing without her shoulder behind them.

Of course, she'd expected more get up and go from her sons, more sense of purpose. But Oliver was a good boy, and pulling his weight in the office. A son she could be proud of. She'd hoped Ben would shape up, and with training might cope, but he was showing some of Stephen's negative manner. Stephen was as lazy as his father. Edwin had told her he was grateful he'd married a wife who did his work for him.

'Without you, Beatrice, Shearing's Shirts would have gone to the wall years ago.' Thirty years of marriage to Edwin had taught her exactly what he was like. Beatrice's lips tightened, making her face seem harder, less handsome.

She let herself into Ben's office and closed the door softly behind her, mindful that Edwin and Oliver were close. Not that she felt there need be any secrecy about what she was doing, it was for the good of the business. Ben was tetchy when she asked. This way she'd spare his feelings.

Sliding into the chair behind his desk, she opened a drawer. She had learned by now where he put the files he was working on. She lifted the top papers out, wondering why he'd hidden a birth certificate amongst them. She turned it round and studied it.

'Rose Evadne Quest' she read, with a further surge of annoyance. Hadn't she pleaded with Edwin not to take her on?

'Her uncle has asked me to, as a favour.'

'I'm asking you *not* to as a favour to me! It's bad enough knowing of her existence, without having to see her every day.'

'It's not easy for the girl. She's got to have employment. A trade . . .'

'Honestly, Edwin, you've no sense. You've no consideration for me. How do you think I feel about her?' He'd had his way, of course, but at least Rose Quest had learned to sew. Beatrice stifled a smile. She'd forgotten when she'd told the girl to bring in her birth certificate that she'd been born in the workhouse. She understood now why Rose hadn't brought it immediately. She wouldn't want that to become general knowledge. She was ashamed of it.

Beatrice understood another thing: Ben was sympathetic and trying to protect her. A secret shared such as this was not a good thing. She wanted no emotional ties between them.

She went to his file cabinet and found Rose Quest's application to join the pension scheme. Then she ticked the box to confirm her date of birth was correct, and countersigned it.

On Ben's desk, she found what appeared to be the envelope the certificate had been kept in all these years. She slid it back inside, and put it in her pocket. She'd give it back to Rose herself. If her secret had engendered any intimacy between them, that should blow it sky high. Definitely the best way to handle Rose Quest.

Beatrice delved deeper into the drawer and found what she'd come for. Ben's figures were still written in ink. The fact that he hadn't had them typed meant he didn't consider them complete. She turned up what seemed to be the balance sheet, and felt the blood drain from her face. With a sinking feeling of disbelief she found she was looking at the results for the shirt business for 1936.

They'd had a decade of thin profits. The depression had dogged them, trade of any sort had been flat then, but by last year business generally had begun to pick up. She'd worked very hard, and made every single employee and every member of her family work hard too with the express aim of bringing profits up.

Beatrice had worked out a careful strategy. They'd expanded the workforce, bought more efficient sewing machines, and kept their prices keen. They'd attempted to cut out wholesalers by selling more direct to retailers. Yet they'd made less profit than the previous year!

Beatrice truly believed that hard work and hard thinking brought its own rewards. Never had this happened to her before. She had never even considered that her strategy might fail. Fifty years of always getting it right brought its own confidence. Of course they'd had their good years and their bad since she'd started taking an active interest in the shirtmaking in 1916. But when she had decided what could be done to improve profits or turnover and worked towards it, her methods had never failed. Till now.

She felt cold, ill even. She'd had a strange feeling during the second half of that year that although turnover was up, profits would not be. But because she hadn't been able to put her finger on the reason, she'd dismissed the feeling as fanciful.

She sighed, knowing well enough why Edwin encouraged her to take an active part in the business. Perhaps he'd loved her when they were first married, but that wasn't what gave her such a hold over the family now. It was her ability and her energy he wanted now. That brought its own bitterness.

Ben went slowly upstairs still thinking about Mary Green, and what a poor waif she was. He opened his office door and pulled back in surprise, every nerve in his body jangled with shock and annoyance when he saw his mother sitting at his desk with his documents spread out in front of her.

He felt his hands clench, and the angry words rise in

his throat. He swallowed them back, fought to hide his screaming irritation. It wouldn't do any good to have a blazing row with her about this. He'd told Stephen that fighting with mother only shook him up and furthered her aims rather than his. He knew he himself would fare no better.

'These figures can't be right, Ben,' she said, not one whit abashed. 'You've made a mistake somewhere. Come and explain exactly what you've done.'

'Mother, I don't like you coming in and looking through my papers behind my back. It's a violation of privacy.'

'I'm worried about these figures.' She frowned. 'I'm sure you'll understand and forgive my impatience.' He fought to appear quiet and reasonable.

'I understand, but it's unforgivable, Mother, and I don't intend to put up with it.'

'Ben! I need to know where we stand. I may have to take steps . . .'

'I've been thinking too. Perhaps there *are* one or two points. Since you're here, you might as well hear them now.' She was glaring up at him. He felt he'd taken the initiative from her.

'May I have my own chair?'

She seemed surprised to be asked but eventually stood up. Ben put out a hand to ease her back to the chair he provided for visitors. Her hip was granite hard. It seemed she spoke the truth about wearing her own corsets. He did his best to stop his mouth from turning up at the corners.

'As far as the corsets are concerned, you've made a slightly increased profit.'

'For heaven's sake, Ben, I know that. I see to those figures. I gave you a copy as a courtesy.'

'I know,' he said. 'Profits there were in line with expectations.'

'It's not the corsets I'm worried about.'

'Hear me out.' He shuffled into his drawer the papers she'd been studying. Spread others out where she could read them. 'There's nothing wrong, your corsets are showing a reasonable profit, but you aren't exploiting the market properly.'

'Oh!' She looked almost shocked. 'In what way?'

'I tried to tell you the day you showed me round.' He leaned back in his chair and fought to appear more at ease than he was. His mother's dark eyes were searching his.

'You're making old-fashioned corsets for the elderly and middle-aged. Of course, from time to time, they need to replace what they have.' Her fingers were jabbing impatiently at the figures, pointing out the profit she'd made.

'But they don't replace what they've got as often as younger people. Probably wear them until they're falling to pieces, and since the cloth you use is the next thing to canvas, that takes some doing. It's a declining market, Mother. Every year, the number of ladies wearing corsets such as you make lessens.'

'Brassieres are doing well. Our best line.'

'True, but you'd sell more of those if they had a more . . .'

He took time to phrase what he had to say. How did he tell his mother he thought ladies' underwear should have an erotic quality?

'If they were more attractive. You know, lacy.' She was looking at him strangely. He felt his criticism was striking home.

'And you've a real gap in your product range – suspender belts for the young. As you said, they have to hold their stockings up too.'

'I thought of roll-ons,' Beatrice said slowly. 'Could be difficult, all elastic. The girls aren't used to working with it.'

'They'd get used to it – they have in other factories. Elastic is the latest thing. Lighter to wear, cheaper to make. Did you know they make roll-ons in one-way and in two-way stretch?' She was staring at him in amazement. 'How long is it since you went round the big stores in town to see what the competition is making?'

'I come here every day,' she said, and he caught the first defensive note in her voice.

'And flog yourself hard,' he agreed. 'I went last Saturday. It was quite an eye opener.'

'Really?' She seemed to be looking at him with more respect.

'Just to see what was on display. I think you should go too. Corsetry is changing, and you aren't keeping up to date. Your profits won't keep pace unless you keep up with fashions. Use satin and lace instead of that canvas.'

That brought a half-smile to her face. 'Perhaps you're right, Ben. I'll have a look round the shops. Thank you for your suggestions, but it's the figures for shirts that are bothering me.'

He rocked upright in his chair. The figures for shirts were bothering him too.

'I haven't had time to finish them yet,' he said coldly. 'You'll have to be patient a little longer.' He stood up as a signal for her to go.

She sighed and stood up too.

'Why don't you spend this afternoon going round the big stores? Liverpool as well as Birkenhead. Do for suspender belts what you did with the Kestos brassiere back in 1929. After all, you can try them on, examine them closely, get a good look at how they're made.'

When the door closed behind her Ben was bursting with exultation. He strode to his window and back again twice, rattling the change in his trouser pockets.

He'd made a suggestion about her precious corsets and she'd agreed to it! She'd meant to grill him about the lower profits for shirts, and he'd diverted her attention. He felt he might cope with Mother after all, and laughed outright at his success.

It came to him then like a deluge of cold water that he'd pushed Rosie's birth certificate amongst his figures. He'd not seen it as he'd spread them out for Mother. He bounded to his desk and shuffled through his papers again, letting one sheet flutter to the floor.

The birth certificate had gone. Ben wanted to kick himself. He should have known Mother would get the better of him.

Slowly, he went to his filing cabinet and took out the first of the few files he'd made so far. On Rosie's application form to join the pension fund was his mother's signature. He felt sick.

He could guess what she intended to do now. Deliver the certificate personally to Rosie for maximum embarrassment. It was Mother's way of getting back at her because Ben had tied her hair ribbon. That was Mother all over.

He went racing down to the sewing room and threw open the door. His eyes went down the row of machines to Rosie's back. Her copper-coloured head was bent lower than usual. From that and the dejected droop of her shoulders, he knew Mother had been too quick for him. It would only make matters worse if he went in now. It would rouse the curiosity of her colleagues, let them see there was something strange about Rosie's birth certificate.

He was shaking with fury as he strode to the cubicle in which Beatrice worked. He crashed back her door without his usual preliminary knock. Her desk had been cleared, she was not there. He opened the communicating door to the next-door cubicle she'd meant him to occupy. Her secretary, Miss Gibbons, had moved into it.

Her grizzled grey head came up from her typewriter. 'Mrs Shearing's gone out.' She was looking at him over the top of her spectacles. 'Said she wouldn't be back till late this afternoon.'

'Thanks,' he said between his teeth. Perhaps it was just as well. They'd have had the battle he'd wanted to avoid if she'd been there.

Ben went back to his office and tried to concentrate on the problem of the shirt figures. He'd given up hope of finding some simple explanation, something he'd overlooked. The problem was definitely more sinister than that. He needed to know exactly how many shirts had been made in the sewing room last year.

He opened the book Flora Pope had kept during 1936, and started to add her figures on his Comptometer. The shirts were pressed and packed away in dozens, and Flora entered the daily figures, attributing them to each machinist by name. At the end of each week, the book went to the accountant to make up the wages.

Ben knew the figures had to be correct at this stage because the machinists were paid on piecework. They would complain if their wages were less than they expected.

On the third page he wondered if some of the figures had been altered. Taking the book to the window he held the page up to the light. The original number entered for 5 February certainly had. There was no doubt about it: more work had been paid for than the number of shirts made indicated.

Ben felt the adrenaline kick into his system and the blood course through his veins. This was the first indication he'd found that the figures had been tampered with. Now he knew what he was looking for, he found several other suspicious entries.

Somebody had tried to make it appear that fewer shirts had been made, but not by anything like enough to cover the number being lost.

He got to his feet so abruptly his chair fell over backwards and headed down to the sewing room to look at the figures in the current book.

'Flora,' he said, 'if you make a mistake in this book,

what do you do? Rub it out?'

'Cross it out,' she said, taking some pins out of her mouth. 'And put the right figure above it. Like I have here.' Her plump finger pointed out an instance.

Ben went slowly back upstairs. He'd checked every new employee they'd taken on in the previous three years. Most were not in a position to take liberties with the stock. There was no hard evidence pointing to any employee. Now he was coming to the hard part – his own family.

Dad was convinced that more shirts had been made, and Stephen that he'd sold more. They had not all gone through the books.

Ben shuddered as he remembered Oliver's white knuckles and tightly controlled voice this morning. He must have something to do with it.

He'd never got on with Oliver. Was it his own jealousy that made him suspect his brother of stealing from his own family? It wasn't always easy to see one's own motives.

'Motives be damned,' he said aloud. Somebody was stealing. He had to look closely at everything Oliver had done last year. Either it would clear him or it would not. He still couldn't see how anyone could spirit so many shirts away. He couldn't just load up his car and drive off with them. Ben felt like a second-rate spy.

He'd barely got back to his desk when Stephen, grim-faced, came to his door.

'I can't believe Mother's gall! Suggesting she take me by the hand to visit customers I know. Customers I've dealt with alone for the last few years. Don't think she wouldn't have the nerve. Nothing embarrasses her, but it would send me through the floor. She'd get their orders too.'

'Show me your order books,' Ben said.

'I already have.'

'Again. I must get a clearer picture. You have an order book, and write every order in that?'

'No. Only if a customer gives me a verbal order when I'm in his office. Then I'd write it in my book, and give Oliver a copy. But two of the wholesalers we deal with regularly send in orders on their own forms. Other customers type their requirements in letters, and send them through the post.'

'And Oliver keeps all those?'

'Yes, he initiates the purchase orders.' Weeks ago, Ben had seen Phyllis Quest typing them up on pads of multicoloured forms and asked her to explain how they worked.

'Five copies, all right? One on file, one posted to the customer for confirmation. The remaining three go to the storeman to make up the order. He sends two out with the order, and the van driver gets them signed when he makes delivery. Then one stays with the customer, and the other is brought back to you.'

Ben nodded, he eventually used it to bill the customer. He took out the two bundles he had in his desk. The forms used for corsets were identical except for a different numbering sequence and the word 'Corsetry' on top. He pushed those back out of sight.

The range of sizes carried made the orders complicated. Many more shirts were made and sold in sizes to fit the average man, but retailers had to stock the full range. The exact proportion varied from retailer to retailer.

'Where do we keep the stationery?' he asked Stephen, who took him out on the landing, opened the large cupboard there, and handed him five different coloured forms attached together. There were two stacks of forms waiting to be used, each with its own series of numbers already printed on. The system ought to be foolproof.

'I think Oliver takes a set down with the order he wants Miss Quest to type,' Stephen said. Ben pushed his hair off his forehead. It seemed Oliver was involved with every step, though he still didn't understand how he got the shirts out of the building without anybody seeing him.

His father came to the door and said: 'It's lunch-time, are you two coming down?'

Ben was glad to push the files he was working on back in his desk and turn the key. Mother would not go through his papers again if he could help it. He even locked his file cabinet before following the others downstairs.

But he was worried. He'd looked through the figures for 1935 more closely, and was almost sure he could see the same phenomenon. Certainly more shirts had been manufactured than sold. That year a lot of stock had been written off. He could remember his mother's fury even after all this time.

'Dad, tell me about the stock that was written off in 1935.'

'You mean from water damage?'

Ben caught him up at the bottom of the stairs. 'Yes, but what caused it?'

'Burst pipe during a spell of frosty weather.'

'In a bedroom?'

'There was a bathroom above, it came through the ceiling.'

'It ruined a lot of stock?'

'Our bad luck. Too much had been stored in that room. Some of it should never have been there.'

Agonised, Ben wondered if it had been deliberate? If stock had been written off to mask a discrepancy in the accounts?

'Who decided what should be written off and what was still saleable?'

'Your mother. Though Oliver said she wasn't fussy enough and slung out more when she turned her back. The insurance paid up, of course.'

Ben felt even more worried. Should he see this as another incidence of the same fraud? If it was, he hadn't the faintest inkling how it was being done.

As they approached the kitchen, he could hear the buzz of chatter. This was the social hour of the day, filled with noisy prattle. He saw Rosie Quest the moment he went through the door, sitting at a long scrubbed table with a bowl of soup in front of her. The table was almost full, but Dad was leading him exactly where he wanted to go, towards two empty places on the opposite side.

Rosie looked troubled. Long golden lashes rested against faint shadows under her eyes. She looked up. Her emerald eyes met his unseeingly, she seemed engrossed in her thoughts. Everybody else seemed to have plenty to say.

'Hello, girls,' his father said as they pulled out their chairs. The machinists were known collectively as girls, though most were long past girlhood and one or two approaching retirement age. Ben knew his father was popular. The girls said he had 'no side'. They rather admired the seedy tweed suits that Mother said were more suited to the grouse moor.

'Have you seen "Morning Glory", Mr Shearing?' Kitty Harmon sang out. 'Katharine Hepburn and Douglas Fairbanks?'

Kitty's false teeth were perfect porcelain beads set in brick-red artificial gums that could sometimes be seen to move. Her own paler gums showed above them when she smiled.

Mrs Pratt brought them three bowls of broth and set a plate of ham sandwiches between them. Sandwiches were available for everyone, but most brought their own because it was cheaper. He noticed Mary Green, still pale and wan, had brought only dry bread to dip in her soup, and she was not the only one. Rosie was nibbling on a meat sandwich. She looked well nourished by comparison.

'As a matter of fact, I have,' his father said.

Ben was surprised. 'When did you ever go to see a film?'

'I do occasionally,' said Edwin, spooning up his broth.

'I'd no idea. With Mother?'

'No, she thinks films are a waste of time.'

'It's at the Palace this week. Lovely, wasn't it? Oh, I

did enjoy it.' Kitty had worked most of her fifty-two years in Shearing's sewing room. Ben tried not to watch her false teeth when she spoke.

'You went to see it last night, didn't you, Flora?'

The light flashed on her thick bottle glass spectacles and in that instant Ben thought he saw something pass between the sewing room forewoman and his father.

He listened with half his mind, the rest of it mulling over the problem with the figures. He must examine the returns from the sewing room, see if fictional shirts were being added to push piecework payments up. He didn't think it a likely cause of the problem. Flora Pope had started in their employment as a fourteen-year-old apprentice, and Father thought highly of her. She'd have to push up the earnings of all the machinists to have this effect.

'Lovely film,' she laughed, making her two chins quiver. 'Thoroughly enjoyed it.'

Some employees, mostly the men from the cutting room, sat chatting across the tables for the full hour. Others, usually the married women, rushed out to the shops to buy provisions for the evening meal. Flora and Kitty got up and went out. The table was gradually emptying.

'Fancy a walk down to the Crown?' his father asked. 'A beer?'

Stephen agreed readily, but Ben shook his head. He was desperate for a word with Rosie who was eating her apple and still looking into space, and anyway he needed a clear head for the afternoon. After Stephen and his father had gone, he moved up two chairs till he was directly opposite her.

'Would you like to see that film?' he asked on the spur of the moment. 'Kitty makes it sound quite good.' Startled, her green eyes swung to meet his. He saw fleeting emotions there: distrust, fear and surprise. 'I'd like to take you.'

'Me?'

'Why not?'

'No, thank you,' she said. She sounded cool and withdrawn. 'I don't think we should.' She was getting to her feet, making her escape.

Ben pushed back his chair hastily. 'Walk down the road with me, Rosie, we can't talk here.'

'We've nothing to talk about.'

'Yes, we have. I want to explain, to apologise. Come on, get your coat, there's still twenty minutes.' She disappeared into the room that was used as a cloakroom, but was out again in seconds with her coat.

'You promised,' she said accusingly. He was overwhelmed with the knowledge that he'd failed her. He'd promised to keep her secret from his mother, and he had not.

'I know, and I'm sorry. I meant to keep it, Rosie. You were with me when Mary Green fainted, you saw me push it in my drawer. My mother went rummaging and found it. Honest. I feel bad that I hadn't given it straight back to you, I knew your date of birth was correct.' She was keeping her face turned away and stepping out briskly. 'Did she give it you back?'

'Yes, she came marching in and flung it on my machine. "Your birth certificate, Rose," she said, so contemptuously. It carried right up the room. "I quite understand your reluctance. I wouldn't want anybody to know either." '

Ben sighed and they strode on in silence. At last he said: 'There's nothing else she can do, Rosie.'

'Flora asked me what she meant, then Kitty. I heard them talking about me . . .'

'It's finished, over with. The end of the matter.'

'But she knows.' Rosie let all her fears and anxieties show. They made her seem painfully vulnerable. Ben could not understand why other men did not want to sweep her up in their arms to provide comfort.

'What does it matter now? She's used that knowledge to hurt you, so she's done her worst. Put it behind you.'

'She could let everyone know.'

'She won't, though I don't see why you're so worried. The girls would be sympathetic. They're all on your side anyway.'

'But if . . .'

'She won't. I know how Mother's mind works. She knows you'll worry yourself sick that she might. And knows she inflicts more anguish on you this way. If she let it become public knowledge, other people would think her underhand. Dad would. Right?' Rosie nodded shyly looking at him through her lashes.

'Come with me to the pictures? Wouldn't you like to see "Morning Glory"?'

Her green eyes met his. 'I don't know that I could. I always help with the milking in the evenings.' Something in the way she said it suggested she was tempted.

'What time does that take place?'

'About six. Then I help bottle the milk. We're

CHAPTER SEVEN

Ben was opening the back door of the Albert Hotel for Rosie when the bell signalling the end of lunch hour started to ring. 'I'll have to run,' she said, taking to her heels.

He followed more slowly, and was passing the kitchen when he saw Mary Green push herself upright against the table and come slowly to the door. She looked ill.

'You're still not feeling well?' he asked. She shook her head miserably.

'Go home then. Better if you rest. Don't come in tomorrow. It's Saturday, and a half day anyway.'

'Will that be all right?' Her eyes were heavy. She looked a decade older than she was.

'Of course. You aren't fit to work. Get your coat and hat.' He found a paper bag, and put six eggs and half a pound of butter into it from the fridge. She'd come back and was leaning against the door, grey-faced and listless. He pushed the bag into her hand.

'You must eat, Mary. See you have breakfast before you come to work on Monday.' She was trying to thank him when he saw Eric drive the delivery van round the back. 'Where do you live? Is it far?'

'Spencer Street.'

'Let's see if we can get you a lift.'

Eric the van driver, pimply with acne, was coming towards them with the long bouncing stride of youth. 'Have you got anything urgent to do?' Ben asked. 'Could you run Mary home?'

'I was just bringing these in for Mr Oliver.' He pushed three delivery notes into Ben's hand. He saw the girl into the passenger seat before going back to his office. He knew Oliver routinely passed the notes on to him to invoice the customer, so he tossed them into his own tray.

He took the accounts out, spread the pages across his desk to mull over again, though he could have re-written the figures from memory.

Then something made him reach for the delivery notes in the tray. He noticed now that one had a number that differed more than it should. It was printed in the same place on the form and had the same number of digits, but it was a sequence he'd not seen before.

Its significance dawned on him. He sat upright in his chair, his heart thumping. He knew now how Oliver managed it. He had two different numbering sequences!

Oliver kept a tight control on both. When he wanted delivery notes typed, he took the forms down to Phyllis. She sent them up to the storeman to be made up and the shirts were delivered by their own vans, in the normal way. If their employees had noticed the difference, they hadn't questioned it. Why should they? The number was a device for following up sales and accounting procedures, and Oliver handled any queries personally.

All he had to do was to remove the rogue numbers later, so no invoices were made out for them. No gaps were left in the normal sequence for him to check out.

Ben studied the rogue form. The delivery was large and had been made to a wholesaler. He guessed payment would be made direct to Oliver instead of to the company. He had an accomplice there, he must have.

Stephen was right; he had made more sales this year, but some of the orders hadn't gone through the books. What Oliver was doing made Stephen seem unsuccessful. It had brought him discredit and family censure. Ben knew now he should have believed Stephen, should have supported him.

He shook his hair back from his forehead, and felt horror gnaw at his entrails. He couldn't handle this. It wasn't straightforward work. He'd had no training for accusing family members of fraud. He couldn't bear to think about it, yet he had to.

He heard a door slam across the corridor and footsteps heading towards the stairs. Oliver was going somewhere. Ben went to the head of the stairs, and watched him say something to Phyllis on his way to the door. He peeped into his office then, and saw he'd cleared and locked his desk. Well, there was no desperate urgency for what he had to do. It gave him breathing space.

It was Friday. He decided he could give himself the weekend to think out the best way to handle things.

That brought a faint trickle of relief; he'd distanced himself from the nightmare. He found it impossible to settle to routine work after that. He couldn't get what Oliver had done out of his mind.

On Saturdays they always went home for lunch. Afterwards he went up to his room. He was drawn as always to the window, but today the tide was low. Beyond the expanse of exposed mud were the brown waters of the Mersey, with the Liverpool docks almost lost in mist.

As an indulgence, he opened the box he'd brought and settled down with the annual company accounts for Shearing's Shirts, starting with its inception in 1865. To Ben they were doubly interesting because they were tracts of family history.

For hours he strained his eyes over yellowing paper, fading ink, and old-fashioned copperplate figures. Curiosity about his forebears drove him on till he was totally fascinated. There were reports which Ben didn't find easy, some words used were no longer in daily use, but the general message was clear.

In the early years profits were small, then steadily they began to increase. Year on and year about the figures went up. Shirt making had been very profitable for Ainsley Shearing, his grandfather. Taking into account the value of money in those days, his grandparents had been rich.

Ainsley had started by employing out-workers who stitched the shirts by hand. He'd made nightshirts, morning shirts, work shirts, boil proof shirts and evening shirts. There were figures for high collars and wing collars. Grandfather had acquired his own premises in 1874, and had had sewing machines from their very early days. By then he employed more workers, who made more shirts than they did today using twentieth-century sewing machines and the latest business techniques. Prosperity was greater in Victorian times than it had been since. It was a fantastic success story.

Ben was excited when he went down for tea in the drawing room. Grandma was buttering a hot scone for herself.

'You must have been very proud of Grandpa,' he said. 'The company thrived under him.'

'I wouldn't know about that.' Her frosty tone surprised him. 'I never worked in the business.'

'But you must have heard all about it,' Ben said. 'Grandpa must have shown you the accounts.'

'No, he never did. In my day, ladies were not expected to work.'

'But Mother enjoys it.' He knew she would consider an existence like Grandma's very boring.

'Things were different for your mother,' she said tartly. He thought she seemed ruffled.

'I bet you were proud of the money he made, though. This house was bought from company profits in 1880.' He could see her lips tightening and she sat more upright in her chair. 'It was top of the market then, in what was a high class district. Only the best was good enough for you, Grandma, and it could be afforded.'

'I expected him to provide the necessities of life for me,' she retorted. 'Ladies did then. It was considered their right.'

'What was he like?' Ben wanted to flesh out his picture of a business paragon.

'Nothing out of the ordinary. Just a man.' He was brought up short. He'd expected her to show pride in what her husband had achieved.

Ben admired anyone with the talent to start a business and make a success of it. He had similar ambitions for himself, and Ainsley Shearing's genes were part of his inheritance. He wanted to know much more about him.

'Was he a gentle person like Dad? Kind to his workers?'

'I don't want to talk about him.' His grandmother's face was sombre and closed. She finished her tea and marched upstairs, where she had a sitting room as well as a bedroom. Mother called it her boudoir, and said she didn't spend enough time in it. Usually she was to be found in the drawing room, or the less formal sitting room the rest of the family favoured.

Gran was never an easy person, often moody and ill tempered and inclined to find fault. Father attributed it to age, and Mother to the total emptiness of her day. But to be so offhand about Grandpa, her husband! Ben found that very strange. He went back to Ainsley's accounts to try to find out more from them.

He spent more time on them than he'd intended. He had to rush to bathe and be ready in time for the guests Mother had invited. He didn't make it and heard them arriving before he was quite dressed. From the landing window he saw the expensive new car on the drive.

His mother was coming out of the drawing room as he crossed the hall.

'Ben!' Her face was outraged. 'That suit will never do. Run and put on your grey. I want you to look nice for Sarah.' She put a hand on his arm to stop him entering the room. He shook it off.

'Mother, I'm old enough to decide what I shall wear.'

He went in and knew instantly their guests had heard the exchange. He found they were looking at him closely.

To embarrass her and prevent her doing it again, he said: 'My mother would like me to be laced in a set of her corsets. She wants to mould me to her will.'

He heard a soft, half-suppressed giggle, and turned to the girl. She had her hand in front of her mouth to hide her laughter.

'This is our second son, Ben.' He knew his mother was furious from the frost in her voice. He had told her several times in private that he resented her interference in his choice of clothes.

'Mr and Mrs Michelson and Miss Sarah Michelson.'

It was on the tip of Ben's tongue to tell Mr Michelson that his mother would approve of his shirt, but he knew that would be going too far. It was their own best quality Egyptian cotton, and an exact replica of the one Dad was wearing. Sarah Michelson's hand was warm and firm. There was amusement in her hazel eyes. A handsome girl. His brother Oliver and wife Lydia had come for dinner too.

Lydia was a platinum blonde with painted finger nails. She hung on to Oliver's arm and listened avidly to every word he uttered. Her large blue eyes, filled with adoration, gazed up at him.

She was Mother's choice but Oliver had every reason to congratulate himself. Now he was not only a favourite son but an adored husband and respected son-in-law.

What were they all going to say when Ben accused him of stealing from the business?

He studied Oliver across the room, wondering if such a thing as brotherly love existed. His manner was supercilious, his gaze openly combative when it met Ben's. His instinctive reaction was to fold his fingers into fists. He felt the old urge to raise them.

He thought of his childhood as happy, but it had not been idyllic. As an infant he'd had his hair pulled and his arms twisted to impossible angles by Oliver, two years older, lording it over the nursery.

His earliest memories were of mutual hostility, breaking out in sparring, bickering and outright fisti-cuffs at the slightest excuse. As they grew older it could smoulder below the surface for weeks as they went about their everyday lives, but could and would explode like a volcano if some spark should set it off. And when open warfare broke out, Stephen was always in the thick of it, fighting on Ben's side. If Oliver attacked Stephen, Ben supported his younger brother without questioning whether he was right or wrong. It was their survival tactic.

Oliver had the advantage of four years' seniority over Stephen, and could lay him out with his fists in seconds. As they grew older they all used cunning and words instead of fists, but the sparring didn't stop. Both he and Stephen were relieved when Oliver went away to prep school and the nursery became more peaceful. It didn't stop major battles taking place in the school holidays.

Ben had loved Bessie, the nursemaid who had looked after them as infants. Grandma had taken an interest in their welfare, taught them nursery rhymes and the alphabet. When Mother came home from work every night, they had story time with her. There had been swimming and sailing and rides in the cars at weekends . . .

At breakfast the next morning, Mother looked victorious. 'You liked Sarah Michelson, didn't you?'

Sarah had spent half the evening talking about the work she did in her father's factory. He'd proudly told them she ran his office for him, and everything went like clockwork. Ben had been impressed, he'd found her interesting. He'd even liked her. The chemistry was wrong for anything more. Her lashes didn't cast shadows across her cheeks like Rosie's did. Her eyes were not shy, vulnerable woodland pools.

Constance Shearing sat up in bed with a jerk. Her heart was thudding with a violence she could both feel and hear. Panic fluttered at the edge of her mind. Already the grey light of dawn was showing through her curtains.

She told herself firmly she was all right, she had nothing to worry about. She was safe at home in her own bed. It was just the bad dream again. Probably due to the cheese she'd eaten last night. In her dream she was never given anything but bread and water. She shivered as she remembered the biting cold, and the thin rags she'd been wearing. Always she was in the same bare cell with bars on the high window. She must put the wretched dream out of her mind!

Constance climbed out of bed stiffly, every muscle aching with tension. She always felt drained and nerve-racked after she'd had this nightmare. She pulled back her curtains to let in the day and looked at her clock. It was six-thirty, almost an hour before she could expect her breakfast tray.

She shivered again and made herself get back into bed. She must not catch cold. Her fear was receding; in daylight it seemed foolish. She put on her spectacles and opened the book she'd been reading last night. It was three months since she'd last had that nightmare. She'd hoped it was gone for ever, and that she was over it. But the truth was she never would be over it. She'd done such terrible things.

It was guilt, of course. Some would say she'd got away with it completely, had gone unpunished, but she'd come to realise God punished in different ways. The implication of her nightmares was all too obvious: He sent them so she would never forget.

She'd never been able to cope with the guilt. She didn't think she could ever resolve it now. It wasn't just what she'd done, it was the effect it had had all her long life. The effect it was still having on her family, the business, everything, even to this day.

She read half a page but it made no sense. She started reading it again. She didn't need the recurring nightmare to remind her, when she had Beatrice here every day. She'd allowed her to come into the family and manipulate them all. She was still manipulating them, ordering the Shearings about their own business. Constance knew the blame would be with her till the day she died. She'd ruined everything for her children and their children.

She wanted her breakfast, more for the diversion it would create than for the food. But now she was dependent on a succession of girls hired on a daily or part-time basis to assist the housekeeper, Mrs Roper, and they were a law unto themselves. The days when she'd had a personal maid and resident housemaids had long since gone.

The tap on her door came at last, and her breakfast tray was set across her legs, with the welcome pot of tea and her newspaper.

'Good morning, Mrs Shearing, I trust you slept well?'

'Yes.' She hadn't intended to be so sharp, this girl was pleasant enough.

'Mrs Roper asked me to remind you to be dressed and ready by quarter past ten.'

Constance frowned. She couldn't think why, she hardly went out these days. She daren't ask the girl or they'd laugh about it in the kitchen, and think her senile. There was only room for one thing in her mind this morning. She busied herself pouring tea.

'Lucky you, it's a nice clear morning,' the girl prattled on.

Girls didn't know their place these days and it seemed even Beatrice couldn't drive it home to them.

'I do envy you going to the big launch.'

So that was it. 'Such an important occasion,' Constance said, cutting the top off her boiled egg. 'The launching of the *Ark Royal.*'

'My little girl is going with her school. They do so much with them these days. They're even getting ready for the Coronation.'

'Another important occasion,' Constance mused. Outings were becoming a rare treat for her, and she'd be glad of one today because sometimes the weight of her bad dreams could linger all day. 'You'll be able to see something of it from the windows at the front,' she said.

She started dressing in plenty of time, put on an extra under-bodice of cobweb fine wool to keep her warm because the day seemed fresh and she was not used to the open air now.

She went down to the drawing room just before the appointed time and stationed herself at a window. A blustery wind was whipping up the incoming tide and making it choppy. She could see foam all over the muddy Mersey estuary. The waves were racing in to crash on the shore.

Many of the ships in the river were dressed overall with bunting that strained and flapped in the strong breeze. It was a day of celebration for the people of Birkenhead: Cammel Laird's shipyard had an important naval vessel to launch. There was work for all. The long, lean years of the depression were over.

Edwin returned to pick her up. It was a pleasure to see him in a formal suit, looking like a gentleman for once. He was friendly with one of the shipyard managers, a neighbour here in Rock Park, and they were invited to view the launch from the stand and go afterwards to the reception.

'Where is Beatrice?' Constance despised herself for asking. It almost seemed she couldn't enjoy the relief her daughter-in-law's absence brought.

'She'll go straight there in the other car.'

Constance grimaced. She knew why. It was a waste of Beatrice's time to come home to pick her up. A waste of her time to sit about waiting for the ceremony to begin. Beatrice couldn't relax and enjoy herself as Edwin did. She would allow herself one glass of champagne at the reception, and then want to get back to work.

The crowd was gathering. Constance looked round, enjoying the naval band and the air of expectancy and excitement. Bunting fluttered from the shipyard buildings, faces crowded every window. People were thronging every vantage point. Grimy workmen had downed tools, schoolchildren were being marshalled into crocodiles.

The managers of the yard were seated immediately in front of her. Beside her, Edwin seemed to know everybody, nodding and shaking hands over the back of the seats. The vessel waiting to be launched seemed a strange shape. Workmen were knocking out chocks that had held it in place. It made her feel old to think aeroplanes would land on that deck. She felt more at home with sailing vessels; they were certainly more graceful.

Beatrice came briskly down the line of seats, a moment before the First Lord of the Admiralty and his lady who was to launch the vessel. She wore a new smart hat, and looked smug and self-satisfied at being invited to take her place amongst the leading dignitaries and prominent business people of the town.

This was what had motivated her from the beginning – the need to climb the social ladder, to be seen as belonging to the middle class. She would see this occasion as a personal triumph as well as a celebration for the town and shipyard. Beatrice had achieved what she wanted. Constance felt bitter. She had never achieved any of the goals she had set herself.

Always when the wind blew up river the deafening clatter of riveting and the creaking of cranes could be heard in the garden at home, but today the yard was quieter. A hush fell on the crowd as the ceremony started.

There was a prayer from the chaplain, a tinkling sound as the bottle broke on the ship's stern. Constance held her breath and it seemed the crowd around her did the same. As they waited silently she saw the ship begin to slide, very slowly at first, but gathering momentum. There were deafening cheers as the *Ark Royal* splashed into the Mersey. In the river, ships' hooters blared a deafening welcome.

'Isn't this exciting?' Beatrice turned to her in a pseudo-friendly fashion. Constance knew it was all for show, to demonstrate to anyone watching that she was a thoughtful and caring daughter-in-law.

Today, Beatrice was pleased with herself. She saw herself as cleverer than all of them. Constance reminded herself she only had herself to blame. She had allowed her to do this to the family.

Rosie felt herself cringe every time she thought of

what had been said in Edwin Shearing's office, but it was not Edwin's knowing that she minded. She'd felt his sympathy. It had been Oliver who in his arrogant manner had made her admit all her upsetting secrets and lay them bare before his disdainful gaze.

It had been a painful interview. She heard his voice again saying: 'The law doesn't recognise illegitimate children.' He had made her feel a social outcast, almost beneath contempt.

She would have said nothing to her uncle if he had not pressed her about the outcome.

'I should have gone in to see Edwin myself,' he fretted. 'I meant to, and then I thought . . .'

'I am of age.' Rosie tried to smile. 'Got to stand on my own feet now.' She saw from his face he blamed himself for the embarrassment she'd faced.

'Of course I'll give you the money,' he said.

'It's rightfully yours according to the law, Oliver won't be wrong about that.'

'What does the law know about it? Our Grace would have wanted you to have it, and you shall.'

When Edwin came into the sewing room, Rosie cringed with embarrassment and wouldn't look him in the face. After all, he'd been there listening to it all. She kept her head bent over her work.

'Rosie?' He paused at her machine. When she did look up he was smiling encouragingly. 'The matter's in hand,' he said. 'Don't worry about it.'

Worrying wasn't what she was doing exactly, she was more on an emotional knife edge. Since her birthday the even tenor of her life had been shattered by arguments and embarrassing interviews.

She was glad to be at work. It was routine, and that was what she wanted most of all. She felt she did her job well and enjoyed sewing, but the hours were long and like everyone else she looked forward to the weekend.

On Saturday, which was a half day, she made up her mind to look for the house she had lived in with her mother. The address, 15 Hoop Lane, was on Grace's papers and Rosie had borrowed a street guide from Eric the van driver to find out exactly where it was.

Maud provided a cooked dinner at one o'clock, and Rosie sat at the table with Tom and the rest of the family to eat it. Phyllis was hurrying to catch the bus into town where she wanted to buy a new dress. Rosie cleared away and washed up before setting out. It was a murky day, damp and unseasonably chill for spring, with drizzle blowing in her face. She walked quickly to keep warm, pushing her hands deep into the pockets of her coat.

She didn't know what she expected to see, but Hoop Lane turned out to be a terrace of redbrick houses with bay windows. It was not grand, not what she'd expected from the fine clothes in the trunks. It seemed further proof that her mother had not been a kept woman. Even Aunt Maud would have to admit that if she was, no great fortune had been lavished on her. It was an ordinary house with respectable net curtains. There were hundreds like it in Birkenhead.

As she stood outside, the front door opened and a middle-aged woman came out with three children swinging round her. She was shabby and tired-looking. As Rosie turned away, disappointed, she saw the woman look in her direction. But she'd know nothing of Grace, it would do no good to talk to her.

Rosie went home feeling restless and unsettled. Uncle Will was out about the farm somewhere, but the day was miserably damp. Maud had built up the fire in the range and was relaxing on the settle. Rosie knew she would stay there till it was time for Will and Tom to come in for tea.

Rosie no longer felt comfortable sitting in the same room as her aunt, and certainly didn't want to tell her where she'd been. She'd felt Maud's resentment directed towards her too often. She debated whether to go out again and climb on top of the hay in the dutch barn where she could be guaranteed privacy.

But she was keen to have a closer look at the books that had belonged to her mother. So, knowing Phyllis was out and she'd have the room to herself, she went upstairs to her bedroom. Taking both books from the shelf, she kicked off her shoes and threw herself across her bed.

The books felt slightly damp. She wrinkled her nose at their musty smell. She had brought *The Longest Journey* and *Where Angels Fear to Tread*, by E.M. Forster. She opened the latter. Her mother would have read it, and she wanted to do the same. She wanted to know what sort of a person Grace had been. She became engrossed, no longer noticing the drizzle that pattered on the window.

It must have been half an hour later when she turned over and resettled herself. Lowering her book to the counterpane, she turned a page.

An envelope slithered out and floated down to the

bedside mat. Rosie leaned over and picked it up, eager to see anything that might throw light on Grace's personal life. It was addressed to Miss G. Quest at 15 Hoop Lane. Her heart lurched as she recognised the writing. Surely it was her aunt's hand? Her fingers were shaking as she drew out the single sheet.

She was right! The letter had the Ivy Farm address at the top. Rosie felt her knees go weak as she read:

Dear Grace,

I'm sure you will understand that Will and I have to refuse your request. I don't know how you find the nerve to come crawling to us now. You always knew what you did was wrong and would bring the family name into disrepute.

You've upset Will so badly he cannot bring himself to reply, he's asked me to do it for him.

We are not surprised at your present difficulties, and can only say you've brought them on yourself. If you are really as desperate for a roof over your head as you say, I suggest you seek help from those responsible for your trouble.

We cannot possibly have you back under our roof in your present condition, not even temporarily. It could not be hidden from our friends and neighbours, and we have no wish to offend them.

Maud

A rush of bitter hatred made Rosie sit up with a jerk. It was a heartless letter, Maud at her self-righteous worst. Grace must have been at her wit's end to ask for help, and this reply must have come like a kick in the teeth. Rosie's anger boiled up anew. Her mother had had no one else to turn to.

She was looking for a date on the letter. Tears were blurring her vision, but she made it out at last, January 1916, two months before she'd been born. If Maud had helped, Grace need never have gone to the workhouse at all.

Ivy Farm had two more bedrooms on this floor, but they were over the parlour and the dining room which were never used and were consequently thought to be very cold. A certain amount of heat came up from the kitchen below, and in theory the bedrooms in use should have been more comfortable. There were two attic bedrooms as well, in need of redecoration now but anything would have been better than the workhouse. Rosie felt herself about to explode with rage. She sprang off her bed and went headlong down to the kitchen.

Her aunt was still on the settle, at first not deigning to look up from the newspaper she was reading. Her apron was off now the main work of the day was over. Rosie flourished the letter in front of her startled eyes.

'You wrote this to my mother,' she accused, letting the rancour she'd felt for years roll out. 'You could have prevented her going to the workhouse. I suppose you always hated Grace as you've hated me?'

'What has come over you?' Maud was instantly on the offensive, her anger more than matching Rosie's. She was up on her feet instantly.

'You could have helped her, given her a home for a few months. I could have been born here. It was your fault she had to go to the workhouse. All your fault!'

Rosie found herself screaming in frenzy.

'Stop this nonsense,' Maud said, but there was less fire behind her words than usual.

'I hate you for this,' Rosie couldn't stop herself lashing out again. 'Have you no feelings for anyone else? How mean, how disgustingly mean, can you get? Turning Grace away when she needed help. You appal me.' She backed off, panting, horrified at her own outburst. She'd never dared speak to her aunt with a fraction of this venom before.

She was expecting retaliation, Uncle Will would be sent for to discipline her, but Maud's face was grey. There was terror in her eyes. 'Give that letter to me,' she said.

Rosie's anger left her as quickly as it had come. Another thought came to her.

'Uncle doesn't know you even wrote, does he? He didn't know Grace ever asked for help. He'd never have refused her. Never have stood aside and let his sister go to the workhouse. It was a vile thing to reject her when she had no one else. Barbarous.'

It took Rosie a few moments to realise Maud was pursuing her. 'Give me that letter, do your hear?'

'No,' she said. 'What makes you think you're so superior to everyone else? What you did makes you despicable.' She was taken by surprise when Aunt Maud tried to snatch it. She was not as tall as her aunt, but many years younger and more active. She evaded her grasp.

'Wait. Just wait till I tell my uncle.'

'Don't!' said Maud, her bony face screwed up in desperation.

'He feels guilty about what happened to her now. What's he going to think when he sees this? He'll never forgive you, will he?'

Rosie ran back upstairs, slammed her bedroom door and leaned against it, panting. The letter was crumpled and twisted now. She must not let her aunt touch it. She would have it behind the fire in an instant, then there would be only Rosie's word it had ever existed. She looked round for somewhere to hide it.

There was nowhere in this bedroom, her aunt would take it apart systematically while she was at work. Rosie changed into her old farm clothes. She found a small flat tin that had once held crayons but now contained a few foreign stamps. She tipped them into a drawer and folded the letter into the tin. She would hide it outside where Maud would never think of looking. She put it into her skirt pocket and went downstairs, keeping her hand firmly on it as she crossed the kitchen.

Maud was agitated, rushing from pantry to table with the tea cups. She crashed them down on the table.

'Rosie, don't tell your Uncle Will.' Her mouth drooped with misery. 'You'll only upset him. Haven't you caused enough trouble in this house?'

'You caused the trouble. I didn't like finding out I'd been born in the workhouse. I don't suppose my mother enjoyed being there. None of it need ever have happened.'

'Have I ever asked you to do anything for me before?' her aunt was pleading.

'You've expected plenty, and I've done it willingly. But finding this letter changes everything.'

'I'm asking you to give it to me now and say nothing to anyone.'

'What did you do? Hide her letter from Uncle? I find that very hard to forgive. She could have come here. There would have been no disgrace in that.' The kettle came to a rumbling boil as it swung on its chain over the fire, filling the chimney place with steam.

'Of course there would. Things were different twenty years ago. I had to preserve our good name.'

'What about *my* good name? What about Grace?'

'Give me that letter.' Maud held out her hand.

'No.'

She stood with her arms barring the back door. 'Give it to me, you little hussy,' she spat. Rosie saw Maud's gaze fix on her pocket. She knew her aunt was going to take it if she could. At that moment, she heard Uncle Will's step in the porch. He was talking to Tom. She saw Maud freeze.

'Get out of my way, Aunt Maud, or I'll tell my uncle this minute, in front of Tom. You won't have time to burn anything.'

Maud slid away as the door opened.

'It's a miserable afternoon.' Uncle Will was wiping his boots on the doormat, letting in a blast of cold air. 'We're not too early for tea, are we, Maud?'

Already she was banging bread and strawberry jam on the table. Rosie snatched her coat from its hook behind the door and slipped out without another word. She ran across the yard. The stable or the cow shed? Where could she hide it? Where would it never be found?

Flash was in on this damp afternoon and thought

Rosie had come to pet her. She rested her forehead against the mare's neck, still damp from the drizzle, and tried to think. Her mind was in turmoil. She mustn't put it in the loft where Uncle Will had put Grace's things. That would be the first place Maud would look now she knew Rosie had brought it out of the house.

Not the dutch barn either. Too many of her paintings were pinned on the beams, telling everybody it was her favourite place. Maud would take it apart, probably rummage through Grace's trunks. Rosie remembered the apple loft that had at one time been one of her private hideaways. As a child, she used to hide silly little things she didn't want Phyllis to take behind a loose brick in the wall there. Sweets sometimes, and her Saturday halfpenny if she hadn't spent it straight away.

She went through the cowshed to a building on the far side of the yard. Uncle Will brought his potatoes and carrots here when he dug them from the clamps. There were always a few sacks of them, cleaned free of soil and ready for sale.

Upstairs in the airy loft last year's apple crop had been laid out so that none of the fruit touched. Very little remained now, but the whole building was redolent with a fresh tang. The loose brick was above the window. She had to stand on a wooden crate to reach the one brick that came right out. She pushed the tin box containing the letter to the back of the hole and slotted the brick back in place. It didn't quite go home, but the bricks were uneven and it wasn't noticeable. She jumped down and moved the crate.

She'd never told anybody about the loose brick, and nobody had ever found what she'd hidden there in the past. Even she hadn't been near it for a decade. She could be sure the letter would be safe now.

She didn't want to destroy anything that had a connection with Grace, even things that had brought her pain. She had so few. Though she had no plans to use it, she didn't want to think Maud's secret was safe as it would be if the letter were destroyed.

When she went back indoors, her aunt cut herself on the bread knife and seemed more agitated than ever.

CHAPTER EIGHT

Rosie didn't sleep well that night. She couldn't get Maud's face out of her mind, twisted and ugly as she'd demanded the letter. Phyllis's regular breathing seemed to taunt her.

Rosie wanted revenge on her aunt. She wanted to see Uncle Will lash out at her in fury too, but couldn't show him the letter. He was guilt-stricken now. If he knew what his wife had done he'd feel a hundred times worse.

Rosie wondered if he loved Maud. The relationship did not seem to bring contentment to either of them. Maud's irritation could bubble up at her husband as easily as it could at her niece. Her tongue could be waspish at his expense. Rosie had never seen Maud show affection to anyone but Phyllis, though they'd all rubbed along without too much friction till now.

The argument on her birthday had created a rift between Maud and Will. He was aligning himself with Rosie but she could see it was tearing him in two. He wasn't sure where his loyalties should lie. If she were to show him the letter, he'd be furious with Maud and an unbridgeable gulf would be created between them.

Uncle Will's interests would be best served by letting
things settle back to where they'd been before her
birthday. They all needed to get back on a normal
keel.

The sensible thing for her to do would be to take
Maud's letter from its hiding place behind the brick in
the apple loft, tear it into tiny pieces and flush them
down the lavatory. She'd have to forgo revenge on her
aunt if it would hurt Uncle Will. Anyway, it was a
horrible letter, it had upset her to read it. She didn't
want to be reminded of it. Rosie made up her mind to
do exactly that at the first opportunity.

At breakfast the next morning, she noticed her aunt
still seemed nervous. She dropped and broke a plate.
Maud was treating Rosie as though she was a time
bomb, likely to explode in her face. Only then did she
realise she was causing her aunt more agony by
keeping her in suspense. Maud expected her to show
the letter to her uncle sooner or later. That would be
her revenge! She would keep her aunt expecting the
worse. Rosie would never tell her she didn't intend to
use the letter against her.

Once the breakfast things had been cleared away
and she had time to herself, Rosie put on her coat. She
went first to the stable and climbed to the loft over
Flash's stall. It was empty now but she'd left lines in
the dust and ancient hay when she'd dragged the
trunks out. There was no way of telling whether Maud
had been here searching for the letter.

From first opening the back door her intention had
been to go to the dutch barn. Her mother's things were
drawing her like a magnet. She felt she shouldn't walk

straight up there in case Phyllis or Maud were watching. She didn't want to betray her hiding place, if they hadn't already guessed it.

With one last look round to make sure they were not watching, Rosie headed in that direction and climbed the ladder. The hay was soft, fragrant and warm. She looked round, full of suspicion, but there was no sign anything had been disturbed here either. Rosie knew she was secretive, but couldn't stand the thought of Phyllis or Maud searching through the possessions in her own private hideaway.

She burrowed into the hay and found Grace's tin trunk, took out the dress of midnight blue to admire again. She decided she'd take the lizard-skin handbag over to her room and use it.

She threw herself down on the hay. It made a soft yielding bed from which she could pick out dried buttercups, still yellow. She turned over. She was close to the open rafters here. They were festooned with silken cobwebs that were never disturbed.

She heard a shower start, softly pattering on the old roof at first, but drumming and swishing through the gutters the next instant. She could smell the rain falling on the wet earth beneath and yet feel snug and warm here.

She reminded herself that pleasant things were happening too. Ben had invited her out this afternoon. But when the time came to get ready she felt shy again, and would have preferred to spend the afternoon pottering about the farm as usual.

Since she had agreed to go, she changed into her green dress, tied back her hair with the green ribbon, and pinned Will's birthday brooch to the lapel of her best coat.

To see the Shearing Rover, immaculately polished, waiting at the kerb in Gordon Drive came as a shock. Ben got out of the driving seat to greet her. His wide smile was disarming. She found herself ushered into the front seat where she'd seen Beatrice Shearing sit. The polished wood fascia met her eyes as it must Beatrice's. Rosie couldn't believe Mrs Shearing would allow her inside this splendid vehicle.

'I thought we'd have a run out to Parkgate.' Ben's dark eyes never left her face.

'Sounds wonderful. Your mother's let you borrow her car to take me out?'

'We have two cars. On Sundays I usually take one and Stephen the other. Mother likes to stay at home.'

Rosie sank deeper into the soft leather seat. She might have known his mother would have no idea who he was with. The thought didn't put her at ease. 'You're lucky.'

He smiled at her. 'She sees it as an economical use of resources. Cars are used by family members instead of each of us having our own. Stephen needs a car to visit customers, but I just like cars. Do you?'

'Yes, but I can't remember when I was last in one. Uncle Will keeps a horse and trap.' She laughed. 'Well, the trap's still there, but the horse hasn't been in the shafts for years. We use buses. This is wonderful.'

Already they were out in country lanes. She couldn't remember when she'd last seen anything but the suburban roads of Rock Ferry, and the busy shopping streets of town. The River Dee was very different from the Mersey. Rolling fields ran down to its banks. There was no sign of industry here.

Ben drove the length of the quay at Parkgate while Rosie gazed about her entranced. 'I'd no idea it was such a beautiful place. Such ancient buildings.'

'Nothing much existed in Birkenhead before Victorian times. Here it did.'

He parked the car near the south slip, and they got out to walk. It was a fresh blustery day. A cold wind tore at Rosie's hair, and the tide raced in across the mud of the estuary. A biplane was towing a banner across the sky, advertising Bile Beans.

She paused to admire a building with a dramatic black and white façade. 'It looks like an illustration from a book of fairy tales.'

Ben laughed and took her arm in friendly fashion. 'Oliver's prep school, Mostyn House. We used to be brought here to see him.' He told her about the Grenfell family who ran the school, and their famous son who went to Labrador as a medical missionary, and about Lady Hamilton who spent a lot of her childhood in the town.

Ben seemed relaxed. He was pointing out the Watch House that jutted so far out it narrowed the road to half its width.

'In the eighteenth century,' he said, 'customs officers lodged there and kept watch on the vessels that came up the river.'

Rosie felt at a loss, stiff and shy, and quite sure he would find her dull. She noticed for the first time that he had an attractive cleft in his chin. It gave his face strength and character. Yet . . .

'You're so like your mother. More than either of your brothers.'

'I hope you don't find that offputting?' She could see from the quirk in the corner of his mouth that he was half teasing.

'Of course not,' she said hurriedly. But it was. If Ben was like her on the outside, he could have her tough inner core too. It might not show yet.

'I only have her good traits.' His smile was broader now. 'I quite admire her, you know, Rosie. She keeps us all on our toes, makes us work. Shearing's owes it success to her.'

Rosie hoped he didn't notice the shudder she gave. What had she in common with a man like this? Yet his lightest touch against her hand made her every nerve tingle. She was acutely aware of the wind lifting his heavy locks of dark hair, and his long loose stride. She knew he was trying to please her.

'Balcony House,' he said, pointing it out. 'In the eighteenth century this was the Assembly Room, but it didn't have its elegant cast-iron balconies till much later.' Ben seemed to know how to make conversation; Rosie felt halting and dull in comparison.

He led her inside the Boathouse Café for tea and cakes. They had a table in the window.

'Modern,' he said. 'But there has been an inn on this site for centuries. Once it was the Ferry House for the daily sailing to Flint. I think the packet boats for Dublin used it too, but when the roads improved passengers preferred to sail from Holyhead and cut the sea journey in half.'

Rosie was fascinated by him, he knew so much.

Back in the car, she tried to thank him.

'You've taken so much trouble, given me a lovely treat.'

He laughed. 'Mother used to recount local lore to us when we came to take Oliver out. She thought it educational.'

'I've loved it all.' She was aware of her own short-comings, felt sure she'd not demonstrated enough interest in all he'd been pointing out. She'd been unable to unbend.

Her voice was a whisper: 'You've been very kind, but why me?'

She should have realised what that would do, should have known from the shivers running up her spine, but she was unprepared. He pulled her round to face him, bending across from his seat. Rosie closed her eyes as she felt him slide an arm around her shoulders. His warm lips were planting light butterfly kisses on her own closed mouth. She kept it closed and stiff and straight.

He drew back. 'I like you, Rosie.'

She wondered for a moment if it was a cruel tease, but Ben didn't seem cruel. She wanted above all to show him how much she liked him, but could not. She felt in a straitjacket, unable to get out.

His dark eyes shone with tenderness. 'You're beautiful, Rosie.'

'What? With my ginger hair? Phyllis calls it frizz.'

'Have you never looked in a mirror? You hair is lovely.' He touched it gently, pulled it against his cheek. Then, urgently, he was burying his fingers in it, and kissed her again.

163

Rosie felt on fire. She was pushing him away. Ben looked at her, glorious red-gold curls tossed and windblown. She had a light sprinkling of golden freckles across her straight nose, and gorgeous deep green eyes. He wanted to break down her reserve, get her to open up. She was so shy.

Such a stilted beginning to the afternoon. Her shyness had inhibited him, made him cast round for something to talk about. At best he must have sounded like a guide showing tourists around, at worst a knowall.

'Tell me about yourself,' he said. There was so much he wanted to find out.

'Not much to tell.' She was looking at him through her lashes.

'Bet there is. What have you got to hide?' She was tantalising him.

Rosie sank deeper into her seat. 'Nothing you don't already know.' Her smile was tremulous.

'Relax,' he said. 'I don't care where you were born. It's what you are now that counts.'

'I can't,' she said with a little moan. 'I only wish I could.'

'Rosie, you've built a wall round yourself. You won't even let me peep over the top.' His voice was soft as he pulled her closer, holding her against him.

'I've noticed,' he went on slowly, 'not many of us want to be seen clearly for what we are. People have an instinctive urge to hide their true feelings: They play roles, pretend to be what they're not.'

He had to talk her round. He felt her nervousness. He was afraid he'd frighten her off altogether if he kissed her with half the passion he felt.

'We Shearings pander to it when we advertise our shirts. "Shearing Shirts for Gentlemen". "Feel a Toff, be a Toff in a Shearing Shirt".

'Clothes help us all present ourselves to the world. Men play at being gentlemen when they're not. Hiding their real persona behind a front they project. Women improve their figure by lacing themselves inside Mother's corsets.

'Those who have something to hide live in fear that it will be accidentally revealed. Fronts take time and energy to maintain. That's why you should be glad the spectre of where you were born is out in the open. You don't need to worry about it any more.'

He was talking too much. He paused, looking at her instead. She was staring out across the estuary to the Welsh bank. Rosie hadn't even got her front firmly in place. She let all her fears and anxieties show, making her seem infinitely vulnerable. He kissed her gently. Even now she couldn't relax. He could sense her unease because it was broad daylight and some stranger might see him kiss her.

'Will you show me round your farm?' he asked as he started the engine to drive back.

'Of course.' She was smiling, but he could see she was shy even of that. 'But you'll spoil your shoes.'

'I have wellingtons in the boot.' He wanted to know what her life was like when she wasn't at her sewing machine. He didn't intend to delay finding out.

When they'd arrived and he'd put his wellingtons on, she hurried him past the farm house itself. He followed her into a paddock and immediately an ancient pony ambled towards them. Rosie was patting his neck and fussing him. Ben made himself do the same. He wasn't mad about horses, never having had much to do with them. The pony's dim old eyes seemed to see little, he was afraid it would step on his foot if he were not careful. It was also enormous.

He was taken to see the trap, now disintegrating and covered with dust. He saw the dairy, with crates of clean bottles piled one on top of the other waiting to be filled. He bit back a comment about lack of equipment, which meant so much having to be done by hand.

'Do you pasteurise the milk?' As a business it looked pitifully small.

'Our herd is TB tested,' she told him proudly. 'The vet comes to attest that the cows are TB free.'

An ancient border collie with a faded black coat barked until Rosie called to him. The dog was torn between warning his owners of the approach of a stranger and bringing the cows in for evening milking.

'He stands no nonsense from cattle,' Rosie said, as they saw him give a laggard a nip on the leg to speed her along. 'Not every farm dog can work cattle.'

Ben watched the cows streaming across the cobbled yard and into the cow shed for their evening milking. Rosie was animated at last, pointing out Tinkerbell and the hated Marigold. Two old men followed in the rear. Rosie waved to them. Ben couldn't help but notice the affection with which they greeted her.

'Here, Jake,' she called as the last cow went through

the door. Wagging his ragged tail, the dog came to be patted and made much of. He had tufts of grey in his coat.

'He's a soft old thing really,' Rosie said. 'Sleeps most of the day now. Under the old cart on wet days, in the stable with Flash at night.'

Ben bent to pat the dog, feeling he had eased Rosie over her first stiffness. He watched the two elderly men taking in churns and buckets. He wasn't sure which one was her Uncle Will and which the hired help till Rosie introduced him.

'Ben Shearing?' The old man with the pocket half torn off his coat was pumping his hand. 'You must be Harry's nephew? Harry Shearing?'

Ben tried to kick start his mind. He hadn't heard the name mentioned in his family for the last two decades, yet . . . He remembered the name Harry from somewhere in the past.

'We were close as boys.' Will's eyes shone. 'He used to come here to the farm to play.' Ben met Rosie's gaze. There was a strange look in her eyes.

'Your father mentioned Harry to me only the other day,' she said. 'He'd told me he'd been here as a child too.'

Uncle Will laughed. 'Your father was much younger, at least five years. He didn't interest us much at that time. We thought him a mere baby.'

'I don't remember Uncle Harry,' Ben said. 'Was he a good friend of yours?'

'The best. We had a lot of fun as boys. He used to come here to help with the hay harvest. We taught him to milk, and he loved it. We were at school together,

Birkenhead School. We were more prosperous in those days.'

'I went there too.' Ben was surprised but heartened. It seemed the social rift between Rosie's family and his was not as wide as his mother was trying to make out. Not if his family and Rosie's had once been on visiting terms. 'What was Harry like?'

'Very like your father to look at – hard-working, upright, a good man. We're going to have tea before we start milking. Come in and join us.' Ben accepted gratefully, knowing Rosie would have been too shy to invite him on this first occasion.

He took off his wellingtons in the porch, and had to bend his head to get through the kitchen door. He thought the low-beamed farm kitchen was warm and homely. He was introduced to Aunt Maud, who seemed affronted by his presence until she heard his name was Shearing.

'You didn't tell us, Rosie, who was taking you out,' she chided her niece. 'We could have put the lace cloth on the table if we'd known.'

Ben turned to the young girl sitting by the fire, wondering why Rosie didn't introduce her too. 'Of course – Phyllis,' he said. 'I didn't recognise you for a moment.'

He knew immediately he'd said the wrong thing. He was seeing her without make-up for the first time. Her dress was nondescript, not the smart scarlet one he'd got used to seeing her wear in the office. He found himself sitting at the table while Rosie's Aunt Maud hurriedly brought out the best china and cleared away the crockery she'd set out earlier.

'Funny you should know my family, Mr Quest,' Ben said. 'I can't get over that. Did you ever come to our house?'

'Many times. More often than Harry came here.'

'Did you know my grandfather?'

'I met him once or twice.'

'I'm reading his old company accounts at the moment, and finding them absolutely riveting. They give a very clear picture of his business, but there's nothing about him personally and nobody talks about him at home. What was he like?'

'He did a lot with Harry, I think he was very wrapped up in him. Theatres, cricket matches, sailing, that sort of thing. Harry thought he was wonderful.'

'He invited you too?'

'No, he didn't take much interest in Harry's friends. Barely tolerated me. He was rather an aloof man, I think.' Will was spreading his bread with home-made strawberry jam. 'You know he shot himself?'

Ben was lifting his cup to his lips. Some of his tea slopped into his saucer. 'Shot himself? No, I didn't know.' He felt astounded. He'd never heard so much as a breath of it. 'What happened?'

'It's such a long time ago,' Will said, smoothing his thin grey hair across his scalp. 'I'd have been about eighteen when it happened. Harry and I were drifting apart by then. I left school at sixteen to work on the farm. He stayed on of course. I found it lonely. I missed Harry. I tried to keep in touch, and we did see something of each other in the school holidays. Harry was shot too.'

'You mean he killed . . .?' Ben couldn't get the words out.

'Your grandfather killed himself.'

Ben had a queer feeling in his stomach. He sat staring across the room towards the old-fashioned range. He could hardly believe it – yet it did explain why nobody ever mentioned Ainsley. Not even Gran.

'And Harry?'

'He got over it.'

'But what happened to him? I've never even heard him mentioned at home.'

'I heard rumours on the milk round. Some of my customers worked at Shearing's. I went round to the house to find out what had happened. Harry was in hospital and his father dead. The curtains were drawn and Harry's mother was in bed resting. It was the gardener who told me. He remembered me, you see.'

Ben swallowed. The cake stuck in his throat.

'I went round again a few days later, when I knew Harry would be home. He was all right, only been in hospital for four days. They'd taken the bullet out, but he wouldn't talk about it. An accident, that's all he'd say. Nobody's fault. I was hurt that he didn't confide in me. It was the first time he hadn't.'

Ben saw the old man shiver. 'What happened to him after that?' He was asking himself why Harry was never mentioned by his own family. Surely Dad or Grandma had memories they'd want to share as Will had?

'We saw less and less of each other, but I was asked to his wedding. He was running the shirt factory by then.'

'He must have died quite young?'

'It was some time in the war.'

'He went to the front to fight then?'

'No, it happened here. Whatever it was.'

Ben was finishing his cake when Maud said: 'There was a bit of a mystery about that, too.'

'What sort of a mystery?' He watched Will chewing slowly.

'I never did find out.'

'What?'

'I don't know whether he died or not. There was nothing in the papers. No rumours about Harry in particular, just that he'd gone and your dad was managing the factory.

'The war was on, of course, there was bad news and lots of it from the front. Deaths in plenty there. Why should the papers search for local news? Anything could have happened to him.

'I called in to see Edwin, but he wasn't at work that day. It was years before I saw him again, and though I asked he seemed too upset to talk about Harry. It was only then that I realised he was dead.'

'Must have been an accident.' Ben made up his mind to find out.

'It was sudden. Did you know he was one of the first to own a motor car in Birkenhead? Harry always cut a dash.'

'It was all so long ago,' Ben said. 'I would have been only a baby then.' He was shocked at what he'd heard, and amazed to learn so much about his family from Rosie's uncle.

★ ★ ★

Rosie came out to the car with him to see him off. She hadn't put her coat on and was tucking her hands under her arms to keep them warm.

'Will upset you. I'm sure he didn't mean to.'

'It came as a surprise, Rosie, but it's history now. I'm not upset. I want to know more, and now I can ask. Will has explained a lot.' He unlocked the car door and turned to drop a goodbye kiss on her cheek. A formal sort of peck, the sort he gave his grandmother from time to time.

Rosie smiled, put her hands up on his shoulders and pressed her lips against his in involuntary response. He felt pure pleasure surge through him.

'Rosie! You can kiss then?'

'Of course.' But she was too shy even to look at him.

'You're good at it too. You've come out of your shell. I've thawed you out at last.'

'I'm still freezing,' she whispered as he swept her up in his arms and hugged her.

'Ice maiden!' he laughed. 'Will you come out with me again?'

Her lips parted in a delighted smile. 'I'd like that.' The smile reached her eyes, bubbled out in laughter. 'Thank you.'

Ben felt a glow of relief. 'Can't take you to see that film "Morning Glory", though, we've left it too late. The programme's changed.'

'I don't mind what the film is.' She gave an excited giggle. 'I'll enjoy anything I see with you.'

He kissed her again warmly. 'I'll see you tomorrow at work. Goodbye.'

Rosie watched Ben drive round the corner before running back to the kitchen. She felt intoxicated, high on a wave of elation because he found her attractive. She couldn't stop smiling, as she danced to the fire to warm herself.

'You're aiming high,' Aunt Maud sniffed from the settle. 'Boss's son.'

'It won't come to anything.' Phyllis was in front of the mirror, putting on her hat before going out. 'He's just playing around with you. Soon get fed up, I should think.'

Rosie shivered. She felt as if she'd been doused with cold water. 'You're jealous,' she retorted. 'You rather fancied him yourself.' The back door slammed shut behind her cousin.

'I just hope the same thing as happened to Grace doesn't happen to you.' Aunt Maud rustled the pages of her newspaper as she spread them out. She seemed to be getting over her worry about the letter and was needling Rosie again. 'You'd better be careful. It's in your blood.'

She ran upstairs to change into old clothes for milking. The intoxication had gone, leaving a sour taste in her mouth. She wanted Ben, desperately needed someone she could call her own. He delighted her. She could see his face again, an inch above her own as he'd teased: 'You can kiss then?' She could hear his laughter, deep and masculine.

Phyllis might be jealous but she could also be right. So could Aunt Maud. Something like this must have happened to her mother, and it had brought the most awful consequences. In her heart she wanted Ben, but her head told her to be cautious.

Ben drove down Gordon Drive feeling light-headed. Rosie's reserve had melted once she started showing him the farm. He felt again that surge of elation when she'd raised her lips to his. It proved she felt for him what he felt for her.

He'd seen her home, and met her family, and amazingly he'd been told by her Uncle Will that he'd been friendly with Dad's elder brother. His own family never mentioned Harry. The little he'd learned only made him more curious. It seemed there were secrets in his family history that were being kept from him.

Ben had deliberately closed his mind to the problem of the fraud all day. Now he made himself think of it. He intended to call in at the Albert Hotel on the way home. He wanted to look round Oliver's office and the storerooms while there was no one about. He'd asked Dad for the master key to the building, and had brought the key ring with duplicates to the cupboards and files.

So far, all he had by way of evidence was one document showing a different number sequence, which Oliver would surely have pointed out to him if all was above board. He could understand now how the stock was leaving the factory, but not how his brother was collecting payment personally, if indeed he was. He wanted to find more evidence to convince Mother that Oliver was responsible.

He slowed down, pulling into the pavement to park in the street because they kept the large iron gates locked when the factory wasn't open. His footsteps sounded loud on the short drive, and the building was eerie in the growing dusk.

He let himself into the entrance hall feeling like a common thief. The silence seemed heavy now he'd grown used to so much noise and bustle here on weekdays. It was cold because there'd been no heating all day.

He hurried upstairs to Oliver's office, not putting on a light till he'd closed the door. There was an air of settled comfort about it that his own office lacked. Oliver had a decent carpet, a bookcase and a large mahogany desk. Ben sat in the swivel chair in front of it, searching through the keys on the ring. None would turn in the ornate keyholes. The drawers remained obstinately locked.

He sat back exasperated, his eye coming to rest on the bench with its padded velvet seat. Did Oliver loll on that when he read his newspapers? It hardly seemed like office furniture. He went to the file cabinets and opened both without difficulty. Methodically, he checked through every file. It was boring and time consuming. He was heartily tired of it before he'd worked through all the files and found nothing out of the ordinary in any of them.

Where else was there to look? The files were kept in position in the drawers in expanding cardboard pockets. On impulse, he pushed them back and felt underneath, working through the drawers again. In one, his fingers closed on a pad of forms. He pulled it out. The familiar pad, but with an alternate number sequence. He felt a surge of exultation. What a find!

The pad needed to defraud them was hidden away in

his office. It must be considered proof of his guilt. Ben sped downstairs, locking up the building as he went. He felt lifted up on a wave of triumph as he took the incriminating forms out to his car.

Darkness had fallen, it was much colder now. When he pulled up outside the front door of his home there were lights showing at several windows. He thought it looked welcoming.

He took the pad straight up to his room. On the way down he looked into the dining room. On Sunday nights a cold supper was laid out on the sideboard for the family to help themselves. The room was empty though somebody had eaten and gone. Ben had had tea and cakes twice during the afternoon. He needed a drink more than food. His mind was still spinning.

The lights were on in the drawing room. He pushed open the door to find his grandmother toasting her toes against the white marble fireplace. Orange flames were leaping halfway up the chimney, and casting a glow across her regal figure. A glass of sherry stood on the table beside her.

They never pulled the curtains unless it was stormy because the room enjoyed the same view as his bedroom above. Ben paused to look out of one of the three tall windows. The garden fell away in terraces, making it possible to see over the wall that separated it from the Esplanade.

Liverpool was a myriad of sparkling lights spread across the opposite bank. The ships at anchor in the Sloyne were lit by their riding lights. The landing stage was as bright as day, and just as busy.

'I don't know where everybody has gone,' Grandma

complained. Ben knew his father often walked down to the Royal Rock Hotel for a drink on Sunday evenings, and thought she knew too.

'Mother will be here, busy at something.' He poured himself a generous measure of his father's whisky and sat down on the opposite side of the fire. He could hear the waves breaking against the sandstone wall and the rocks below. It was high tide and the breeze had freshened.

'Busy Bee,' his Grandmother said. 'You're all out every week day at that factory. You'd think on Sundays one of you would be glad to stay home and keep me company.'

'I'm here now, Grandma.' He got up to top up her glass. Her hand on the stem had papery thin skin, and the diamond rings on her fingers flashed prisms of coloured light. 'Has it always been like this for you? Left at home by yourself? Didn't you ever want to go to the factory and help?'

'Certainly not! A lady doesn't work. Neither does she set foot in a factory.' Her voice rose on a note of querulous disgust. She had silver hair, and plenty of it, piled up on her head. With her high cheekbones and boomerang eyebrows, Ben thought her still beautiful at seventy-four.

'It's bad enough having a family that has to go to such a place to earn their living, without being required to go oneself. It's something I've had to put up with.' Ben had been going to ask her about Harry. He decided he'd have to lead up to it gradually.

'At home, as a girl, things were very different for me.'

'At Hendlesham Hall,' he prompted. 'Was it better than this house, Grandma?' Looking out at the night sky studded with stars and the lights shimmering on the river, he couldn't imagine any house being pleasanter.

'Much larger, Ben, and entirely different. We owned all the land round it. My father thought this a mere villa. There are hundreds like it. He was a baronet, you know.'

'Yes.' Ben sighed, he'd heard it many times. 'Sir Alfred Hendlesham.'

'I was Miss Constance Hendlesham. We owned eight hundred acres.'

'As much as that? I didn't realise . . .'

'At one time, yes. My family lived there from the sixteenth century. Long before all these merchants started moving here from over the water.'

'But you didn't own all that land in your day, Grandma.' He'd heard Sir Alfred had been in an impoverished state when he'd died, and Lady Hendlesham had been glad to get their daughter off their hands. He could see by the way Grandma straightened up in her chair that she didn't want to be reminded of that. The passage of time was adding a rosier tint to her memories.

'There was still enough land for me to ride over. My father kept a decent stable.'

'Did you miss that when you married and came here?'

'Of course I did. My mother thought I was going down in the world.'

'It would have been thought a very pleasant house,

Grandma. A good address then.' It was an imposing one even today.

'My mother would not have countenanced my marrying a man in trade had he not been able to provide a home suitable for a person of my standing.'

She sat upright in her chair, holding herself ramrod straight as though learning deportment with a book on her head. Her black taffeta skirt rustled as she moved, and with her black velvet blouse provided an elegant backdrop for her four-strand pearl necklace, her cameo and pearl brooch, gold bracelets and ear rings. She dressed with as much formality for a cold supper as she did for a celebration dinner.

'When I was small you used to show me your jewellery. You had so much I thought you were a queen, and that your tiara was a crown. Did you inherit it from your family?' That brought a guarded look to her face, and he guessed immediately Ainsley had given it to her.

She ignored the question. 'Mother was very much against the marriage.'

'Mothers can be socially ambitious for their children,' he said. His own mother was certainly ambitious for him. 'But you got your own way, and you didn't want for anything, did you? You had a long and happy marriage.'

He was surprised to see her gulp down her sherry. He got to his feet to refill her glass. 'Thank you, Ben.'

She was lifting the full glass to her lips when he said: 'Tell me about Harry. I've only just realised I had an uncle.'

She slammed the glass back down on the table,

spilling a little, and struggled to stand up. 'I haven't had my supper yet. I think I'll go now.'

Ben took her glass and followed her to the dining table. Will had been right, nobody wanted to talk about Harry. There must be something they were trying to hide.

As he filled his plate with cold pork, he mused that Grandma was another who put on a false front with her clothes each morning. It seemed there was a tremendous edifice of family folklore she was trying to live up to. He was intrigued. He couldn't begin to imagine what it was she was hiding.

CHAPTER NINE

Constance picked at the food on her plate. She was not hungry. She waved away the salad Ben passed her, and then the bread. She hated Sunday, it was the hardest day of the week to get through. All her life she'd gone to church on Sundays, sometimes twice. It would draw attention to her troubles if suddenly she stopped, but her sin was yet to be forgiven. The older she grew, and the nearer to meeting her maker, the greater it seemed. Tonight it had weighed heavy, oppressing her, making her feel irritable and out of sorts, even before Ben had started raking up the past.

'You must have come to love this house, Grandma,' he said. Constance wished he'd let her alone. She should never have let Edwin bring his family here all those years ago. Now they treated her house as their own, never giving her a moment's consideration.

'Overlooking the river like this, it's a beautiful position. And you've lived here so long.'

'Since I was seventeen.' She didn't want to talk of those long distant days, but he was probing again. Making it impossible to shut out the hurtful memories. She'd eaten almost all her meals since, sitting here at the bottom of the big mahogany table. The furniture had been Ainsley's choice. He had brought her here after their honeymoon in 1880.

The clock, small white face set into a mammoth-sized black marble replica of Britannia, had been a wedding present from one of Ainsley's friends. She'd always hated it, almost as much as the black marble urns that flanked it. They seemed more suited to provide ornament to a grave.

'You married Grandpa when you were seventeen? That was very young.' Ben was pretending to care, but it was plain to see his mind was busy with something quite different.

'Far too young to marry at all,' she snapped before she realised how much it would give away. She'd been totally ignorant of what marriage to Ainsley Shearing would be like.

'You must have loved Grandpa or why rush into it?' His needling provoked her. He was pretending to humour her, but there must be a purpose behind it.

'Yes,' she agreed. She wasn't going to dwell on how hard life had been for her. She didn't want Ben's pity. No point in telling him her father had died only months earlier, and left them with nothing but debt. Father had lived as befitted a gentleman of his standing, even when he must have known he was drawing on his capital. The stable could have gone years earlier and saved them something. Her mother had been frantic, reduced to selling up her home and taking a room in a hotel.

She herself had been faced with the choice between marriage and finding a job. Ladies of her station in life didn't work for a living. Couldn't anyway – she'd never been to school. Her mother had suggested she might become a governess, and had even suggested the name of an acquaintance who might employ her should she apply, but Constance couldn't think of facing the sort of harassment she'd given her own governess.

'How old was Grandpa then? He must have been much older than you. He'd started the company in 1865 and built it up every year after that.'

'What makes you say that?' Constance was filled with misgivings. Ben was stirring up her past, raking it like old leaves, turning up memories she wanted to keep buried.

'I've been reading his company reports. I could tell you how much he made all through the early years.'

'What for?' she barked at him. He was beaming with an innocence that sent fear fluttering through her.

'Dad thought they might teach me something, interest me. I find them absolutely fascinating. Grandpa had a wonderful grip on finance.'

Constance couldn't swallow. Ainsley had had a vice-grip on everything. Including her.

'The company was wonderfully prosperous under his management, far more so than it is now.'

'People could afford to buy shirts then. The country was well off in the days of the old Queen.'

'They were all hand sewn to start with,' Ben said. 'Can you imagine? All stitched by out-workers. And Grandpa had a shop through which he sold them.'

She'd have been even more ashamed of him if he hadn't progressed beyond that. Well, she couldn't have married him at all.

'Grandpa was one of the first to have sewing machines and open a factory. He could keep you in comfort, Gran.'

'Yes, every comfort.' That was why she'd married him, not because she'd loved him. How could a delicately brought up girl of seventeen feel passionate about a shirtmaker of forty-three? He was more tied up with his shirtmaking than she'd ever imagined. After all, her father had never worked. She had hated the smell of the factory that hung about him. Hated his greying hair and lined face. He seemed so old – only two years younger than her own father. She'd been conscious of his sagging flesh from the first moment.

Ainsley saw her as a mark of his success. A lady by birth whom he could show off to his fellow merchants, the elite of Birkenhead. Someone of taste and fashion. She knew he indulged her to buy her favours. He showered her with clothes, jewellery, flowers, and the best house and furniture he could afford. She had meant to play fair with him. Do the best she could to please him in return.

'I'm proud to be his grandson.' Ben was smiling at her. 'I hope I manage the company as well.'

Constance felt sick. 'You don't know what he was like,' she said. Ben was little more than a child after all.

'What was he like? Tell me.' He was waiting, watching her like a cat watches a mouse. He tossed his heavy straight hair back from his forehead. His smile was meant to encourage her confidence. 'I'd love to know more about him.'

Constance shuddered. She hated being pressed for

details of her past. She couldn't tell him she'd been ashamed of Ainsley Shearing and his uncouth habits.

'He must have loved you. You must have been very beautiful then.'

She'd thought she was going to be a rich man's darling, truly a bird in a gilded cage. She couldn't tell Ben that the marriage had gone sour at an early stage, and certainly not why.

'Why won't you tell me about Harry?' Ben's gaze brought her up with a jerk. 'We were talking about him today. I'd . . .'

'What were they saying?' She pushed her plate away. 'Who was talking about him?' She felt panic rising in her. Ben must suspect something. He always seemed to be probing painful memories these days. She couldn't talk of Harry. She'd loved him, depended on him. He'd meant so much to her.

Even to think about the way he'd disappeared, frightened her. Beatrice had been jousting with him for years, but Harry didn't realise how malicious she was, nor the evil of which she was capable. She must have caught him off guard.

Constance had often gone round to his home. Alice, his wife, had said one day, right out of the blue: 'Harry's gone. I suppose you know?'

'No!' She'd felt the first prickle of apprehension then. 'Gone where?'

'I'm telling everyone he's left me. That's the official story.'

'Harry would never go away without saying goodbye to me,' she'd said. 'He'll be back.'

'He can't come back. I don't want him anyway. You

know how things were with us.'

Constance had known they hadn't been getting on, that they'd had a terrible row at Christmas. She remembered asking, her mouth dry: 'Another woman?'

'Beatrice has seen him off.'

'Beatrice?' What's she done to him?'

Alice had shrugged. 'You know Beatrice.' Constance shuddered. It was only after that she'd found out he hadn't been to the office for a few days.

When Edwin came home from the front, she'd tried to tell him Beatrice had done something terrible to Harry. He'd laughed at her. Nobody would listen.

When Edwin left Beatrice accosted her, clutching at Constance's shoulders, eyes blazing like black sloes.

'So it was you who started all those rumours?' she'd raved. 'I might have known! Don't you dare go round saying such things. Not to anyone. Killed Harry indeed! You're a right old scandalmonger. Always trying to make trouble for me. Don't ever let me catch you talking about Harry again, do you hear?'

Beatrice never forgot anything. She'd be furious with Constance now if she told Ben what had happened to Harry.

'Will Quest, do you remember him? He said he was Harry's friend.'

She felt her head begin to swim. 'Yes. Yes, I think so. When he was at school he had a friend he used to bring here a lot.'

'That would be him.'

'What did he tell you?' She was shivering in dread.

186

'What did Harry die of? Will said he was only thirty-five?'

'I can't think, Ben. It's such a long time ago. I'm tired, I'll have to go to bed.' She was pushing back her chair, levering herself upright against the table.

Ben stood too. 'Are you all right?'

'Yes. It's been a long day.' She'd got as far as the door.

'Shall I bring your coffee up?'

'Ovaltine,' she said. 'Perhaps Ovaltine.'

The stairs seemed to be getting steeper with time, and she shouldn't have asked him to bring up a drink. It gave him the chance to put his questions again. Beatrice had said she must not talk of Harry.

Her own two small connecting rooms seemed a haven when she reached them, though the atmosphere of the nursery still clung to them. When the children grew up, Beatrice had suggested she move to them. She'd been reluctant at first, because she was reluctant to do anything her daughter-in-law wanted.

Beatrice called the tiny sitting room her boudoir but that didn't make it comfortable. Constance sighed. She should have done more to it. The big nursery fireguard had been removed and a free standing electric fire put on the hearth in its place.

'Too much to expect Mrs Roper to run up and downstairs with coal except in very cold weather.' Beatrice had warned. The chairs were too low. Constance found it hard to get out of them.

The adjoining night nursery was now her bedroom. At least it was her own. She'd never had to share it with Ainsley, and that made it comfortable and very safe. It was dominated by the big white cupboard in which she'd once stored napkins and baby binders. She opened it to take out her slippers and dressing gown.

She removed her jewellery and replaced each piece in its case. Harry's bed had been where hers stood now, but she didn't want to think of Harry. Especially not of losing him.

There were so many things she could no longer think about. Ainsley's death had not been a loss, but she couldn't think of that either, not if she wanted to stay sane.

It was guilt, of course, because she hadn't been able to love him. She could sense his lust as soon as he touched her. It seemed impossible that she, a lady, should be subjected to such indignities.

He'd told her she was a total failure in bed. She'd hated sharing it with him, but it was part of the bargain she'd settled for. Especially, she'd hated this morning passion. Ainsley had been a morning man, usually being too tired after a day at the factory. At first she'd prided herself that he didn't know how much she dreaded his thrice-weekly show of love.

Pregnancy had seemed even more horrific when it came. She'd felt continually sick and full of terrors about the birth. The child in her arms had helped her forget the worst discomforts. At last she'd had something she could love. They'd both adored Harry. He'd been a beautiful child. Like all the Shearings he'd had sandy-coloured curls, a round baby face and wide-awake eyes.

Constance let her mind drift back over the years. She had followed the fashion of the day and dressed him in frilly dresses like a girl. They'd both indulged him.

For a time, she'd thought they might be happy. Certainly those had been the better days of their marriage. She found herself pregnant a second time within four months. The thought of going through it all again appalled her, but she'd made herself look on the bright side. If it resulted in another child like Harry, she could endure it.

But it was not to be. She miscarried at three months, and found it an exhausting and depressing experience. An experience she went through twice the following year and once the year after. It didn't make Ainsley's morning passion any easier to take. She'd hoped the novelty of having her in his bed would fade and he would leave her alone, but that didn't happen.

After three more miscarriages, her doctor advised Ainsley to give up trying for another child. Constance was more than willing.

'Separate beds?' she suggested hopefully when the doctor had gone, but he wouldn't hear of it.

The best she could hope for then was that with age his appetite for sex would fade. After his fiftieth birthday the frequency fell from thrice-weekly to twice. Constance had hoped age would have greater effect.

She had yet another miscarriage the following spring. It left her weary and feeling, at twenty-five, old before her time; that the bargain she'd entered into was not so much to her benefit as she'd expected.

Harry grew more precious because it seemed he was to be the only one. A headstrong child who was never scolded, the apple of Ainsley's eye too.

All the time the shirt factory grew and prospered and Ainsley denied her and Harry nothing. The effort to hide her repugnance of his sexual advances became too great. Fear of another short-lived pregnancy added to it. She was pregnant for the ninth time when she discovered he was taking Harry's nanny to bed too. She turned a blind eye to it. She had to or face the increased demand herself. Her continued pregnancy surprised her, though she felt anything but well. It resulted in a live birth, a rather puny five-pound son she called Edwin.

She'd given up expecting to have another child, and felt little for him. Pity was the strongest emotion as she shut the nursery door against his wailing, leaving him to Nanny. There was over six years' difference in her sons' ages, and Harry had taken all her love. She'd felt guilt ridden that she couldn't love her husband, guilt ridden she couldn't love her second son. She'd felt very unhappy, and blamed Ainsley for it all.

She was in bed when Ben knocked and brought in her Ovaltine. Hard to believe he was Edwin's son. Harder to believe Edwin had turned out a greater comfort in the long run than Harry. But then, Harry had been cut off in his prime.

Ben perched on the side of her bed. He was like Ainsley in many ways. The shape of his head, for instance, the way he held it. She sipped the Ovaltine.

'Just as I like it.' Hot and bland.

'Grandpa fascinates me. I'm reading through his early business accounts, written in his own hand. When I think that he lived in this house, and you were his wife, it's history coming alive. I wish you'd tell me more about him.'

Constance knew she had stiffened. She couldn't tell him anything. Couldn't talk about Ainsley. Just to think about him frightened her, made the soles of her feet curl in horror.

'Careful, Gran, you'll spill your drink. Are you all right?'

She took a firmer grip on herself. 'Just tired, it's getting late. I can't talk any more tonight.'

'Good night then, sleep well.' He stood up. 'You must tell me about Grandpa some other time.'

Constance closed her eyes in agony. His words told her she'd postponed the inquisition, not prevented it. She finished her drink, put off her light, but she couldn't even lie still in the bed. Sleep was a lifetime away.

It upset her just to hear Ainsley's name. 'History' Ben had called it. The events of those days were starkly clear in her mind compared with what had happened yesterday. How she wished they were not.

Ben's mind was on Rosie as he got ready for bed. To think of her immediately blotted out the worry of how to deal with Oliver's fraud. In some strange way he felt he derived strength from her. She helped him stand up to his mother. He was growing more certain that he loved her, he wanted her with an urgency that would not wait.

He wanted to tell her all this. He was almost sure she felt the same way about him, but he wanted to hear her say it. He wanted their relationship accepted by friends and family as permanent. He felt drawn to Rosie. He understood her.

He would take her to the cinema in Birkenhead tomorrow because he thought she'd enjoy it. For himself, he just wanted to be with her. It was enough to talk to her, to look at her and touch her. That night he slept soundly.

He was dressing the next morning when he saw the pad of delivery notes on his tallboy. He'd spent time mulling over his Uncle Harry and why nobody in the family would talk about him. He'd spent hours day dreaming about Rosie, but he should have been considering what he could do about his suspicions.

As far as he was concerned they were more than suspicions now, but had he enough evidence to convince Mother? He didn't think so. She was convinced Oliver could do no wrong.

He could take the pad down with him to breakfast and outline his suspicions to the family, but they would certainly confront Oliver with them and he would be warned and then no real proof would be forthcoming.

He stared out of his bedroom window deliberating on whether to tell his father, but Dad would not keep anything from Mother. What he ought to do was put the delivery note he'd got from Eric on Oliver's desk, and then see if his brother sent it back to him to bill the company. He could get Phyllis to copy it first. Would she see anything strange in that? He made up his mind to do it as he went slowly down to the dining room.

'Really, Ben, you're very late this morning.' Beatrice's voice was sharp. His father concentrated on buttering some toast.

'Sorry,' he mumbled. For once Stephen had reached the table ahead of him. His smile said clearly: 'Your turn today, mate.'

Their housekeeper, Mrs Roper, her hair in an efficient-looking grey bun, brought in the morning post and put it by Edwin's plate. Beatrice was silent till the dining room door closed behind her and Edwin had handed an envelope over to Stephen.

'What time did you go to bed last night?' she demanded. 'I didn't hear you come in.'

'I was in all evening,' Ben was saying, when suddenly Stephen let out something between a whoop of joy and a triumphant crow. He was laughing out loud.

'I've done it!'

'Done what?' his mother demanded impatiently.

'I've got a job. As from May the first. At the bank.' He gave another whoop of joy, his face wreathed in smiles.

Ben was aware that his parents were staring in shocked silence. 'Stephen,' he said quietly, 'what about our company?'

'Don't be silly, you can't do that,' his mother admonished.

'I've done it.' He smiled, brandishing his letter. 'A firm offer in writing. I had an interview last week.'

'You didn't tell us you were . . .' Ben had never seen his mother so flustered before.

She had no time for false fronts, she was too busy. She was manipulative and didn't give a toss who saw her moves, carrying them out by sheer force of will. She went after personal power and didn't care who saw it. At least she was honest.

'What sort of job? Anyway, you can't take it.'

'Bank clerk.' Stephen laughed again. 'And I'm definitely taking it. Very definitely.'

'What about us? Surely the family firm means something?' Edwin asked.

'I've had it up to the back teeth. I want to get out.'

'You'll never earn much as a bank clerk,' Beatrice rounded on him. 'Surely you prefer . . .'

'No, Mother. It'll get you off my back.'

Ben couldn't take his eyes off his mother. Her face was scarlet. She'd been thrown into total confusion.

'It was not my intention to upset you, Stephen. I was only trying to help, both you and the firm. Who is going to do our selling?'

'Mother, it's all yours. You couldn't wait to get started on it last week.'

'Don't be ridiculous, I can't do everything.'

'Last week you thought you could. You've never been satisfied with what I did. "Pull your socks up, Stephen. Put your heart into the job, work harder." That's all I've heard from you. I never pleased you. Now you can do the job exactly as you want, and I wish you joy of it.'

'I was trying to show you a better way of working.' Beatrice looked stricken. 'I don't want you to be a bank clerk. There's a better future for you with us.'

'Mother, I can't live with you on my back, your permanent heckling. I've been trying to get myself another job for almost a year.'

Stephen had been forced by Oliver to put up his fists and fight for survival. Ben had always thought he was too young, too brash, to see that fighting Mother called for different tactics. With her he needed a more subtle, roundabout way to achieve his aims. To take a new job would certainly get her off his back, but Ben was afraid opting out would be to Stephen's disadvantage in the long term.

'Stephen, don't do anything about this till you've slept on it. Give yourself time to think it over,' Dad was advising.

'I've already thought it over a dozen times. There's no other way for me. I'm not going to miss this opportunity, it's taken me too long to get it. If you want to know, I applied for a job abroad, but they say I need at least a year's experience in this country. This is it as far as I'm concerned. You can keep your corsets, and your shirts are getting up my nose.'

Ben was shocked at the effect his brother's desertion was having on their mother.

'I know I pushed my sales up last year, but no one believed me. I met the targets you set, Mother, but still you weren't satisfied. You wanted to come with me, to see my customers. I'm not putting up with that.'

Ben saw her mouth open. 'The figures prove . . .'

He was wracked with guilt. He should have told Stephen he believed him. That the increased sales he'd claimed he'd made were genuine. He should have told Stephen he suspected Oliver of creaming off the profits. Slowly he forked up his last mouthful of bacon.

'Stephen, you aren't starting your new job for a month. There's no reason why you can't work out your notice. I want you to,' he said.

'Mother won't want it, not now.' He was looking at her belligerently.

'Tell him,' Ben insisted. 'Mother, tell him somebody has to sell our stock.'

'I'm sorry, Stephen. Of course I want you to work your notice. It's only right you should.'

'We've got to find a replacement for you.' Ben tried to think. 'What about Charles Avery? He's been working in sales. You know him, you've worked closest to him. Do you think he'd be any good in your job?'

'Yes.'

'Then show him where our customers are. Take him round with you for a month. Introduce him to them. Show him what you do, please,' he said. 'For the sake of the firm.'

'All right,' Stephen agreed reluctantly.

'After all,' Edwin reminded him, 'we'll still be paying you a share of the profits at the end of the year.'

'I don't see why,' Beatrice was boiling over. 'Letting us down like this.'

'It's only fair,' Edwin said, getting to his feet. 'It's getting late. Come on, we've got to go. If you insist on keeping the keys, Beatrice, we have to get there on time. It costs money to keep staff waiting outside.'

Ben got up slowly and followed them out to the car. Stephen's defection had shaken them all. He doubted if the family would ever be the same again.

They had a family conference in Dad's office, and talked to Charles Avery about taking over Stephen's job. That at least was settled.

Ben sat at his own desk with a file open before him, routine work that shouldn't need much thought. He couldn't even start. He sipped at a cup of tea, glanced at the headlines in the paper, and came to the conclusion he couldn't hope to concentrate this morning. Too much had happened.

Suddenly he was jerking to his feet again. How could he have forgotten? He went bounding back to his father's office.

'Dad, can you spare a moment? I want to talk about Grandpa.'

'You're finding his old account books interesting?'

'Fascinating, but Rosie Quest's uncle told me Grandpa shot himself.' Ben suddenly realised his father was staring at him.

'Who?'

'Rosie Quest from the sewing room. She took me to her home.'

'I'd heard you'd taken a fancy to her.'

'It was her Uncle Will, do you know him?'

'Yes.'

'Is it true Grandpa shot himself? I tried to ask Gran last night . . .'

'I wouldn't do that, you'll upset her. She won't talk about him.'

'Is it true then?' He hesitated. Was it his imagination or had his father gone pale?

'Yes, it's true, your grandfather shot himself.'

'Why didn't somebody tell me? Strange to hear things about one's own family from somebody else.'

'A painful subject as you can imagine, we none of us want to remember. Anyway, you know now.'

'He just shot himself?'

'Yes.'

'He was very successful. Why should he shoot himself?'

'It was an accident, Ben.'

'And what happened to your brother Harry? Nobody ever mentions him. Dad, I didn't even know you had a brother.'

'It all happened a long time ago. There are some things we have to put behind us, if we are to survive.'

Ben frowned. He still found it hard to understand. He could see his father looking back over the years, on his face a look of infinite sorrow.

A flash of lightning momentarily lit the Liverpool skyline, and, once gone, the storm clouds seemed even darker. A crash of thunder followed, rolling and tumbling, reverberating through the house. Constance shivered and moved stiffly to pull the curtains against the threatening sky. She was not afraid of thunder, of course she wasn't. Just a little nervous because she was alone. She had seen worse storms than this.

She would have her tea, make herself forget the foul weather outside. She switched on a table lamp and was comforted by the glow. The coals dropped in the grate, causing the flames to leap higher, making the drawing room seem cosy. She helped herself to a cake from the plate on the trolley. Where was everybody? On Sunday afternoons she expected to see the family at tea. Another roll of thunder reminded her how open was the aspect of this house. It had always borne the brunt of the weather, and made her more nervous of storms here than anywhere else.

Once Hilda had said the same: that the house was

very exposed to gales and storms because bad weather gusted up river straight off the Atlantic. That was a long time ago, when Constance would still have been considered a bride. In those days you were referred to as a bride for six months, as though serving a probationary period for full wifehood.

'I would like to be your friend,' Hilda had said, letting her cold hand rest against hers. Hilda's hands were beautifully manicured but always cold.

How she'd needed a friend that day! How she'd yearned for someone to tell her how to cope with Ainsley! She'd thought him deranged. A monster with appalling appetites. Constance quaked now, remembering too how youth had coloured her perception of age. She couldn't understand how Hilda could be thirty-one and still look young. Her skin was pale and smooth, her hair of such a rich deep red it seemed to glow through the lace of her cap, and so curly that tiny corkscrews bounced round her hairline.

Neither could she understand why Hilda, beautiful as she was, remained a spinster. Spinsters had no status at all, and to reach thirty in that state signified failure. Even Ainsley had said it was a great pity his sister had missed her chance.

'How are you getting on?' Hilda had asked in her gentle fashion. 'Is Ainsley treating you well?'

Constance had so wanted to pour out the feelings of terror that choked her. Her tongue-tied response was still vividly with her. How did one speak of a total horror of one's husband, especially to his sister? She could see Hilda's green eyes smiling down at her now.

'Dear Constance, something is worrying you.' The

cold fingers twined themselves round hers.

What words could she use to communicate the awfulness of Ainsley's passion? No one ever spoke of such things. Hilda was a spinster and would not fully understand the nature of men. Constance herself hadn't till her wedding night. Yet she felt a need to speak to someone, find out if Ainsley was perverted or whether all men behaved like wild animals in bed. She had to try. She chose her words with care.

'Hilda, there is a darker side to Ainsley that makes me nervous. I would like your opinion.' The cold fingers tightened with a knowing jerk.

'I know there is, my dear, and I've wondered whether I should try to explain.'

'You have?' Constance felt a joyful surge of relief that Hilda understood.

'I'm glad you've spoken of it. It was his grief, Constance, that made him turn to it. Grief at losing Dinah.'

Puzzled, Constance pulled her gaze away from the earnest green eyes to the large gilt-framed portrait above the marble fireplace. It showed a woman in a red dress with an overblown figure and heavy shoulders. She thought Dinah looked well advanced into middle age, and even the kindest must call her plain.

'He loved her. It shows the measure of his loss that he turned to the darker side, as you call it. It was his way of mourning. He couldn't accept death meant the end.'

'No.' She'd had a sinking feeling in her stomach as she'd agreed. That had worried her too, but not so much as Ainsley's unbridled passion.

'The bond between husband and wife can be like that. I didn't like him going to spiritualist meetings but it comforted him then. You must try to understand.'

'He goes still,' Constance choked. It was all part of Ainsley's complicated character, but not the part she hated most. Not the darkest, though Hilda might think so. She loved her brother and would not believe ill of him.

'He wants me to go with him.' She swallowed. 'He urges me to come, and I'm frightened. He says Dinah wants to meet me, that I could learn so much from her, that she has advice for me. I know I would faint if she so much as tried in front of others.'

Constance felt her scalp prickle. The nature of that advice had been made very clear to her, though she was not making it so to Hilda. He'd been angry when she'd failed to please him in bed. The inference had been hurtfully plain. Dinah had given more satisfaction in that respect.

'I refused to go. He speaks of her as though she's still alive. As though she's still part of his life. As though she's living here with us.'

'Now he's married to you, you'll change all that. Just give him time.'

'How could Dinah have such a hold on him?'

'He loved her. We all loved her, but we love you too, Constance. Certainly Ainsley does.'

Her scalp was tight again, she could hardly get her breath. Dare she mention the other?

'Ainsley wanted to cross the great divide to be with her,' Hilda continued.

'He doesn't see it as a divide at all,' Constance answered tartly.

'Her death was so sudden. When a man has had thirteen years of marriage he is lonely without a wife.'

'He wants her still. He speaks of her as though she's just gone out of the room, as though he can call her back.' Constance raised her eyes to the portrait again. She would dislike Dinah with her self-satisfied smirk if she were alive, she knew she would.

'I am not like her. Why did he choose me?'

'Because you are so different. Dinah helped him build up his business. Her father was a gentlemen's outfitter, she understood the trade. When they married he had a shop which she managed for him. It gave him time to set up the factory. He's different now. He's successful, rich. You complement his success. Of course he needs someone different now.'

Hilda smiled. 'We have always thought of ourselves as middle- class, but to you we must seem lower down the social scale?'

Ainsley certainly did. There was a greater refinement about Hilda. She would have fitted better into the life Constance had been brought up to at Hendlesham.

'Do you ride, Hilda?'

There were stables in Rock Park, maintained for the convenience of the householders. Some kept their own horses there, but it was possible to hire a carriage or a hack to ride round the park or along the prom.

Constance remembered her green velvet riding habit upstairs. She'd learned to ride – side saddle of course, Papa would not have allowed any other.

Ainsley disapproved of her riding, and had forbidden her to go alone.

He'd said: 'I doubt they keep ladies' saddles there. Hire a carriage if you wish to go out, and be sure to take a maid with you.'

'No,' Hilda said. 'I never had your advantages.'

Constance felt caged. There was so little she could enjoy in her new life. In an access of frustration she burst out: 'I don't like seeing Dinah's picture here, dominating my drawing room. My predecessor.' She bitterly resented it, but felt she had to be wary of showing such strong feelings to Hilda.

'Tell him how you feel then.' Her green eyes sparkled with kindliness. 'He's a good man, he'll understand. I'm sure he'll humour you in this and put Dinah up in the attic. He'll find another picture to take its place.'

Constance shuddered. She couldn't admit she'd already asked him on the night they'd returned from their honeymoon. She'd been a very new bride of two weeks, and a little shocked at what he expected from her; bruised and sore too. Already disillusioned because she knew Ainsley had not enjoyed his honeymoon and was disappointed in her. It had been a night like this one. Stormy, with lightning flickering through the curtains, thunder rolling up the river and rain hurtling at the windows.

The morning had felt hot and sticky when they'd started the journey back from Windermere. The inside of the hired carriage had been filled with an overpowering smell of leather. The sky was like lead, her new clothes were sticking to her, and Ainsley was taking up so much of the seat she felt squashed and almost overcome by the heat.

'Could we not stop and spend another night somewhere?' She'd fanned her burning cheeks with her glove, wanting to get out of the carriage so she could breath again, yet dreading the seclusion of another bedroom.

'I must get back to the factory,' he'd replied. 'We've been away long enough. Aren't you eager to see your new house?'

'I have seen it, Ainsley, I like it very much.'

'So you should. I've gone to a lot of trouble and expense to fit it up to the highest standard. We'll soon be in Liverpool and once there it'll take next to no time to get home. There'll be a cooling breeze on the river. You'll enjoy the ferry.'

But the storm had broken by then. She'd shivered as she'd watched the torrential downpour dance off the deck. She'd had to huddle in the saloon with the other passengers, and the smell of leather was replaced by that of smoke and wet wool. She'd seen the brilliant flickers of lightning even through closed eyelids.

As the ferry tied up, Ainsley had opened her umbrella, taken her arm and hurried her up the pier, leaving two porters to follow with their luggage. They'd waited in the ferry house for two hansoms to be brought to the door, and after the cases had been loaded in one, had got into the other. From there it was but a few hundred yards to the door, but by then she'd been cold and damp and glad of the cheerful fire and hissing gas lights.

She had visited the house several times before her

marriage. Ainsley had chosen and ordered the furniture and hired staff to get the place ready. All she was expected to do was to approve his choice. She had seen it taking shape but never actually finished till now. She'd thought the drawing room perfect until she turned round and saw Dinah's portrait dominating the fireplace wall. She'd felt affronted. What new wife wouldn't be, to see her predecessor given such a prominent place?

It was late at night. The servants welcomed them home with hot soup and sandwiches. Constance had found her honeymoon trying and was hoping things would be better once they settled down. Cocooned in the warmth of the drawing room, comforted by the hot soup, she had dared to ask him to remove Dinah's portrait. Tried to explain that she could not meet her gaze every day.

He'd responded like a wild animal. 'Dinah understands me! I want her to see you are no threat to her. I want her to see you are little more than a child and can't inspire love as she did. I want her to understand you have not taken her place in my heart. There is so much she can teach you about the duties of a wife, Constance, you must listen and heed.'

'She's dead, Ainsley.' The hairs on the back of her neck stood upright with fear. 'Dead and gone. She knows nothing now.'

'I feel her here with me always. There's no great rift between life and death. She's in the after-life. Dinah tells me . . .'

She couldn't stop herself. 'Are you trying to frighten me?'

'Silly child, you're frightened of life and frightened of death too.'

'Everybody fears death.'

'I do not.'

It had frightened her more that he so obviously spoke the truth. It made her shout at him: 'I fear for people who imagine they can talk to ghosts. You're unhinged. Dinah's dead, Ainsley, dead and buried and gone for ever.'

She hadn't seen his hand swing out, but the slap pushed her sideways and her cheek was stinging. It had made her collapse on to a chair, sobbing more from shock than hurt. He'd hauled her to her feet, frog marched her up to their bedroom and slammed the door.

'You're a heretic! The bible says there is an after-life. Do you not believe in the bible?' He pushed her towards the bed. She could feel her heart pounding. His anger and physical strength were terrifying.

'Dinah is here with us, do not doubt it. Her spirit, and her soul. Only her body is gone. She knows that is the only reason I need you.'

On his bedside table was a silver-framed photograph of a younger Dinah, wearing a crinoline. Constance snatched it up and hurled it across the room. As the glass shattered he sprang at her, tearing her blouse, ripping her clothes like a wild animal.

'For the relief of the flesh,' he said. 'And it's damned hard to get it from an iceberg like you!'

CHAPTER TEN

Rosie could see dust motes dancing in the shafts of
sunlight that shone through the tall and gracious
sewing room windows. Each had a faded pelmet above
it, though there had never been curtains all the time
she'd worked here. Having once been the lounge of
the Albert Hotel it was a pleasant room. Its finely
moulded ceiling had two magnificent ovals of fern
leaves and flowers in relief plasterwork. Now they
were dusty and yellowing and showed two stumps of
chain where once two chandeliers had swung. Bare
fluorescent tubes had been installed to provide light
for the workers.

They sat at sewing machines which had been
installed in rows of eight. A moving band took power
up the line from an engine on the wall at the end.

Rosie had just had another dozen soft collars, cut
out and ready to sew, booked out to her. She took the
pieces that made up the first, lowered the foot of her
machine on to the grey and white striped cotton and
started to sew. She'd done it so many times, her fingers
guided it automatically, leaving her free to think about
Ben.

'He's a very kind person,' Mary Green had whispered this morning. 'Have you noticed the way he looks at you? I think he likes you.' Rosie was beginning to think she was falling in love, and daring to hope that he loved her in return.

Almost every play she listened to on the wireless, every film she saw, every book she read, was about falling in love. It happened to almost everyone she knew. Most of the girls Shearing's employed were either married or had boyfriends. Phyllis was engaged, but Rosie had never expected it to happen to her. She was a loner, and afraid she always would be.

But, unbelievably, Ben was showing real interest. He'd wanted her to kiss him. She felt a delicious quiver of anticipation. The fact that he was a Shearing made it even more unbelievable. It was a secret she was hugging to herself, mulling it over whenever she sewed or milked or lay in her bed. It was the most exciting thing that had ever happened to her.

Phyllis was treating her in a more friendly fashion for a different reason. On Monday morning Ben had walked straight up to Rosie's machine and asked her: 'Can you come to the pictures with me tonight?' The machines around her slowed to a halt to allow their operators to catch the drift of his words.

She'd had to tell him she'd not had time for anything more than a hurried sandwich before meeting him, because she'd helped with the milking first.

On Tuesday morning, he'd come to her machine again to ask: 'How about coming to the Royal Rock with me for a meal tonight?'

'I will,' Kitty Harmon who worked at the next

machine sang out. 'Yes, please.'

'I was asking Rosie.' Ben beamed, not one whit perturbed.

Flora Pope, on her other side, gave a gutsy laugh: 'Rosie had her turn last night. Give somebody else a chance – I'll come.' Her double chins quivered with fun.

'Who said anything about turns?' he joked. 'You and Kitty go together, there's good girls. I won't be able to give you much attention. Not if I'm with Rosie.'

She felt herself blushing, wondering why he had to make such a public display of their friendship. Edwin Shearing happened to come into the sewing room at that moment.

'What's all this ribald laughter?' he wanted to know.

'Your son has just refused to take me out for dinner.' Flora's giggle exploded into laughter.

'Flossie, I'll feed you any time. You and the other thousand, just as long as you get this order finished.'

Flora laughed so much tears ran down her face and she had to take off her spectacles and dry them on her overall.

It had lasted for a couple of weeks now. Rosie was going out almost every night. She felt she needed more clothes in order to enjoy her new social life, and spent every spare moment she had at home sewing for herself. She bought a length of blue cotton and made herself a sun dress with a matching bolero.

By way of appeasement, Aunt Maud offered to buy another dress length for her. Phyllis went shopping with her and chose linen in a warm peach shade Rosie had never worn before.

'It will set off your hair,' her cousin had said. Rosie draped the material over her shoulder and looked in the mirror. She was surprised to find it was a paler tone of her hair colour. 'It'll really suit you,' Phyllis insisted.

She made the dress with the latest heart-shaped neckline, and as she slid it over her head to wear for the first time, was very pleased with the result. Just thinking of meeting Ben in twenty minutes brought a frisson of excitement.

She combed her hair out, deciding to leave it loose tonight the way Ben liked it. She would take her mother's lizard-skin handbag. It went well with her dress and it brought Grace nearer.

'You look wonderful,' Ben said when he came to pick her up. Rosie knew he was taking her to the pictures because for some reason he felt he couldn't ask her to do the same thing two nights running.

'I don't want you to grow bored with me,' he'd said. 'And the Royal Rock lounge is nothing special unless you're keen on drink.'

At first, Rosie was afraid he found the much acclaimed Charlie Chaplin film not to his taste. His gaze seemed to be on her more than on the screen. She was very conscious of his hand holding hers.

Later on she saw him laughing a lot, and they both gorged on the chocolates he'd bought in the foyer.

Shearing's Shirts began to buzz with the news that Ben Shearing was taking Rosie Quest out and not hiding the fact. Young girls from every department eyed her enviously, the older women and the men with more respect. Rosie felt her stock had risen generally.

'It worked then.' Ben's mouth had quirked at the corner when she told him. 'I hoped it might.' It was only then she'd realised that had been his intention all along.

'You're trying to counterbalance what your mother does to me?'

One Wednesday, everybody in the sewing room knew he was picking her up an hour later than usual and they were going for a drink.

In the Royal Rock that night Rosie nursed a glass of orange juice while Ben sat over half a pint of beer, and they talked and talked.

'I'm getting hungry,' said Ben towards ten o'clock. 'Come with me and have a bite to eat. There's usually pork pie and ham put out for late snacks. Mother's gone out for the evening – with Dad.'

'I don't know.' Rosie wanted to see his home but was suddenly stiff with reluctance.

'Stephen's always out. There'll only be Grandma there. It'll be quite safe. Come on, it's only round the corner from here.'

She clung to his arm as they went up the front steps. She had an impression of space and solidity. The massive front door opened on well-oiled hinges. It was far more gracious and formal in style than the farm, though perhaps not quite so old.

The hall was redolent with the scent of furniture polish. Ben helped her off with her coat, hung it with his in a cloakroom.

'No need to be afraid, Rosie.' She followed him

towards a door. When he opened it, she caught a glimpse of a large airy sitting room with a fire dying in the grate. Though the light was on, the room was deserted. Ben was backing away.

'Come upstairs. Grandma has her sitting room up there,' he explained, and then laughed. 'Mother complains she doesn't stay in it nearly enough. You'd better meet at least one member of my family.'

The staircase was wider and shallower than at the farm, with a gracious curving handrail and a thick red carpet that deadened their footsteps. 'She likes a bit of company.'

Ben gave her a reassuring smile before knocking on a door on the first floor. Rosie heard no response, but he went in. Taking a deep breath, she followed. The old lady was sitting bolt upright with an open book on the wooden arm of her chair. The standard lamp at her shoulder turned her hair to spun silver.

'Grandma, I've brought a friend to see you.'

'How nice, Ben.' She took off her spectacles, blinking at Rosie in confusion. 'These are my reading glasses.' She got to her feet, knocking her book to the floor. She wore a black silk dress that fell to her ankles, relieved only by a white lace collar. Rosie bent to retrieve her book, while Ben stepped to the mantel-shelf and picked up another pair of glasses.

'Are these what you want?'

'Ah, yes, that's better.' She smiled vaguely and swung round to face Rosie. 'I'd have known you anywhere, my dear,' she smiled. 'The likeness is very strong.'

Ben said: 'This is Rosie Quest, Grandma, a friend of

mine. What likeness are you talking about?'

'The family likeness, of course.' Rosie felt rooted to the carpet in shocked surprise. 'The Shearing colouring.' She caught Ben's agonised glance, then his embarrassed laugh.

'Shearing hair is usually a sandy colour, Grandma. Nothing like Rosie's. Finer and with less curl.'

The old lady took her glasses off again, polished them on a lace handkerchief before replacing them. Rosie felt her scrutiny. 'Not just her colouring. Her face too. That's a Shearing nose.'

'I'm no relation,' Rosie stammered, feeling at a loss.

'Nonsense, Gran. You're embarrassing Rosie.'

'She's the spitting image of Hilda.' Rosie felt her heart turn over. It was beating like a drum.

'Who's Hilda?' Ben demanded.

'Ainsley's sister. Hilda Shearing.'

'Ainsley was my grandfather, but I'd never heard he had a sister,' Ben told Rosie. She could see he was shaken too.

'You wouldn't have. She's been gone a long time. Passed away at the turn of the century.' Constance walked round Rosie. 'You're very like her, same build, but Hilda wore her hair up, and a lace cap. Always a lace cap.'

'You're imagining it, Grandma. You can't remember what she was like. You tell me you can't remember much about Grandfather.'

'Oh, I remember him all right. Hardly likely to forget.' There was a note in her voice that further disturbed Rosie. 'He looked like your father.'

'But not like him in other ways.' Ben was humouring

her now. 'Grandfather had a good business brain, didn't he?'

'Oh, he had.' Suddenly his grandmother was cackling with uncontrollable laughter. 'And he had a passion for guns. Duelling pistols particularly. Did you know he used to go to Bisley? He won one year.' Rosie saw a strange light shining in her eyes.

'No,' Ben said. 'I didn't know he'd won at Bisley. So he was good at other things, not just business?'

'He knew all there was to know about guns.'

'He couldn't have, Gran.'

'He did, I tell you. He gloried in his guns.'

Ben frowned. 'Are you sure? I mean, he'd hardly be likely to shoot himself by accident if he was an expert, would he? Tell me more. I want to know all about Grandpa.'

'No!' Rosie could hear the desperation in the old woman's voice.

'But only you can tell me, Grandma. Why shouldn't I know about my own family?'

'No, Ben, no.'

Rosie thought Mrs Shearing looked like a cornered animal. But if her husband had shot himself, she could understand why the old lady didn't want to talk about it. Rosie put her hand on Ben's arm to stop him. He got the message. 'Do you want to come down for your supper, Grandma? Come and eat with us.'

'I've had all I want to eat tonight, dear,' she said, sitting back in her chair and closing her eyes.

Constance felt his lips brush her cheek in apology, but it was too late. Angry tears were scalding her eyes.

It was Ainsley's voice that said in his half-mocking tone: 'Isn't it beautiful, Constance?' She felt the cold metal in her palm. 'Go on, look at it. Surely you can appreciate its beauty? Hold it properly.' Towering over her, he would twist her unwilling fingers into position. 'See how your hand moulds round the handle.'

She shuddered. 'They're deadly weapons,' she choked. It seemed obscene to decorate cold steel with engraving, put pistols in satin-lined cases like jewellery. Pistols were for killing people.

Ainsley loved his antique pistols more than he loved her. He'd collected so many. Some had come from the Continent in mahogany cases with linings of different colours. His personal favourites were English duelling pistols, of which he had many. He often took them from their cases to admire and clean and polish.

'I can teach you all about firearms, Constance. I can make you an expert.'

'I can't bear them. I don't want to know anything about your guns.'

But he had dragged her by the wrist into his study where he had laid out four guns in a row. He'd demanded she learn the difference between the matchlock, the wheel-lock, the flint-lock and percussion-lock. He'd stood over her, made her tell him what sort they were as he pointed to each lock in turn. There had been no escape for her till she did it.

It was a deadly hobby and one that frightened her. Ainsley kept the guns in specially fitted cupboards in his study, some on display through the glass fronts. She never went in the room unless he forced her. He knew just how much they frightened her.

'Hold it steady, Constance. I'll teach you to shoot.'

'I don't want to shoot. I don't want to touch the things. Why do you do it, Ainsley? You know I hate your guns.'

'I like them. I could say it was an accident, Constance.'

Her mouth suddenly dry, she'd whispered, 'An accident? What do you mean?'

'If I were to shoot you. Kill you. Don't think I wouldn't dare.' It had taken her breath away.

He turned the gun on himself, the muzzle only three inches from his head.

'Would you rather I killed myself?' Mesmerised with horror, she watched his finger tighten on the trigger.

'No,' she was screaming. 'No, no, no!' She'd had her eyes closed and her hands over her ears.

The dull click brought sweat to her forehead. He'd made a fool of her again. It hadn't been loaded.

'I don't know why you stop me, Constance.' His voice was cold and mocking. 'I would have thought you'd be glad to see the back of me. You don't love me. One of us will have to go.'

In the mornings, she would lie still and tense, feigning sleep, praying he would get up and leave her alone. One day he left a note on her bedside table. 'Pretending to be asleep is pointless. I'll wake you if I need your services.'

Edwin was six weeks old, her second child but tenth pregnancy. She'd begged him to leave her alone. When he went to the factory, she'd had the bed made up in a spare bedroom and moved her things. Told him on his return he was no longer welcome in her bed. He'd got out his guns to taunt her.

'Shoot me. Go on, it's what you'd really like to do isn't it?'

She'd shrunk from him. She hated his guns and she hated him.

'I don't understand you, Constance. You were brought up with guns. I know your father kept them too.' But Father's guns had been sporting rifles. He'd kept them locked away in the gun room. He never took them out except on his way out of the house for a day's shoot. He cleaned them and locked them away again on his return.

No lady was expected to touch such things. Never would Father have kept them in a glass case. Nor brought them into the drawing room or, worse, her bedroom as Ainsley did.

He played with them as gunmen in the Wild West of America were reputed to do. He would put his finger in the trigger guard and spin the gun, making it look like artless play. Then, with one deft jerk, he could be holding it so that she was looking down the barrel.

Constance remembered how she'd tried to steel herself to accept Ainsley's ways. Close your eyes, she'd told herself. Don't let him see how frightened you are. Because you show your fear, and how much you hate his guns, it gives him a way to taunt you. Pretend you don't care. Don't give him the satisfaction of seeing your terror.

But it didn't stop her heart racing or the feeling of panic fluttering like a bird in her throat. She couldn't hide it. Her white face and shaking fingers told their own story. He continued to tease and torment her.

'A wife has certain duties, Constance. A husband certain rights. They cannot be withdrawn or altered to suit your whim. Today you will move your things back to my room. You will return to sleep in my bed.'

She had dared to disobey his order, terrified of him yet frightened too of further pregnancies.

Another of her duties was to pour his tea for him when he arrived home from work. That day he'd brought a pair of duelling pistols to the drawing room when the tea trolley had been pushed in. He'd twirled one round his finger, making her feel threatened.

'Did you know, Constance, that the slightest suggestion that a man's conduct is lacking in honour is sufficient to call forth a challenge? In France duels are still fought.' Then, with a buttered scone in one hand and the gun in the other, he'd levelled it at her. She'd felt the stark jolt as she found herself looking into the barrel. He knew she always would.

She'd tried to take a tighter grip on her own terror; tried to calm herself by looking out at the calm river, concentrating on the gentle swell and the small sailing boats seeking the light breeze. All three windows were open on this summer afternoon.

'I know you're only playing. I know you do it to frighten me, Ainsley. I know it isn't loaded.'

With the speed of Bill Cody, he'd dropped one gun and snatched up the other. The blast when it came shattered her ears with its reverberations. The smoking gun swung back to point at her.

Constance was sure her last moment had come. Her

mind was empty of everything but shock, numbing blinding shock.

'I hit it,' he said, quite calmly.

With a great shuddering sigh she opened her eyes. Next door's white tom cat lay on the terrace in a widening pool of blood. She felt vomit rising in her throat.

'You don't know whether they're loaded or not, Constance. Don't challenge me so I have to show you. Now go upstairs to the bedroom and take off that damned tight dress and corset and lie on the bed. In future, do not deny me my rights.'

With a shudder she remembered what a sobbing nervous wreck she'd been. She'd had to comply. Shivering, she'd slid between cool linen sheets, pulling the covers round her neck.

She heard his slow measured steps coming up the stairs. The bedroom door opened and closed with a firm click. The key turned in the lock. She closed her eyes and buried her head in the bedclothes, pulling them closer. She knew from his grunts and sighs that he was undressing. Suddenly the bedclothes were whipped off her, leaving her shivering and almost naked.

'Stand up,' he ordered.

She stared up at him without moving. He reached for the pistol he'd put down on the bedside table and started to twirl it again. She slid off the bed and jerked upright, rigid with terror.

'Take off your shift, everything. I want to see you naked.'

She couldn't do it, her fingers were all thumbs. She

was reduced to a quivering mass of nerves. In the end, he had to put the gun down to pull her clothes over her head. She tried to cover her nakedness with her hands but he pulled them away, positioned them on her head, and made her walk up and down with them in that position.

'Now, let's make love,' he'd snarled. She felt demeaned and humiliated. For her there was hatred and a burning need for revenge, horror and terror and shame, but no love.

'Don't ever refuse me again,' he'd snarled as he lay across her, spent at last.

Rosie felt Ben's hand on her arm as he led her downstairs again. 'I'm sorry. I've never known her like that before.'

'You shouldn't keep asking about your grandfather. It upsets her to talk about him. You're bringing back bad memories.'

'But I want to know. Even Dad clams up when I ask.'

'Did he commit suicide?' Rosie ventured. 'That would explain it.'

'I don't know.'

'I'm more worried about the other thing.' Her mouth felt dry. 'What did she mean about me having the family likeness, the Shearing colouring?'

'Taken leave of her senses,' Ben said, frowning. He took her into the dining room, sat her down. There was pork pie and roast ham on the sideboard. He filled two plates.

Rosie's mind whirled with conjecture. She made

herself put it into words. 'Was she saying your father . . .? He's always been kind.'

She saw Ben shake his head. 'He's like that to everyone. It's his normal manner.'

Rosie had to agree. 'The girls in the sewing room all liked him, but . . .' She remembered the feeling she'd had when he'd first seen Grace's bank book. She tried to put it into words.

'You're imagining things,' Ben said firmly, putting mustard on his plate. 'If my father were yours also, then you'd be my half-sister.'

'Yes,' she said. 'That's what I'm afraid of.'

He laughed. 'You can put that idea right out of your mind. I don't want you as a sister.'

'It seems to add up to that.'

'It doesn't. What I feel for you, Rosie, is not brotherly affection.' He started to eat.

Rosie tried to do the same. She chewed and chewed, but the ham wouldn't go down. She kept telling herself that if Edwin was her father, he would never have let her mother go to the workhouse. He was far too kind and considerate of others.

Haltingly, she began to tell Ben how little she knew about her father, and all the tragic circumstances of Grace's life and death.

'I knew there must be something like that to make you put up such a wall against everybody.' She caught his half-smile. 'Even against me.'

Rosie began to feel better. He understood how she felt. She'd never opened up like this to anyone before. 'It's better to talk about the bad things, not keep them all as dark secrets,' he advised.

'You aren't the only one with secrets, Rosie. While we're in the mood for confidences, you might as well hear about this. I'm worried stiff.'

She found herself listening with growing horror to Ben's problems with the company results for last year, and heard how difficult it was going to be to convince his mother that Oliver could be defrauding them. They sat on over the table long after they'd finished eating.

Suddenly she realised how late it had grown. 'I'd better go,' she said. 'I don't want to be here when your mother comes home.'

'I'll take you in the car.'

'I could walk. It isn't far.'

'I'd rather see you home. Anyway, it's late and you have to get up for work in the morning.'

Hurriedly, Ben got their coats and led her outside to the Ford Ten. Rosie slid into the passenger seat, watched him start the engine and nose the car out of the drive. Outside on the road the green Rover was slowing down ready to turn in.

'Only just in time,' he murmured, before lowering his window and calling to his father: 'Just taking Rosie home, Dad. I won't be long.'

Rosie caught his mother's malevolent stare, and shivered. 'She knows now you've brought me here.'

'I'm not sorry. She'd have had to find out some time.' In the subdued light from the dashboard, she saw him half smile in her direction. 'She has to know we're getting serious.'

Rosie felt comforted. 'Do you feel serious about me?'

'Yes, very. How do you feel about me?'

She smiled. 'Serious. And closer now we've talked.'

'Good.' One hand crept across the seat to give hers a momentary squeeze.

'About what your grandmother said, that I've got the family likeness – it bothers me, Ben.'

'I expect she was thinking of Hilda Shearing when we walked in. To the very old, the past is more real than the present.'

'She's not that old. And she seemed very sure.'

'Mother thinks she's a bit strange.'

Rosie smiled. 'Your mother thinks *I'm* a bit strange too!'

It was late when he got home. Ben had expected the family to be in bed but saw a light still on in the study. He was afraid his mother was waiting up for him. The hall was full of shadows, with only one small lamp lit.

The front door closed softly on well-oiled hinges. Ben re-locked it behind him and was creeping quietly towards the stairs when the study door flew open and his mother swept out, her floor-length bronze skirt outlined against the light. 'Ben! Whatever made you bring that girl here? She quite upset your grandmother. One of our machinists!'

It took his breath away.

'What have you got against Rosie?'

'She was born in the workhouse!'

'If you hadn't gone snooping in my desk, you would never have discovered that. I blame myself for leaving the certificate there.'

'You're a Shearing, and I've told you before I don't like you playing around with the work girls.'

He felt his resentment building. 'I'm not playing around with the work girls. I'm very serious about Rosie.'

'Ben! Don't be ridiculous. She isn't good enough for you. What's the matter with you boys? Letting yourselves down. I don't know what this family is coming to.'

His mother's face was like thunder, and she hadn't heard the important part yet. Why couldn't he say outright: 'I'm madly in love with her, obsessed'? He felt his hackles rising.

'You might as well get used to the idea, I'd like her to be a permanent fixture.'

He heard her gasp.

'Nonsense, Ben. You'll soon grow tired of Rose Quest. Perhaps she's all right to play around with, but quite unsuitable to fill any permanent place in your life. I've no doubt you'll come to your senses sooner or later.'

He went straight upstairs, shaking with cold fury, all pleasure in Rosie's company chased from his mind by his mother's aggression.

Rosie heard the familiar creaking of the old stairs as she ran down for breakfast the next morning. Maud was turning crackling bacon in a frying pan that had a handle like a bucket, designed to swing on the hook over the range. She was poking up the morning fire beneath it and didn't turn round.

'Is that you, Phyllis?'

'She's not finished dressing.' Rosie felt she could run circles round her cousin this morning. Already she'd done her share of the milking, and the drizzle on her face had thoroughly woken her up. She'd run upstairs to toss off her old clothes, and wash and change into a blue jumper and skirt for work.

'Please give me a hand, Rosie. Dish up the porridge, would you?' She marvelled at the change in Aunt Maud who always asked politely for help now. Her attitude had changed completely since Rosie had found the letter to Grace. She took the bowls that were warming on the hob and started to fill them.

'I don't want any of that.' Phyllis, heavy-eyed, somnolent and yawning, had come down and was eyeing it distastefully. 'Count me out, Rosie.' She picked up an envelope from the doormat as she came to the table. 'The postman's been. For you, Dad.'

Uncle Will was giving more attention to his food than to his post. It was several minutes before he slit open the envelope and spread the letter on the table before him. Two more spoonfuls of porridge rose to his mouth, then suddenly the spoon crashed down on his plate.

'What's the matter?' Maud wanted to know. He was reading the letter through again. Rosie saw his face tighten as her aunt repeated: 'What's the matter? Who's it from?'

'The landlord – well, his agent. He's giving us notice. I can't renew the lease again next year.'

'What a cheek!' Phyllis leapt to his support. 'After all the years we've rented.'

'He's got planning permission, the land is to be sold for building,' Will said. His bushy dark eyebrows stood out against his white face. Rosie thought he looked stunned. 'I've been dithering about it for years. All he's done is force my hand. I suppose I should be grateful for that.'

Maud snatched up the letter. 'Doesn't he offer you alternative land? I don't see why he shouldn't. Your family has rented from him for generations. He can't just put you out.'

'He has, Maud, but it's out Spital way. Too far to do the milk round from there.'

'You could start another.'

'No, it wouldn't be easy to find new customers. Tom wouldn't want to look for a new house, either.'

'What about us?'

'We can still rent this house,' he said.

'I'm not bothered about the house,' she retorted. 'You said when you retired we could buy a place of our own, further out in the country. Heswall, perhaps, or Greasby.'

'Yes, but I thought if I retired they'd find another tenant. I expected Ivy Farm to keep its land, and that we'd have to move. Don't you see? If we can stay here it makes it easier.'

'Not for me,' said Maud. 'I don't want to end my days in this old place.'

'The girls can still go to work. If we moved further away . . .'

'Rosie will be off our hands before another year's gone.'

'Well, I don't know . . .' she protested. Talk like this could still sting her.

'The Shearings don't drag their feet once they've made up their minds,' Maud said. 'They don't have to

226

save up first like our Phyllis's . . .'

'You can leave Gerry out of it,' she snapped. 'I'm getting tired of waiting for him.'

'I thought you were all set, Phyl, with your bottom drawer ready,' Rosie said.

'I was never very keen on the Bentleys,' Maud said. 'He was no great catch.'

'All the more reason to rent this house then,' Will said victoriously.

'Dad, I can get the bus, or even another job. I'm getting fed up with Shearing's too. A change wouldn't hurt me.'

'Don't you dare give in your notice till you've got another job,' her mother said firmly. 'You've got to be sensible.'

Recently Phyllis had started to walk to work with Rosie. As they were crossing Bedford Road Rosie said, 'I'd no idea you weren't happy at work.'

Phyllis grunted: 'It's boring, and Mrs Shearing would try the patience of a saint.'

Up till now Phyllis had crowed about her office job, claiming it was pleasanter and paid better than Rosie's job as a machinist. It hadn't bothered her, she'd always been content in the gossipy atmosphere of the sewing room. Flora Pope was always fair in her dealings, and everybody liked Edwin Shearing. What Rosie didn't welcome was Beatrice Shearing's interference, and it was obvious that in the office Phyllis received more than her fair share of that.

CHAPTER ELEVEN

Ben knew he was wasting time. With files spread across his desk, he'd spent the last half hour staring at his figures. He'd come to the conclusion that increased sales were probably being made but there was no trace of them in the books. And no trace of payment for them either. Their profit for last year was very much reduced and if there was anything worse than that, it was that he was doing nothing about it.

He'd delayed telling his family in the hope of finding out exactly how the fraud was being carried out, but he was so worried he could delay no longer.

He had some evidence that Oliver was involved, but if he voiced his suspicions it would put his brother on his guard and Ben would learn no more. He'd copied the delivery note the van driver had given him, and then he'd put the original in Oliver's in-tray. He'd hoped his brother would bring it in to him and thus allay his suspicions. Oliver hadn't done so.

He must assume that next year's profits were already being eaten into, since it was logical to suppose the fraud would continue until he uncovered it.

For the last few days he'd kept his office door ajar so

he could keep an eye on Oliver's movements. Now he heard his brother slam out of his room and come bounding across.

'More work for you.' Oliver tossed a bundle of blue delivery notes on his desk. Ben felt tension twisting his stomach. He had to fight the impulse to grab them, see if at last the rogue note was amongst them. If Oliver didn't want him to bill the wholesaler, it meant he'd received payment personally. Ben made himself fold his hands in his lap and sit back.

'How did we do last year then?' Oliver's fine eyes were on the papers laid out on the desk. 'Are those the figures? Let's have a look.'

When he realised Oliver was coming round to his side of the desk, Ben snapped the files shut. All the old antagonism came welling up again.

'You're dragging your feet a bit over the results, aren't you?'

'They're not good.'

'You'd have been shouting them from the roof top by now if they were. I'm surprised Mother lets you get away with this. She must be showing clemency because it's the first time you've done them.'

Ben thought Oliver seemed ill at ease, striding up and down. But did he feel guilty? He could see no obvious sign that his brother felt responsible for their poor results.

'You're in a hurry to find out?'

Oliver was certainly impatient to see the results, but so was Mother.

'Just thought it would be nice to know how things stood before I went off.'

'Ah, yes, you're going away for a few days.'

'Just a little break.'

'You'll have to wait till you come back then.'

As soon as he'd gone, Ben grabbed at the notes Oliver had brought. He sifted through. The one he wanted to see was not among them. He made up his mind to delay no longer. He went to his father's office, closing the door carefully so that there was no chance of Oliver overhearing.

'Will you be in tonight, Dad? I want to talk to you and Mother.' As soon as they'd had dinner, he'd lay it out for them. He couldn't worry about this on his own any longer. A good time to do it if Oliver was going away. They'd have time to think about it and make up their minds what to do. They could even force his desk and see if there was anything else there to incriminate him.

Ben went back to his own bleak office to collect the evidence together. He'd have preferred to tell Dad by himself, but he was bound to insist on Mother knowing, and that would mean recounting the same tale twice. Better get it over at one sitting. He'd take them into Mother's study after dinner and get it off his chest.

When the factory closed that evening, he went out as usual to the car. Father was already in the driving seat, and Ben had hardly slammed the car door when his mother turned round from the front and said: 'What's this about a meeting tonight?'

'There's something I want to tell you.'

'What about?'

'Oliver,' he said reluctantly, 'He's worked out a system with delivery notes, giving them a different sequence of numbers.' He opened the briefcase on the seat beside him and handed her the pad he'd found hidden under Oliver's files.

'What are these for?'

'I'm trying to explain. There's a problem . . .'

'With delivery notes?'

'Yes. I believe by manipulating them it's possible to defraud the company.'

'Nonsense!' Beatrice snapped. 'They've worked well for years. They're efficient. The pad of notes was my idea. The system's foolproof.'

'It isn't,' he said. 'That's what I'm trying to tell you. I believe Oliver has worked out an alternative number sequence . . .'

'Changing the system would cause trouble. It takes time for the staff to grasp any change, and the forms have to be printed specially. A waste of money too.'

'It's not the system I want to change,' he said patiently. 'It's how Oliver uses it. Now I've taken over so much of what he used to do . . .'

'I know you think you're doing the lion's share of the work now.' He heard the impatience in her voice. 'I pl   to hand on other responsibilities to Oliver. Don't imagine he'll be idle. This is your handing-over period.'

'Mother, will you listen? I'm not bothered about any handing-over period.' Ben felt exasperated. He was not getting the scale of the problem over.

'That's right, let Oliver get on with his own work. It's more important to concentrate on yours. It's time you came up with last years' results.'

'I have them here. They aren't typed yet, but I've

got the figures ready to show you.'

'Just put them on my desk, Ben. Your father and I will look through them. We'll be having our regular monthly meeting next weekend, we can discuss them then.'

His father was turning into the drive. He said in his jocular fashion: 'Come on, Ben, don't keep us in suspense. What figure do you have for net profit?'

'We hardly made a profit, that's what I'm trying to tell you.'

'What?' His mother turned right round in her seat, shocked.

'You saw the figures some time ago when I caught you looking in my desk, Mother. I think I know where our profits have gone – that's what I want to explain.'

Beatrice was already out of the car. 'Let's get this over with now, Ben. We'll go into the study straight away. I'll tell Mrs Roper to delay dinner.'

Ben was hungry, he'd never known dinner be delayed for any reason, but now he'd got through to her at last, he wanted it over too. His father paused at the drawing-room door to speak to Gran. Stephen had arrived home a few moments earlier and had already poured her a glass of sherry.

'Come on in, Stephen,' Ben said. 'You'd better hear this too.' Within three minutes his family was crowding into the study after him.

He launched into a full explanation of what he'd discovered, and laid out on the desk the copy of the delivery note he'd been handed by Eric the driver. He demonstrated how it tied in with the number sequence on the pad he'd found hidden in Oliver's file cabinet.

'This is just an old pad,' his mother said. 'Isn't it, Edwin? Nothing very significant about this.'

He turned it over. 'I remember him ordering a new supply from the printer. We must have started on the new ones without finishing up the old.'

'Why change the numbers?' Ben wanted to know. 'Whose idea was that? They should have carried on consecutively.'

He told them how he'd found the pad hidden in Oliver's cabinet, pointed out that the difference in the numbers allowed him to extract them from the system, after the staff had packed and delivered the orders. He'd brought last year's sewing room books to show them the erasures.

Edwin's face was grey. 'It's like history repeating itself,' he breathed. 'Like . . .'

'No,' Mother snapped. 'He wouldn't do such a thing. Not Oliver.'

Ben said levelly: 'Oliver ordered the reprinting. Oliver sees that the orders are made up correctly, he's in charge of deliveries, he's running the system – it's his responsibility. Every time he wants an order made out, he tears off a set of delivery notes – which means he selects the number – and takes it down to Phyllis Quest. Wouldn't it be more usual to give her a whole pad of the things, or let her take them from the cupboard as she does the rest of the stationery?'

'Are you accusing your own brother?' Beatrice sounded outraged.

Ben understood how she felt. He'd been worried sick, fearful it was his own imagination that made him attribute their lack of profit to fraud. It had taken him weeks of re-checking, of seeking an error of his own making, before he could accept the truth.

'It was easy for him before I took over the accounts,' he said. 'Stephen made sales that weren't put through the books. Didn't he try to tell us?'

'I did, Mother.' Stephen was anything but upset. 'I knew I was meeting my targets.'

Beatrice turned on Ben in a fresh outburst of anger. 'Why didn't you tell me before now? You suspected Oliver and said nothing.'

'It's my job to sort out anything to do with accounting procedures. I had to be sure before I said anything.'

'You took a lot on yourself. I told you to keep me informed. I kept asking for the figures.'

'I'm telling you now.'

'It's thin evidence for such a serious accusation.' She sounded furious. 'We'd better get Oliver here and see what he says.' She picked up the phone and asked the operator to connect them. 'I'll get him to come over right away. We've got to clear this up.'

Ben knew he'd failed to convince. They could all hear the ringing as Beatrice waited for someone to pick up the phone.

'Hello, Lydia. How are you? Is Oliver there? I'd like a word.' They saw her impatience spill over.

'He's not home yet? Get him to ring me, will you, when he comes?' Ben watched her face mirror her feelings as she listened. He was afraid that after all the effort he'd put into tracing the missing profits, Mother would discount the truth of what he said.

'Yes, well, as soon as you can.' She crashed the

phone back on its stand. 'He's taking her out to dinner. He'll have to come here first.'

'Let's have ours,' Edwin said, getting to his feet. 'While we wait for him to ring back.'

Constance was hovering in the hall. 'Beatrice, Mrs Roper is afraid the dinner will spoil if we don't eat soon. What's kept you all in there?'

'I thought you'd be glad to have it a little later tonight,' Beatrice said tartly as she bustled forward to lead the way to the dining room.

Ben felt too angry to eat. He could barely sit still. Mother was blaming him for the upset, Stephen was crowing, and as usual Dad was not committing himself either way.

Before the pudding was served, his mother got up to telephone Oliver again, and this time his housekeeper told her they'd gone out to dinner. She returned in a furious temper.

The meal over, Ben hardly knew what to do with himself. He spent ten minutes staring aimlessly out of the drawing-room window. Stephen had gone out. Mother had retired to her study again. His father looked up from his newspaper.

'You're restless, Ben.'

He released a sigh. 'I'm sure you know why.'

'Come down to the Royal Rock for a drink with me?' Ben didn't know what he wanted, but he didn't want to sit in a pub mulling over the same ground with Dad. He shook his head. His mind was whirling, he felt full of energy, but resentment smouldered in him too, that Mother had favoured Oliver in this.

A long walk perhaps? But it was a dull and drizzly evening.

'Dad, can I have your office keys? I've finished reading all Ainsley's old account books. I'd like to get on with the story and see how Harry fared.'

'He didn't do as well. Here you are, the keys to my cupboard. Put back the books you've finished with.'

'Course I will, Dad, thanks. You won't be wanting the car?'

Once in the Ford he changed his mind again. It was Rosie he wanted. He'd told her he couldn't see her tonight. At four o'clock he hadn't been able to see beyond the difficulty of explaining Oliver's fraud to Mother. It had seemed likely to fill the entire evening. Now he felt an urgent need to be with Rosie, pour out his anger and justify his accusations against Oliver.

As soon as he put his hand on the gate of Ivy Farm, Jake appeared from nowhere to bark ferociously. It brought her aunt, gaunt and miserable, to the front door before he reached it.

Maud directed him dourly round the back to the dairy. It was not yet dark but night was drawing in and the light had been turned on. He heard Rosie's voice above the swish of water as he approached; could see Will swilling down the floor, sweeping water out over the step.

Suddenly Rosie appeared behind him, her cheeks pink, her green eyes shining. Tiny beads of moisture clung to her thick red hair, making it sparkle under the naked bulb. She smiled with such radiance when she recognised him, it lit up her whole face.

'Ben!' There was pleasure in her voice, her face, in every line of her body because he'd come when she hadn't expected him.

'Can I take your helper away, Mr Quest? That's if you'd like to come out for an hour, Rosie?'

'We've just about finished for tonight.' Will's voice was gruff.

'Oh, yes. Yes, please,' she laughed. 'But I'll have to change.'

'No need.'

'I can't come in these old things.' For the first time he noticed one of her elbows showed through the sleeve of her cardigan. 'I must look a mess.'

'You look wonderful.' He meant it.

'I'll only be five minutes,' she said, running towards the house.

'She's a good girl,' Will said, turning the head of his broom up and leaning it against the wall outside. 'I'm very fond of Rosie.'

'So am I.' Ben shifted his weight from one foot to the other. He felt he could jump over the moon now she'd agreed.

'You be kind to her, lad.' Will switched off the light and closed the dairy door.

'Of course I will.'

'She's not had an easy time, our Rosie.'

'I know that. I'll take good care of her.' Ben knew at that moment that he wanted to take good care of her for the rest of her life.

Rosie was bubbling with pleasure as she shed her old clothes on to her bed and put on a clean blouse and skirt from her wardrobe.

'He didn't want to come in,' Uncle Will told her as she ran down to the kitchen. 'Said he'd wait in the car for you.'

When she slid into the seat beside Ben, he hugged her with unusual strength, clinging to her as though for comfort.

'I thought we'd go for a walk,' he said. 'Along the Esplanade in front of our house is as good as anywhere.' As he headed the car back towards the ferry, all his worries came out in a torrent. How certain he was that Oliver was siphoning off profits, though exactly how he received payment instead of the business Ben had no idea. He was telling her everything: that his parents didn't believe a word of his story, that he couldn't convince his mother Oliver could do any wrong. By the time he'd parked the car near the river, the drizzle had become a heavy shower and he hadn't a coat with him.

'It'll pass over in a few minutes,' she said to calm him. He seemed confined in the car, restless, like a caged animal. All the time Rosie felt an undercurrent of excitement building inside her.

'Perhaps a quiet place where we can talk?' he said. 'A view of the river would be nice too.'

It was impossible to find. The ferry buildings blocked most of the view. If Rosie craned her neck she could glimpse through a side window the lights of Liverpool shimmering and reflecting in the water, but all distorted in the driving rain.

'It's too close to the ferry,' Ben sighed as boat passengers came and went in a steady stream past the car. 'Rock Park is the quietest place I know because cars have to pay a toll to enter but it's too close to home. We don't want Dad thumping on the window as he walks back from the Royal Rock.'

Restlessly, he put the car into gear and moved off. 'We'll go to Parkgate. I should have driven there in the first place.'

Rosie sat back in the seat, enjoying the drive along dark deserted country lanes. Parkgate promenade was almost deserted at this time of night. Ben parked the car facing directly down the estuary. The rain had stopped, the night was very black and the tide far out, a silver strand against the Welsh shore.

'I love you, Rosie,' he said as he took her in his arms and kissed her. It was the first time she'd heard him put it into words. She was breathless with pleasure and excitement. 'Do you love me?'

'You must know how I feel.' Rosie looked into his face. 'You're smiling, why?'

'Because I still have to ask how you feel.'

'I've never loved anyone before. I don't know what you want to hear.'

'Just the truth.'

'I like the feeling, it lights me up.'

He laughed again and hugged her closer. 'You'd definitely say it was love?'

'Yes, it's love. I do love you, Ben.'

'Thank goodness for that,' he laughed, and pulled her closer still. 'Now I'm wondering whether you love me enough to consider marriage? Could you be persuaded?'

'Is this a proposal?'

'Yes. I can't get down on one knee in a car.'

'I would like to marry you. You could persuade me with no trouble at all.'

'Wonderful! I'll try and make you happy. Take good care of you.'

They stayed parked on the promenade a long time. It was very late when Ben drove her back to Gordon Drive. 'Shall we go in and tell your Uncle Will?'

'Not tonight.' Rosie felt too full of joy to speak about it. 'I want to keep it to ourselves.'

'You're still too shy,' Ben said. 'We've got to tell everybody, give them time to get used to the idea. Otherwise I'll never get you to the altar. Tomorrow then, we'll tell either your family or mine. And you must have a ring. We'll choose that tomorrow too.'

Rosie found her family had already gone to bed, and a note from Aunt Maud reminding her to bolt the front door once she was in. Phyllis was breathing deeply, curled up in the bed nearer the window. Rosie undressed in the landing light coming through the open door, hugging to herself the knowledge that Ben loved her. She felt full of love for him, and very lucky. She wanted to be Ben's wife more than she had ever wanted anything in her life.

On the way home, Ben decided he might as well call in at the office and exchange all Ainsley's old ledgers and account books for more recent ones. He was far too excited to sleep. He'd proposed to Rosie on the spur of the moment and was very happy she'd accepted. For the first time he could see what he hoped to achieve in life becoming possible.

It was bedtime for most people. Some houses had

lights in their upper rooms, some were in total darkness. There were few people about and the roads were still wet. He turned into the road in which the Albert Hotel was situated and pulled up outside. There were several other cars already there.

Suddenly all his nerves were jangling. Parked just ahead of him was Oliver's new silver SS Jaguar.

Ben leaned over the steering wheel for a few moments. He hadn't expected to confront Oliver, but now the opportunity had presented itself and they would have the building to themselves. There was nobody to overhear or burst in on them. Had his mother already been in touch with Oliver? He didn't know. His brother might be expecting trouble or he might not.

Either way, he must know it was only a matter of time before the family started asking awkward questions. He could hardly expect to keep his activities hidden for ever. Ben decided he was in the right mood to challenge him.

He got out of the Ford, letting the door click shut as quietly as possible. Oliver had not locked the gates. He slid between them. The blackened brick façade loomed above him in the dark sky. In the dim glow from the security lights he could read the sign: A. W. Shearing and Sons, Shirtmakers, behind which he could just make out the words Albert Hotel which had been painted out.

A light had been left burning in the hall. Ben paused at the bottom of the stairs, listening. The silence was unnerving. He strode up quietly. A strip of light showed beneath the door of Oliver's office. The key, large and ornate, waited ready to secure the lock as he departed. Ben slid it out as quietly as he could. He needed the upper hand if he were to accomplish anything. Then, taking a deep breath, he gave the door one sharp rap and flung it open.

His eyes went immediately to the desk, but the chair was empty except for a neatly folded jacket on each arm. He heard a scuffling sound behind the door. Suddenly he realised Oliver was embracing somebody on the padded seat there. A woman's face with dark enquiring eyes peered over his shoulder. Ben had never seen her before.

He knew he was gaping. His heart was thudding like an engine. His plan no longer seemed feasible with a woman present. The sight of the stranger was numbing, he couldn't think.

'What the hell do you want?' Oliver was more aggressive than usual. It helped to see him looking downright shocked. He was buttoning his shirt up. Stephen's case of samples was open on the floor. The woman, older than Oliver, was hitching down the skirt of a smart blue suit as she came towards him. Ben turned the key in the lock, dropped it into his pocket and went over to the desk.

It was the sight of the cheque that jolted his mind back into running order. Oliver's desk was bare apart from that and a familiar blue delivery note. One glance told him it was of the alternate sequence of numbers, and showed the same address as the previous one he'd seen. Ben pounced on the cheque. It was for the same large sum as shown on the delivery note, and made out to Oliver Shearing Esq.

The method Oliver used to convert shirts to personal cash was now clear in Ben's mind. They were packed up and delivered in the same way as bona fida sales. Payment was made direct to Oliver, and the alternate number sequence both allowed him to extract the notes so they did not go through the accounting procedure and covered up the fact that other deliveries were being made. With Oliver in charge of accounts, it had been only too easy.

Last year what he'd taken had gone unnoticed. This year he'd been greedier, yet Oliver had known for a long time exactly when Ben would take over all the accounting. He surely must have realised it would make it more dangerous? Ben looked at the signature on the cheque, E.F. Watson.

'Miss Watson, I presume?' He looked at the woman, overblown now in middle age but once she'd been pretty.

'Mrs.' She was nervously defensive, revealing more than she should.

'And is there a Mr Watson?'

'That's none of your business.' She turned to Oliver. 'Who is this?'

'I'm Ben, his little brother. Did he never mention me?'

'You can't come bursting in on us like this,' Oliver protested. Ben was pleased to see him almost wringing his hands. 'You don't have to tell him anything, Esther.'

Ben went deliberately to the chair behind Oliver's desk and handed each of them their jacket.

'Better get dressed, I'm afraid the fun's over for

tonight.' He sat down, trying to look more at ease than he felt.

'So it's Mrs Esther Watson? Please cross out Oliver's name on this cheque and make it payable to A. W. Shearing and Sons Ltd.' He pushed a pen across the desk to her. 'Do as I say. You must know you've been handling stolen goods. Well, there won't be any more from this source. You've initialled it? Good.'

He stared into her slightly protruding dark eyes. 'If I want to find out if there is a Mr Watson, all I have to do is to lift the phone tomorrow and ask for him. Your telephonist will either put me through or not. Oliver has your company's address conveniently on this delivery note. If there is a Mr Watson, I could tell him I saw you kissing Oliver when I walked into this room.'

'There is,' she admitted.

'You're business partners?' She nodded. 'And what sort of business does W. & E. Watson's carry on?'

'We're men's outfitters, five shops. We do a bit of wholesaling to smaller retail outlets too.'

'At our expense, I suppose?' Ben said. 'I don't care whether you do it for love or money, it's a criminal matter. I could call in the Fraud Squad, you do realise that?'

'Would you want your own family name pulled through the mud?' She was trying to stand her ground.

'No, but bear in mind there's enough evidence to incriminate you if this gets out. You can go now.'

She looked to Oliver for guidance. 'I don't want to go.'

'You'd better,' he muttered.

Ben got up and unlocked the door. As she went he

said: 'Keep your mouth shut, if you want to keep out of trouble, and never come to this office again.'

He re-locked the door. As he slid the key in his pocket and turned, he saw Oliver coming at him like a raging bull. He felt his brother's fist jolt into his stomach. It sent him staggering, he only just managed to stay on his feet.

'It isn't two against one this time.' Oliver's face leered into his, twisted and ugly. 'Stephen isn't here to help you.'

Ben felt blind fury. He'd been itching to lash out at Oliver for months. Now he flew at him, fists flailing. His right hooked against Oliver's jaw, sending him sprawling into the corner. Ben felt the force of the impact in his own arm. His temper was out of control. He wanted to thrash Oliver within an inch of his life.

'Get up,' he choked, shaking with the effort it took him to stand back. 'And don't be stupid. Fighting won't settle anything, and the age advantage is on my side now. What good will it do if we give each other black eyes?'

'Right then.' Oliver slowly pulled himself to his feet, rubbing his chin. He staggered a little, supported himself against the back of his chair. 'I'll go home.'

'Not so fast. Sit down. I want to make the position clear.'

'What do you mean?'

Ben slid into the chair behind the desk again, thankful he seemed to have the upper hand once more but not quite sure how he'd manage it. It gave him the courage to test his will against Oliver's. Struggling to appear calm, he said: 'Have you spoken to Mother tonight?'

'What do you mean tonight? I haven't seen her since I left the office. Look, Ben, couldn't you keep quiet about all this?'

'Too late for that. I'm sure Lydia must have told you Mother was trying to phone you. I tried to tell her how you were siphoning off our profits, but I couldn't explain how you collected the cash. Now I know. You have an accomplice who helps.' Ben could see his brother physically curling up.

'This alters everything, Oliver. She'll believe me when I show her this cheque.'

His brother was breathing heavily, his eyes plaintive. 'Please don't say anything. I won't do it again.'

Ben couldn't keep the disgust out of his voice. 'She was suspicious anyway. You've dug too deeply into the till, made our loss only too obvious. The family will have to know what you've done.'

'No. They'll be happy if profits go up next year.'

'Oliver, you're in big trouble. The party's over.'

'Esther Watson means nothing to me.' Ben could see him sweating. 'I know you think you saw . . .'

'I always thought that bench looked out of place in here, not the usual run of office furniture, but I understand now. Your office doubles as a bedroom in the evenings.'

'Of course it doesn't!'

'A nice wide padded seat, a cushion for the head . . . Why didn't I see it before? She's your mistress, Oliver.'

'No, she isn't! It's a business relationship. All right,

so she likes a bit of a cuddle on the side. That's all it is.'

'You'll no doubt be able to convince Lydia of that?' Ben remembered seeing her looking at Oliver with adoring eyes. He'd envied him his happy marriage.

'Lydia mustn't know anything about this.' Oliver had never looked more shocked.

'It depends whether Mother can hold her tongue. It depends on a lot of things.'

'You've got to keep quiet about Esther. Think what it would do to my marriage.'

'Then there's a price you'll have to pay.'

'What's that?' Ben could see fear in his face now.

'First, after you leave this building tonight, you never set foot inside the door again.'

'That's nonsense, I work here.' Oliver's face went scarlet. His temper frothed up again.

'Not any more. How can I be sure you won't figure out another way to milk the company?'

'I can't leave just like that. What would Lydia think? It would be suspicious. She'd be bound to ask questions.'

'I couldn't trust you behind this desk again.'

'What am I supposed to do then?'

'Hasn't Lydia's father offered you a job? Tomorrow you tell Mother you've decided to take it.'

'It was just a suggestion he made. It isn't all cut and dried.'

'I'm sure you can spin him some story to speed things up, Oliver. You're good at that sort of thing. Or was the job on offer all a story in the first place?'

'I can't leave right now. Be reasonable, Ben.'

He closed his ears to any plea. 'There's another stipulation. You must pay back what you've taken.'

'How can I do that without a job?' His brother was incredulous. 'I wouldn't have taken the money in the first place if I hadn't needed it.'

The gall of it took Ben's breath away. 'What can you possibly need money for? A house and a wealthy wife, you're set up for life!'

'I can't pay it back. I won't.'

'The money comes back or I tell Lydia everything tomorrow. She wouldn't want her father to give you a job if she knew. And I'll tell Mother what a success your arranged marriage has turned out to be. It should stop her meddling in my affairs. Now, it's the middle of the month so we owe you a couple of weeks' salary. Are you due for holidays?'

'You've forgotten, I'm taking a few days off now to go to Gloucester.'

'Ah, yes, so that's how you meant to spend our cheque? On a trip to Gloucester.'

'It's Lydia's grandparents' Golden Wedding.'

'Yes, well, any money due to you will be offset against your debt to the business. How much did you take?'

'Good God, I don't know!'

'Don't be such a fool. You must know what you've taken.'

'I don't. I didn't keep any running total.'

'What about the delivery notes?'

'I destroyed them as soon as she'd paid up. They were incriminating. Couldn't keep them, could I?'

'What have you spent it all on? I know you've

bought a car, but that won't account for more than a fraction of it.'

'I've got to live.'

'So have the rest of us.'

'I've got to run a home. Lydia's used to living well, I can't ask her to economise.'

'She has her own money, Oliver. You told us that.'

'So she has, but her family are generous. I have to return their hospitality. I can't look mean, can I?'

'Because they throw money about, you don't have to. They know your circumstances.'

'They expect the best.'

'Would they expect you to steal from your own family? How long did you expect to get away with it? It's as well for all of us that I have found out, otherwise you'd have gone on to bankrupt the firm.'

'No, I wouldn't have done that.'

'Give me the keys to this desk, Oliver.' Ben put out his hand. 'Come on, let's see what else you've got in here.'

'There's nothing, I've told you.'

'Watson's are big customers?'

'Yes, I suppose so.'

'Does anybody else make cheques out directly to you?'

'No, of course not.'

'That's it then. All I have to say. I think I'll use this office now you're going.' He looked around. 'Much more comfortable than mine, but that bench will have to go.'

'You'll say nothing about Esther Watson to Mother?'

'I'll not say I saw you smooching, provided you stop working in the business and you pay back what you took.'

Oliver's face registered doubt. 'You promise?'

'You're in no position to bargain, Oliver, but I'll imply it's no more than a business arrangement if you agree to my conditions.'

'I agree, but Mother will have her own ideas. She'll want it handled her way.'

'She's already working on that, Oliver. You know what she's like.' He re-locked the desk, he hadn't the patience to search it properly tonight. It didn't matter. He could look through it at his leisure tomorrow. He had other evidence anyway.

'Ben, just give me one more chance,' Oliver was pleading. 'Look, I'm worried about what you're going to say to Mother.'

'She already knows most of it, and she's hell bent on sorting you out.' Ben didn't even try to stop his contempt showing. 'She'll be devastated, because she thinks the world of you. She's given you everything she could, and this is how you repay her. Has it gone on gambling or drink?'

'Don't be so bloody sanctimonious. Anyway, it's none of your business.'

'Get out.' Ben stood up threateningly. 'Get out and don't ever come back.' He followed Oliver to the head of the stairs and watched him go out of the building. Then he went down and locked the front door behind him.

Ben was thankful he'd not had time to think over what he'd done. Better that he'd been catapulted into it before he'd had time to consider the pros and cons. Oliver had won too many rounds in the past, but his luck had been out tonight. To catch Oliver kissing that woman had given him a double hold.

Ben went back upstairs. He'd always known Oliver was a bully, but he hadn't expected him to be such an abject yellow-bellied coward when he was up against it. If his brother had realised how nervous he'd been, how uncertain of his facts, how he'd been casting round for some way to handle the whole ghastly business, then Ben would never have got away with it.

He entered the cheque in the company's paying-in book and locked it away in the small safe in Dad's office. It helped to be doing routine work. Except that it wasn't routine to alter the number on a delivery note, before it could go through the books. He locked the delivery note into his own desk. It was important evidence. His mind was still crawling with shock and horror.

He went back to his father's office, took out the accounts for the years 1912 to 1918. He had to go out to his car because the box with the books he was returning was still locked in the boot. The cold night air seemed to clear his head.

Oliver's behaviour was irresponsible. He was betraying his own family and even his wife. He seemed to have no loyalties. His brother was another who played a role. He had hidden himself behind a wall of polish and sophistication, but once caught on the wrong foot, the whole edifice had come crashing down. Tonight Ben had seen the real Oliver for the first time.

He was glad he'd succeeded in pushing him out. As far as he could see, Oliver had not accomplished much for the business. The family had thrown up a maverick. Ben felt ashamed for him.

CHAPTER TWELVE

The next morning, Ben woke feeling tired and heavy-eyed. He ought to feel on top of the world – he was going to marry Rosie. He ought to feel triumphant that he'd been right about Oliver, and kicked him out of the business. But he'd been gripped with rage when he'd confronted his brother last night, and had forgotten Mother would expect him to explain and justify any further action he took. He hadn't thought it through. Once Mother knew of a problem, she expected to deal with it herself. She'd look upon what he'd done as interference.

It was as well he had those delivery notes with the alternate number sequence to show her. When he went down to breakfast, she was still fulminating.

'Your father and I have talked over what you told us, Ben, and you've not got much to go on. You gave us a bad night, neither of us slept well. Are you sure you're not just stirring up trouble for the sake of it?'

'Have you spoken to Oliver?'

'No, you boys are all the same, totally lacking in consideration. He didn't ring back, and he wasn't home all evening.'

'There have been developments,' Ben said, starting on the plate of eggs and bacon the maid put before him.

'Oh?' Dad looked up.

'What?' demanded his mother. He waited till the girl had closed the door behind her.

'I've given Oliver the sack. Told him he must never set foot in the office again.'

Stephen gasped with pleasure.

'You've done what?' His mother's eyes were like saucers.

'Sacked him. He's admitted everything.'

'Ben, you're going to have to tell us exactly what happened,' his father said.

He told them how surprised he'd been to see Oliver's car outside the factory so late at night. He told them everything except that he'd seen his brother kissing Esther Watson and giving every indication he meant to go further.

'You can't sack him just like that! It was very high-handed of you. Poor Oliver.'

Ben was outraged. 'Mother, Oliver is living above his means. He's a disgrace to the family.'

'That is for me to decide.'

He growled back, 'You mustn't let him get away with this.'

'The firm is shedding family members fast,' Stephen chortled. 'You haven't asked him to work his notice?'

'He's dishonest. We can't afford to have him there.'

He could see Stephen was elated that the family idol was proved to have feet of clay. He felt pleased about that himself.

He couldn't understand why Mother had so little regard for Stephen, who had twice Oliver's guts. He'd always resisted pressure to make him do what he didn't want to. Nobody was going to push Stephen around. He hoped the same was true of himself.

'I kept trying to tell you. Didn't I, Mother?' Stephen was beaming at her.

'Don't let's get sidetracked on that again. Ben, we aren't sure yet that he's taken anything. We only have your word for it. It's very inconvenient when he's going away like this.'

Dad said: 'Surely he could come in for half an hour first, so we can talk to him?'

They were late again arriving at the Albert Hotel. Their employees were waiting in groups at the door. Ben could hear Mother's heels tapping behind him as they all trooped upstairs to his office to see the evidence. He was pushing his desk keys into the lock when he saw the fresh scratches on the dark oak.

He froze, knowing somebody had forced it open. It had to be Oliver. He tried the drawer before turning the key. It opened easily. The strength seemed to ebb from his legs. He knew without looking the delivery note he'd kept as evidence would be missing. It was.

Pointing to the scratches did not convince Mother that Oliver had returned last night to steal it. Even Dad frowned and looked sceptical. Ben slumped into his chair, feeling beaten. His mother's dark eyes accused him of fabricating the whole story.

He leapt to his feet when he remembered he'd put the cheque in the safe. Although he'd taken the precaution of altering the combination when he'd re-locked it last night, he half expected to find it had been spirited away too. It was still in the paying-in book. It was passed from hand to hand. Held up to the light, turned over and passed back to him.

'This proves nothing, Ben,' his mother said firmly. 'Certainly the cheque was made out to Oliver, but it could be a genuine mistake. There's nothing to prove he didn't ask for it to be corrected himself.

'I'm going to ring Oliver now. We're going to have to straighten this out,' she said. She was getting to her feet when the phone rang on Ben's desk.

He picked it up, and Miss Gibbons told him Oliver was on the line wanting to speak to his mother. Beatrice went bounding downstairs to take the call in her own office. His father followed her out.

Ben collapsed at his desk, knowing he'd failed to convince. He felt trapped. What a fool he'd been not to put everything in the safe or take it home with him. Anything but leave it where Oliver could reach it.

The only crumb of comfort he had was listening to Dad systematically turning out every drawer and cupboard in Oliver's office, searching for more incriminating evidence, but his brother was too wily to have left anything where it would be found.

Ben was still sitting there when he heard his mother come back upstairs. He heard her speaking to Dad. She sounded excited. Her voice had a carrying quality. Moments later his door banged open and Beatrice came in like a hurricane. The victorious look on her face told him things had taken a turn for the worse.

'I've spoken to Oliver. He's quite upset, says you

accused him of terrible things.'

'Mother, I've explained exactly what he did and how he did it. Is he coming in?'

'Not now. He rang from the Felthams' home. As you know they're all going down to Gloucester together, and were just about to set off. He'll come in on Tuesday when he gets back.'

His father came in quietly and closed the door.

Ben said: 'You don't believe what I say?'

'I want to hear what Oliver has to say too. We've heard your side of the story, we have to hear his before we decide anything. We mustn't be hasty, Ben.'

'I suppose you comforted him, told him he could still work here?' Her manner told him she had.

'He says you handled it like a military coup, waiting until he'd arranged to be away before you started your campaign against him.'

'Mother, our profits have gone, our shirts are disappearing from our stockrooms. There has to be some explanation. It's been going on in front of our eyes for the last few years, yet nobody has seen it. I've outlined Oliver's system. Doesn't it explain everything exactly? Doesn't it sound feasible and true?'

'What he says sounds feasible and true as well. You've always been very aggressive towards him, Ben. And if it is true, why didn't you say something sooner? I did ask you.'

Ben felt like giving up. He'd been so sure he'd got his brother tied up.

'You can't show me proof, Ben.'

'The cheque.'

'Oliver says Mrs Watson made it out to him without

259

thinking what she was doing. He asked her to alter it. That's all there is to it.'

'But where are the supporting documents for that order?' He was triumphant, quite sure he had Oliver on this. Hadn't he destroyed them because they were numbered on a false sequence? 'Not one shirt leaves the factory without an order or a delivery note.'

'They were in his desk, Ben.' He was at her heels as she crossed the corridor to Oliver's room. There on top was the familiar blue delivery note. All the right stamps had been inked on to it. In addition, Oliver had written across it diagonally 'Do not invoice, Paid in full', giving the date.

Ben couldn't believe his eyes. Everything was as it should be, its number was from the standard sequence. He went out to the cupboard in the corridor, where the blank delivery notes were kept. It was the last delivery note to be used.

He started to explain how this alone was proof of abnormality.

'Oliver must have come back last night and typed this copy himself on Phyllis's typewriter.' It wasn't a bad effort either, only one crossing out.

His mother said sharply: 'Oliver said Watson's wanted the order in a hurry. It was delivered yesterday. He met them at some golf club dinner last night, and Mrs Watson gave him the cheque. He brought it into the office on his way home because it's substantial and he knew he'd be away for some days. You walked in while he was here and accused him of all sorts of dreadful wrongdoing. He's quite hurt.'

Waves of cold fury were washing over Ben. 'Not as

hurt as I'd like him to be. He's been robbing the business blind.'

'Ben, we've heard your side of the story, we'll hear Oliver's when he comes back. In the meantime, the less fuss made about this the better. We don't want to start a lot of embarrassing rumours going round the office.'

It was as much as he could do to stop himself kicking the stationery cupboard door. It had been a bad mistake not to relieve Oliver of his keys to the building, and he'd quite overlooked the fact that his brother might have two keys to his desk.

'What does Dad think?'

'He agrees we should discuss it calmly together when Oliver returns.'

Ben sighed. That meant Dad was sitting on the fence as usual, and Oliver had days to perfect his story. 'What do you think has happened to our profits then?'

'Leave it, Ben.' Her voice was weary. 'You're getting on my nerves.'

As she went clattering downstairs he turned back to his own office and sank into his chair. 'Damn Oliver,' he said. 'Damn him.' He felt depressed, disillusioned and angry.

Apparently Mother cared more for him than she did for a profitable business. He'd judged her wrongly there, but there was no doubt she was fraught. He'd never heard her mention nerves before. She still had the will-power to overrule him because he hadn't consulted her, but for the first time Ben wondered if her self-confidence was slipping just a little.

He tried to work on for another hour, then in a

surge of exasperation flung down his pen on the pile of papers in front of him. Today he was not making the best use of his time. He would have a go at Dad, make him come down from the fence. Ben stormed across the corridor to his father's office.

'Dad, do you have a minute?'

Edwin finished writing a sentence before he spoke. 'I was going to come and see you when I'd finished this. Have a seat.' He leaned over and pressed the electric bell on the wall. 'We'll have a cup of tea.'

'Dad, I'm fed up. After weeks of hunting down the missing profits, nobody believes me.' He'd promised Oliver he'd say nothing about his relationship with Esther Watson, and he'd kept that promise so far, but Oliver was trying to brazen this out. He wondered whether he should tell his father now.

Edwin looked up from the file he was working on, and felt for the cheroots he liked to smoke. 'Ben, I believe you, I know you've worked hard to ferret out the facts, I'm sure it hasn't been easy.'

He felt a little better.

'I'm proud of the way you're handling this. Calmly, giving us facts. Clearly this must be the explanation.'

'Mother isn't convinced. I gave Oliver an ultimatum to get out, and she's telling him he can come back. She wants him to carry on working here.'

Ben watched his father exhale blue smoke. He looked weary and unwell. His office was impregnated with the smell of cheroots.

'Come back but not necessarily to work. It's like this, Ben. In her heart of hearts, your mother knows what you've told us is the truth. She was worried stiff because the profits we expected weren't coming in. She's no fool, she'd worked some of it out for herself. We do discuss these things.' He brushed ash from the front of his pepper-and-salt tweeds. 'But she can't accept that Oliver would steal from the business. You know how she's always been with Oliver. The sun shines out of him, has done since the day he was born. Always far more engrossed in him than I was, but even I find this difficult to swallow. Oliver stealing from the business! How would you feel if someone you trusted did that?'

'I did trust him. At least, I trusted him with company money till now.'

'Bide your time, Ben. We'll all listen to what Oliver has to say. Your mother will question him closely. Then we'll decide. Do you know what he spent it on?'

'High living.' The word 'women' hovered on his tongue. It remained unsaid.

'Your mother was working on the same theory, that the shirts were going out of the stockrooms.' Ben saw his father's slow smile. 'I think she finds it hard to believe you could come up with the right answer before she did. That makes it harder for her to accept, too.'

Ben didn't want to be appeased. 'If Oliver continues to work here, he'll find some other way to rook the business. All my time will go on watching him, wondering what he's up to.'

'It won't come to that. Give us time to accept the facts, then we can deal with them properly. It's a hard blow, Ben. Too close to home. It's not just business, it's family too. We hoped for a lot from Oliver, your mother especially.'

Mrs Pratt brought in the tea tray at last, her bulk swaying slightly on her dainty feet.

'I always felt you had more business acumen than your brothers. Did you know that, Ben? You've much more stability, more interest in the business. Just bide your time, we'll sort this out.'

Ben was writing at his desk later in the morning when a distant scream jolted him to his feet. Panic-stricken, agonised, he thought it sounded like a wild animal caught in a snare.

As he put down his pen he heard another shriek, full of terror and pain, and knew it came from the sewing room below. He heard running feet and somebody shouting for him.

He skidded down the stairs and knew it was a bad accident as soon as he saw the crowd gathered round Flora Pope's machine. 'She's run the needle through her thumb,' Rosie told him when the crush of women parted to let him through.

'I feel sick,' Flora gasped. Beads of sweat stood out across her nose and chubby cheeks. The needle had penetrated through her nail, and was pinning her flesh to the cloth. He felt his gut writhe painfully at the sight.

'Don't look,' he told her, taking off her thick spectacles. He pushed them into Rosie's hand. 'Take care of them for her.' He could see the colour draining from Flora's face.

'She's fainted,' a voice said, but with her weight

against him, he didn't need to be told. He held her against the machine.

Once, long ago in the school holidays, he had seen this happen to someone else. Since it was necessary for the machinist to guide the material under the sewing foot with the fingers, it was easily done.

He'd watched his father take the sewing foot off the machine, wind the needle as high as it would go, then push the thumb down hard to free it. Father had said then it was the inexperienced who had accidents of this sort. It surprised him to find it had happened to Flora, who had been sewing here for decades.

'Switch the power off, Rosie,' he said, trying to think. They had the latest power driven industrial sewing machines now.

'It's off,' she confirmed, but he was concerned now that Flora was coming round. She was moaning as she jerked her trapped hand. It took all his strength to keep her half-conscious body from sliding to the floor.

When he heard the needle snap, Ben knew the worst had happened. He should have held her hand firmly in place so it couldn't. Now, though Flora was no longer attached to the machine, half the needle was embedded through her thumb nail with only a tiny fraction of it showing.

'Bring me the tool box, Kitty. Do you know where it is?' He could feel the sweat standing out on his own forehead as the open tool box was held out to him. He selected a small pair of pliers. He could see tears of agony on Flora's eyelashes and her face was putty grey.

'Keep her hand steady.' Three other girls came to

anchor it to the machine. It took him a long time to get a good grip on the tiny stub of steel sticking out of her nail. He braced himself, then taking a deep breath gave it a sharp tug. Flora screamed again, screwing up her face in agony.

'It's all out,' he said thankfully. 'Here you are, Flora.' He pushed three-quarters of an inch of needle along the machine top. A few drops of blood oozed out of the wound. He wiped them away. Flora was crying. It was a deep puncture wound right through the nail and into the flesh. Just to look at it twisted his stomach again.

Last time, his father had run cold water on the injured thumb but there was no way he could mobilise Flora's bulk to a tap.

'Iodine now,' he said to Rosie who had the first aid box open beside him. He daubed it on liberally, trying not to get any on the shirt she'd been working on. He pulled it clear, tossed it to willing hands. 'Sponge these drops off before they dry.'

There had been little blood from the wound, but it was welling up under the nail now. Flora was doubling up in agony. She would have slid off her chair if he had not held her on it.

'Hey, Flora, it's over. All out. You'll be all right in a minute.' But her eyes were rolling up in their sockets. Her face was clammy.

'She's real bad,' he heard someone say. There was a babble of excited voices. One lifted above the rest, strong and urgent.

'She's fainting again.' She was a dead weight against him. He lowered her to the floor as gently as he could.

Ben was perplexed. It hadn't been like this last time. Once the needle was out, the girl had had a cup of tea and gone back to work an hour later. He didn't know what to do for fainting fits like this. Somebody was patting Flora's hands, someone else had smelling salts under her nose. She was coming round again. Dark agonised eyes were fixed on his face until another wave of pain made her bring her knees up to her chest.

'I think you'd better go home, Flora,' he said. She didn't look as though she could do any more work today. 'Will there be any one there to look after you?'

'She's got rooms, lives by herself.' Kitty's false teeth whistled as she spoke. 'There might be someone else in the house, I don't know.'

'No,' Flora managed. 'No.'

'Rosie, go with her and light a fire. Make her a cup of tea, see she's all right.'

Rosie's green eyes looked into his, panic-stricken. 'She can't walk.'

Ben heard his mother's voice coming down the room. 'Flora Pope is it? What's the matter with her? What's she done now?' He knew why his mother didn't like Flora. It was because Dad did. Stephen had told him of rumours he'd only half believed at the time.

'Can I take her home in the car, Mother? She's ill.'

'No, Stephen has taken it. Gone to Chester.'

Flora was struggling to sit up. Suddenly he thought she was going to vomit.

'Hospital,' she gasped. 'Hospital.'

'See if there's a van in the yard, Rosie.' Ben shivered. He didn't know what to do to help. He ought to learn more about first aid if he was going to be put in this position. It was frightening. He was grateful to see someone had fetched Eric the van driver to the door. Somebody else had fetched Flora's coat and was fastening it round her shoulders. Somehow she was transferred to the passenger seat of the van.

'It must be shock,' he said. Her hands felt icy. 'Go with her, Rosie.' He pressed a few coins into her hand. 'Take her to the hospital and stay with her. Get a taxi to take her home afterwards.'

'She looks like death,' Kitty said, and he had to agree. He watched the van jerk out into the road, with Rosie squashed in the back.

Rosie tried to anchor itself to the back of the seat to stop herself from sliding across the van. She didn't miss the nervous glance Eric shot in Flora's direction.

'Is it the Borough you want to go to?' he asked over his shoulder.

Rosie knew nothing about hospitals. 'Isn't the General Hospital the right place to go?'

'Yep. Me mother still calls it the Borough. Can't get out of the habit. Yep, the General. You all right, Flora?'

She seemed to be doubling over with pain again. 'Yes,' she managed through gritted teeth.

'We'll soon be there.' Rosie put a hand on her shoulder to comfort her. Flora felt rigid with pain. She wished they were safely there.

Eric drove into the car park in front of the hospital and shot out of his seat. On his way round the back he opened the doors for Rosie. She slid along the metal floor on her backside and jumped down. Eric was already helping Flora out of the passenger seat, and once Rosie had a firm grip on her arm, he would have gone.

'Help me get her inside first,' she protested, knowing she could never hold Flora's bulk upright if she were to faint again. Flora weighed twice as much as she did, was taller too, and now as another paroxysm of pain gripped her, it was difficult enough with one each side.

Once they got through the door of the Casualty Department a nurse pointed out a row of chairs where they might wait. Flora pulled herself upright.

'I'll be all right now, Rosie. You can go back with Eric.' She felt awash with relief, there was nothing she wanted more, but she knew she mustn't.

'Ben told me to see you home afterwards. Light your fire for you. I'd better.'

'No, really, I'll be perfectly all right. You're losing time.'

'Ben will make my wages up, Flora.'

The nurse was coming back with a card to fill in, her apron crackling with starch. Rosie, conscious of the smell of antiseptic, watched as she went through the routine. Flora roused herself to give her name and address.

'And how old are you?'

'Thirty-nine,' she gasped, doubling up again.

'And what seems to be the trouble?' Flora was bent over, unable to speak.

'She drove a needle through her thumb nail at work,' Rosie tried to help. 'It broke, but . . .' She stopped. Flora's face was grey and sweating. It was obvious now, her problem was much greater.

'I think I'm having a miscarriage,' she gasped out, desperation showing in every line of her plump face. Rosie felt she'd been turned to stone. She was shivering. Not Flora Pope! What man could do this to Flora?

'You'd better come and lie down.' The nurse's voice was matter- of-fact. She was helping Flora to her feet, leading her off round the back. 'The doctor's here now. He'll need to examine you.'

'What about me?' Rosie asked, feeling equally desperate. 'Shall I come too?'

'No.'

'You want me to go?'

'Better hang on a bit till we know . . . If you don't mind.'

Rosie sank back on the hard chair, her head in a whirl. She couldn't believe what she'd heard. Not Flora Pope!

She couldn't have said how long she sat there, only half aware of patients coming in, of wounds being bandaged and injections given. She made herself think of being married to Ben. It brought a swirl of pleasure. The same nurse came back.

'You brought in Flora Pope?'

'Yes.' Rosie got to her feet.

'We're going to admit her. We'll want you to take her clothes home. Come and get them and say goodbye. She's feeling a bit better now.'

Rosie followed her to the small day ward behind, and slid between the screens that had been pulled round Flora's bed. Her eyes flickered open as Rosie approached.

'There.' She indicated the large paper bag of clothes on her locker. Rosie noticed her thumb had been bandaged. 'Can you take them home for me? They're sending me up to the ward.'

Rosie nodded. 'Shall I bring your dressing gown in? Slippers, that sort of thing?'

'Please,' Flora whispered through colourless lips. 'My handbag.'

It was on the locker. Rosie handed it to her, hardly knowing what to say. Flora was pressing a key into her hand. Telling her how to find the house. 'Nightdresses. Soap and towel too.'

'Do you want me to bring a book or some sewing for you to do?'

Flora slowly shook her head, and gave a wry smile. 'Could do with a rest from sewing.'

'Something to pass the time here, I meant,' Rosie whispered.

Flora heaved herself up urgently, propping her head on one massive arm. She was wearing a white hospital gown. 'Don't say anything at work. Nothing about this, do you hear?'

'Yes, Flora. Just about your thumb.'

'The pains started, I got careless. Please don't ever let the girls know.'

'I won't,' Rosie promised. 'Not a word to any of them.'

'I'm glad Ben sent you with me. You won't be working there much longer.' Flora's eyes settled on Rosie's left hand. 'You've not got your ring yet?'

'This afternoon. He's taking me to choose it this afternoon.'

'You'll want to keep your mouth shut for the sake of the family.' She fell back on her pillow, and Rosie tiptoed out with her clothes.

She couldn't stop thinking of Flora. The way her two chins quivered when she laughed. In the sewing room that had been often, a gutsy laugh clearly audible above the whirring machines. Rosie had never known her without a joke on her lips before. Today, Flora wasn't telling jokes.

Rosie would have crossed the car park and never noticed the green Rover or Edwin Shearing getting out of it, if he hadn't spoken.

'Rosie, how do I find Flossie in this place?'

It took her a moment to pull herself together and direct him. The significance of his coming here, and the anxiety in his eyes, was not lost on her. She was glad to turn away and get herself to the bus stop.

Her own face must be showing what she felt. The intimacy of the pet name Flossie! Yet she was plump. No, more than plump, fat. Hard to believe any man would find her attractive; utterly incredible that Edwin Shearing did, and had made her pregnant.

Rosie was waiting for the bus to take her to Flora's rooms when another thought almost poleaxed her. Hadn't the back of her neck crawled with horror the day she'd shown Edwin her mother's bank book? The sight of it had dumbfounded him. She'd watched the colour drain from his face.

He'd known Grace, she'd felt sure, but he'd dismissed it with such ease when she'd asked. She'd wondered then if he might be her father. She'd gone hot and cold at the idea but dismissed it. Now she thought of it again, and it didn't seem impossible.

She felt icy with shock. Was Edwin Shearing the father she'd told herself she hated? No, she was being foolish and fanciful. The implications of that were too awful to contemplate. She had to force the idea out of her mind. Make herself concentrate on Flora's needs.

Her rooms were comfortably furnished. Rosie hung the clothes she'd brought with her in Flora's wardrobe. Found a handsome dressing gown and some slippers.

When she returned to the hospital, she took Flora's things up to the ward but was not allowed in to see her again. They told Rosie she was comfortable and to telephone that evening. It was Saturday and the factory would close at midday. Rosie saw a public telephone and rang Ben to give him the news, then went straight home for lunch.

By the time she'd eaten and changed, excitement was beginning to fizz inside her again. Ben was waiting at the kerb to drive her into Birkenhead when she ran out of the house.

Streamers of bunting and flags were decorating the main streets, making them look festive. 'For us?' Ben asked, his mouth quirking at the corner.

'Getting ready for the Coronation,' Rosie said.

'Dad keeps asking me what I think Shearing's should do to celebrate it.'

'Let those who have them bring their wirelesses,' she said promptly. 'It's the first Coronation ceremony ever to be broadcast. The girls are all dying to hear it.'

'Good idea,' he said.

When he led the way into Pyke's the jeweller she found he'd already paid an earlier visit to the shop to pick out a selection of rings. A tray was put on the counter in front of her, glittering with an array of traditional diamond engagement rings, so that she could make her choice.

'Thought it might be less embarrassing to do it this way. You can't see what they cost, and I know it won't be too much.' Rosie tried on a solitaire.

'Or if you prefer something a little more unusual . . .' The sales assistant slid another tray on to the counter, shining with emeralds, rubies and sapphires. Rosie's eye went immediately to an opal mounted in platinum with a small diamond on each side.

'Mexican fire opal,' the assistant said. 'Very unusual, very nice quality.'

'I love it.' Rosie smiled up at Ben. 'It's so beautiful.' Iridescent fire smouldered back from her finger.

'You're sure? I like it too, it's a generous-sized stone. If you'd wanted diamonds, they'd have to be smaller.'

'Quite sure. They're all lovely, Ben, but I like this best. I shall be proud to wear it.'

She watched fascinated while he took out his chequebook. The ring was polished and put into a small leather box.

'Don't bother wrapping it,' Ben told the assistant as he was reaching for paper.

Rosie felt so happy as she watched him open the box and slide the ring on her finger.

'There, now it's official.' He pushed the box towards her. 'Put this in your bag.' She felt like a queen as she walked out of the shop, her arm through his.

'A cup of tea, I think, now.' They got back in the car and drove to the Connaught Tea Rooms. Rosie still felt bemused as her feet sank into the thick carpet. The table was tiny with a single rose in a stem glass. Around her was a low background murmur of conversation from the predominant female clientèle. The diamonds in her new ring flashed fire in the dim light.

A waitress in a black dress and frilly apron, a matching cap covering her hairline, brought a delectable selection of cakes on a silver platter: macaroons, rum babas, confections of chocolate, cream and icing.

'Aunt Maud makes cakes but nothing like these,' Rosie said, helping herself to a chocolate éclair.

It was the second time she'd poured tea for Ben from a little silver teapot. It seemed a very smart way to serve it. Would it be like this, she wondered, when they were married?

'Do you have little teapots like this at your house?'

'We use a family-sized one in the dining room, but Grandma has one just like this for her tray. Rosie, I've got tickets for the first house at the Argyll. Flanagan and Allen head the bill.'

She was thrilled. 'Lovely.'

'A day for indulgence, Rosie, we've just got engaged. We'll have supper somewhere afterwards.'

She had never been to the music hall before. The inside of the Argyll Theatre was a revelation. Ben explained that the décor in the auditorium was a copy of the Parthenon Frieze in the British Museum, and the staircase was of white Sicilian marble. Rosie sat beside him in the stalls, taking in the scent of disinfectant, the plush seats, and the air of expectancy as the velvet curtains swished apart. The tunes danced in her head even after it was all over.

She was seated at the table in the Royal Rock dining room when he said: 'What about telling your family?'

'I suppose we'd better.'

'They'll see your ring.' He smiled. 'They'll know, Rosie. What is there to wait for? Just be a waste of time. You don't want a long engagement, do you?'

'We'll need to save up, and there's so much to decide and arrange. Where we'll live, for instance.'

'Not with my mother.' He broke into a wide smile. 'Is that what's bothering you? I don't want to start married life with Mother breathing down my neck either. I wouldn't suggest we live with her.'

Rosie laughed. 'I give thanks for that.'

'The understatement of the year.' He was laughing with her. 'We'll get a place of our own. I think I could afford to buy a small house on mortgage, or we could rent somewhere to start.'

'We'll tell my family tonight, then.'

'Will they be pleased, do you think?'

She laughed again at his diffidence. 'Uncle Will thinks only of my happiness, of course he'll be pleased for me. He seemed to take to you.'

'I took to him.'

'Aunt Maud will be delighted. She can't wait for the day I move out. She gave me a pair of double sheets for my birthday, to start my bottom drawer.'

'And Phyllis?'

'Her bottom drawer is full to overflowing and has been for ages. She's engaged to a Merchant Naval officer, but I've noticed she doesn't wear his ring every day like she used to, I think she's having second thoughts.'

'But she'll be pleased for you?'

'More likely to be jealous.'

They were all in, seated round the fire, when Rosie took Ben into the kitchen. He seemed too tall for the room. Everyone was stiff and formal, but they said they were pleased. Uncle Will shook his head. Ben didn't stay long because it was already late.

When Rosie returned from seeing him to the car, Uncle Will said: 'A nice young man, Rosie. I hope you'll be very happy.'

'Quite a catch,' Phyllis told her. 'And it didn't take you long to get a proposal once you got started, I'll say that for you.'

'Opals are said to be unlucky,' Aunt Maud sniffed. 'I think you're asking for trouble choosing one as an engagement ring.'

Phyllis's dark head bent over Rosie's hand. 'I've heard they're unlucky too, but it's more a dress ring, wouldn't you say? You can always keep it if he changes his mind about marrying you.'

'He won't,' said Rosie. At least she felt confident about that.

CHAPTER THIRTEEN

On Sunday afternoon Ben took Rosie out to New Brighton. They walked along the promenade and watched the ships crossing the bar as they came into Liverpool.

'I'd like you to come home with me,' he told her. 'We need to tell Mother.'

Rosie felt a shiver of apprehension. 'She doesn't like me.'

'She'll love you, Rosie, once she knows you. Try not to be shy. Try to open up and let her see what you're really like. If we show her your ring, she can start getting used to the idea.'

'It's going to take her time.'

'You're going to think I'm calculating . . .'

'Why should I?'

'Because I am. Strategically, this is the right moment. Mother is feeling low, things aren't going her way. First, Stephen has just told her he'd rather work as a bank clerk than let her dictate how he should sell our shirts. And I've told her Oliver, her favourite, is feathering his own nest at her expense. She hasn't accepted that yet, but she'll have to.

'She has plans for me, Rosie, and you aren't part of them. Now is the moment to let her know I'm not going to be dictated to. She's bound to feel she's losing control, put up less of a fight.'

Rosie laughed. 'You've got it all worked out!'

He put out his hand and felt for hers. 'Only with Mother.'

He had her arm hooked firmly through his as he drew her in by the front door. The only sound in the lofty hall was the ticking of the grandfather clock. Rosie felt full of trepidation at the thought of coming face to face with Beatrice Shearing on her home ground. She was being guided towards a door of solid oak.

'Mother will be in her study, I expect.' Ben seemed to be keeping his voice deliberately low. There was a brooding silence that reminded Rosie of church.

'Mother?' he called as he opened the door. 'There you are.' Rosie caught a glimpse of an affronted Mrs Shearing peering at her over the top of her spectacles.

'I've brought Rosie in to see you. To say hello. We've something to tell you.'

'At this time of night?' Rosie's heart seemed to roll in her chest. She watched Beatrice rip off her spectacles as though about to leap into action.

'We've come to tell you we're engaged,' Ben said smoothly, turning to smile encouragement at Rosie. She felt his fingers gently unfurling her own, turning her hand over so that the opal was displayed.

Beatrice's gasp of displeasure was audible. She leapt to her feet. 'This is ridiculous, Ben! You hardly know each other.'

'No, Mother, I've asked Rosie to marry me and she's agreed.'

'Oh, I'm sure she jumped at the chance.' Rosie felt herself flinch at the full force of hatred. 'What a step up in life it would give you, Rose.'

She made herself ignore that. She'd been deciding over the last hour what she must say. She took a deep breath. 'Mrs Shearing, I love Ben. I'll try to make him a good wife.' He was squeezing her hand, showing his support.

'I know I'm not the person you would have chosen for him yourself . . .'

'You're certainly right about that!'

Rosie quailed, hardly daring to look into her imperious dark eyes. She found everything about Beatrice offputting, from her neat brown chignon and elegant clothes to her inbuilt arrogance. She forced herself to go on as calmly as she could.

'But now that Ben has chosen me, I hope you'll be able to accept . . . That perhaps we could turn over a new leaf and be more friendly.'

'What could be fairer than that, Mother?' he said. 'Do say you'll try.'

'Friendly! We're not talking about being friends.' Beatrice's eyebrows lifted in amazement. 'You'll be a member of this family. My daughter-in-law.'

Rosie was stung to stand her ground. 'You aren't the mother-in- law I'd have chosen either, and I say it as politely as I can because I've no wish to upset you. I've known you as my boss, and it hasn't been the easiest relationship. I hardly remember my own mother – I'd have liked to share Ben's. I'd have liked you to be friendly and motherly and welcoming towards me, but we can't help what we are, and we're stuck with each other. Why don't we make the best of it?' She put out her own hand. 'We might find it possible to be friends.'

She saw Beatrice turn further away from her. 'You've infuriated me for years, Rose Quest. God knows I've tried to teach and guide you in your work, but you stand in front of me looking aloof. Giving the impression I'm a cross you're determined to bear.'

Rosie straightened to her full height. As she saw it, Mrs Shearing had metaphorically speaking kicked her into the corner of the sewing room on an average of three times a week. 'I've always tried to be polite,' she faltered. 'To learn . . .'

'Mother, you'll have to get used to the idea. We're engaged, and I hope we'll be married fairly soon.'

'No, Ben! You must take time to think over something so important to your future.'

'I'm going to take Rosie up to see Gran. We'll tell her.'

'Don't be silly, Ben. She's been in bed this last hour or more.'

'Dad?'

'He's in bed too. Do you know what time it is? Stephen's still out. Goodness knows where he's got to.'

'It seems we've chosen a bad time to make our announcement.'

'You've chosen badly in every respect,' Beatrice retorted, tight-lipped.

'I'll take Rosie home then.' She felt his hand drawing her away. She was glad she hadn't taken her coat off. She buttoned it up as they went out to the car.

'I'm sorry, Rosie, that was awful. I should have made sure Dad was around. I thought he would be. She'd not have been rude like that if he'd been there.'

'I knew she'd take it like that.'

'Rosie, you were magnificent.'

'I tried.'

'I know it took a lot for someone as reserved as you to speak up. You came right out and offered friendship. Thank you for that.'

'She's always the same with me, Ben. I thought about it, the best way to greet her, the best thing to say.'

'You were wonderful. I couldn't believe my ears when you spoke up for yourself like that. I've still a lot to learn about you.'

'It didn't do the trick.' She smiled sadly. 'I wasn't good enough.'

'It made her look churlish. You were so generous. She's much older, and should be wiser, yet she wouldn't even agree to meet you halfway.'

'I wish she had.' Rosie shivered.

Ben was furious with his mother and felt sleep was impossible until he'd calmed down. He felt like walking through the night, perhaps along the Esplanade until he'd got it out of his system. It was sober habit that made him drive straight home, with the intention of going to bed.

He locked the front door quietly, and turned to tiptoe across the darkened hall. He could see a shaft of light showing under the sitting-room door. His heart sank. Surely his mother wasn't waiting up to renew the argument? He strode across the hall and threw the door open with his weight behind it. His mother had been about to snatch it open. The door rebounded against her shoulder. Her face was tight with pain and temper. 'Look what you're doing, Ben!'

'Sorry, I didn't expect you to be lying in wait for me behind the door. You were very rude to Rosie. She was bending over backwards to be friendly to you.'

'You can't marry her.' His mother's voice shook.

'Why do you hate her so? She's sweet-natured and . . .'

'No, Ben, she's not suitable. You'll have to tell her you made a mistake.'

'Mother! You're the one who's making a mistake. Why should it bother you so much? You won't have to live with her.'

'The girl is impossible.'

'Mother, she's agreed to marry me. It's what I want, we are engaged. It's a fait accompli.'

He climbed three stairs, aware that his mother's dislike of Rosie had grown in proportion to the amount of attention he had shown her.

'It's . . . it's out of the question.' She was so enraged she could hardly get her words out.

'Mother!' Ben felt his fury boiling up to match hers. 'It's not a matter in which you have any say. We are both of age.'

He hadn't heard the front door open again. Stephen had come in and was unbuttoning his coat.

'What? Our Ben in revolt too? Mother, you have got trouble on your hands. What's happened now?'

'I've asked Rosie Quest to marry me,' he said through clenched teeth.

'And Mother doesn't think it a matter for congratulation?' Stephen laughed. 'Well, I do, Ben. I wish you all the best.'

'This has nothing to do with you, Stephen.' Beatrice turned on him.

'I think it has. When my brother gets engaged, it has everything to do with me. I want to congratulate him. Rosie Quest is a very attractive girl, and Ben has had the guts to make up his mind to marry her even though you don't like her. You'll have to go along with it, Mother. Accept it.'

'It's not a question of my accepting anything. I'm trying to prevent trouble. You think you know everything but you've hardly lived yet, either of you.'

'Rosie Quest has more power over Ben than you have,' Stephen crowed. Ben was afraid his success in getting another job was making him too daring. 'Is that what you don't like about her?'

'I'm telling you to leave Rose Quest alone. You can't marry her.'

'Mother! Don't be silly . . .' Ben was choking with rage as he saw his father's slippered feet descending the stairs. He wore an old dressing gown over his day clothes, his habitual mode of dress on chilly evenings.

'What's all this racket on the stairs? You'll wake your grandmother. It's after midnight.'

'I've asked Rosie Quest to marry me.' Ben felt as though he'd said it a hundred times already. Suddenly he felt dead tired.

'Now you've woken your father!' Beatrice exploded.

'He didn't feel well when he came home. He wanted an early night.'

'She's agreed, has she, Ben? Well, Beatrice, this probably calls for a drink. Why don't we go into the sitting room and have it in comfort? A little brandy might do me good.'

Ben watched his mother spin on her heel and run upstairs. Above him her bedroom door slammed, showing just how far she'd lost her temper. He shuddered. He would have preferred her approval.

'Oh dear.' His father led him into the small sitting room and slumped on to a cretonne-covered armchair. 'I'm afraid your mother isn't too pleased that you've chosen Rosie Quest.'

'Why?'

'It's a long story . . .'

'I'm pleased.' Stephen came in juggling three glasses and a bottle of Martell.

'I hope you'll both be happy.' Edwin raised his glass. 'I'm sure she'll make you a good wife. A nice girl.'

'What has Mother got against her?' Ben saw his father's eyes go to Stephen.

'There's something I ought to tell you, Ben, but not tonight. I feel a bit under the weather, and it's high time we all got to bed.'

'Something private?' He was curious. He'd have pushed it further if they'd been alone, and his father hadn't looked so exhausted.

'It shouldn't be after all this time. Bring Rosie round sometime and I'll try to explain.' The brandy burned Ben's throat. Stephen's high spirits couldn't lift his own. Nothing could blot out his mother's blank refusal to accept Rosie into the family.

All weekend, Beatrice had felt she was having a crisis of confidence. Ben hadn't told her he'd sent Flora Pope to hospital, she'd only found out on Saturday, when she'd asked the van driver to account for his time. With Edwin missing from his office, and Ben's lips clamped in an obstinate line, she'd immediately been suspicious, so she'd telephoned the hospital.

The ward sister had been economical with information, too, but she'd found out Flora had been admitted to the gynaecological ward, and would go down to theatre that afternoon. The news did nothing to quieten her mind.

'I hear there's more the matter with Flora Pope than a needle through her thumb,' she'd greeted Edwin when he came home for lunch.

'Yes,' he'd said.

'What exactly?'

'Women's trouble of some sort, I believe.'

'You haven't got her pregnant?'

'Don't be silly,' he'd said, heading for the dining room.

It had stayed on her mind, but she told herself Edwin couldn't be that stupid. Beatrice found Sunday no easier. All the family except Constance had gone out immediately after lunch, and stayed out all afternoon and evening. She felt Edwin was taking advantage of her. Neglecting both her and his business.

She'd tried to work at her desk in the study but achieved nothing. Her mind had been on anything but work. Beatrice felt things were blowing up in her face.

Recently everything seemed to be going wrong.

It had been quite late when Edwin had come home. She'd felt no patience with him when he'd announced he wasn't feeling well. Serve him right. She'd told him to go to bed, and deliberately stayed downstairs out of the way while he did.

He hadn't gone to bed at all, he'd been curious enough to come down and see what all the fuss was about when Ben came in. Then he'd felt well enough to stay up and drink brandy with him. She'd had time to take a bath and wash her hair.

Now, as she buttoned her nightdress to the throat, she was watching Edwin's reflection in her dressing-table mirror. He had come upstairs to slump on the red velvet chair, and was still no nearer getting ready for bed. He'd pulled the chair up to the bedroom hearth though no fire had been lit tonight.

Edwin was no help at the best of times. Thirty years of marriage had taught her exactly what he was like. He spoke of being a responsible person because seventy-one people replied upon him for their living. He spoke of a wife and three sons to provide for, and it all seemed to weigh heavy.

Beatrice knew it was lip service. She'd always taken care of him. She'd brought up the boys. She ran the house and the factory, and both of them knew Edwin was merely a figurehead. If from tomorrow he never went in to the factory again, nothing in throughput or output, profit or loss, would be altered one jot. Unless one counted a small increase in profitability from the saving of his salary.

Edwin's problems were self-indulgence and laziness.

Beatrice's lips tightened. He went about his work as though he had all day, as though no great care was needed, and as though the outcome was a foregone conclusion. Edwin was the child of well-to-do parents who had been brought up with every need met before he felt it. It had made him soft, with no urge to succeed. She had tried not to make that mistake with the boys.

Beatrice hadn't grown up like that. She had been full of needs, and they had given her a hunger for success that had never abated. They had also given her nightmares about making no profit, being short of money and going hungry, and of seeing herself a failure. She consoled herself with the thought that everybody carried some mark from childhood experiences.

Oliver's defection had seemed unbelievable when Ben accused him, but deep down in her own mind the seed had already been sown. She hadn't wanted to dig deeper into Oliver's figures. She'd known something was dreadfully wrong. That was why she'd been worried, why she'd pushed Ben. She'd hardly been aware of her own motivation at the time, but looking back, perhaps she'd pushed him to do the dirty work for her.

Tomorrow Oliver would be coming home from Gloucester, and she'd told him to come round to see her and Edwin after dinner. Now she was dreading it. Since Ben had demonstrated the method Oliver had used to cheat them, she'd been unable to think of anything else. Edwin couldn't stop talking about it, maintaining Ben was right and Oliver was trying to lie his way out of trouble.

'Ben has done our dirty work for us,' he'd told her. 'He's told Oliver he'll have to go. Don't let him persuade you otherwise.' Impossible to accept that her eldest son could lie and cheat and steal from her. She'd loved and trusted him. The hurt was draining her and making Edwin ill.

She felt raw about Stephen, too, she'd lost him completely. And Ben was changing, challenging her authority at every move. Taking up with Rose Quest of all people. He hadn't learned sense yet.

Edwin was even less use to her than usual. Only last week he'd had a nasty turn in the office. Phyllis Quest had found him slumped over his desk when she'd taken some letters up for him to sign, and gone running in to Ben to raise the alarm. Fortunately, it had been almost closing time when it happened. Beatrice had brought him home and he'd gone to lie on the bed for an hour. Then he'd said he felt better and had come down for supper. She'd been surprised when he'd said he was going out afterwards.

'For a drink, and a breath of air. I'll just walk down to the Royal Rock.'

. Now she heard him stir and groan softly on the spoonback velvet chair.

'I think you ought to see Dr MacFarlain.' She tried to keep the anger and frustration out of her voice. She couldn't cope with sick people at the best of times, and really Edwin seemed to be making a fuss about nothing. His gentle eyes met hers in the mirror. He gave no sign he objected.

'What exactly is the matter with you?'

'I've no energy, Beatrice.' He was as vague as ever.

She would have laughed if she'd not felt in such a turmoil.

'You never have had.'

'I've less.' He did look exhausted, and he'd done next to nothing all week. 'My heart seems to race. Makes me feel dreadful.'

'It's nerves,' she said. 'I'm not surprised with all the trouble we've had recently. Oliver, Stephen and now Ben.' It could be that he was worried about Flora Pope, too, and trying to keep it to himself.

'Ben's all right.'

'The best thing for you is to stay in bed in the morning. I'll get the doctor to call.'

'Perhaps that would be best.'

'Your mother's acting very strangely too. I'll ask him to look in on her at the same time.' He gave no sign he heard. Beatrice put down her hair brush, barely in control of her temper. She was ready for bed, and Edwin still hadn't moved from the little plush chair.

'Come on,' she chivied. 'You'll do yourself no good sitting there.'

She watched him push himself upright. Suddenly he seemed old. Slowly and stiffly he undressed, dropping his clothes back on the chair.

'Where are my pyjamas?' He had tossed aside the pillows and the bedclothes from his side of the bed, without finding them. Edwin expected to find everything he needed instantly to hand.

He was standing looking helpless. She opened the huge wardrobe that had belonged to his father. Behind the beautifully polished mahogany doors were drawers and shelves, hanging space for his suits and racks for his ties. Beatrice jerked open a drawer and pulled out a neatly ironed pair of pyjamas in maroon and white striped silk.

'Those are my best ones,' he demurred.

'Put them on, Edwin.' She'd never cared for the flannel ones he favoured anyway. Slowly, he obeyed in silence.

The big brass bed had belonged to his parents too. She didn't doubt he'd been conceived and born in it. It was made particularly high by its goosefeather underlay, and it seemed to take more effort than usual for Edwin to climb into it. He lay back, his face grey and sweating against the white pillow.

'All right now?'

He sighed 'Yes. Good night.'

Beatrice curled up on her side of the bed, aware even as she felt sleep stealing through her that he was more restless than usual.

She didn't know how long she slept, but a clumsy movement in the room jolted her back to consciousness. The noise came again. The room was in darkness, but she knew instantly that Edwin was out of bed. She leaned over to switch on her bedside light. Blinking in the sudden brilliance, she saw a swirl of stripes move more confidently towards the door.

Almost every night Edwin got up to go to the bathroom. He was irritatingly apologetic, trying to manage without putting on the light. He always woke her, of course. Who could sleep while he blundered across the room in the dark?

She had told him often enough to avoid drinking so

much before he came to bed, but he would not listen to sense. She heard him stumble across the landing to the bathroom. She heard the light click on.

He'd had beer tonight, she'd smelled it on his breath when he came home. Edwin had some very proletarian tastes considering his middle-class upbringing. He'd had brandy afterwards with the boys.

Beatrice could feel herself drifting off again, till suddenly there was a noise like a tree being felled. A dull resounding thud that shook the floorboards, even in this solidly built house. She couldn't place the noise and raised her head to listen closely, but there was nothing further. Had Edwin fallen? Bewildered, and half comatosed, she slid out of bed. The sight of him lying in a crumpled heap on the bathroom floor banished sleep.

She found herself shaking with horror and the sudden cold. He must have banged his head on the bath or something as he fell. His chest was rising and falling as he struggled for breath, his face cold and sweating. She tried to lift him. Even his arm was a dead weight.

She ran back to her bedroom, pulled on a warm dressing gown and slippers. Her teeth were chattering as she ran up to the floor above to shake first Ben awake and then Stephen. She sped back to Ben's room.

'All right, Mother, I'm coming.' His voice was calm and collected. It soothed her rising panic. Ben seemed suddenly solid and reliable. She followed him back to the bathroom. He was crouching on the bathmat, cradling the crumpled heap of maroon and white striped silk in his arms. He laid Edwin down gently.

'Mother,' he said, looking up at her, his face pale and shocked, 'I think he's dead.'

He got back to his feet and she felt the weight and warmth of his arm pulling her close in a spontaneous gesture of comfort and sympathy. She was thinking how fitting it was that she'd made Edwin wear his best pyjamas.

It was three o'clock in the morning and every light in the house was burning. Heavy with dread and fear Ben had telephoned the doctor and told him Edwin was already dead. Dr MacFarlain had known them all for years. He said he would come anyway, and seemed concerned for Beatrice.

She was like an uncertain stranger, hanging back, unable to do anything, wearing a baby-blue dressing gown he'd never seen before, with her thick brown hair swinging loose about her drawn and haggard face.

Mrs Roper was also strangely unfamiliar in night attire, her hair reaching halfway down her back. He asked her to take Mother down to the kitchen and make tea.

Stephen looked younger than ever with his sandy Shearing hair standing up round his frightened face. He'd had his old camel dressing gown since he was about fifteen.

'Come and help me lift Father,' Ben said. It was a struggle to lift him from the bathroom floor and lay him on Oliver's bed, the best place since his room was not used now.

It seemed unbelievable that at lunchtime they'd all

sat down together and eaten roast beef. Dad had eaten two helpings of pudding. Now he was dead. No wonder the shock had numbed Mother. Ben felt hollow and empty. He could remember only the good times they'd shared.

'The best way to go. Best for him, anyway.'

'A shock for the rest of us. It's knocked Mother sideways.' Stephen drew in a long shuddering breath.

'Only her and me left to run the business,' Ben said. 'In a few short weeks . . . Do you still want to leave?'

'Mother will be back in the saddle in a day or so. Yes, it's all agreed with the bank. I'll not change my mind because of this.'

'Let's go and have some tea then.' Ben sighed. What else was there to do? The kitchen was warmer, but in the silence of the night the clock ticked obtrusively. He drank half his cup and then went back upstairs to remove the pillows from beneath his father's head. Better for him to lie flat now.

It came to him then that Gran had slept through it all. Better that she stay asleep. Time enough to tell her the bad news in the morning. He heard the soft crunch of tyres outside as the doctor arrived and went down to let him in.

Ben did not go back to bed, though both he and the doctor insisted Beatrice must. Dr MacFarlain left her two pills to help her get back to sleep. She'd protested but had gone eventually. When Ben had taken her up a cup of the fresh tea Mrs Roper had made, the pills were on her bedside table and Mother was staring up at him from the pillow.

'He was younger than me. How could he go just like that?'

'Poor Dad,' he said. But Edwin had still been enjoying life. Really it was the rest of the family he felt sorry for. Especially himself. He sat alone at the kitchen table and tried to assess his loss.

There were so many things he'd meant to ask Edwin but hadn't. About his brother Harry, for instance. Will Quest had raised so many questions but he'd pushed them to the back of his mind. He'd meant to discuss the old company accounts with him. There would be so many more facts that Dad would have known. He wanted his advice about buying a house. There had seemed to be plenty of time for everything.

And hadn't he said only last night there was something he needed to tell him about Rosie? Ben wished he'd made time.

He felt he needed his help and support at work. He hadn't really found his feet yet. Dad's death had come before he'd learned all he should. He'd needed Edwin's help to stop Mother flattening him completely.

Daylight came before he felt ready to face another day. Mrs Roper came down fully dressed, with her hair in its habitual grey bun on the nape of her neck. She raked out the Aga and put on the kettle again. 'It's Finnan haddock for breakfast,' she told him.

He was about to refuse any when Mother appeared at her usual time.

'Come on, Ben.' Her voice was as heavy with morning impatience as usual. 'You aren't even dressed. You'll be late at the office.'

'Are you going in today?'

'Of course. I couldn't mope about here. Be better for all of us if we do.'

She seemed brighter and more alert than he was. 'I thought you'd sleep in. Those pills . . .'

'I didn't take them. What would I want with sleeping pills? The doctor's a fool.'

He went slowly upstairs, took a cool bath to bring him round and dressed for work. He even managed to eat some of the Finnan haddock. If Mother could do it, so could he.

She drove him to work. As usual, there were two or three people waiting on the step ready to go in.

'You'd better tell them, Ben.' She went straight to her cubicle of an office.

He did, but it was shattering to his self-control to see such shocked horror on the faces of their workers. He was asked, time and time again, about every awful detail. Many of the women were distressed.

When Rosie arrived he took her up to his office and clung to her, finding comfort in her arms. He felt truly thankful that he'd settled their future, but guilty too that he'd spent so much time with her over the last few weeks. If he hadn't been so smitten with Rosie, he'd have spent more time talking to his father.

Ben found the day long and draining. He had to make funeral arrangements as well as work. The factory was unusually quiet. The workers seemed to be keeping their voices low, as though they were in church. He did overhear a few comments: 'At least we won't lose our jobs. It'll be business as usual. Mrs Shearing can run the place as well as he could.'

'Bet there'll be no stopping her now.'

'I'll miss the old man. He wasn't a bad sort. No side to him.'

Constance had not seen the house so full of mourners since Ainsley's funeral. She'd worn black ever since his death. Today her best silk chiffon was unrelieved by any touch of white; she'd added her jet necklace and earrings.

The business had remained closed as a mark of respect for Edwin. Most of his employees had come to the church service, stood at his grave, and now seemed to be here. Constance shivered. So much was happening outside her control, she hardly understood what was going on. It was bewildering to outlive one's younger son.

'Did you have to ask that woman here?' Behind her, she heard Beatrice turn on Ben with sudden venom. 'To my house?'

'I'm sorry, Mother.' Ben, in a sober dark suit, seemed chastened.

Constance turned to study the woman of whom they spoke. She was standing alone at the window, staring out at the river, a glass of sherry in one hand and a damp handkerchief screwed up in the other. Overweight and wearing a tight grey suit that strained at the seams, she looked desolate and still wept behind her thick spectacles.

'I only asked the longest serving staff back to the house, Mother. Dad was popular, and would have wanted it.'

Beatrice snorted with indignation. 'You should not

have asked Flora Pope. It's an embarrassment to have her here in my house. And that girl! She's not been with us five minutes. Why ask her?'

'Wouldn't it look odd if I didn't ask Rosie here? I wanted her to come. I'm going to marry her, Mother.'

'You cannot, Ben,' she hissed viciously. 'Put that idea right out of your mind. I've told you, it's impossible.'

Beside her a voice said wryly: 'Beatrice hasn't changed much.' Constance turned, aware that Beatrice would disapprove of Alice's presence in the house too.

'No, I'm afraid she finds having all Edwin's friends here rather hard.' Beatrice couldn't fail to have seen her. Alice was the tallest woman in the room, big-boned and wide-shouldered as well.

'She never took to any of us,' Alice said. 'Edwin's family connections, his friends, yet Beatrice sees us all as enemies.'

Constance's head was beginning to ache. She'd felt confused and out of kilter since that morning five days ago when Ben had come to sit on her bed to tell her Edwin had had a heart attack and was dead. Edwin dead!

She shook her head. Last night she'd gone to the drawing room at five-fifteen as usual, expecting him to come home from work, pour her sherry and drink his glass of whisky with her. How could she have forgotten he was dead?

'So sudden, Mrs Shearing. Such a shock to us all. Edwin was still in his prime.'

'I blame the factory, it's a very unhealthy place,'

Constance replied, remembering too late that Miss Gibbons had to spend her days there too.

Everybody was sad and full of sympathy, just as they'd been at Ainsley's funeral. A man she didn't know came to clasp her hand between his to talk of the dead.

'So sudden, so young. How old was Edwin, Mrs Shearing?' She'd answered that twice already, yet now she was groping, his age gone from her mind.

She tried to think. 'Let me see, he was born in 1889, that would make him . . .'

Somewhere close, Beatrice's voice said briskly: 'Edwin was forty-eight. No age at all. Yes, such a tragedy.'

Constance's mind wandered. The year Edwin was born had been a year of hope, but it had all come to naught. She didn't want to think about it, but the images kept coming. Ainsley had been forty-nine that year. His face was before her now. She could picture it more clearly than Edwin's. A full set of gingery whiskers covered his chin and cheeks in a somewhat darker shade than his hair. A hard glint showed in his pale blue eyes, a vicious streak in the angle of his jaw. He'd been a cruel man.

'A little more sherry, Constance?' Someone refilled her glass. 'Such a sad day.'

She cast her eyes round the mourners filling the drawing room. Nothing had changed since Ainsley's funeral. Then, too, all eyes had sought relief in the view of the Mersey, the tide full and vigorous, the ebb and flow of the waves a background to their voices.

Amongst the acutely painful memories of that day, the worst was of Francis's cold accusing eyes meeting hers across this room.

For a moment, the clusters of guests parted and she glimpsed a man wearing a dog collar. Suddenly her hands were moist with fear. She gripped Ben's arm. 'Is that Francis?'

'It's the vicar, Grandma, Mr Wilson. You know him well.'

Of course it was! The vicar's eyes met hers across the room. His were soft with sympathy. Ernest Wilson didn't have Francis's handsome face and toffee-coloured hair. Ben was patting her hand, trying to comfort her.

'Who is Francis?'

She couldn't answer, her heart was still pounding. She felt caught up in Francis's spell again. His powerful eyes had been full of suspicion and recrimination at Ainsley's funeral. She'd been haunted by that look down the years.

'Is Francis someone you used to know?' the girl asked.

'Yes, Francis Woodley. Years ago – it was another age. He came to call on us here at the house, out of the blue. A courtesy visit, he said. He was a distant cousin, second or third on Ainsley's mother's side. Once he and Ainsley had been close friends. He'd had a curacy down on the south coast, but his wife had died in childbirth and he'd wanted to come back up north to be nearer his friends and family. He knew of Ainsley's whereabouts through them.'

'Someone you were fond of?' Ben asked.

She snapped with betraying sharpness: 'Why do you say that?'

'Because you remember him well.'

It had flared up between them at their first meeting, not fondness but powerful physical attraction, a scorching passion.

'Let Rosie and me take you out of this crush. We'll find a quieter place, somewhere you can sit down.' She felt better as soon as they were out in the hall. There was more air. Then, suddenly, she was backing away.

'Not in there! I'm not going in Ainsley's study.'

'Of course not, Gran.' It took her a moment to realise they were heading instead to the informal sitting room that Ben called the den.

'Tell us about Francis,' he said as she collapsed in an armchair. 'Close the door, Rosie.' The buzz of voices became a distant murmur.

'You ask too many questions,' grumbled Constance. It was almost an inquisition. They must suspect she'd done something wrong to keep on at her so.

'Tell us, Gran.' Ben's young face was close to hers and she could no longer shut out the echoes from the past.

'Francis was a gentle, charming man, devout and steeped in the traditions of his church.'

She felt again the fever that had burned between them. She knew Francis felt it too, that he renewed his friendship with Ainsley so he could see her. They were hardly ever alone together and it was years before he spoke of his love. Yet it was always there. She had never dared speak of what she felt for him before. It was forbidden. It had weighed on her conscience like lead.

'His smile was sad,' she said.

When he was about to leave he had a way of taking her hand between both of his. Polite society allowed them to touch in that way. Francis made it a loving gesture. He wanted more, he had always wanted more, she had seen adoration in his eyes, and was terrified Ainsley might too. They had to hide their feelings from him.

Ben's brown eyes were still watching her. She must not betray what she'd felt.

'Mother will wonder what has become of me. I must go back to our guests,' he said, getting up. 'Rosie will sit with you for a while. Funerals are very draining.'

The girl got up and fetched a cushion for her back. 'Is that better? Edwin was a very kind man. I shall miss him too.'

'Not Edwin,' she said. 'Francis. I still miss Francis.' The years fell away, taking her back.

CHAPTER FOURTEEN

'Who was Francis?' Rosie held her breath. She was afraid she'd broken Constance's line of thought. Constance turned pale blue eyes to her face.

'He was the curate at St Eade's. That's why it was so terribly wrong.' The old lady was wringing her hands. Rosie took one of them between her own to stop her.

'What was?'

'I'm going to shock you.' Constance seemed almost coy.

'No,' Rosie denied. 'Nothing you did would shock me. You're too much of a lady.'

'You always did say that, Hilda.' Rosie felt the hairs on the back of her neck prickle. Constance was confused. She was mistaking her for the long-dead Hilda, Ainsley's sister.

'If I told you I loved Francis, that would shock you, wouldn't it? We've talked of how difficult I found it to love Ainsley, and you comforted me.'

'Did I? What did I say?' Rosie made her voice gentle. Constance closed her eyes and dropped her voice to a whisper.

'Oh, that men are all like that. If they weren't the

human race would die out. God planted in them this urge to procreate. You didn't know, Hilda, that men never tire of it – they go on till they're ninety. It's a terrible burden for their wives.'

Rosie allowed herself another breath. The old lady seemed to have forgotten her, seemed almost to be talking to herself. Her voice seemed changed.

'It brings them beautiful babies, you said, but all I got was one miscarriage after another.'

'You have two sons, Constai.ce, Harry and Edwin.'

'Yes, two sons, but countless miscarriages, too. You must accept it, you said, but I never could. Ainsley is a good husband and a good man, you told me. But he was your brother, you couldn't believe ill of him.

'You said: "Because you dislike a wife's duty, you mustn't dislike Ainsley. If you accept that all men are the same, love will grow with acceptance. If you show him love," you said, "he will return your warmth. And that in turn will make you feel loved."

'You were wrong, Hilda. I never loved Ainsley. His scratchy ginger beard. His bad teeth, and sometimes bad breath.

'Oh, my feelings towards him grew, you were right about that, but it was hatred that grew. The trouble was I couldn't hide it from him, and once he knew it was hatred redoubled because he started to hate me.

'Francis was so gentle, so unworldly. I waited so long for him to come, my youth was gone. I was thirty-six. So cruel to spend all one's youth fighting off a husband you can't love and then at thirty-six be scorched by passion.

'It made me sad, Hilda, when you said: "At least you've had the chance of marriage, I envy you that." '

Rosie waited so long for her to go on she'd almost given up hope. She had to prompt: 'But you had Francis's love?'

'Oh, yes. I never realised love was like that. Francis was young, younger than me. That was rather naughty.' She laughed girlishly behind a wrinkled hand and several diamond rings.

'He loved me, Hilda. I made him love me despite the teaching and example of the church. That shocks you, doesn't it?'

'No.' Rosie heard the nervous squeak in her voice. 'Temptation is great and our bodies lead us on despite the warning voices in our heads. It's the same for all of us.'

'Francis was afraid he'd be defrocked. I was married, you see.'

'And he was not?'

'A widower who needed a wife. I thought the safest thing, the best thing, was to be rid of Ainsley.'

Rosie straightened up in her chair, aghast.

'I didn't want to involve Francis, but . . .' The pale blue eyes were open again and staring into hers. 'You think I was wrong to rid myself of Ainsley?'

The pause dragged out. Rosie was choking, she couldn't get any word out.

'You do, don't you?'

'Well . . . Ye-es.' She felt goose pimples breaking out on her arms.

'It was an easy death. He shot himself.'

'Well then, you weren't to blame.' She felt a trickle

of relief. Constance couldn't realise what she was saying.

It dried up suddenly when the old lady said: 'Oh yes I was. Terribly to blame.'

There was no mistaking her agitation. Rosie made her lie back in her chair and close her eyes. Fetched a footstool for her feet.

Constance had re-lived her first meeting with Francis a thousand times. She had heard the doorbell ring. There had been pikelets for tea that day. Ainsley had a dribble of melted butter running down his chin when the parlourmaid brought in the visiting card. He'd had to hold it at arm's length to read without his glasses.

'The Reverend Francis Woodley. Good lord! Show him in.' He'd been on his feet to meet him before Francis had reached the drawing-room door, pumping his hand in welcome. She'd thought Francis looked a real gentleman in his frock coat and striped trousers. His dog collar added further distinction.

'It's good to see you back up north with us. Though of course,' Ainsley cleared his throat, 'we were very sorry to hear about Clara.'

Constance had wiped her hands on her napkin and gone to greet the guest. He'd turned to her then, hand outstretched. She'd seen the name Dinah already on his tongue. She'd seen too the little jerk of surprise when he realised his mistake.

'My second wife, Constance,' Ainsley had said hurriedly, before diverting his attention with some shared reminiscence. Francis had squeezed her hand in a friendly fashion. His eyes had smiled momentarily into hers. It had been enough to make her cheeks run with heat.

His presence in the room raised the emotional temperature and sharpened her instincts. She knew from the beginning that she was trying to attract his attention with her smiles. Knew she succeeded too. His handsome eyes searched for hers so often she feared Ainsley might notice. She felt truly alive for the first time in years.

Francis had made her see sense, made her see herself as she really was. Not a frigid woman as Ainsley kept telling her. She couldn't be cold and feel this quickening of excitement as soon as Francis came anywhere near her. There was nothing wrong with her. Francis could make her feel like a warm and loving woman.

The boys came down after their tea in the nursery. They'd been young then, with innocent piping treble voices. Ainsley had been as proud of Harry as she was, showing him off to their guest.

'I have a son too.' Francis had smiled at her. 'A year younger than Edwin.'

'You must bring him to meet us.' She'd grasped gladly at a reason for him to come again.

A date was fixed and she looked forward to it with heightened anticipation. When he arrived the second time, leading Clive by the hand, she'd swept the child up in her arms. All the delight and affection she felt for the father she showered on the child.

Clive was a squarely built, sturdy boy who made Edwin seem even punier by comparison. Although younger he was already taller, more robust, with an enquiring mind. Constance wanted to love him, but found she could not. Clive was much more like the Shearings than Francis. He had their build, their sandy hair and green eyes. That didn't endear him to her.

She knew Francis felt the same attraction as she did when he changed Clive's school, sending him to the same one her boys attended. Francis was trying to move in the same circle. It would not seem unreasonable if he saw more of her. She immediately invited the child to accompany her boys home on Thursday afternoons to take nursery tea and do his homework with them.

That meant Francis could come regularly on Thursday afternoons too and take tea with her and Ainsley. To give him an excuse to stay longer, she invited Hilda to come as well to make a four for bridge. They played before dinner, and went home soon afterwards.

'I do hope we aren't taking advantage of Constance's kindness,' she'd heard Francis say to Ainsley. 'I'm very grateful for her help. A motherless child needs a family and a woman's hand. I'm very thankful you and Constance invite Clive so often.'

Constance had no patience with the endless activity children seemed to need. The only child she'd ever found attractive was Harry, but in front of Ainsley she put on a great show of affection for Clive. He was their cover. She and Francis had used him to hide their attraction for each other.

For years she made much of Clive, including him in the family outings and activities only because it allowed her to enjoy Francis's company. Harry treated Clive as he treated Edwin, with disdainful superiority.

He said he was a pain in the neck. At first, Edwin and
Clive had regarded each other with wary caution, but
over the years the friendship she was trying to encourage blossomed.

Constance liked Clive less as time went on. Sometimes the child seemed to understand more than he
should. He certainly came to understand that she only
displayed affection for him in Ainsley's presence. His
quick intelligent eyes seemed to watch her with suspicion, she knew he didn't like her. But by then he'd
grown closer to Edwin and seemed happy in his
company, teaching him to make and fly kites, learning
to make and sail small boats on the garden pool.

She invited Hilda and Francis to come earlier one
Thursday afternoon, and Hilda had laughed and said
to Ainsley in her hearing: 'I do believe Constance tries
to matchmake.'

She'd been overcome with embarrassment, stitching
fiercely at her embroidery, keeping her eyes on it.

'Dear Constance, I thank you, but I fear it's too late
to make a wife of me. I'm too set in my ways.'

'Francis would make a good husband.' Ainsley's
voice had been gruff. Francis was a great conversation-
alist, interested in every topic, so Ainsley enjoyed his
company too.

'I am older than Francis. An unseemly age difference, I fear.'

Constance had to swallow hard. Nothing had been
further from her mind. But it was another explanation
for all the visits Francis was making. She hastened to
say: 'You do not appear much older, so does it
matter?'

'He is staid in his ways,' Ainsley said. Constance almost choked. She could not agree Francis was staid. 'He needs a wife, Hilda. If . . .'

'No,' she'd said. 'No.'

Constance kept her head bent over her embroidery. She'd asked them to come earlier to alter the routine. Hilda didn't come every Thursday, and on the odd occasion when she did not, Constance and Francis would have an hour all alone. Her ploy worked. They had to sit in the drawing room or the garden, and show great propriety because there were always at least three servants in the house in those days. But they were alone together at last. They could talk without somebody else overhearing every word.

To start with, the increase in Francis's company seemed wonderful, but it didn't satisfy her for long. The more she saw of him, the more she wanted of him. Already she wanted him to take Ainsley's place as her husband, but even when they had an hour alone she didn't put her feelings into words. That would be wrong, a terrible temptation to Francis, but her face and her manner must have told him she'd welcome any advance he made. She knew now that unrequited passion feeds on itself, multiplies, grows, burgeons out of control.

On the afternoons Hilda didn't come, Ainsley would take Francis off to his study once tea was over. There they would indulge in more masculine talk, and drink sherry before dinner. Constance felt bitter about being excluded, but it kept Ainsley happy with the visits and she did have Francis to herself during the afternoon.

She felt happy with him, he brought her hope. She

lived for his visits, always sat opposite him so that later she could remember just how his toffee-coloured hair waved round his head. She fed her own passion on the warmth of his smile, the loving look in his eyes. His voice was rich and low with a timbre all its own. She loved to listen to him. He spoke of everything except what she wanted to hear most – that he loved her too.

He showed so much interest in the business that Ainsley took him round his workshops, but Francis admitted afterwards to Constance that it had upset him to see the poor women sewing in the dusty rooms. He hadn't liked the noise or the frantic atmosphere of industry. He and Ainsley were as different as chalk from cheese, even if they were related.

Ainsley took Constance to hear Francis preach and see his church, and it seemed he preached only to her. They dined at his house, not every month but quite often, and it broke her heart to see how much it lacked a woman's touch.

She knew she was tempting him in the way she held her body, holding his gaze with hers. She wanted him to admit that he too felt this overriding passion that was consuming her.

He arrived one afternoon, five minutes before Hilda, and as Constance greeted him with outstretched hand, he raised it to his lips and kissed it instead of giving it his usual friendly squeeze. It seemed a breakthrough. Her hand burned. It took longer, almost another year before she felt his lips touch hers.

But loving Francis made her hate Ainsley more. Made her cringe from his advances. She found the only way to endure him was to make herself believe it was

Francis who touched her body. Yet Francis would never be so rough.

He came earlier and earlier on Thursdays. It was only five minutes' walk along the Esplanade for her to meet him near the ferry. Francis did not keep a carriage, he hired one when he needed it or travelled by public transport. On fine days they could stroll for an hour along the Esplanade before Hilda was expected. Then Constance would return home through the gate on the promenade, and he would walk through the park and announce himself to the parlour-maid at the front door.

From that it was a short step for her to go over on the ferry. He would meet her in Liverpool. It was so much safer to stroll about the city where nobody knew them and there were no servants to carry tales. As she grew more daring, she got into his hired carriage and went for rides with him.

One Thursday night in November a thick pea soup fog had settled in with darkness. Ainsley had sent the gardener round to the stables to fetch the hired carriage as usual, but the horses had all been unharnessed early as the fog was thought too thick for anyone to go out.

Ainsley had ordered the guest room to be made ready for Francis and Clive instead. Constance had been kept awake into the small hours by the ship's fog horns wailing their warnings on the river, but she was excited too at the thought of Francis being so close.

Ainsley went off to work the next morning, leaving them both still in bed. Her personal maid brought up Constance's breakfast tray as usual. She could not eat.

She heard a tray being delivered to the guest room. Heard Clive go to school with Edwin and Harry.

She climbed out of bed to comb her hair at the dressing table, leaving it in a pale golden cloud about her shoulders. Francis had never seen it like this before. She patted a little powder on her nose, made herself as beautiful as she could, and tried to steel her nerve to do what she craved – go to his room. Her heart was pounding with the daring of her own thoughts.

The usual morning routine meant no servant would disturb her again until she rang. They stayed away from the bedrooms until she was up. She knew this was a chance that would not occur often. She was reaching for her new pink dressing gown in the wardrobe when she heard the tap on her door. Guilt made her jump.

'Come in,' she called, full of suspicion that Ainsley had ordered her maid to come up earlier than usual this morning.

Francis slid in, closing the door quietly behind him. 'Forgive me, I couldn't resist . . .'

Joy was pulsing through her. She opened her arms and ran to him, smiling with delight. No need to steel herself to do anything.

'Just say the word and I'll go.'

'Stay,' she whispered. 'You know you must stay.'

It had taken three years to get him to make love to her, though she'd known from the start he would. The waiting increased her pleasure in it.

The fact that he shed Ainsley's pyjamas to make love to her in Ainsley's bed made it seem all the more daring. Now at last Francis was telling her he loved her. How she basked in the pleasure of that, but he said they must never do it again. It didn't lessen her craving for him, nor his for her. They were taking greater risks to be together. Francis could not keep away.

On one of the first Thursdays of the year when it was warm enough to sit outdoors, Hilda arrived first. Constance was always very careful to make her feel welcome. She needed Hilda too, to cover the affair with Francis, and was fond of her anyway.

She had had the chairs and tables taken into the front garden. She remembered now how she'd been watching the dappling of sunshine on Francis's light brown hair when Hilda had excused herself. In the snatched five minutes, while Hilda went indoors, Francis brought out a key ring and jingled it at her.

'A house.' He smiled. 'Where we can be alone.' Francis dared not take her to his home unless Ainsley came too. He kept a housekeeper, it was church property, and appearances had to be kept up.

'The owners, friends of mine, are spending a year in Florence and have asked me to keep an eye on their property. Will you come?'

Her heart turned over with excitement at the thought.

'Monday then?' He whispered the address. 'I've had a key cut for you.' He pushed it across the table towards her. It was safely in her pocket when Hilda returned to her chair.

The house was a rather grand one in Hamilton Square. The curtains were drawn and the furniture covered with dust sheets, but it didn't matter. At last they could be alone without fear of interruption. They were able to make love regularly then. Often they went three times a week. They both knew it was wrong, but it added another dimension. Increased their joy in each other, added to the excitement.

Constance became pregnant for the thirteenth time that autumn. She prayed it was Francis's child and that she would carry it full-term. She did not.

Yet nothing could mar her memories of that wonderful year. She wanted to become pregnant again, she wanted Francis's child above everything else. By the following spring she was pregnant yet again, and was heartbroken when she lost this child also.

Then, all too soon, Francis was talking of hiring a woman to make the house ready for its owners' return.

Her existence seemed bleak after that. Without the empty house to go to, they seemed to have no time together at all. What she gave Francis, or could expect to receive from him, had never been enough. Now she was greedy, wanting to share his every moment. She knew Francis craved more too. She wanted to be his wife and share his life. Nothing less would satisfy their need.

There was one afternoon she particularly remembered. It was midwinter and the weather had been too cold and wet to stroll the Esplanade. She had had a carriage ride with him the previous Friday, but it was almost a week since she'd seen him.

She expected Francis to come on Thursday as usual. She was ready and waiting in the drawing room half an hour before he was likely to arrive, tingling with anticipation. When the doorbell rang, she made herself wait for the maid to answer the door. She was on her feet waiting for him to be shown into the drawing room. But it was Hilda who arrived first. Her cheek was cold when Constance kissed it.

She hurried her sister-in-law to the fire, trying to hide her disappointment that she wouldn't have a few moments alone with Francis first. Hilda was full of small items of domestic gossip. Constance tried to make much of her, rang for tea to be made immediately to warm her, but she was too eager to see Francis again. Half her mind was listening for his ring on the doorbell. She let her eagerness show.

'You're fond of Francis, aren't you?' Hilda asked unexpectedly. Constance was instantly rigid with fear. Unable to move. Unable to look at Hilda. She couldn't even breathe.

'He comes too often to the house.' Her voice had been gentle. 'There will be talk. I wouldn't want Ainsley to hear it.'

Constance couldn't move. She tried to answer but no sound came. This was what she'd been dreading for years. The room was spinning round her when the doorbell sounded again.

'I mention it only as a warning,' Hilda whispered as Francis was being shown in.

With him in the chair opposite, trying to touch her hand as she passed his teacup, his green eyes trying to meet hers, she couldn't shake off her terror. She dared not look at him. Once Ainsley came home too she knew her manner was stiffer than ever. She couldn't unbend all evening.

She managed to slip Francis a note, asking him to

meet her in Liverpool the next day. She had to talk to him. Tell him that after all these years Hilda had noticed.

'Perhaps we've grown less careful,' he worried. 'We must be more cautious.'

But Hilda caught a chill that afternoon. It went down to her chest, and a racking cough confined her to her own house for several weeks.

The following Thursday, he did not ring the doorbell until Ainsley had been home for half an hour.

'I must not show impropriety,' he explained. 'Your neighbours may feel I do wrong by visiting your wife when she's alone in the house.'

'Suit yourself,' Ainsley had said. 'I consider you family. Anyway, Constance would benefit from a little more religion.'

'We do wrong,' Francis told her afterwards. 'For me, it's particularly wrong.' He said their passion was stronger than their will to be honourable. He tried to counsel her as he counselled his parishioners. She found it helped to talk about her feelings for Ainsley, but Francis didn't believe her when she said she was quite sure Ainsley would kill her if he knew the truth.

'You must face his pistols, don't let him see how much you fear them. It gives him power over you.'

Commonsense had told her that. 'I've tried,' she protested. She'd failed too.

'Come with me now,' Francis had said. 'They are merely Ainsley's playthings. He would not hurt you I'm sure. Frighten you perhaps, but actual physical violence, no.' She'd never been able to convince him there was evil in Ainsley. Francis liked his company, and felt more guilty because of it.

Since Hilda was not expected, she had let Francis lead her into Ainsley's study to look at his pistols. She never went alone, and even with Francis's hand in hers she'd had to force herself to look at the weapons squarely.

'Now you are not so frightened.' Francis was smiling at her gently. 'I think some of these are quite beautiful. You will too if you look at them closely.'

'These are not the ones he uses to shoot seagulls or frighten me. These are rare antiques he keeps on show, in this glass case.'

'If you handled them, I think it would help.' She half suppressed her shiver. 'I would like to handle them myself,' he said. 'I find they have a certain fascination.' Constance knew Ainsley kept the keys to all his cupboards in his tallboy in the bedroom, and ran upstairs to get them.

'See, this pair are Queen Anne. The butts are inlaid with silver wire decoration.' He pushed a gun into her hand. She let it lie on her outstretched palm. Panic rose in her throat. She made herself swallow it down. After a moment it didn't feel quite so cold or look so deadly.

Ainsley had another cupboard, stacked with polished wooden cases. Constance opened it and took out several, opening them at random on his desk.

'These are old match-locks.' She pushed an open case towards Francis.

'You already know more about them than I do.'

'Ainsley made me learn.' For Francis, she picked them out now, one by one, like a child performing for

her teacher. 'Wheel-lock, flint-lock, percussion-lock.'
She was trying not to cringe as she touched them.

Francis took one case to the window. 'A more
deadly pair of flint-locks I've never seen, but in a nice
oak case lined with green baize.' It had compartments
inside and was complete with ready cast bullets, a
bullet mould, powder flask, screwdrivers, cleaning
rods and spare flints. He laid them out, inspecting each
item and showing her what each was used for.

'Would these still kill a man today?' Her mouth was
suddenly dry as the thought hammered in her head.

'Ainsley does not intend to kill you. He knows
exactly what he's doing, and he's totally in control. He
would not hurt you, Constance.'

'But they would still kill?'

'Yes, at short range, I'm sure they could.'

It became Francis's therapy for her. When they
could be sure of not being caught by Ainsley or Hilda,
they went together to the study and handled the guns
in the hope she would feel more at ease with them.
Francis found books about guns on Ainsley's book-
shelves.

'Read them,' he advised. 'The more you know about
them, the less fearsome they become.' Constance
tried. Francis too studied them, and explained what
he'd learned to her.

'You see, in hands that know and understand them,
guns are safe.' Constance was afraid that what they did
was kindling an interest in pistols in Francis too.

Always there was something new that caught his
eye. They opened all the polished wooden boxes in
rotation, and had the pistols out, but were very

careful to put everything back just as they'd found it. Constance always re-locked the cupboards and put the keys back in Ainsley's tallboy.

Now the idea had come to her, it seemed the only answer. She couldn't get it out of her mind, though it gave her nightmares. Had Francis thought of it too? She couldn't ask him, dare not. It was too terrible, yet it was the only way to end this impasse.

Francis was particularly interested in the gadgets for loading and cleaning the guns. He liked to experiment with loading them.

'This pair has a supply of bullets made ready in this corner compartment. Feel how silky smooth they are, Constance.'

The deadly ball rolled in a circle round her palm, the tickle made her shiver. She felt the familiar tightening of her stomach muscles, but it wasn't fear of the bullet itself. It was the macabre thought that wouldn't leave her in peace.

She asked: 'Each gun has to have its own bullets made specially for it?'

'Yes, in the days these were made. Each barrel is a different size and they have to fit tight. That's what the mould is for. Lead is melted and poured inside. When it's had time to set, it opens thus and out comes the ball.'

Constance knew she was breathing more quickly. She was gripped with the need to put her idea to Francis.

'I believe it was considered good practice to place the muzzle of the gun in the mouth and blow through the barrel to make sure the touch hole was clear.' It had seemed fearsome when she'd seen Ainsley do it. She couldn't look at Francis's lips closing on the muzzle. She had an overbearing urge to cover her face.

'Wouldn't do to have it blocked with dust or dirt, would it?' Francis looked up and smiled. 'The hammer is then put to half cock like this, and the safety catch put on if there is one. In this case there is. Does Ainsley have gunpowder?'

Constance knew she was biting her lip. 'There.' She pointed to the powder flask. Would he charge the gun?

'Did you know gunpowder is made of saltpetre, charcoal and sulphur?' Constance felt sick. 'All such homely materials. Saltpetre to cure our bacon, charcoal for our sketching. Do you sketch with charcoal, Constance?' She couldn't answer. 'And sulphur . . . Sulphur is good for so many things. Do you use sulphur ointment? The powder should be measured and very carefully poured down the barrel like this.'

Constance could feel her skin crawling with dread. She had to ask him. She must not let this opportunity go. She steeled herself. 'Will you do something for me?'

Engrossed in tamping the lead ball down the tight-fitting barrel, he said: 'You know I'd do anything for you, Constance.'

She had palpitations, her hands were shaking, but she had to say it: 'Will you kill Ainsley?'

His gaze shot up to rivet hers. She could see the colour draining from his face. He looked shocked, sick, horrorstruck. Slowly he laid the pistol on the desk, and backed off. She could see his lips moving, as though he wanted to say something but couldn't get it out.

Her own words came in a torrent. She knew now the enormity of what she asked.

'It's what you want too. You know it is. It's the only way we could be married.' He gasped audibly, his eyes never leaving hers. She was terrified, realising she'd asked too much.

'Constance!' Her world seemed to fall apart as she saw disgust in his eyes. He backed off still further, then without another word swung on his heel and left the room.

'Wait a minute,' she called, as he was crossing the hall to the front door. 'I didn't mean it, Francis. Of course I didn't mean it. Don't go.'

The front door slammed behind him. The revulsion on his face told her he'd gone for good.

She turned and ran upstairs, fighting for self-control. She must not cry. Ainsley would notice red and swollen eyes and taunt her, but she couldn't choke back the scalding tears or stop the convulsive sobs. She'd lost Francis!

Her life would be empty without him. She had been prepared to do anything for love of him, but there were things Francis would not do for her; she'd found that out too late.

She spent an hour splashing cold water on her eyelids, holding a wet face flannel against her red nose, patting herself dry and adding powder, anything to try and hide the distress she felt. The afternoon was wearing on. She could hear the clatter of tea things from the kitchen.

She heard the commotion of hooves and harness at the front. The piping boyish voices and shrieks of sudden laughter were tearing her apart. She was gripped by numbing panic again. She had forgotten all about Clive.

The boys had come home from school and brought him with them as usual on Thursdays.

'Your father had to return home,' she told him as she rang for a housemaid to accompany him over to the estate stables on the other side of the park, and see him safely into a carriage.

'Can't he stay to tea now he's here?' Edwin demanded, but she wanted him out before Ainsley came.

'No,' she said with a rudeness the child hadn't heard before. Edwin started to whinge. She despatched him upstairs for nursery tea with unaccustomed ferocity. It left her shaking, with tears threatening to overflow. She rushed to her bedroom, shutting the door in his face.

Ainsley was due home any minute and she knew she should go down to the drawing room to be ready to pour his tea.

She kept examining her face in her mirror for tell-tale signs. Just when she felt ready to face him, her eyes would be awash again, the tears brimming over and running down her face.

Ainsley was late, and she thanked God for the half-hour respite. She was ready at last and in the drawing room, ready to ring for the tea trolley. She heard his carriage in the front, heard the front door click shut behind him. She knew he would be hanging up his coat and hat, now he would be going to his study. It was his usual routine to take in the papers on which he would work later in the evening and see if any letters had come by the afternoon post.

Suddenly she was gripped with renewed panic. She saw again the horror on Francis's face as he'd laid the gun on Ainsley's desk. She had left it exactly so. The cupboard ajar, his keys in the lock. She was choking in horror, feeling the strength ebb from her knees.

She was waiting with bated breath for his call: Constance, what have you been doing in my study? Instead she heard the rattle of cutlery on the tea trolley as the parlourmaid pushed it up the hall.

His voice was deep. She heard him speak, no mistaking that. The trolley stopped moving. She knew he was asking Lizzie if she'd been in his room. A few more minutes passed while she crawled with dread for the moment she knew must come.

The rattle of the trolley was approaching again, the knock at the door came, then the trolley being pushed in.

'Thank you, Lizzie.' Her voice was a weak whisper. She dared not look at her in case the maid should notice her blotchy face.

'Cook has made sponge cake today, Mrs Shearing, and I've brought toast and gentlemen's relish. Will you want anything else?'

'No, thank you.' She was stiff with tension, could hardly move as she heard Ainsley's footsteps approaching.

'Hello, Constance. What about my tea?'

She was jerking to her feet. 'I'm sorry.' The tea

splashed into the saucer. She made herself pour another cup for him. As she took it over, the teaspoon was rattling in the saucer. When she dared to look at him, he was opening his newspaper.

It came to her then, Ainsley couldn't believe she'd touch his guns. He didn't suspect she had anything to do with leaving them out on his desk. She wouldn't even look at them unless he took her into his study and forced her to confront them.

'Has anyone been here today?' he asked. She saw concern on his face.

'Francis came this afternoon.' She forced her voice to stay steady. 'He brought back the book you loaned him, and thanks you for it. There's some function at his church this evening, so he could not stay.'

'Did he go to my study?' Her heart turned over and thudded on.

Only the anxiety on his face kept her calm enough to say: 'No, I don't think so. He was in here, and the garden. We walked round the front garden. He's very interested in our gladioli, says they won't grow for him.'

'What about Mrs Lewis?' She was their house-keeper.

'It's her afternoon off.'

'Did she have my study cleaned this morning?'

'Monday is the day for your study, Ainsley. You complained Lizzie disturbed your papers and said it did not need dusting every day. You told me to make sure they didn't go in.'

Constance had been acting a part for years, pretend-ing feelings she didn't have, hiding others. It was second nature now. She mustn't show any interest in what Lizzie had told him, though she knew it must have been something similar. She dared to ask: 'Is something the matter?'

'I must have left my cupboards open last night. I don't suppose you noticed?'

'Which cupboards?' A band was tightening round her chest.

'The cupboards in my study.' His irritation was boiling over.

'I haven't been in there.' Relief, utter relief, was flooding through her as she saw he wasn't going to question that. He didn't believe she'd go near his guns, but she must not show her relief and another thought was thundering through her. Had he noticed one of his guns had been loaded? She picked up the teapot again.

'Are you ready for another cup, Ainsley?' Her heart was thudding wildly. She felt terrible. She needed her smelling salts, but they were up in the bedroom. She felt faint, ill even.

CHAPTER FIFTEEN

Beatrice nosed the Rover through the gates of the Albert Hotel and backed it into its usual position facing the front door. Switching off the engine, she relaxed at last. It was over.

She let her head rest against her hands on the wheel, she could feel herself shaking. She'd been dreading the visit to Edwin's solicitor but now she knew the worst. She hadn't expected a bequest to Flora Pope. She'd been listening to Pringle's pedantic voice reading Edwin's will and been suffused with sudden boiling indignation. She really begrudged the two hundred pounds to Flora. He might have warned her, she told herself in cold fury. It was humiliating.

When he'd drawn up the will seven years ago, Edwin had said:' I'll see you don't starve, Beatrice.'

'I'm not afraid of that, I'll always have my corset company.'

'I've been fair. You've given time and energy to the shirts.' It hadn't set her mind at rest. How could it when he'd warned her that he meant to make provision for Rose Quest?

'Please don't do that,' she'd pleaded. 'There's no need.'

'It's done.' Edwin always got his own way when he wanted it, and he'd wanted this. 'There's every need, as you know.'

'No, Edwin. I'm not happy about it.' Rose Quest was an even greater humiliation than Flora Pope, and both were proof she'd failed.

She should have made more fuss at the time. He'd drawn up the new will shortly after the girl had started her apprenticeship. Beatrice would have been even less happy if she'd known Edwin would be dead in seven short years.

She had expected Rose to have left, married, moved out of her life long before Edwin died. She'd not have felt this bitterness, this foreboding of trouble if she'd been gone. It made things so much more difficult with the girl still working in the sewing room. Worse still if Ben insisted on marrying her.

She was back in Pringle's office in Hamilton Square, half choking with impatience to hear what Edwin had done, slithering on the leather chair by the large partner's desk which had been piled high with documents tied with pink ribbon. She'd watched while Pringle selected the family deed box from the rack in the corner. From the moment of Edwin's death she'd worried about this.

Beatrice sighed heavily. The letter from Pringle and Bateson had specifically invited her to bring her sons and Rose Quest with her this morning. She had preferred to go alone and find out exactly how things stood. She had half hoped that Edwin might have listened to her plea. If not, then she'd already worked out how to give Rose Quest something more – and this time it wouldn't be to her taste.

She had always known that not everything was Edwin's to hand on, and that Constance had owned the house outright since Ainsley had died. She also owned one-third of Shearing's Shirts.

Edwin had thought he was being fair. He had left Beatrice the residue of his money and investments. The two-thirds share in Shearing's Shirts that he'd owned, he'd split between her, the boys, and Rose Quest.

She couldn't think of that girl. Didn't want to. Her existence had altered everything. She'd been furious with Edwin when he'd given Rose her apprenticeship.

'I don't want to see her every day,' she'd exploded. 'She'll remind me. How could you do such a thing? For God's sake Edwin! You've no sense.' She'd always known it would lead to more trouble. For seven years the girl's great green eyes had reminded her every time she'd gone into the sewing room. Edwin had had no thought for her. She'd pleaded with him to change his mind, terminate it, even ask one of his friends to take Rose instead. He knew Rose's presence needled her.

'You must be over all that, for goodness' sake,' he'd laughed when she'd complained. 'I can't believe a woman like you still thinks of past affairs. You aren't the fluttering romantic type.'

Beatrice sighed. There were some affairs even women like her could not forget.

Now she said to Pringle through clenched teeth: 'You can write to each of them. Tell them exactly how they benefit under the terms of Edwin's will. I'd be glad if you didn't mention the reason for Rose Quest's inclusion. A lapse many married men make – it's all a little embarrassing now, as you'll no doubt understand.'

'Of course, Mrs Shearing,' Mr Pringle had assured her. He'd gone on about applying for probate, but she was no longer listening. She could feel resentment building like water behind a dam. Why should the girl have an equal share? A small bequest would have been more than adequate, but far better never to have mentioned her in his will at all. It was going to stir up a hornet's nest of trouble.

She would have liked Ben and Oliver to own a larger share. She didn't want them to feel they were getting scant recompense for their work. But Oliver had been taking advantage of them and taking more than he should, and Ben had blatantly disregarded her wishes over Rose Quest and needed to be put in his place. Better by far if Edwin had left it all to her. She would reward those who in the long run did most of the work. It would have been a fairer arrangement.

Beatrice sighed again. For once she couldn't pull herself together. Her head was pounding. She felt no better, but had to get back to work. As she got out of the car she looked up and saw Ben watching her from the window of Edwin's office, and reflected it was just as well he couldn't know what she'd been thinking.

Hurrying into the building, she let the front door swing back behind her and found herself face to face with Flora Pope. She felt her fury and hatred boiling up again.

Every time she came face to face with Flora's rolls of fat and sagging bosom, Beatrice thought how much she needed her one piece corselet, the strongest with the most body control. Flora had a figure that cried out for help. A decent corset would make her look younger and more attractive.

'Good morning, Mrs Shearing.' The light was reflecting off her thick spectacles. 'I was wondering if . . .'

Perhaps Flora preferred to look the ragbag she did when she came to work, believing it would throw everybody off the scent. Indeed, it had taken Beatrice years to believe the rumours she heard. Perhaps Flora had worn a corset when Edwin had taken her out. He'd meant to be discreet, of course, and had always taken her over to Liverpool where they were less likely to meet someone who knew them. Even so, people had told Beatrice of it, and she knew he went to her spinster's room when he told her he was walking down to the Royal Rock for a drink.

Hurt washed over her in waves. That Edwin could have lain down in Flora Pope's bed then come home to her! And the woman had been pregnant. She was almost certain of that. It made her stomach churn with disgust.

'Not now, Flora,' she snapped with more than her usual venom, pushing past her to the stairs. Flora Pope had no protection now and had better watch out. Beatrice could give her her cards any time she liked. It was just a question of deciding who should be forewoman in the sewing room before she did it. No point in cutting off her nose to spite her face. She'd give the

matter some thought when she calmed down. Flora
had it coming.

As she went into Edwin's office, Ben turned round
from the file cabinet.

'There you are, Mother. I thought this morning we'd
agreed to look through the work Father handled?
Decide who is to handle each file from now on.'

'Yes, that's what I'm here for.'

'First thing, you said.'

'I've come as soon as I could. I had an appointment.'

'Who with?'

Beatrice bit back the words 'Never you mind'. It was
her automatic reaction. She would have to rely more
on Ben now. 'It wasn't important. Shall we get on with
the job?'

'All right.' He was looking at her strangely. He'd
noticed she'd side-stepped the question. He was going
to find out eventually anyway. Would it be better if she
told him now?

He waved his hand towards the desk. 'I've picked
these out for myself. I'll take them over.'

'I'm sorry, Ben.' She felt crushed with fatigue. She
knew it was in her voice. 'I had to see the solicitor this
morning, about the will.'

She saw the sympathy in his eyes. 'It's a difficult
time for you, Mother. I could have come with you. It
might have helped.'

'Nothing helps, Ben.' She felt full of sadness. It was
all too raw. She made herself say more briskly: 'Send
the rest of the files down to my office, Ben. I'll see to
them.'

★　★　★

Ben followed her to the door. 'Don't go for a moment, there's something else. We ought to talk to Oliver. Straighten out what . . .'

'Not now, Ben.' That banished the sympathy from his face.

'It has to be done.'

Oliver had come back in the hubbub of Father's death. He'd helped shoulder his coffin, attended the funeral and family meals. Ben had never intended to bar him from those, but now Oliver was coming to the office as well. Actually doing a little work, nothing too strenuous, trying harder than ever to ingratiate himself with Mother. And she was carrying on as though she'd forgotten he'd done anything wrong.

Ben felt he'd lost his father's support as well his affection, and now he was standing alone against Oliver and Mother.

'I can't cope with any more trouble now. Can't even think of it,' she exploded.

'Let me think of it then. Let me deal with it. It's all I've ever asked.'

'You're in too much of a hurry, too aggressive with Oliver. We're all bruised by your father's death. Let it ride for the moment, let us get over this.'

Ben studied her drawn face. He'd never known Mother put anything off before. Never known her so tight with tension. Suddenly he was sure she was holding something back.

'The will was straightforward? What you expected?'

He saw something of her old determination come into her eyes. Her chin lifted. 'There is something, Ben.'

'Yes?' He felt suddenly cold.

'It's very complicated. Mr Pringle is writing to you to explain.'

'Explain what?' He felt some sixth sense filling him with foreboding.

'As you know your father owned two-thirds of the business. He's divided that into six shares.'

Ben forced himself to think. 'Three for you and one for each of us sons?'

'No. Two for me, one goes to Rose Quest.'

'No!' It took a moment to sink in, then he felt he'd been kicked in the gut. He tried to speak. His voice was a croak. 'Why?'

'Why do you think?' His mother's voice was louder, harsher. 'He was her father. He wanted to be fair.'

He knew he was staring at her. 'I don't believe it.'

'It's true.'

'Why didn't you tell me before? You know what this means? Rosie and I . . .'

'I tried, Ben.'

'You accused me of playing about with the machinists. You said she was not the right sort because she'd been born in the workhouse. Why didn't you tell me she was half Shearing?'

'I said, leave her alone, she's not for you. It was very difficult with your father alive.'

'That's total humbug. Nothing has ever stopped you saying exactly what you wanted to before. You knew I loved her.' Ben felt his way back to a chair and sank down, appalled.

His mother's laugh tinkled like splintering glass. 'Why else would he part with a share of his business,

Ben? Rosie is Edwin's daughter by his mistress, Grace Quest. She's your half-sister. It's impossible for you to marry her.'

Ben knew he sat at his desk for a long time with his head in his hands. He felt physically sick. He could not believe Rosie was his half-sister.

He heard his father's voice again on the night before he died, saw the old camel dressing gown he'd worn pulled to his waist with the twisted cord.

'I hope you'll both be happy,' he'd said. 'I'm sure she'll make you a good wife. Rosie's a nice girl.'

If he'd been Rosie's father too, he'd have known marriage was out of the question. He'd never have said that, Ben was convinced of it. There had been more. He tried to recall Edwin's exact words.

'There's something I ought to tell you, but not tonight. It's a long story . . .'

Ben remembered asking if it was something private. He'd meant personal really.

'Shouldn't be after all this time. Bring Rosie round sometime and I'll try and explain.' So there was a definite connection. She must be Harry's daughter, a half-cousin not a half-sister.

Ben lifted his head an inch and sighed. If only he'd known his father was so near his end, he'd have persuaded him then to tell him. He remembered the way Edwin's eyes had gone to Stephen. If they'd been alone that night . . . But what was the use? Dad couldn't tell him now.

He got to his feet. Mother was adamant Rosie was his sister. She had been terrified of this ever since

Grandma had said she had the Shearing likeness. He had to talk to her before she got her letter from the solicitor. That would convince her, as it would everybody else, that she was Edwin's illegitimate daughter.

His mother was in her cubby hole of an office dictating to Miss Gibbons. He opened the door.

'I'm going out, Mother,' he announced. 'And I'm taking Rosie. We have things to talk over.'

'What about your work?' She seemed outraged that he should leave it now. It heartened him.

'There are more important things. I'll take the Rover.'

'No, Ben. I want to use it.' Her voice was chilling.

'The Ford?'

'Charles Avery has it. He's out calling on customers.'

'Damn,' he said. 'We're going anyway.' He strode down the sewing room to Rosie's machine, and whispered that he wanted to talk to her. Heads were lifting all round, he was conscious of being watched by many eyes as they walked up the room together.

'I should ask permission before I go out.' She was wary.

'Not any more.'

'I must at least tell Flora. She'll wonder where I've gone.' He waited by the cloakroom as she turned back, held the door open as she reappeared, saw her snatch her coat from the peg. He hurried her down the front steps.

'What's happened?' she asked. He took her arm and hurried her across the car park. It was raining. 'Where are we going?'

Ben stopped. He didn't know. 'There's something

we've got to talk about. Is there somewhere we could get out of this rain? A café?'

He saw her hesitate. 'If it's important . . .'

'It's very important.'

'I know a place. On the farm.'

'Not with Will. Somewhere private.'

'It's very private, nobody will disturb us. What's the matter?'

He told her about the letter she'd soon be receiving. That his father had left her a share in Shearing's Shirts. 'An equal share, you'll own as much of the business as I do.'

She pulled him to an abrupt halt. 'Then he was my father!'

'I don't think so, but my Uncle Harry could have been.'

'I can't believe . . . He must have been my father.'

'No, Rosie, not necessarily. If Harry had once owned a share of the business, my father would want to hand it on to you. He'd see that as fair and right.'

'But if Edwin was my father, that means . . . Oh my God!'

'Rosie, I don't believe he was.'

'With the population of Birkenhead running to a hundred and fifty thousand, why does he have to be one of your family?'

'I'm not saying he is. Just that it seems likely, with Dad willing you an equal share of the business. And it could be why Grace didn't tell Will. He'd been Harry's friend. They might even have met through him. Where are we going?'

'To our dutch barn. We won't go up Gordon Drive

and pass the house. I don't want us to be seen going there.' She led him along streets he didn't recognise. Then up a narrow path to a six-bay barn built of old sandstone. The whole front was open to the weather. Five of the bays were empty. Scythes and pitchforks hung on the wall.

'Nothing much left now. Just this last bay. I'm glad Will hasn't had to use it all, or we'd have nowhere to go.'

'Is this hay?' It rose like a solid wall in front of him. A ladder led upwards.

'It's old hay from last year. Our lease is up in October. Rather sad. I don't know whether we'll be making hay this year. Come on.'

'Up there? I'm not much used to ladders.' Her brows lifted slightly. He could see from her expression that climbing ladders was taken for granted on a farm.

'I'll hold it for you,' she said. 'Up you go. You'll like it up on top. I've never brought anyone here before.'

He climbed awkwardly. The ladder seemed perpendicular, and also old and fragile. It was propped across the cross beam of the barn. He then had to get off the ladder on to that. He felt anything but nimble.

He turned round to assure Rosie he'd keep the ladder safely supported from up here, but she was close behind him, coming up at twice the speed he had. She was light and lithe, and climbed through the cross beams with ease.

'I used to come quite a lot when I was small. Will and Tom knew I came here to get away from the rest of the family. Sometimes they'd call up that a meal was ready, or Aunt Maud wanted me for something, but nobody ever came up here on the hay.'

She took off her hat and coat, shook off the raindrops before spreading them across a beam. 'Let's have yours.'

'Won't we be cold?'

'Not here.' He watched her scrambling across the hay and started to follow. The soft loose hay gave beneath his weight. Every so often one foot would sink through as far as his knee. He was stumbling after her. Right in the centre, up against the far wall, she threw herself down.

'If you're cold you can burrow down a bit. It's lovely and warm even in midwinter. Haven't you heard of cooking in a haybox?'

He bounced down beside her in the fragrant hay. His thigh was touching hers, the feel of it sent shivers down his spine. The rain was drumming on the tiles above and gushing through the broken gutters.

She looked troubled and pensive when he pulled her closer, wrapped his arms round her. 'It's logical, Rosie, that Harry was your father.'

'But equally logical that it was Edwin.' She looked stricken. 'I'm thinking of Flora Pope. He kept a mistress towards the end of his life, and managed to get her pregnant. Wouldn't it be even more likely to happen when he was young? Edwin always treated me in a fatherly manner, and your grandmother recognised a family likeness?'

'The likeness would be there whether it was Harry or my father.'

'The trouble is, your mother is saying . . .'

'Yes, and I don't know how we're going to prove otherwise.'

Rosie was frowning again. 'Why should she say that if it isn't true?'

'You know Mother, she has this God-given assurance that she knows best. She doesn't want us to marry.'

'But surely, even for her . . .? What if she's right?' Her deep green eyes were wide with apprehension. 'I'm frightened, Ben.' He put his cheek against hers in a gesture of comfort.

'She isn't, and we've got to find some way to prove it.' He snuggled lower in the hay, knowing she'd taken pleasure in bringing him here. 'This is a wonderful place. What are all these pictures?'

All along the great beams were water-colours painted on curling paper, held in place with rusting drawing pins.

'I used to paint a lot at one time.'

'You did them?'

'Yes.' She smiled and lay back in the hay. 'I did these.'

'They're good, Rosie. Far too good to pin up here.'

'I wanted to go to Art School once – my mother went. I've some that she did, portraits were her strong point. Would you like to see them?'

'I'm more interested in your paintings. You've got enormous talent. Can I have one to take home?'

'Of course, take what you want.'

'This one. It's the view from here across the fields, isn't it? It's full of tranquillity. I shall have it framed and think of you every time I see it.'

'It's weathered a bit.' She took out a drawing pin and the rust mark showed. 'I could paint the same view again for you.'

'You shouldn't be spending your days sewing, not when you can paint like this. Did you never think of night school classes?'

'Yes, but they clash with evening milking.'

'Do you want to go on sewing all day and every day?'

He watched her frown. The rain had made her hair curl more tightly than ever. 'I think you should do more painting, and think seriously about taking classes. Once we're married, you could.'

'I don't know whether I'd ever be good enough to earn a living painting landscapes. I'm really more interested in design.'

Ben smiled. He loved seeing Rosie like this, enthusiasm beginning to bubble out of her as she forgot her troubles. 'I'd really like to know more about it.' Her green eyes were shining as she pointed out designs for printing on cloth hanging amongst the landscapes. 'And about designing clothes.'

'You must. I'll keep you to that.'

'I reckon I could design shirts now. I know you make short- sleeved summer shirts, but have you never thought of making real sports shirts? From new materials like Aertex.'

'We could, I suppose. You're right, Rosie, I should be thinking about it.'

'So many more people are going hiking and camping and playing sports.'

'It's a good idea, Rosie.'

'I reckon I could make the patterns. I know exactly how the pieces go together, I've been sewing them for years.'

'Do drawings for me. Let's see if you can come up with something really new.'

Now she was serious again. 'Is it going to make a lot of difference to me? Owning a share in the business? It's going to churn Will up when he finds out.'

'Don't tell him then.'

'You're forgetting, Phyllis works in the office. They'll find out there, sooner or later.'

'Sooner then, I'll tell them. I was forgetting about Phyllis. This is going to stir up problems all round, Rosie.'

'You think I should refuse it?'

'No, Dad must have had his reasons. He wanted you to have it.'

Ben watched the rain gust across sodden fields. The cattle clustered for shelter against a hedge.

'Oh, Rosie!' He wanted to give comfort, but he wanted to receive it too. He'd been shaken apart by what had happened in the last few days.

He kissed her, feeling a wave of passion wash over him. He told himself to slow down before he frightened her off. Instead he let his lips flutter lightly across her face and down her throat. The top button on her blouse was constricting. He slid it open and caused the next one down to slide out by itself. Her soft white skin made his fingers tingle as he ran them downwards. He felt her body respond to his touch, and it brought a feeling of greater urgency.

He pulled at the ribbon his mother insisted was

essential wear in the sewing room. Her hair sprang loose about her face and shoulders in bouncy curling tendrils. He loved the luxurious silky feel of it, the rich deep colour and the faint scent of her, fragrant and feminine.

He felt love welling up in him. It was tinged with lust and pleasure and excitement, and a need to put the misery of the last few days behind him. He knew he was kissing her with more abandon than he ever had before. He made himself stop, lifting his head, fearful Rosie would shy away from his advances.

Her lashes lay thick and gold against her pale skin. Her eyes were closed. He watched her raise her face to his, till the softness of her cheek warmed him. He gathered her closer. Never before had he felt so filled with love. As he kissed her again he felt passion taking over, a passion he was almost unable to control.

He was shrugging out of his jacket, loosening his tie, almost before he realised his intention. He felt he was being swamped by his need of her, but he was still in control – until one of her fingers gently smoothed the hairs on his wrist. Suddenly he was trembling. He put his head down on her breast.

'Push me off, Rosie,' he moaned, but her arms held him tight. He could feel the length of her body against his, soft and yielding. An insect was crawling up his bare arm, the irritation lost in the urgency of his own need.

Trembling in stunned after-shock, Rosie whispered: 'I've done exactly what my mother did.' She could see Ben's face above her, looking horror-stricken.

'Rosie, forgive me. I didn't mean . . . I went too far, much too far. I meant to hold back, cool the pace. I was afraid I'd frighten you off.'

'Frighten me off?' She giggled nervously. 'You couldn't *shake* me off. It wasn't your fault.'

He pulled her closer, wrapped himself round her. 'I love you, Rosie, you know that.'

She loved him. But: 'I've done what Grace did. I couldn't understand why she let it happen. I swore I never would. Now I have. I can't get over that.'

'It was my fault, Rosie. We'll set the date and get married. After all, we are engaged.'

'You're forgetting,' she choked, 'your mother says I'm your half-sister.'

'Listen to me.' He sounded vehement. 'What happened to your mother won't happen to you. For one thing, I'm going to hold on to you. For another, you've got your share in Shearing's, you'll always have a little income from that.' The corner of Ben's mouth lifted again into its habitual quirk. 'Provided I can make a profit.'

'Ben, that's . . .'

'We're half-cousins, I'm sure. Remember that, Rosie, half-cousins and no more. We'll fix the date and call Mother's bluff.'

But she felt uneasy. They got dressed, brushed the tickling hay off each other and went back to the Albert Hotel. All afternoon, Rosie tried to lose herself in the routine of sewing and found it impossible. Ben had loved her and she'd found it wonderful. She felt wrapped in the warmth of his love, protected by it. Now at last she could appreciate why her mother had found herself in the position she had. It was only too easy.

The atmosphere in the sewing room had changed with Edwin Shearing's death. Flora was white and shaken. Just as she'd always sent waves of jollity and good humour eddying round the room, now she was lowering the emotional level with her apathy and tear-stained misery. Poor Flora. She'd hardly had time to recover from her miscarriage. Rosie knew Edwin had been the father of the child she'd lost.

None of them had recovered from the shock of his death. The girls couldn't stop talking about him, and of the changes his absence would inevitably bring. The worry of what those changes would mean for her gnawed at the back of Rosie's mind, detracting from the contentment she would otherwise be feeling.

By way of compensation, Edwin had meant to give her something of value. Instead he'd taken away what she valued most. Her breathing felt tight every time she thought of it. If he was the secret father who had killed her mother and let Rosie herself be born in the workhouse, she wanted to hate him. It made it ten times worse that Edwin had had enough money to prevent any of it happening. He could have helped Grace find a room, paid her what he paid a seamstress. That's all it would have taken.

Until now Rosie had let a mountain of contempt build inside her for her unknown father. She tried mentally to heap it on to Edwin's head, but couldn't. She wanted to hate Ben, too, because he was his son. She couldn't do that either. She loved Ben.

She tried to think it through calmly. She must not be

persuaded by Ben, though she didn't want to believe Edwin had been her father. She'd liked him, he'd been kind, understanding even. She couldn't believe he would have abandoned Grace.

Beatrice knew the facts, she didn't doubt that, but Ben didn't think she was telling the truth. His grandmother probably knew too. Ben should ask her.

With Edwin gone, Mrs Shearing was spending more time in the sewing room. That alone was enough to upset the girls, but in addition she was carping more and finding fault with everything they did.

The following day, Beatrice Shearing was even more irritable. Rosie could feel the nervous reaction she was bringing about. As feelings were heightened, output went down. Early in the afternoon Beatrice exploded in a fit of ill temper.

It seemed that their flannel work shirt in red and grey check was proving more popular than expected, and the stockroom had run out of large sizes. Orders were waiting and could not be made up. The cutting room had been alerted, and had altered production, but Flora had not. She had had a week off work, and seemed unable to get on top of it now she'd come back. There was always a back-log of shirts cut out ready for making up, and Flora had not switched the machinists from these. Beatrice came in and discovered the large sizes were still being kept waiting.

It brought a tirade of abuse down on Flora's head that shook them all. It took Rosie's breath away. They could all see the forewoman was not functioning to her usual standard, but there was no call for such a humiliating dressing down. Even Beatrice seemed to realise it was all too public because eventually she ordered: 'Come to my office, Flora.' In silence they both walked up the room. 'Get on with your work, girls,' Beatrice barked from the door.

For five minutes every sewing machine whirred at top speed. Then a grey-faced Flora stumbled to her place to retrieve her handbag. Beatrice, with heightened colour and arms folded, stood at the door watching her. The machines slowed in alarm.

'Rose.' Beatrice's voice carried up the room. 'Rose.'

'Yes, Mrs Shearing?' She felt her heart pounding as she turned.

'Come to my office, please.'

She got to her feet reluctantly. One thing Rosie was sure of, Beatrice would hate her having a share in the business. She didn't want to discuss it with her in this bad mood.

Rosie was not invited to sit. Beatrice slid into the chair behind her desk and barked: 'Have you received a letter from our solicitors?'

'Not yet, but Ben has told me what to expect.'

'Good.' From the expression on her face, Rosie thought it was anything but good. 'It saves me from going into long explanations.'

'It doesn't really.' She tried to rally her flagging courage. 'I don't understand why Mr Shearing should leave anything to me.' She shifted her weight from one leg to the other as she saw the colour flare again in Beatrice's cheeks.

'The circumstances of your birth were an unfortunate mistake on his part, and he wished to make amends. That should be simple enough for you to understand, Rose. He has treated you very well, the same as his legitimate children. That was his wish not mine.'

Rosie made herself say: 'I'm not convinced he was my father.' Really it was Ben who was not convinced. She was becoming more certain by the minute.

'Why else would he give you a share of our business? Don't be so ridiculous.' Beatrice raised one eyebrow. 'Of course I know why you say that, but you have no need to marry into the business now. You have a share in your own right. That was Ben's attraction for you, wasn't it?'

'No.' She was choking. 'No.' Rosie was searching for words to convince Beatrice she really loved Ben, but she went on talking.

'I've sacked Flora Pope for inefficiency. I'm appointing you in her place, so you can play a greater role in the running of this business.'

Rosie could hardly believe her ears. She felt knocked sideways. Events were moving too quickly for her to grasp.

'Well, what do you say to that?'

'But Flora's very efficient. I'm sure I'll not . . .'

'I'm not asking you to run the whole business, just the sewing room.' Rosie flushed at her sarcasm. 'Only right you should take more responsibility. You feel capable of acting as forewoman, don't you?'

'Of course.' She wasn't at all sure, but she knew she mustn't show her misgivings to Beatrice, who'd despise her. Beatrice didn't know what misgivings were.

'But the girls will never believe you've given me Flora's job.' She sensed a show of aggression would get her further with Beatrice, but it was alien to her nature and hard to summon. 'They don't know yet I'm supposed to be Edwin's daughter. Do you want it to be generally known?'

'We'll tell them now.' The next moment Rosie found herself trying to keep up with Beatrice's staccato heels drumming across the hall. She banged back the door of the sewing room. The girls had all been speculating on what was happening. In the sudden hush, the two with the fastest reflexes started to sew.

'Girls,' Beatrice announced, 'I've had to dispense with Flora Pope's services. I cannot tolerate inefficiency and insubordination. Rose will be your forewoman in future.'

With flaming cheeks and head down, she stumbled back to her machine, slumped on to her chair, and prepared to carry on with her work.

'Bring the books to my office, Rose. Now, if you please. We'll need to go through them to make sure you understand what to do.'

Rosie got to her feet again and fetched Flora's books from the cupboard. She hoped she already knew how to keep them because she was in no state to take in Beatrice's instructions now. She felt drained. All she wanted to do was to settle back into the routine and try to regain some of her equilibrium.

When she came back again, the girls were agog that Flora had been so summarily dismissed after twenty-five years' service. They knew of course about her liaison with Edwin Shearing, and there was much whispering and speculation with hands in front of mouths.

'Never thought she'd pick you to take her place,' Kitty whispered. 'Always thought she had it in for you, too.'

'She has,' Rosie sighed. Today there was no way she could relax and get on with her sewing. She had to think about her new duties. On her first afternoon as forewoman, output had been low from everybody. Although she was able to send some outsize shirts up to the stores, she knew not enough were ready to complete the orders waiting there.

Rosie was glad to get out in the fresh air and familiar streets. She wanted to throw herself back into the routine of milking and forget the upsets of the day. She felt soothed when at last she could rest her forehead against Tinkerbell's flank, and hear the swish-swish of milk in the pails.

CHAPTER SIXTEEN

For once milking didn't soothe Rosie. Her head ached. She'd thought the facts through ten times, and there was no way round them.

The last thing she wanted was a share of the Shearing business. She'd refuse to have it if it would put her relationship with Ben back to where it had been before Edwin's death. Ben might as well have shouted from the roof tops that he loved her. He'd let everybody know how they felt about each other.

'No point in keeping it secret. I want Mother to know,' he'd laughed. But now it had rebounded on their heads.

'Good job you found out in time, Rosie,' the girls in the sewing room had commiserated this afternoon. 'You can't marry your long-lost brother.'

'Narrow escape there, Rosie,' Eric the van driver had whispered at tea break. 'Not much fun marrying your own brother.'

'He doesn't feel like my brother,' she'd snapped back. 'I'm not sure he is.'

'Naughty, naughty.' He'd grinned. 'That will never

353

do.' Rosie found it hard to cope with. It was all too new and painful.

Old Tom was complaining that his chest felt tight, and she heard him coughing. When milking was finished she persuaded him to go home, saying she would bottle the milk for morning. Uncle Will scalded the buckets and churns, and would have put the cardboard tops on the bottles if she hadn't sent him in. She wanted to be alone to think, but thinking didn't help. She felt angry and frustrated, and was afraid she might lose Ben. A share of Shearing's Shirts was no compensation for that.

She went indoors only because she feared supper would be ready, and Aunt Maud cross if she kept them waiting. As soon as she closed the kitchen door and saw Maud's cold grey eyes, she knew Phyllis had told them.

Uncle Will turned round from the table which hadn't yet been set for supper. He looked as though he'd been kicked.

'Is it true? Edwin Shearing's left you a share of his business?'

'Yes.' She took off her old coat, went to the sink to wash her hands. If only Edwin were still alive. She and Ben had had no time to enjoy each other.

'Why?' Her uncle's voice was strangled. 'Phyllis says he was your father. Is that right?'

'Ben says not.'

'It's what they're saying in the office.' Phyllis was at her most intense.

'Could be just gossip.' Will scratched his balding head.

'Mrs Shearing is hardly likely to say that about her husband if it isn't true.'

'Oh, her!' Maud spat. 'She'd say anything to suit her purpose.'

'The Shearings could have stopped our Grace going to the workhouse. They always had plenty of money.' Uncle Will's shocked gaze met hers.

'You've got to be related to them.' Phyllis's eyes seemed to reassess her. Rosie's stomach turned over as she felt the hurt again. She'd already come to the same conclusion.

'Edwin Shearing? I'd have broken his neck if I'd have known. How could he do that to our Grace? Everybody looking up to him. A factory owner. A married man.' It was easy to see Will was troubled. 'He would have been married then, wouldn't he, Maud?'

'Of course he would.' There was bitterness in her voice. 'He married Beatrice Spring almost straight away. Indecently soon.'

'Indecently soon after what?' Phyllis asked, looking from one to the other. The silence was fraught with tension.

'After he broke off with my friend Mildred.'

'You knew one of Edwin Shearing's girlfriends?' Rosie asked, surprised.

'His fiancée. They were engaged for a year – the wedding date fixed and everything. She was a lovely girl. Mildred Patterson she was, her father owned a string of shoe shops. I met Edwin Shearing socially at her house several times.'

'Really?' Phyllis said, amazed.

'What makes you think the Shearings were a class above me?' Her mother rounded on her. 'I was his equal once.'

'Why did you never say? I didn't know you knew him.' Phyllis was still agog with surprise.

'We've come down in the world since I married your father. I'm not cut out for this. I've had a life of drudgery.'

'What made Mildred break it off?' Phyllis was recovering. 'He'd have been quite a catch.'

'Too good a catch, that's why Beatrice Spring wanted him. She got her hooks into him.'

'Well now, Maud, it could just have been Edwin changing his mind. He saw someone he thought suited him better.'

'She poisoned him against poor Mildred. Told him a pack of lies.'

'Beatrice Shearing gets what she wants,' Phyllis said slowly. 'Steamrollers over everything in her way. Nobody stands a chance against her.'

'Her father drank, the Springs were nothing, the whole road looked down on them. Socially, her family was beyond the pale. I'm surprised the Shearings even looked at her.'

Rosie heard the bitterness in her aunt's voice. She could see envy in her face. Maud hated to think Beatrice had done so much better in life than she had.

'Come on now, Maud. She was a good-looking girl then.'

'Are you saying Mildred wasn't?'

'No, Maud, I'm not saying that,' Will protested. 'Oh God!'

356

'She never got over it. Went into a decline she did. Poor Mildred, she's been in her grave these last twenty years. I blame him for that.' Maud swung round on Rosie. 'Edwin Shearing had a cruel streak in him. A very cruel streak.'

'What do you mean?' she gasped.

'He didn't care how he hurt her. Quite heartless. A selfish man. It broke her heart.'

No, Rosie wanted to protest. No, he wasn't like that at all. He was kind and considerate. She'd always known Maud was bitter.

'You ought to get your own back on them for what they did to your mother.' Maud put her face close to Rosie's. 'Get your own back on them for what Edwin did to my friend.'

'No, Aunt Maud. You must know I'm not the sort to seek revenge.' Anyway she couldn't do anything that might hurt Ben.

'Don't be a fool. Break it off with him before he throws you over. You'll have to now anyway. Nobody can marry their half-brother.'

Rosie wanted to push her aunt away. She could almost feel Maud's hatred, white hot and intense. It dragged at her face, deepening her furrows of discontent.

Rosie could see Phyllis eyeing her, looking almost pleased at the ways things were turning out. 'What are you going to do then?'

'We've got to find out who your father was,' Uncle Will said. 'No two ways about it, you've got to know now.'

Rosie felt she was being torn in two. She could no

longer think calmly about her own father. Ben was telling her he was convinced it was Harry, but clearly he was worried. She knew she was growing obsessed with the need to find out for certain one way or the other.

That night, Rosie re-read the letter she'd had from the solicitor. It occurred to her that Edwin's will might give the reason she'd been left a share in his business. She mulled this over for a few hours at work the next day before the need to know drove her to take action. She wanted to discuss it with Ben, but when she went up to his office he wasn't there.

'He's in with his mother.' Phyllis nodded towards the cubicle as Rosie walked past her desk in the hall. Rosie wavered for a moment, but she needed to do more for herself, not wait for Ben to do it. He had enough to see to now two members of his family no longer worked in the business.

She could see the solicitor herself, couldn't she? She had a perfect right to know why she was in the will at all. Surely she had guts enough to ask?

'Tell them I've gone out for an hour or so, Phyllis,' she said, and then headed quickly to the cloakroom to get her coat before she lost her nerve. Ben would be delighted if she could sort this out. She caught the bus into Birkenhead.

Every other time she'd come to Hamilton Square she'd been impressed by the finely proportioned buildings of Storeton stone, the well-maintained gardens, and the impressive clock tower on the town hall. Today she hardly noticed them. She was trying to summon up courage, trying to formulate the questions she'd need to ask, and to get her nerves sufficiently under control so they would not show.

She wandered round the square, trying to find the office of Pringle and Bateson, Solicitors. When she realised she was going the wrong way she turned back. Her heart was beating too fast when she saw the brass plaque beside the front door and she hurried straight past it, making up her mind to circle the whole square again. When she came to the office a second time, she forced her feet up the front steps. The clerk in the outer office looked up politely.

'Do you have an appointment?'

'No.' She was filled with confusion. What had she been thinking of? To make matters worse, a door was opening further down the hall and a client was being shown out.

'You couldn't have timed it better,' the clerk said. 'I'll tell Mr Pringle you're here.'

Moments later she was being shown in and her hand was being shaken. His office overlooked the square. From the chair she'd been offered Rosie could see out over the shrubs and formal flowerbeds. The partner's desk seemed intimidating, the atmosphere rarefied and legal. Rosie fixed her gaze on Mr Pringle's face which was puffy with a bulbous nose. She drew out the letter he'd sent her and pushed it across his desk.

'I'd like to know why Mr Shearing left me a share in his business,' she told him. 'It came as a surprise.'

'But you knew him?'

'I worked for him. He's left nothing to the rest of his workforce.'

'It could be that the relationship is a little embarrassing.' He cleared his throat, seeming embarrassed himself.

'I was wondering if you could read me the relevant part of his will?' Rosie got into her stride. 'I mean, doesn't a will say "To my wife I bequeath . . . To my son I leave . . ."? I'd like to know how he describes me. What was I to him?'

Mr Pringle seemed discomfited, even uneasy. 'I suppose there would be no harm in that.'

Rosie watched him slowly get to his feet and fetch a deed box with the name Shearing on the side. He took out the will. It seemed to take him a long time to find the relevant place.

'Here it is,' he said, but he was looking up at her again. 'I did explain in my letter, didn't I? Under the will of Ainsley Shearing, who was Edwin's father, one-third of the business went to Mrs Constance Shearing for her lifetime. Then it will revert to the members of the family who are being given a share now. Thus it will increase your share too.'

'Yes.' Rosie tried to keep the impatience out of her voice. Mr Pringle began to read: ' "The remaining two-thirds of the business to be divided into six equal parts. Two parts of which I leave to my wife Beatrice. One part each to my three sons, Oliver, Benjamin and Stephen, and one part to Miss Rose Evadne Quest, of Ivy Farm, etc." '

'It doesn't help,' Rosie said, cold with disappointment. She got slowly to her feet, and then sank back on her chair.

'Do you know?' She'd wanted to be able to go to

Ben and tell him she'd cleared it all up. 'Did he ever say anything about me? What I was to him?'

He was scratching his flabby cheek. 'Why don't you have a word with Mrs Beatrice Shearing?' he suggested at last. 'I'm sure she'll be able to explain it to your satisfaction.'

'I already have. I just wondered if there was some way I could confirm . . . It seems so unbelievable.'

He smiled reassuringly. 'There's no necessity to confirm anything. The will is legal, I drew it up for Mr Shearing myself. Of course, it has to go to probate, but you're a very lucky girl to be remembered in this way. Very fortunate.'

'Yes.' She stood up. 'Thank you anyway.' All she wanted now as to make her escape. She'd drawn a blank.

'Flash! Giddyup! Come here.'

In Kelvin Close Will Quest clicked his tongue for his horse's attention. He didn't get it.

The houses here had little patches of grass in front of them which meant he had further to walk to get the milk on the doorsteps. He always went up one path taking his carrying crate, stepped over the fences which were only eighteen inches high to put down his bottles, and returned to the road by a different path.

Flash knew she should walk on to meet him. It was only fifty yards, and she'd been doing it every morning for years. Today, he could see her standing where he'd left her, her nose drooping forlornly an inch or so from the road.

'Flash, come here.' At last he saw the horse strain

against her harness to make the wheels turn, but he went towards her covering the ground more quickly than she did. 'What is it, old girl?' He patted her dull grey coat as he went behind the float.

This morning it was taking him hours to get round. Flash was probably as fed up with it as he was. Of course it was Friday. The round always took longer on Fridays and Saturdays because he had to knock on doors and ask to be paid.

He was glad he no longer had to worry about renewing the lease on the farm. His mind had been made up for him. He wouldn't be able to go on doing this, year in year out. He'd made up his mind to keep on the house, and the agent had offered to buy his herd of cows at independent valuation if he should so wish. He would do that too. His was the last of the independent farm milk rounds in the district, there was no possibility of selling it. His customers would turn to the big multiple dairies and soon forget him.

Old Tom was too old to work and so was Flash. He would be lucky if they both lasted out this year. If Flash lasted longer he would ask if he could keep grazing for her until building on his land got underway. He was glad the decision had been made.

At this part of the round, he had a few hundred yards to ride. Will hauled himself up to the seat in front of the cart, glad of the chance to tip some of the jangling change from the leather bag he wore across one shoulder into the box he kept under the seat. It could get very heavy.

He was not happy about Maud. She was dead set

against staying on at the farm. But how could he move to another house when generations of Quests had lived and died at Ivy Farm? He couldn't bear the thought of uprooting himself now he knew he didn't have to. It was another disappointment for his wife, one he was hoping she'd accept in time.

She'd never taken the slightest interest in the farm, making out she was too much of a lady to soil her hands milking. Even when she was young and they'd been first married she'd only come out at haymaking or harvest with the worst possible grace. She'd even resented the fact that her housemaid, when he'd been able to afford one, had to help scalding the churns and bottles.

He'd never been able to provide the standard of living she'd expected when she married him. Worse, he'd gone down in the world and Maud was a snob. She always spoke of her father's occupation as that of master builder, though everybody knew he mended broken gutters and renewed rotted window sills. But he had been in business on his own, and had made a better living than Will was doing.

'We never went short at home,' Maud had complained years ago when he'd had to ask her to cut down on household expenses. 'Cut down on what?'

'Hetty's leaving to get married. We can't afford to replace her.'

'No help in the house? How can I manage on my own? Surely you can afford wages for one girl?'

'It's not just her wage, it means another mouth to feed.'

'You shouldn't have saddled us with Rosie. She's another mouth to feed and she makes more work for me,' she'd fired back at him. 'I suppose you'll want me to cut down on clothes and presents and all the little luxuries of life too?'

It had filled her with resentment that eventually they'd come to that too. She certainly felt socially superior to others. She never went into the street without wearing her hat and gloves, because she counted those the accoutrements of a lady. It had made her frosty and ill tempered, unable to show affection except to Phyllis.

Maud's family had had a wide circle of business acquaintances. She'd been expected to marry well; most of her friends managed it. She'd known the Shearings socially and her expectations were based on the standard of living they enjoyed. He'd always known Maud had had richer suitors before him. He'd never been more than a tenant farmer, but at one time he'd seemed more prosperous. As the years went on, he'd been a disappointment. Now, she saw him as a failure.

He'd had to stamp back on the needling of envy he'd felt for the Shearing family in his youth, and for Harry in particular. He had felt envy, there was no reason to deny it now. Life smiled on the Shearings, everything came easily to them.

Once he'd sworn revenge on the man who'd harmed his sister. Now Rosie's new trouble was bringing back the heat he'd felt eighteen years ago, making him want to close his hands round Edwin's throat and strangle the life out of him. Or should he be thinking of strangling Harry?

Will found he was trembling, savage old fool that he

was. Edwin was already dead, and as for Harry, he was probably dead too after all this time. It was too late to think of revenge. He should think of helping Rosie. Of course her father had been one of the Shearings, that was why Grace couldn't tell him. She'd had to keep her mouth shut. She knew he'd have slaughtered the man.

But if only she had, Rosie wouldn't be in this predicament now. She'd looked radiant when she'd brought Ben to be introduced that Sunday afternoon. They'd seemed so much in love, and now this. Unbelievable that she had got herself mixed up with the same family. It was the wheel turning full circle.

But, he told himself, Ben was a decent lad. He liked him. Another thought made him shiver. Hadn't he been very fond of Harry too? Wasn't Edwin a decent man? The more he thought about it, the more afraid Will was.

'Uncle Will, you've got to help me,' Rosie had said last night when they were finishing off in the dairy, and there'd been agony in her voice. 'You knew the Shearings. Which one do you think was my father?'

Her face showed how desperately she wanted it to be Harry, but how could he say whether it was more likely to be him than Edwin? The worst part was knowing he was the connecting link. It made him heavy with guilt that the Shearings had known Grace through their friendship with him.

Yet Grace had not been born when he'd been on friendly terms with Harry. She had been fifteen years younger than he was. Edwin had never come to the farm much, nor known the Quests well. Yet one of them had used Grace as his mistress. He didn't know when or how that had come about.

'Tell me what you remember of them Uncle Will. There must be lots of details.'

He'd tried, but his mind had been like Mersey mud last night and nothing much had come. 'I do remember his home.' Rosie had listened patiently though he knew he was telling her nothing she hadn't seen for herself.

'What was Harry like?'

'A lot of fun, quick at lessons, cleverer than I was. He went to university when I started work on the farm. Everybody expected big things from him, but I don't think they materialised. The world was his oyster but he failed to open it, Rosie. A bit wild perhaps at times. He got me into a lot of trouble at school, one way or the other, though he seemed to have the luck of the devil when it came to avoiding it himself.' Except of course that he'd disappeared when he'd been about thirty-five, leaving a young wife. The weight in the pit of his stomach grew heavier when he remembered Harry had been married.

'I went to his wedding. A real slap-up do. It was in the summer, a hot day. 1906, I think, or would it be '05?' Why would he, a recently married man, take up with Grace?

'We know my father was a married man, Will. He'd have married Grace otherwise. When was Edwin married?'

He had no idea. 'I wasn't invited to his wedding.'

'He was married at the time I was born, because both Oliver and Ben are older than I am.'

'I know Harry's wife,' he said suddenly. 'She buys her milk from me.'

'Really, Uncle Will? Why, that's marvellous news. Do you know her well? Can you find out if she knew Grace?'

Rosie had been really excited, and he wanted to help but didn't know how to. After all, he didn't know for sure that Grace had been Harry's mistress, and even if she had, it was possible Alice Shearing had never known. Either way, she certainly wouldn't want to be reminded of it after all this time.

They were coming to her house now, number thirty-six Elmhurst Road. It was considered one of the better roads in the district, and the Victorian redbrick terraced houses were a little larger than average. Number thirty-six came at the end of the row and was twice the size of the others.

Will gave a good knock on the polished brass knocker. The white net curtains gave the house an air of respectability. He remembered her moving here in her widow's weeds. Before that they'd lived in a big house in Prenton, too far away for him to deliver milk. It had bothered him at the time that she'd apparently retained so little of the Shearing affluence. She'd never wanted to talk about Harry.

He heard her heavy steps on the hall linoleum before she opened the door six inches. Her eyes sought his, then the door creaked open wide.

Alice Shearing was a large woman who wore her short grey hair permed in tight waves to hug her head. She seemed to fill the narrow hall of her house, but behind her he could see a wheel chair manoeuvring in

the tight confines of a doorway. In her youth Alice had
been a hospital nurse and though she'd given it up
when Harry married her, she still had something of the
old starched efficiency in her manner.

He'd been delivering her milk for more than twenty
years now. She was a good customer because for years
she'd supported herself by taking in gentlewomen in
their declining years, and milk occupied a large part of
their diet. Also, she was the sort of woman who always
had the sum owing to him ready on the hall table when
he knocked on the door. It was in his bag too quickly
for him today.

'My niece Rosie is to marry Ben Shearing. I brought
her up. I'm very fond of her. They're engaged.'

'Really?' She wasn't one to pass the time of day
gossiping. He'd never spoken to her about anything
but her milk order before.

'I think I told you I was a good friend of your
husband when we were boys at school?' She was
drawing herself up to her five foot eight and looking
him in the eye.

'I don't have much contact with the Shearing family
now.'

Will went on faster, 'Ben and I have been talking
about Harry.' The door was closing slowly. 'There are
things he'd like to know . . .'

'I'm sorry.'

'I'm sure you could help.' The gap had narrowed to
eight inches.

'You're asking the wrong person. Ask Edwin's wife,
it was all her doing. Ben's mother. Tell him to ask her,
she knows.'

The door jerked home and the latch caught, but not before he'd seen brooding resentment in her face. He turned away sadly, suddenly blinded by memories. He'd heard rumours all those years ago from other customers. Some working for Shearing's said Harry was dead. Others that he'd gone away after a family row and Alice had decided not to go with him.

When she'd first moved here in 1916, she'd been wearing widow's weeds and he'd assumed they were for Harry. He'd tried to tell her how sorry he was, expecting her to show grief. Instead he'd seen the same burning resentment on her face he'd seen now. At the time he'd wondered if he'd put his foot in it. He hadn't known what to believe. Death had been commonplace then. Perhaps she'd been in mourning for another relative?

Resentment must have smouldered in her for twenty odd years. Her memories of Harry were obviously not happy. Will felt suddenly more hopeful that Harry was Rosie's father, but he was no nearer being sure of it. Certainty was what Rosie needed. Guesswork was no good to her.

'I need the car, Ben.' His mother was coming out of her study as he ran downstairs. 'The keys, please.' Arrogantly assured, she put out her hand. 'You'll have to manage without it tonight.'

He handed them over. 'Are you going straight away?'

'You can see I am.' Her abundant hair was beautifully groomed into its chignon. She was wearing a red fox fur across the shoulders of a pearl grey suit.

'You couldn't drop me in Gordon Drive? I told Rosie I'd be there at seven, and it's five minutes to now.'

'No, I couldn't, I'm late already.' She was running down the front steps. 'The little madam might lose patience with you if you keep her waiting.'

Ben gave in without a fuss. He had a pact with Stephen that if Mother insisted on using one car, they took it in turns to use the other. Tonight it was Stephen's turn to use the Ford.

It was not that he minded so much, Ben told himself. Rosie understood the situation, and they could go into Birkenhead on the bus to the pictures or walk back to the Royal Rock. She was easy to please, happy just to walk along the Esplanade on fine nights, but tonight his face was soon wet with drizzle.

In any case, Ben knew he didn't want to do any of those things. He wanted to take Rosie to the top of her hay barn again. When he wasn't worrying about Oliver or Mother's spiteful ways, he was dreaming of Rosie. Just to think of undressing her there in perfect privacy made him tingle. It was forbidden but it was exciting, and the thought alone was exhilarating.

But he wouldn't suggest it. He must not pressurise Rosie into forbidden things. If she did not wish to make a habit of it before marriage, he would understand and be patient. As he hurried on as fast as he could, he wondered if perhaps, just perhaps, she might suggest it herself? If she did, it would be an entirely different matter. He ought to call in at a barber's and get some french letters, just in case. She wasn't waiting for him in Gordon Drive, so he went up the path to the farm house and knocked on the door. It opened almost immediately and Rosie was laughing up at him.

'Sorry I'm late. Mother wanted the car but she didn't tell me until I was about to set out.'

'Doesn't matter, you're here now.' Rosie was pushing her arms into her best coat.

'What would you like to do? We could still go to the pictures as planned, if we go on the bus.'

Rosie looked at her watch. 'We've just missed a bus, and it's getting late. We'd miss part of the big picture.' They were outside in Gordon Drive, the air heavy and damp. There was a misty thickening to the night, but he would hardly call it drizzle now.

'I want to talk, I have something to tell you.'

Ben caught his breath hopefully and made himself suggest: 'The Royal Rock then?'

'Why don't we go to the dutch barn? We can talk in peace there.'

Suddenly his heart was pounding and seemed to be working at twice its normal speed. 'We might do more than talk, Rosie.' He pulled her round in the street and kissed her with pure joy.

'We need somewhere private to kiss,' she whispered. 'We can't do it here.' She was pulling away.

'Your dutch barn is too private,' he said. 'I might be tempted to do more than kiss.'

'Yes.' She pushed her arm under his. Ben could hardly breathe. He must have pleased her last time. He couldn't believe his good luck.

'We're walking the long way round.' Rosie gave a little giggle. 'Couldn't take you through the farm yard. Uncle Will might have noticed.'

The narrow path between high hedges seemed very dark. Ben felt himself squelching in the mud underfoot as he held on to her hand. Rosie stepped out confidently, keeping to the grass verge. He felt he was being towed along. Suddenly the dog was barking. She stopped and called to him softly in the night. He came towards them wagging his tail, as if in apology for barking at her. Rosie fondled his ears before sending him off.

'We don't want him sitting at the bottom of the ladder,' she whispered. 'It would tell Uncle Will we were up on top.'

'Isn't he indoors now?'

'Not yet or the dog would be tied up.'

The huge bulk of the barn cut out every glimmer of light. Ben could see the ladder leading upwards. 'The dog won't come back?'

'No, Jake does as he's told.' He saw her start to climb, and felt the ladder shake slightly under her weight as she seemed to run up.

'Are you coming?' Her voice was a stage whisper. He could no longer see her. Ben had to feel for the rungs, it was too dark to see anything. He climbed, feeling ungainly and unsafe, glad he's already done it in daylight. The hay seemed to smell more strongly in the night. He was sinking into its fragrant softness. Rosie had his hand again, pulling him over to the far wall. She was giggling as his feet sank under his weight. He was glad to throw himself down.

Now he could see out into the night. From up here Birkenhead was a thousand orange lights, blurred and indistinct in the gathering mist. They sent an orange glow up in the sky. He heard the hay rustle as Rosie moved beside him. He turned to kiss her.

'Let me tell you first.' She was half laughing as she pushed him away.

'What?'

'While we were bottling the milk tonight, I tried to get Will to remember more about your family. He said Harry was married and knows where his wife lives now, but he thinks his wife left him. There were rumours about another woman. It sounds hopeful, doesn't it?

'Grace could have been the other woman.' It was what Rosie desperately wanted. 'I mean, Harry would have had a share of the business if he'd been alive. Wouldn't your dad want me to have it if I was Harry's daughter?'

'That will be it,' Ben agreed.

'I just wish he'd said so.' She told him about seeing Pringle, but not about Pringle's embarrassed hints that Edwin was her father. She wanted to forget those.

'Couldn't you talk to your grandmother about what happened all those years ago?' He could see Rosie supporting her head on one elbow. 'She must know, Ben, she lived through whatever happened.'

'It was something traumatic.'

'Then she can't possibly have forgotten.'

'You're right.' He turned over on his back and stared up into the blackness of the rafters. It was essential he and Rosie found out the truth about her father. But this was his family too, and he had an overpowering interest in what had happened to them.

He started to tell her about the old company

accounts he'd been reading, and of the picture he'd gained of a very successful company up to the time of his grandfather's death. A business that seemed to be teetering on the verge of bankruptcy a few years later, once Harry was in charge.

'It's the only way we're going to find out what really happened,' Rosie urged.

'I just wish I'd thought to ask Dad before he died. He'd have told me right out.'

'Why shouldn't your grandmother do that?'

'She's hiding something, Rosie. I'd like you to be with me when I do it. Two heads are better than one.'

'Go to your house again, you mean?'

'Yes. Why don't I tell Mother I'm bringing you home for dinner on Saturday night? It won't be anything grand, just the family.' He had been about to add: 'You're one of us now', but bit the words back. 'Oliver and his wife will be there, so you'll meet Lydia. You know the rest of us from work.'

'But your mother?' she said apprehensively.

'I'll tell her you're coming. I expect we'll have a meeting first. Usually it's held in the office, but Stephen isn't there any more. The talk will all be about the lack of profit and why. You've a right to be there, Rosie. You've got to stand up for your rights or Mother will kick you into a corner.'

'I don't know.' Her voice was thick with reluctance. 'To eat dinner with your mother . . .'

'She'll be your mother-in-law soon. You'll have to get used to it when you're one of the family.'

'If we're allowed to marry . . .'

'If we aren't, then it's because you're already one of

the family. Will you come?'

He heard her sigh. 'I'll do anything to find out who my father was.'

'Rosie, you've got guts. You're even ready to face Mother. I do love you.' His arms closed round her and he pulled her closer.

CHAPTER SEVENTEEN

Constance slid the dress of fine wool over her head and buttoned it up to the plain round neck. It was taking her longer to dress these days, but she liked to change for her regular Wednesday afternoon outing. All week she looked forward to it. She very rarely went anywhere else except to church on Sundays and to a Mothers' Union meeting one afternoon each month.

Her interests were getting fewer. Once she'd enjoyed shopping for clothes, but having to try things on in the shop made it tiring and she never found exactly what she wanted. She'd worn black and nothing else since Ainsley had died, which ought to make it easier to find something to suit her. But it didn't.

She'd always had clothes made by a dressmaker. Now she never considered any alternative. She liked to stipulate high necks and pin tucks on the bodice. She was never comfortable in clothes that were short, and ready made clothes seemed outrageously so these days. Her legs felt cold if they were not decently covered.

'It's a bit dowdy, Constance,' Beatrice had said when she'd first seen this dress. 'The cloth is superb, the workmanship good, but those big leg of mutton sleeves date from before the war. And just look at the length.'

She'd had to make come concessions to modern fashion, but clearly not enough to please Beatrice. Once it would have been thought daring to go out with one's ankles on show like this, almost immoral. She still had slim and shapely ankles.

She sank down on the stool in front of her dressing table, and felt in her jewel case for the four-strand choker of pearls in the style made popular by Queen Alexandra. It was feeling uncomfortably tight these days when she fastened it round her neck, but it hid the folds of crêpey skin and made her hold her chin up. It seemed to cast a milky light on her face which she found more flattering than dark shadow from her dress.

Her reflection stared back at her. Something in the way she twitched her head from side to side reminded her of a nervous horse about to bolt. Once she'd been thought handsome, but age had made her pale blue eyes look washed out.

It came again. This time she saw as well as felt the tell-tale jerk low in her cheek. Her fingers automatically lifted to hide it, smoothing the thin papery skin near her mouth. A nervous tic the doctor had said when she'd sought his advice, which only served to make it occur more often. She hated it. To be afflicted with such a thing labelled her a nervous wreck, and it wouldn't go away. She had so many wrinkles too, but could anybody be pleased with the way they looked at seventy-four?

Every Wednesday she went to Alice's for tea. It still seemed a slightly daring thing to do, even after all these years. There would be cup cakes and cucumber sandwiches. Beatrice did not approve of her continued friendship with Alice. Nor the fact that she played bridge there.

'Have you nothing better to do with your time than play cards? Such a waste.'

Constance knew she said it to put her down. It was all part of Beatrice's plan to break her nerve, rob her of confidence. Going to Alice's helped to counteract that. Alice showed affection. Constance was good at bridge, she could win if the cards fell right.

She shook out her white cotton dressing cape and put it round her shoulders before unpinning her hair. Very necessary if one wore black. Her long white hair uncurled and fell halfway down her back. She brushed it vigorously. Once she'd given it a hundred strokes every night to make it shine. It was getting thinner, and she was finding it hard to make it cover completely the horsehair pads she used to puff out her upswept style. She had seen her own mother take the hair left on the bristles of her hairbrush and wrap them round the pads to make them the same colour. It was a trick she had used since her hair went white, but lately in a mirror she could sometimes glimpse the dead matt finish of the pad.

She sprayed herself generously with eau de cologne from one of the cut glass bottles Ainsley had given her as a wedding gift, and tossed off her dressing cape. She was pleased with her hat, though Beatrice had sniffed at that too.

'Positively Edwardian, Constance. Far too big, and all that decoration is a little vulgar.'

'I like the flowers.' The large brim was covered with fluttery silk petals in black and white. They even climbed up the deep crown.

'Hats are worn smaller today, much smarter. That dwarfs you.'

'Perhaps we all like what we wore in our heyday,' she'd retorted. She imagined now a younger face beneath it, the hair that showed golden blonde instead of white.

'You do cling to the past so,' Beatrice had sneered.

Constance shivered. Did she? There was no logical reason why she should, her past had been painful, traumatic even. She would like nothing better than to slough it off as a snake sloughs off its old skin. She would love to emerge free of it, but her past came to haunt her when she least expected it, echoing on and on down the years.

Often she'd get up in the morning feeling happy and content with her lot, yet she had only to reach for her corsets to bring Beatrice's face before her. Beatrice had made and fitted her corsets for as long as she could remember. They were good corsets, she knew she'd not find better anywhere else. Beatrice kept her styles up to date.

But beneath her fingers her modern stays could turn into the rigid padded corsets of the turn of the century, designed to produce the fashionable hourglass figure. She'd had corset covers too in those days, trimmed with frills of broderie anglaise to fill out her bosom.

She'd never been as buxom as the fashions of those days required.

Constance jumped to her feet and paced to the window. Beatrice and her mother had been fitting her for new corsets on that most dreadful of days. She knew she was breathing more quickly, she could feel her heart beginning to race. She had promised herself she'd never think of that day again, but she couldn't help it. She made herself take deep breaths. The garden below looked serene, the lawn freshly cut, the borders bright with summer flowers. The mature trees of Rock Park cut them off from their neighbours, making the houses seem further apart than they were. A garden could restore serenity and an easy mind. It had not changed since the days she had played there with Harry when he was a baby.

'You do cling to the past, Constance . . .' She could hear Beatrice's strident bossy tones now, though she was safely out of the way at work. It made it easier to go about the things Beatrice didn't like, knowing she wouldn't have to face her in the hall. Constance went back to her dressing-table to continue dressing; added a pearl and gold brooch, some pearl earrings. She wore her rings always.

She heard the front doorbell and pushed herself upright. Her black alpaca coat was ready on her bed. She slid her arms inside and buttoned it up. Mrs Roper's step sounded on the stairs.

'Your taxi is here, Mrs Shearing.' She found her calfskin bag.

'Thank you. I'm ready.' In the hall she picked up the large bunch of gladioli she'd had the gardener cut for poor Alice earlier in the day.

The driver was opening the door of his cab as she went down the steps. She didn't need to tell him where she wanted to go. He'd been taking her to Alice's house for three o'clock on every Wednesday afternoon for several years, and collecting her for the return journey at nine. She liked having the same man. Though his manners left something to be desired, she need have no worries about his not finding the house, or taking her elsewhere, or robbing her or something. She never felt secure with strangers.

It was pure delight to see something of the outside world, the highlight of her week. Constance sat back to enjoy the ride. It was never long enough and took her through streets that were sadly poor. Alice had nothing to thank Harry for. The Shearing men made disastrous husbands. Harry had been as bad as his father.

Her cab was drawing up in front of a redbrick house at the end of a terrace. At the front there were two bay windows behind a privet hedge and low wall. The front door was at the side of the house, and was opening before she'd had time to get out. Constance stepped straight off the pavement into the lobby. Alice, big-boned and gentle, was kissing her cheek and drawing her down the narrow hall.

'Your hands are cold, do come to the fire.' Alice knew she appreciated a fire even on a summer day. She had a lovely manner that seemed to cosset. Constance followed her into the small sitting room, and marvelled that Alice had achieved gentility here. She had the right décor, and the carpets, curtains and furniture had come from the home she'd shared with Harry. Everything in the best of taste and of good quality. A maid was handing round cups of tea and cucumber sandwiches.

'How are you, Emmeline?' Constance bent over the wheelchair to kiss her cheek. It did her good to see poor Emmeline, decades younger but with arthritic hands that found a teacup hard to hold. Alice was helping her to sandwiches, putting her plate in easy reach.

Two other old ladies greeted her with pleasure. They'd both been here for over a year so she was getting to know them. They all enjoyed an afternoon of bridge, and Emmeline said she'd sharpened up their game. They were chatty and friendly and of her own generation. Once she would not have considered women such as the widow of a schoolmaster her social equal, but things had changed.

They were all ladies, Alice was very particular about who she took in, but of course they had to come from straitened circumstances to find Elmhurst Road acceptable.

'Do come and talk to Emmeline,' Alice encouraged her. 'She so looks forward to your visits. Little enough to look forward to these days.'

'Then it's a good thing she enjoyed her youth,' Constance said without bitterness. Emmeline had deserted a good husband to run off with another man. Nobody dared ask where he was now.

'I don't think she considers her illness a retribution.' Alice smiled.

Emmeline's cards had to be set up in a stand in front

of her. It tired her poor hands too much to hold them through a rubber or two.

Constance sighed. Edwin had done his best to make her see her life as idyllic. 'You're in your own home, cared for by your own family. What could be more comfortable than that?'

'I always feel at a loose end.'

Beatrice had exploded with impatience when she'd heard her say that. 'You have time to please yourself. Time to do all the things you want to. You said you enjoyed embroidery . . .'

But her fingers had grown stiff, it was years since she'd tried, she no longer wanted to. The trouble was she was lonely. The family went about their own business and mighty busy they were. Especially Beatrice.

She'd always thought of Alice as young, but already she was middle-aged. How transient this life was.

Alice said: 'Someone was asking about Harry last week. It bothered me a bit. I mean, after all this time, who would be interested in Harry?'

Constance froze. 'Who?'

'My milkman. Said he was a friend of Harry's.'

'No, he couldn't be. What did he want?' Constance felt her palpitations start, her pleasure in the afternoon fading.

'I don't know. He said his name was Will Quest. Do you know him?'

'Quest?' Where had she heard that name before? 'A milkman? No.'

Alice had gone, the two old ladies were talking, but Constance heard nothing but echoes from her past.

They must be on to her now. Somebody certainly
suspected her if they were asking questions. She'd
been wrong to think she was safe, even though it must
be twenty years . . . She felt a headache coming on.

When Alice came back into the room, she asked:
'What did you say the man's name was?'

'William Quest.'

'I do remember him now, but they told me he was a
farmer. He was Harry's friend.' She must not let it
frighten her, must not let it show.

'And Rosie, Ben's fiancée, is his niece. She's really
one for delving into the past. Ben asked me to say she
wants to meet you both,' Constance said. 'They're
both badgering me. They think she could be related to
the family. Perhaps you'd know, Emmeline?'

'I can't think . . .'

'Bring her with you some time, if you want to,' Alice
said, on her way out to the kitchen.

Rosie opened her wardrobe to assess the clothes
swinging on their hangers. She didn't want to wear her
pale green wool because all the Shearings had seen her
wear that to work. She took out her blue dress, but
she'd spilled orange juice on it. She flung it on her bed.
She'd have to take it to the cleaners.

The thought of going to Ben's home made her feel
fluttery. That he wanted her to attend a business
meeting too turned the screw.

When meetings had been held in the office, the staff
tiptoed round and behaved with deference, never
interrupting. But it was an ordeal she had to face. If
she insisted on keeping her distance, it was possible

she'd never find out who her father had been.

Rosie's first encounter with Ben's grandmother had been unnerving. His brother Oliver could reduce her to pulp with his arrogant gaze, but the thought of sitting down to eat a meal with his mother as well was frankly terrifying.

'You have a new dress,' Ben said when she asked his advice. 'That peach-coloured one with a shawl collar. You look very nice in it.'

'Will it be all right?'

'It'll be fine, Rosie. Don't let Mother put you down. She'll try.'

Rosie wondered why she should feel so much at ease with Ben, and so much at odds with the rest of his family. Of course, she had liked his father, and she could get along with Stephen, but Ben must have traits in common with the other two. She tried to pinpoint them but failed. Ben was different, she loved him.

She spent Saturday afternoon washing her hair. She would leave it loose about her shoulders to make it look as different as possible from the way it did at work. She was glad Ben had said he would come and fetch her in the car. It meant she wouldn't have that awful moment of waiting for her knock on the front door to be answered.

'Don't forget we're going to ask questions about Harry and Grandpa,' he said as soon as she was in the car. 'Between us, we'll pin them down. Don't let them change the subject. Aim your questions at Grandma, she'll give in more easily than Mother.'

As Ben drove through the gates, Rosie saw Oliver

and his wife getting out of their SS Jaguar on the forecourt.

'Lydia's wearing a full-length dinner dress.' She was shocked. Lydia also had a smart fur cape round her shoulders.

'I never dress up, nor does Stephen. It's ridiculous, just for the family. Dad wouldn't be pushed into it except for formal occasions so we get away with it too.'

'Are you sure this is all right?' Rosie looked down at her peach linen. She was afraid Ben had said it would do because he knew she hadn't an evening dress. She'd felt good in it until a few moments ago.

'Quite sure.' He was smiling at her. 'You look very pretty. Grandma dresses as though for a banquet every night of the week, and Mother affects those full-length skirts. Oliver will probably be wearing black tie. Take no notice. Come and meet Lydia.'

Rosie felt dazzled by her platinum hair and elegant clothes, but Lydia smiled easily at her and put out a slim hand tipped with scarlet nails. She was friendly and unaffected. Rosie wanted to respond, shake off the shackles that still bound her. 'Lovely to meet you' was all she had time for.

She was being swept into the hall with the others where they were greeted by Beatrice Shearing wearing an elegant floor-length dinner dress in brown and cream stripes.

As Ben had predicted, Oliver was wearing a dinner jacket. He kissed his mother, as did Lydia who even seemed pleased to see her. Rosie hung back, knowing a kiss would not be expected of her.

'Good evening, Mrs Shearing,' she managed when

her turn came, and was glad Ben chose that moment to help her off with her coat. It allowed her to shut out Beatrice's unwelcoming manner.

'I'm afraid Ben has brought you on an inconvenient evening. We're having our monthly meeting. With Stephen no longer working at the office, it's easier to have it at home now.' Beatrice's smile was frosty.

'Well, now we're all here,' she went on, 'we'll go to my study. Lydia, will you take Rose into the drawing room for sherry? She can help you entertain Constance. We won't be more than half an hour, dear.'

Rosie could see Ben was about to protest, but he'd told her to stand up for herself.

'Ben brought me so I could attend your meeting, Mrs Shearing,' she said as politely as she could. Beatrice's dark eyes, full of shocked affront, fixed on hers. Never had she looked more formidable, more straight-backed.

'We'll discuss whether you should be invited to future meetings.' Her voice was icy. Rosie felt she was being cut out and looked to Ben for support. His dark eyes said: Don't let her get away with that, Rosie. Stand up to her.

'The way I see it, Mrs Shearing, if I'm being given an equal share of the business, I'm entitled to equal rights too.' She was heartened by the look of rage on Beatrice's face.

'Of course she is, Mother. It would be a waste of time to discuss whether Rosie is entitled to attend.' Ben was hovering at her shoulder. 'She must be treated exactly as we are.' Rosie realised then that Oliver was bristling with indignation.

. 'It may be possible to dispute the will. Really, Mother, you've been very high handed. I should have gone to the solicitor with you in the first place. I'm legal adviser to the company. I went yesterday to see old Pringle about this. He told me he's already applied for probate.'

Beatrice blushed. 'You had no business to go. I can assure you the will is legal. There's no way round it. We can't talk here, we'd better go into the study.'

They followed her in. She immediately pulled out the chair behind an enormous desk and sat down in the position of power. Oliver commandeered the only other upright chair. By Rock Park standards it was not a large room, but it was not small either. There was a fire in the grate, and as in all the other rooms a high ornate ceiling with heavy plasterwork.

Rosie found herself heading for the only armchair overlooking the garden. She drew back. It would place her apart from the others. Stephen flung himself into it, and lit a cigarette.

'Hang on,' Ben said, 'I'll get us some chairs.' A moment later he brought two from the dining room, and Rosie found herself next to Oliver. He turned on her belligerently.

'Father must have been out of his mind, leaving a share of the business to you!'

'Just a minute,' Ben said. 'I think we ought to start by discussing how you creamed off last year's profit. Your position needs clarifying. I gave you an ultimatum: stop working in the business, get out and I won't got to the police. In the upset of Dad dying your future has never been resolved.'

389

Ben looked round at the others. 'None of our shares will be worth much if Oliver is allowed to get away with this.'

'We must keep this orderly,' his mother put in firmly. 'We do have an agenda. What about the minutes of the last meeting?'

'Put this top of the agenda,' he retorted. 'Oliver does little useful work. The business can't afford to pay him the salary it does now. What about the job Lydia's family is offering?'

'This is a bit much in public,' Oliver choked. Rosie was surprised to see how easily Ben shattered his brother's veneer of self-confidence.

'We're all shareholders, it's our money you took,' Ben retaliated. 'This is as private as we can get. I should have called in the police. None of you is taking it seriously enough.'

'Ben, we've had too much trouble recently. We've lost both Stephen and your father from the office. We need Oliver. He's going to apologise, and pay back what he took.'

'*You're* making that decision, Mother? I think we should have a vote on it: should we exclude Oliver from the office, Stephen, what do you say?'

'No!' Beatrice thundered. 'Doesn't the family mean anything to you? It's nonsense to talk of the police. This is a family matter, and we'll keep it that way.'

'We should vote on it,' he persisted.

'We are evenly split,' his mother snapped back. 'I have two votes, don't forget, Oliver one. We are three against three.'

'There's Gran.'

'She's never been brought into business matters. She wouldn't understand what we are talking about. I know you could persuade her to vote on your side, but half an hour later, I could persuade her to reverse it. Not fair to involve her. Anyway, she'd think you were trying to harm Oliver. He won't touch delivery notes in future.'

'How do we know he won't think up some other method of lining his own pocket?' Ben was shaking with rage. It was a side of him Rosie hadn't seen before. 'Are we to waste our time making sure he doesn't, instead of getting on with real work?'

Rosie thought Oliver apologised gracefully and at length. It surprised her how quickly he recovered and turned on her again.

'I do think Father should have thought twice about including you as a beneficiary.' His eyes were raking her up and down. 'It means there's less for the rest of us. Quite unfair.'

Stephen was sitting next to him. Rosie was afraid from his expression that he felt much the same. It was only natural, she told herself, that they should resent her. If Edwin had left her nothing, life would be a lot simpler.

Oliver and Stephen said a good deal more in the same vein. Rosie cringed silently, feeling their resentment directed at her and finding it very unpleasant. She was opening her mouth to tell them she'd never asked for a share and didn't want it when she saw Ben shake his head almost imperceptibly. The moment passed. She'd only have prolonged the argument if she'd spoken up.

'You seem to have got yourself an interest in several estates, by one means or another,' Oliver said pointedly.

'Is the other nearing settlement?' It seemed a good opportunity to ask. She'd been wondering about it.

'No, an intestate estate takes a long time to sort out. You'll have to be patient.'

'You'll let me know when it is?'

'I'll let the beneficiary know.' His manner was as cold as his mother's.

Rosie shivered. The meeting was dragging on beyond the half hour Beatrice had estimated. The enmity she saw sparking between Oliver and Ben was making her colder still. Much was being said about profits and their lack that she didn't understand. They seemed to be talking a different language.

At last they were moving out to the drawing room. Rosie found the dancing flames in the white marble fireplace cheering, and was careful to choose a seat near Lydia and Constance, hoping they would be more friendly. Her mouth felt dry and the glass of sherry Ben put in her hand did nothing for her thirst. He was edging on to the sofa beside her.

'Grandma would like a game of bridge.' Lydia was smiling. 'Do you play, Rosie?' She had to shake her head.

'We could teach you,' Ben said. 'We often used to play a few rubbers when Dad was alive. We enjoyed it, didn't we, Gran? She's a pretty astute player, Rosie, better than the rest of us.'

'I've been playing longer than the rest of you,' said Constance.

'We had to split Gran and Dad. As partners they were unstoppable. You taught us all, Gran, would you teach Rosie? Easier then to find four.'

'Yes, if she'd like to.'

Rosie knew he was trying to make further opportunities for her to see Constance. 'I would,' she said eagerly. 'Yes, please.'

'Did Harry play bridge?'

She recognised that as Ben's opening shot in questioning his grandmother once more. She wondered where he found the energy after the fight he'd put up at the meeting.

It took Constance longer to answer. There was a frightened look in her pale blue eyes. 'Yes, I believe so.'

'Was he a good bridge player?'

'Can't remember after all this time.' Her voice was irritated. 'What does it matter now?'

'Just interested. I've been reading the company accounts and reports, Gran, going back years,' he said with a smile. 'I'm fascinated with my antecedents. Tell us about Harry.'

Constance grunted with distaste. 'The past is best forgotten. No use raking over old troubles.'

'Did Harry bring troubles?' Ben was leaning forward. 'That would be 1916, wouldn't it?'

'We all had troubles then.' His mother jerked to her feet. 'The war was on. I think it's time we had our dinner.'

'The company had its troubles too?' he persisted. 'Was there war work?' The wind had risen. It rattled at the three arched windows and carried rain against the glass to blur the distant lights of Liverpool.

'We made shirts for Tommy. Thick khaki flannel, as many as we could turn out,' his mother said.

'So there were no company problems?'

Beatrice seemed to notice the blustering wind for the first time. Clucking with impatience, she went from window to window, pulling the heavy velvet curtains to shut out the night. 'There are always problems in a business like ours. It's time we had dinner.'

Rosie trooped out behind the others to the dining room, thinking Ben's efforts to find out more about Harry had come to naught. His grandmother seemed more in command of herself tonight than on the first occasion Rosie had met her. She was keeping a tight rein on her tongue.

Beatrice indicated where she must sit. Fascinated, Rosie watched the Shearings' family meal routine. The old lady said a long and formal grace. Silver and glass glittered against the stiff white cloth. Across the table Ben's eyes were telling her to keep questioning his grandmother.

Beatrice was filling bowls with thick fragrant asparagus soup. Rosie marvelled at the speed with which she floated a whirl of cream on top then added asparagus tips before handing the bowls up the table.

'Would you pass me the pepper, please?' Constance asked, and Rosie moved the heavy Victorian cruet of malachite and cut glass up the table to her.

Constance sprinkled pepper generously on to her soup, wondering what had happened at the meeting to charge the atmosphere with such tension. She could feel it sparking round the table. Nobody would explain the cause to her, she was an outsider who didn't understand business, but she could see Ben fulminating, and Beatrice had dripped soup on the clean cloth which was not like her at all.

Constance guessed somebody, probably Ben, had challenged Beatrice's authority. She had prayed that one day it would happen, that the next generation would mature and snatch back the power Busy Bee had built up for herself. Hadn't she seen it happen before? Tonight Beatrice looked strained, scowling up the table at them all. Constance smiled to herself.

The young girl with the auburn curls was leaning closer. She too looked tense as she said: 'I'd like to know more about my father, Mrs Shearing. I know nothing of his early life.'

Constance tried to remember who she was. 'Hilda?' Not Hilda Shearing, but so like her.

'It's Rosie,' Ben said across the table. 'Rosie Quest. Mother says Edwin was her father as well as mine.'

'Really, Ben, this is not the place!' Beatrice had a face like thunder. 'Not a suitable topic for conversation at the dinner table.'

'Why not? We're all family here, and Rosie and I need to know.'

'There's Lydia. Not in front of her, it's not right.'

Oliver's wife laughed. 'My generation is not so delicately brought up.'

One of the daily women they employed was bringing hot plates to the sideboard. She turned to the table and started to collect the soup bowls. Harry was blustering:

'Of course she's family.' No, it wasn't Harry, it was Oliver.

Mrs Roper brought the saddle of mutton to the table, and Beatrice's angry eyes were signalling that nothing more must be said on the subject in her presence. Constance tore her bread roll to tiny pieces. She was mistress of this house. It hurt that no one seemed to remember that.

Busy Bee had her own ideas about how it should be run. She'd changed everything, taking every decision herself and never consulting Constance. She'd resented it, was that so surprising? Edwin had resented it when Harry . . . Ben was saying something else, but she couldn't catch it. 'I beg your pardon?'

'I just said I know nothing of Father's childhood or early life. He had a boat, didn't he, once? You must have lots of anecdotes to tell about him.'

Constance jerked nervously. She didn't want the family to think her mind was always running in its own grooves. She often had to claw her way back to the current conversation in a hurry. She tried to do so now.

'Edwin was a good boy. An upright man with a conscience, a church-goer. Always doing his best for the family and the business. Made sacrifices for both.'

Constance saw the girl look to Ben for reassurance before saying: 'That's the way I saw him.'

'Where is Edwin tonight?' Constance asked querulously, looking round the table. 'Always going off on his own. Never tells us where he's been.' He'd not come to the drawing room for drinks either.

She was suddenly aware that six pairs of eyes had

swung to stare into hers. There was blind horror in all of them.

'Gran,' Ben was reaching for her hand and saying gently, 'he died two weeks ago.'

Constance felt her heart jolt and a wave of panic wash through her.

'Of course! How silly.' Every stark detail of Edwin's funeral was in the forefront of her mind now. How could she have forgotten?

Living in a household of busy people all rushing about their own business only served to underline how empty her life had become. They had so little time for her. She was often alone and naturally thought of times gone. She saw Beatrice watching her, eyes full of contempt, and felt a terrible urge to get even with her.

The girl was talking to her again, but she pitched her voice so low it was an effort to hear her.

'You must be my grandmother too.' Constance looked into her earnest green eyes. Not Hilda, Rosie. That was it, Rosie.

'No, no,' she replied.

Ben said: 'Whether it was Harry or Edwin, they were both your sons. Surely you know? Was it Harry?'

'Harry couldn't help it. We loved him to distraction, even Ainsley did. He wouldn't have shot himself if . . .'

'Stop it, Constance!' Beatrice's words came slashing up the table like a whiplash, leaving her gasping.

'Stop it all of you.' Beatrice was on her feet, her face scarlet. 'You're upsetting her, can't you see? Confusing her with your silly questions. Rose, I can't have you here in my house again if you're going to . . .'

'Mother!' Ben was on his feet too. 'You're overstepping the mark. This has more to do with me than with Rosie.'

Constance was still smarting as she struggled to her feet too. It was now or never.

'Beatrice, I have had enough of your domineering ways. Let me remind you this is not your house but mine. I've been wanting to ask you to leave. Trying to think of a polite way to do it. But politeness never bothered you. So just go, will you?'

Nobody moved a muscle. In the dead silence, Beatrice's mouth hung open with shock. She slumped back into her seat. Constance felt triumph flood through her.

CHAPTER EIGHTEEN

It was the moment she had lived for: to see her daughter-in-law cower before the whole family.

Beatrice had raised her voice to scold and to scream at them. Constance kept hers low and well modulated. She wanted to sound reasonable and in control.

'I want you to leave. I invited Edwin to make his home here when he married. It was a bad mistake. Not the worst I've made in my life but bad all the same. You came in and changed everything. You took all my authority, arranged everything to suit yourself.'

'I did it to help you.' Beatrice's voice was plaintive. 'Take the routine running of the household off your shoulders. It was getting too much for you, you wanted me to.' Constance knew she had the upper hand at last. This was a moment to savour.

'No, I wanted nothing from you. Now I want you to leave. Now that Edwin's gone, there is no reason for me to house his wife.'

Mrs Roper came to the door bearing a huge trifle. Beatrice struggled to assert control. 'We won't be wanting pudding tonight.' All her pent up rage spilled out. 'Leave us.' The woman was hesitating just inside the door. 'Immediately,' Beatrice barked.

Constance saw the shocked surprise on the housekeeper's face. 'Please do, Mrs Roper,' she added more gently. They all watched her leave.

'Really, Beatrice, you don't know how to treat people.' The door closed with a careful click. Ben had an arm round his grandmother's shoulder and was settling her back in her chair.

'Gran, don't be hasty, think things through.' She knew he was trying to soothe them over a bad moment.

'You can't live alone, Constance, not at your age. I take it you're putting Stephen and Ben out too?' Beatrice challenged.

'No, they'll both have a home with me. For as long as they want it.' The silence felt uncomfortable.

Stephen said: 'I'm hoping I'll manage something for myself.'

'Me too,' Ben added.

'Yes, of course, you're planning to marry.' Constance knew she must show no sign of weakness now.

'I don't want to be left with you, Beatrice. You've been a cross I've had to bear for half my life. I'm weary of it. I see no reason to put up with you any longer.'

Oliver stirred himself. 'Grandma, as your eldest grandson, I think of myself as head of the family now. I'm telling you, Mother is right. You need someone living with you.'

'I've thought of that. I shall still have Mrs Roper.'

'This is a big house, Gran,' Ben reminded her. 'Unmanageable for one.'

'I know. I've had time to think of that too. I've decided to sell it.'

She saw she'd cut the ground from under his feet. The others looked astounded.

'I've decided to get something easier to run, and more comfortable. This is a very cold house in winter. I've asked an estate agent to call and value it. He'll be here at two o'clock tomorrow. Ben, could you be here then?'

She could see him swallowing his surprise. None of them had thought her capable of making any decision for herself.

'Yes, of course, if that's what you want.' He was quick to recover. 'But you love this house, Gran. You've lived here since you were seventeen. Dad said he couldn't ask you to leave, that you'd never want to.'

'Edwin loved the house and so do you, but I hate it. I always have.'

'Gran! The river, you'll miss that.'

'No. Anyway, my rooms look over the park, I don't see much of the river now.' She looked down the length of the table. Beatrice has resumed her domineering stance. She needed another reminder.

'If I sell it, you'll have to find somewhere of your own, Beatrice. If I keep it you'll hang on and tell everybody I didn't want you to go.' Beside her, she heard the girl gasp with shock.

'Perhaps it's not such a bad thing to sell,' Oliver put in. 'The district's going down . . .'

'What do you know about anything?' Oliver's superior way had riled her as much as his mother's. 'You're just another Harry. A fool looking for the main chance.'

That brought him to his feet. 'I think I'll take Lydia home. Grandmother is routing us all tonight. I expect she'll change her mind in the light of day.'

'Is that what Harry was?' she heard Ben needling at her again.

'You know he was,' she said. 'But it's taken me a lifetime to see it. He was a spendthrift and a fool. Didn't he cause terrible trouble years ago? Didn't it all blow up in our faces?'

'Hold your tongue, Constance. We agreed that was best forgotten. It's been a trying evening, let me help you up to bed.'

'I'm perfectly capable of getting myself to bed, Beatrice.' She kept her voice cold. They were all on their feet, breaking up for the evening more quickly than she'd expected, but she needed no help. 'Good night.'

She climbed slowly, dragging herself up on the gracious curving handrail with one hand, and holding up her long black skirt with the other. The stairs felt steeper than they ever had before, the carpet thick enough to pull at her feet. She was getting old. Old and frightened. Perhaps Beatrice was right, she had left it too late to set up house on her own.

She was breathless when she reached her own rooms, but it was a relief to close the door and rest with her back against it. She ought to feel safe here, with the nursery bars still on the windows, though they did make it prison-like. Away from the restless tides of the river and the constant wind that rattled the windows there.

Strange to think she'd been reluctant to move here at first, but she'd had to get away from the main bedroom she'd shared with Ainsley. She could see her face reflected in the mirror over the nursery grate. Pale and frighteningly old, her skin paper thin.

She had been keying herself up for two days to tell Beatrice she'd have to go. It was a relief she'd done it, and done it in front of the whole family so that her daughter-in-law could not deny she'd been told.

She knew better than to trust Beatrice who was doing her best to make her feel senile. Telling her she hadn't done things she knew she had. Telling her she must have forgotten other things that deliberately she'd never mentioned. Beatrice was trying to convince the rest of the family Constance was too old to matter.

Slowly she began to undress. She'd be glad to lie down. She had so little energy left these days.

Rosie was shaking as she watched Constance climb the stairs.

'You'd better go too,' Beatrice said nastily. 'You've caused enough trouble here for one night. Picking on a poor old lady like that.'

'Don't try to blame Rosie.' Ben headed to the cloakroom to fetch their coats.

'I'm sorry.' Rosie was trying to calm herself. 'I didn't mean to upset anyone, but I'm sure she knows who my father was. I just want her to tell us.'

'I've told you. Constance won't tell you any different.'

'Why were you trying to choke Gran off?' Ben

asked. 'She was about to tell us why Grandfather shot himself. Why don't you want me to know? Why has it been kept quiet all these years? What is this great secret?'

'You're trying to get a confused old lady to say something that isn't true.'

'Just trying to get confirmation, one way or the other.'

'You ought to be ashamed of yourselves,' Beatrice snarled. 'You're brother and sister. You can't marry, not ever. Don't delude yourselves. It would be incest.'

Rosie flinched. The word cut her like a razor. And it was worse than Beatrice supposed: it had already happened.

She watched Ben's face drain of colour, his lips tighten. Then she felt his arm go protectively round her shoulders as he pulled her close in a gesture of comfort and affection.

Two nights later, Ben waited in the car for Rosie. He was going to suggest they went to the cinema. When she came running out, she had her sketch book with her.

'Couldn't we go to the top of the hay again? I've got something I want to show you.'

'Of course, as long as you don't think we're going too often.'

'No,' she laughed. 'I've done a few designs for sports shirts. What do you think?' He took a sketch book from her, laid it across his knee, and turned the pages slowly. 'They'll look very different from anything you have in current production.'

'Anything *we* have,' he corrected. 'The business is as much yours as mine now.'

'Aertex material makes up very differently.' He could see she was keen. 'I've seen some in the shops made from it. Expensive shops like Robbs.'

Rosie was right, the designs looked very up to the minute, high fashion. Shearing's ought to be making shirts like this.

Ben made up his mind. 'I like this one, and this. We could make up a few as samples and see if our wholesalers are interested. I'll have to get patterns made.'

'I could make the patterns for you. I could adapt them from the ones being used now.'

Ben knew he let his doubts show.

'Let me try,' she protested. 'Then you'll see. I spend all my time putting pattern pieces together. It does give me some understanding.'

'Yes, of course it must.' He smiled. 'I'll take you to Percival's. We buy most of our materials from them. You can see what they've got in Aertex and we'll order a few yards.'

'I can start work on the patterns then?'

'Yes, where will you do it?'

'In the cutting room.' She seemed surprised he should ask. 'Bert Davies will help me.'

'All our shirts have fastened down the front till now.'

'I can soon alter that.'

'But what about the range of sizes?'

'That's why I want to adapt a pattern already in use, and why I want Bert Davies to help me. He's working with patterns all the time.' She was knitting her brows in concentration. 'He makes new patterns from those we already use.'

'Yes, I know.' He was surprised at the confidence she was showing. Rosie was shy with people, but not about what she could do.

'Are you going to say anything to your Mother?'

'Not yet. She won't want to try it. She hasn't thought of it, you see.'

He gave her the sketch book back, and put the car into gear. As he drove near, but not too near, the lane that led to the dutch barn, Ben realised he could have taken her to the cinema after all. He'd agreed to Rosie's plans for sports shirts without leaving the car. They were better than he'd expected.

'You go first,' she was saying moments later. 'I'll hold the ladder steady.' He'd told her it gave him a sense of security. He climbed awkwardly to the top of the hay.

'I don't like to see the barn as empty as this.' Rosie was coming up quickly behind him. Since he'd first seen it, the amount of hay had gone down. 'Usually it's filling up again by this time of the year.'

'Easier to reach the end.'

'I don't feel so safe. It doesn't seem so secluded now.'

'Ouch, what's this?' He'd thrown himself down, expecting to be cushioned by the twenty feet of soft hay beneath him. Instead he felt something hard and cold. He was brushing the hay away so that he could see it.

'My mother's trunk. I hid her things here where

Phyllis wouldn't find them. Let me show you.' The lid creaked open. Ben peered at the contents nonplussed.

'Isn't this a lovely dress?' She was shaking it out and holding it against her, the pleasure it gave her showing on her face. It looked creased and smelled strongly of damp. 'It's beautifully made.'

She turned it inside out so he might appreciate how well the seams had been finished off. It was lined with satin that had not survived as well as the wool. 'Just feel it.'

Obediently, he tested the quality between his finger and thumb, turning his face away so she would not see the compassion he felt.

'Grace would have looked smart in it. It was the height of fashion then.' She was taking out button boots to show him and a huge edifice of a hat covered with wilting and crumpled artificial flowers. Everything smelled horrible. 'Twenty-three when she died, no age at all. Strange to think of my mother never growing old. Never more than a girl.'

'Rosie.' He felt for her hand. 'Don't dwell too much on the past.' It seemed unhealthy for her to have such a passion for it.

'I remember hardly anything about her, you see.' She was earnestly trying to explain, pushing red-gold tendrils of hair away from her face. 'I know she had a very hard time. It would take some getting over, wouldn't it? Being all alone, having to go to the workhouse. I feel this terrible urge to know what really happened.'

He squeezed her hand again. 'I don't think there's

any way you can. If your uncle doesn't know, who would?' She was shaking her head sadly.

'Rosie love, I know it came as a shock – the workhouse and all your mother went through. It would make anyone feel sympathy.' He was choosing his words with care.

'Pity,' she said. 'Pity is what I feel for my mother.'

Ben blinked. 'Yes, well, she suffered. But I think it would be better if you put your mind to the future instead of the past.' He was being as gentle as he could. Pity was choking him, but it was pity for her, that she had to cling so tightly to such mementoes.

He found her distress moving, but couldn't help with this. No wonder she was different from other girls.

'Rosie love.' He pulled her to him.

'I'm afraid,' she whispered. He knew she was not far from tears. 'I'm afraid the same thing will happen to me.'

'It won't.' He was vehement. 'I love you, Rosie, I won't let anything bad happen to you.'

'I have the feeling my father loved her,' she said. 'But it still happened.'

'I'll take care of you, I promise,' he said. It was love he showed her, yet again.

Ben stirred as he heard the grandfather clock in the hall strike one. He was sitting up in bed, feeling half asleep already. His eyes were bleary with trying to decipher old company accounts and reports, but they'd held him enthralled for hours.

The company had been highly profitable during all the years of Ainsley's management. He'd died in 1899 at the age of sixty-two, still in harness, still with a well-run business.

Ben found it hard to believe Ainsley had shot himself. Until he'd asked Dad outright, he'd not heard so much as a murmur about it from any of the family. It was almost as though there had been a pact of silence about what had happened.

The accounts had been signed by a Henry Slocombe for the years from 1899 to 1912. The business had continued to make money, but there had been no expansion, no innovations, no change. Typical, Ben thought, of a business run by an honest hard-working manager unlikely to benefit personally from increased turnover, and without full authority.

Then Harry had taken over, and in four short years he'd run the company down to the point of bankruptcy. Money had started to drain out as soon as Mr Slocombe retired. A large sum had gone from the contingency fund without explanation. Another three months and it was drained dry.

That same year, they borrowed money from the bank for the first time in decades. It was spent on a purpose-built office, a new factory and the latest machines. Salaries and expenses increased by prodigious amounts, particularly Uncle Harry's. Edwin drew nothing from the business once he joined up.

From then on a large slice of their earnings had to be paid to the bank as interest on their loans. There was a shortage of ready cash in the coffers to pay day to day expenses. No wonder Dad had paled when Ben had mentioned his own ambitions to rebuild the Albert Hotel.

Turnover increased in 1913. The company had Government contracts to make shirts for the armed forces even before war began, but it meant an increase in staff and the money it generated was insufficient to solve the cash flow problems.

There were copies of more contracts in 1914. Another dramatic increase in turnover. War should have been good for the business. Certainly the factory was working hard, but it made next to nothing in profit. There had been another bank loan to pay interest on earlier loans.

Ben groaned, it made depressing reading. Undoubtedly the figures showed mismanagement and gross incompetence, but surely nobody could bungle things to this extent unless the shirts had been priced too cheaply for them to make a profit?

Harry seemed to have been taking large sums of money out for his own use, nothing else would explain it. Whatever the money had been spent on, it had contributed nothing and had left the business seriously depleted of capital.

Had he found, Ben asked himself, another black sheep in the Shearing family? Had Harry spent money on high living or gambling or womanising? If only Dad were here to ask . . . but, damn it, his mother must know, and so must his grandmother. He would make them tell him.

Then his mind was off on another tack. Oliver was no businessman. The black sheep trait had come through to the next generation. He mulled over the family characteristics and wondered why Oliver had turned out like Harry while he had turned out . . . like

Ainsley? Well, he hoped he was going to turn out like his grandfather.

Ben heard the clock strike two in the hall below. He put the papers he'd been studying on the floor and switched off his light. His mind still raced with the facts he'd read. He'd spent hours on the years 1912 to 1916, unable to believe what he was seeing.

He knew his father had taken over by then, and Shearing's Shirts had slowly pulled itself back from the brink, but to date it had never been so profitable as it had in Grandfather's day. He could feel himself drifting off to sleep as he thought how good he would feel if he could surpass his grandfather's record.

Beatrice knew she had been sitting at her dressing table for ten minutes doing nothing. This wasn't the first time she had caught herself wasting time recently, and she couldn't understand the change in herself. Suddenly it was an effort to make herself do anything. Her energy had seeped away. She was losing control.

It had been the unexpected sight of the For Sale board erected against the front fence that had done it. She'd not believed Constance capable of going ahead with her plan. Not weak and feeble Constance, who had been so easy to dominate all these years. She felt herself smouldering with indignation again. Ben must have put her up to this. She'd never have got this far without help.

She'd prided herself on foreseeing everything, but she had not thought Edwin would die before Constance. Perhaps it was excusable because in anyone's estimation Constance was overdue to meet her maker. She'd been left owning more than a fair share of Shearing property. All this house, one-third of the business, and had built up a considerable personal fortune because she hadn't spent a fraction of her income over the years. She'd had no need to, Edwin had paid all her living expenses.

Constance was making her feel like a leech. As though she'd been living here all these years on sufferance. Hadn't she worked for it? Without her efforts, the house would have had to be sold years ago. She had a perfect right to be here. She'd earned it.

Beatrice sighed and inspected her reflection in the glass. She'd bathed and changed before dinner. Her long crêpe-de-Chine dinner dress was elegant but black did not suit her, it made her face sallow. It was ageing too. Not only did it show up the tiny wrinkles, it even made her feel older. Black reminded her of Constance. She associated it with enfeebled old age.

Lydia's parents had invited her over. They'd asked Constance too, but Beatrice had declined on her behalf without even telling her. She had more than enough of Constance's company at home.

'About seven,' Alma Feltham had said on the phone. 'Seven till eight. Cocktails before dinner.'

Beatrice sighed. She'd had her dinner, of course. After working all day, she certainly couldn't drink on an empty stomach then wait till eight o'clock for food.

'I know you can't come to a party so soon after – poor Edwin. Not a party, Beatrice. Just a drink with friends. Well, family almost.'

'In-laws,' Beatrice had said.

Now she wished she'd made some excuse to decline.

It would not occur to Alma that it was a long way to go for a drink. It would take her at least twenty minutes to drive each way, and was hardly worth the trouble for the sake of one hour. She'd had to arrange an earlier dinner for the family to fit it in.

She went downstairs, forcing herself to step out in her old brisk fashion, but the moment she'd slammed the car door she was boiling over again with the injustice of it all.

If only Constance had died, it would not have upset the status quo of her life like this. Edwin had been his mother's heir and would now have owned the house. Her hackles were rising. She was blaming Edwin again for leaving her so suddenly.

If Constance had died, it would have eased her lot, taken away one irritation, but nothing was going her way at the moment. Edwin dead, Stephen breaking free, Ben bent on having his own way. And Oliver!

She wanted to weep for Oliver. She'd loved him and he'd let her down. For his sake, she'd done her best to smooth the whole shameful episode over and taken as kind a view of what he'd done as was possible. She'd pretended she wanted to hear his side of the story, even that she believed him. In reality, it had gone against her better judgement to support him.

She'd believed Ben's story from the moment she'd heard it. Truth has a certain ring that makes it instantly recognisable. How many times had Oliver discussed their business objectives, smiled at them as he'd made suggestions, pretended to share their interest in the company's growth? All the time he'd been siphoning off their profits for himself, making it impossible to achieve anything. And he'd been doing it for years. She felt sick when she thought of his duplicity.

She could no longer trust him to do the right thing. Agonised, she remembered saying to Edwin: 'Ben's made him look dishonest.'

'Oliver has stolen from us, he's certainly been dishonest,' her husband had said gently, knowing how it would hurt her. 'Ben's right and you know it. Oliver must go.'

It had been hard to come to terms with that, but she'd agreed they would tell him to go as soon as he returned from Gloucester. But Edwin had died and for once in her life Beatrice had delayed taking any action. The business had been pushed to a back burner for a time. When they'd gone back to it, Oliver had too.

Edwin's death had knocked all of them off kilter. It had also made Beatrice think about the change in the power structure. Edwin had owned two-thirds of the business, Constance one-third, but nobody had ever consulted her about anything.

Beatrice had always known that if she could convince Edwin that a certain course of action was needed, he would be happy to let her take it. Edwin had not been difficult. She'd virtually had a free hand to run the business in her own way.

But Ben had very strong ideas of his own, and she'd no doubt Rose Quest and Stephen would support him. Constance still owned one-third, and would be likely to give Ben her backing whatever he suggested.

Even with Oliver as an ally, her own position was much weakened. The lies he'd told had made a rift between them. She was afraid it would widen with time.

She'd gone up to his office and said: 'If you want this to blow over and keep your job, then you must support me in future.'

He'd looked up and given her his usual charming smile: 'I've always supported you, Mother. Come what may, I've always supported you.'

She wished he would devote himself to the business as Ben did. Wished he had the same flair. But some had it and some had not. The worst part of the whole sorry business was that she could no longer trust her own son.

It was a dark overcast evening, but even so it hardly seemed necessary for the Felthams to have lights in every window. Oliver had been very impressed with their large modern house in Noctorum, a fashionable area of Birkenhead.

Constance had introduced her to Alma's family many years ago. Then her parents had lived in Rock Park too, and attended the same church. Alma's mother had been an enthusiastic organiser of summer fêtes and Christmas concerts. Once Beatrice had thought them very middle-class and nurtured their acquaintance. It had seemed a good thing for a girl needing to rise in the world.

Now she wondered at Alma. In middle age she seemed too fashionable. Her short blonde hair clung close to her head in Eugene waves. She was wearing an elegant backless dress with a pompom on one shoulder.

'Beatrice.' She waved her Sobranie in its six-inch

holder. 'Good of you to come.'

'Been looking forward to seeing you both again.' She smiled, sliding into the role of perfect guest that she'd forced herself to play in her youth.

Alma had been a good-looking girl and was thought to have married well. Her husband Bernard was a good provider, their daughter Lydia had seemed the perfect wife for Oliver. Beatrice was pleased to call them connections by marriage.

Bernard was overweight, and in greeting her was inclined to hold her hand too long. Tonight he kissed her cheek. It was the first time she'd seen him since the funeral.

'How are you, Beatrice?' She thought the sympathy in his eyes rather overdone. 'We've been worried about you. Now then, a cocktail. A Coronation or a screwdriver?'

'A dry sherry, if I may. Really there's no need to worry. I'm quite all right.'

'So much responsibility left on your shoulders. And the business? You're all right there?'

'We're managing, thank you, Bernard.'

'You must be finding it difficult without Edwin at the helm. A worry just now.' Beatrice knew her mouth was hardening. She'd hoped to be lifted away from her own problems, not irritated by their assumption that Edwin had led and she'd followed in his footsteps.

'Fortunately, Ben is just getting into his stride. I'm glad to say he's proving very able. Keen too.'

Alma put in: 'A great pity, Stephen leaving the firm like that.'

'It was all arranged before any of this. He has a job

with the bank. Edwin thought it might suit him better. He wasn't able to contribute as much as the others to the firm.'

'I see. At least you do have three sons, Beatrice. I just hope we aren't taking Oliver's support from you at the wrong moment.'

Beatrice felt every nerve in her body screaming at her, warning her not to say too much now. She sipped at her sherry to gain time. Bernard went on: 'I said to Alma, we must have you over and make sure. I wouldn't want to upset you over this. Stealing your staff, so to speak. Family matters can be delicate.'

She felt suffused with a sudden anger she had to hide. 'Not at all, Bernard.'

Weeks ago, Oliver had mentioned a job at Feltham's as a remote possibility. Clearly it was much more than that now, and he hadn't said another word. Her anger was hardening to suspicion.

'I did ask Oliver if it would be better to wait a few months. So he could see Shearing's Shirts safely through the first year without his father.'

'It won't be necessary.' She knew her voice was beginning to sound angry. What was Oliver up to? She was so terribly afraid he intended to steal more. Why shouldn't he tell them he was about to leave?

'He did tell you how keen we are to have the benefit of his services?'

'Yes,' she said cautiously. Too cautiously. She forced a smile. 'Yes, he did. He seems keen to join you.' She had a sinking feeling in her stomach.

Bernard Feltham smiled in return. 'He did tell us so, but I had to make sure. He's keen to start as soon as

417

possible and suggested next Monday. I do hope that isn't too soon?'

'I wouldn't want to stand in his way.' She slammed down her glass on the table beside her with enough force to endanger the stem.

'Having no son of my own to follow in my footsteps, I'm only too pleased to have Oliver's services. He tells us he's managed your factory accounts?'

He'd dabbled with them. Paid the routine bills. She couldn't have him in the office after this. It was like a slap in the face after she'd gone out on a limb for him.

'Yes,' she said weakly. 'He's a good all rounder, trained in law too.'

'That could be useful.'

'Bernard's very keen,' Alma said.

Her heart was thumping. She'd got out of the habit of thinking on her feet. Oliver had arranged all this behind her back and said nothing. She felt he'd betrayed her again.

It was a relief to see the hands of the clock had reached eight. She had to get out of here. Her cheeks felt on fire. Hadn't Ben warned her Oliver might take more money if they weren't careful? Now she was certain he'd try.

She'd started the car on their drive with a series of kangaroo-like jerks. Once on the road, she was driving too fast. She made herself slow down. She must think.

Of course she was anxious and filled with suspicion, who wouldn't be? What was he up to? She saw now it had been a mistake to let him continue at the office as though he'd done nothing wrong.

She drove to the Albert Hotel. It was securely

locked just as she'd left it at five-thirty. Not a light showed anywhere. She looked round. Everything seemed normal. She went up to Oliver's office and searched methodically through his files. Had everything out of his desk without knowing what she was looking for. She found nothing suspicious.

She felt exhausted as she locked up, but set out then for Oliver's house. Halfway there, she turned back and went home. She'd always despised people who couldn't make up their minds, and now she could not. Beatrice felt she was falling apart at the seams.

She wanted to discuss the problem with Ben, but when she reached home he was still out. She went to bed feeling restless and uneasy. She'd have to wait until tomorrow to deal with Oliver.

Ben felt sleep-sodden. He'd been late coming home last night, and Mrs Roper had brought his morning tea long before he felt ready to get up. It had been an effort to get out of bed at all. He was only half dressed when he heard his mother's quick footsteps coming up to the top floor. She crashed her fist against his door as usual.

'I'm up,' he said. That was what she always wanted to hear. This morning his bedroom door flew open. She was barking at him: 'Did you know Oliver was starting with Feltham's on Monday?'

He buttoned his shirt, trying to throw off the veils of sleep. 'No.'

'He hasn't told us! Why keep it quiet? He's up to something, I'm sure.' His mother was wide awake and so worked up already she couldn't stand still.

'I hope not.' Ben reached for his tie. 'But what's he got to lose if he does help himself again? We already know he's dishonest, and we've condoned it. You shouldn't have stopped me putting him out.'

'I'm sorry.'

That really woke him up. It was very unusual for Mother to be proved wrong. More unusual still for her to apologise.

'He must know we won't queer his pitch at Feltham's. We want him to go. At least, I do.'

'So do I. I can't do with worry like this.'

'Oliver does nothing in the office anyway. He's useless. Makes work for me because I've had to watch him like a hawk.'

'I hope he hasn't . . .'

'Take all his keys, Mother. Tell him to go, and never come back. Watch what he takes away with him.'

'All right, all right, Ben. I know what to do.'

'Then do it. You should have done it as soon as we found out about the delivery notes.'

'What if he's taken more shirts?'

'He hasn't.'

'But if . . .'

'Mother, go away and let me finish dressing. He hasn't, because I've been watching him.' She went at last, leaving Ben filled with surprise at the change in her.

He heard her misgivings over again at breakfast. He was glad they went in separate cars now, in order to have one available for the salesman to use. The Albert Hotel was reassuringly normal, but Mother was at his heels. He took her to the stockrooms.

'There are no shirts missing,' he said.

'Definitely nothing gone from here.' In his own office he went to the safe.

'I couldn't open it last night,' Beatrice complained, she was calmer now but white-faced.

'That's because I keep changing the code. Good security, Mother.'

Everything was as he'd left it. He spread the cheque-books out across his desk for her inspection. 'He's not taken anything else.'

'He's not even in yet,' she complained.

'He will be, in another ten minutes or so. He's always late. You tell him, Mother, and see him out.'

'I certainly will.'

'Don't make too much fuss. No point in letting the whole factory know we've come to the parting of the ways.'

He heard her exasperated grunt before she turned away. Then her heels were beating their usual tattoo down the stairs.

CHAPTER NINETEEN

Constance straightened up in her chair, uncertain whether she'd heard a knock on her door or not, but it was opening.

Ben smiled at her. 'Grandma, I've brought Rosie for her lesson.'

Her mind was a complete blank.

'You promised to teach me to play bridge,' the girl said. 'You did say it would be convenient today? Saturday afternoon?'

'Yes.' She tried to remember making such an arrangement but could not. 'Of course.'

'Where are your cards, Grandma?' Ben was setting up the card table between them. A pack of cards appeared in front of her.

Constance sat back in her chair and smiled, realising suddenly it was a joke. 'Hilda, you've played for years! You're an expert already. We need a fourth . . .'

'I'm Rosie. Rosie Quest.' There was a tremor in the girl's voice.

'You remember, Rosie, Grandma. We're engaged. Going to be married. I'll let you get on with the lesson.'

Constance took deep breaths to still her racing heart, and asked: 'Do you know how to play whist?' It wasn't Hilda! Of course it wasn't Hilda, but the girl was her living image.

'Yes, I think so, though my family only play cards at Christmas.'

'Good, you're halfway there because in bridge we collect suits of cards in a similar way.'

Her hands were clumsy, she couldn't deal the four specimen hands. She dropped two cards face side up and drew in a sharp breath between her teeth. A young, firmly fleshed hand came out in a gesture of sympathy to rest on hers.

'Don't worry about the cards.' Then the slender fingers of the other hand were being held out in front of her. 'I haven't shown you my engagement ring yet. Do you like it?'

Constance touched the hand, moving it into focus to see the pretty opal more clearly. The flesh felt as cold as stone.

'I've heard it said opals are unlucky.' She saw the girl flinch and hurriedly added: 'But, of course, there's nothing in it.'

'Please help us, Ben and me.' She heard the note of desperation. 'I'm sure you know. I'm sure you can. We love each other . . .'

She ought to have loved Ainsley. 'I loved once.'

Constance felt she was becoming a nervous wreck. Francis didn't come to tea on Thursday afternoons now, nor did he allow Clive to come home from school with Edwin.

'I'm so glad you took my advice,' Hilda murmured. 'Though I didn't mean to imply Francis shouldn't come at all. He's unworldly, of course. It wouldn't occur to him that a lady's reputation could be at risk with a man of the cloth. I do hope it didn't upset him to have it mentioned?'

Constance knew Francis had come one night to talk to Ainsley.

'Good evening, Constance,' was all he'd said to her as Ainsley greeted him in the hall. With the drawing-room door open, the cadence of masculine voices had taunted her from the study for several hours. She could not catch their words.

Francis had deserted her and she was worried stiff about the loaded pistol they'd left on Ainsley's desk. She wished she'd told him so that it could be made safe.

He might of course, have noticed and done it anyway, but she needed to know. She felt weak with dread whenever she saw him handling his guns. He continued to plague her with them. One morning she suddenly found a polished oak box open beside her on the bed.

'Look at them, Constance.' Ainsley's face was ugly with menace. She could feel sweat breaking out on her forehead. She couldn't breathe when she saw the same green baize lining, and the bullets ready-made in the corner compartment.

He levelled it at her. Was it one of this pair Francis had loaded? The jolt as she found herself looking down the barrel was worse than ever. Did he know what she'd done? Or was this Russian Roulette in earnest?

'Wake up. Take off your nightdress. I'm not going to shoot you just yet, I want you to do other things first.'

'Shoot yourself,' she dared. She had prayed he'd shoot himself. It would be poetic justice. She wanted him dead now. But the muzzle was prodding through the opening of her nightdress, the metal cold against her bare skin. With shaking fingers, and in mortal terror she tore the buttons apart to comply. He was laughing at her.

'Get up out of the bed. Let me see you hold these guns.' He pulled her nightdress from her, leaving her naked. Her teeth were chattering as he pushed the guns at her. She picked up the first. The safety catch was on, hadn't they left it so? Her skin crawled with horror as she put it off and aimed for his heart.

Ainsley was laughing, his head back so that his grizzled beard pointed at her. He thought the guns unloaded, but was he right? She went forward till she was a yard from him, closed her eyes and tightened her finger on the trigger. It clicked harmlessly. Swiftly she grabbed for the other gun and repeated the performance. Ainsley was still laughing as he pushed her back to the bed.

'You don't think I'd let you kill me?' She collapsed under him in floods of nervous tears.

'I wish I had!' she screamed. He'd made a fool of her again.

When he'd finished, he pushed himself away from her and surveyed her contemptuously. 'You're nothing but skin and bone, Constance. Anybody would think I'm starving you.'

She knew she was losing weight. Her face was drawn, her clothes no longer fitted. She was grieving for Francis. She'd felt depressed and frightened since he'd gone.

'Pull yourself together, woman, do something about it,' Ainsley told her impatiently. 'You look a mess.' She didn't care. She felt ill and wished she knew what had happened to that loaded pistol. She was living in mortal terror that sooner or later Ainsley would shoot her. She wished the moment would come. The waiting was terrible.

When he had gone, she got up, bathed and dressed. She rang for her breakfast. Usually she had it in bed, but this morning the sun was on the balcony. She opened the glass door and went out, wanting to feel its warmth on her face. The tide was full in. She sat looking at the port of Liverpool, through the pretty mock-Regency iron balustrade. It was hazy in the early sun.

She told herself she must count her blessings. She had comfort living here, and money enough to indulge her fancies. It was no use. If she were seventeen and could choose again, she'd rather starve. When her breakfast came, she drank two cups of coffee but ate nothing.

Then she wrote a note to her dressmaker, asking her to call. After a moment's hesitation, she wrote another to her corsetière. She must have new corsets. Her present ones were so loose, Ainsley said she could turn round inside them.

The house seemed full of noise because it was the school holidays. Constance had looked forward to them, wanting Harry's company to fill the void that Francis left. He was the only person who could lift her depression, the only other person in the world she loved.

Edwin was too young to be much comfort. At ten he was more a responsibility, a child to be kept occupied. His piping voice and everlasting questions pursued her round the house, but he preferred to trail after Harry if he could. Harry was the pivot of the family, and they all revolved round him.

He had grown into a handsome lad with the sandy Shearing colouring. He delighted everybody with his constant laughter and energetic ways. He was seventeen now, with only one more year to do at school. He brought his friends home and was often out. His father took him to the factory, to cricket matches and clay pigeon shoots. Constance felt hurt that he so seldom sought her company.

'He's almost a man now,' Ainsley said to her. 'He needs to be cut loose from your apron strings.'

Over the school holidays Ainsley came home to eat lunch with them. 'So I can see more of the boys,' he said, but it was only Harry he wanted to see.

'Would you like to come to Bisley with me this year?' he'd asked Harry one lunchtime.

'Love to,' he'd answered, all enthusiasm. 'Will you be competing, Father?'

'No. It's many years since I tried. My shooting days are over.'

Constance had dropped her fork on her plate with a clatter. She wished it were true.

'Competition shooting is very demanding.'

'I'd like to try it,' Harry said. The very last thing she wanted Ainsley to do was to impart his passion for firearms to their son.

'Why don't you take Edwin too,' she suggested coldly.

'Oh, please, Father. Let me come,' the child asked with eager delight. 'Please, Father, I'd love to.'

'Next year, perhaps. You're a bit young yet.'

'Please, Father. I know a lot about guns.'

'Not enough.' Ainsley was adamant.

'But you can teach me. Tell me what it is I have to learn. You only want to teach Harry.'

Ainsley took them both to his study then, leaving Constance sitting at the table feeling defeated. She wanted neither of her boys to enjoy Ainsley's hobby. Edwin's eager treble travelled clearly. Did she, too, show favouritism like that? she wondered. She knew how painful it was to feel left out.

When Lizzie the parlour maid came to tell her that Mrs Spring her corsetière had arrived, the study door was wide open and the boys crowding round the open gun cases on Ainsley's desk, showing more interest than she cared to see.

'Come upstairs,' she said. She was halfway up before she realised how slowly the woman followed. She'd been coming to Constance for years; suddenly she seemed much older.

'I've brought my daughter to help, Mrs Shearing,' she puffed on the landing. 'She's apprenticed to the same firm and learning the trade.'

Constance let her eyes linger on the daughter. She was as tall as her mother with childishly rounded cheeks and big disturbing brown eyes. Not the eyes of a child at all, but worldly wise, incongruous in so young a face.

'How old is she?'

'Our Beatrice is fourteen, madam.' The mother's glance was affectionate. 'Such a good girl, a great help to me. I hope you don't mind me bringing her with me?' The girl's thick brown hair was drawn on top of her head in parody of an adult style, and her hat could have been one of her mother's. She carried the heavy fashion catalogues as well as a case of samples.

Constance pondered on the unfortunate circumstances of working-class girls as she watched her open the pattern books on the dressing table.

'If madam would care to come and look?' She pulled out the chair in invitation. Constance slid on to it.

'Our corsets are designed to produce the fashionable hourglass figure.' Her voice was deep, too deep and confident for the child she was. She made Constance feel uncomfortable.

'They push the breasts forward but keep them low, madam, giving a pouter pigeon effect.' Constance turned the pages, studying the sketches of rigid padded corsets, while the girl stood behind her chair. 'Our corsets exaggerate every curve of the female form. The fashionable S curve is what we aim to achieve. See how the waist can be pulled in with this model. See how firm and strong is this whale-boning and how tightly it can be laced. It will take four inches off the average waist.'

'Mrs Shearing doesn't need . . .' her mother protested.

'Of course not, madam.' The girl was quick to apologise. 'You won't need pulling in at all. You have a naturally slender waist.'

Constance looked at the girl reflected in the mirror. Such a pity that good looks were wasted on people of her class. Given a few years, this one promised to ripen into a real beauty.

'Not many curves to exaggerate,' she said wryly. She knew the ideal figure for a woman bordered on the buxom.

'They are simple to add, madam.'. The girl was flipping through the pages of another book. 'Our corset covers are trimmed with waterfalls of stiffly starched frills to fill out the bosom. And pads can be added to the hips. It makes them very comfortable indeed to wear.'

Constance made her choice and withdrew to Ainsley's dressing room to remove most of her clothes. She came out in her chemise with only two petticoats. Mrs Spring began running a tape measure round her while the girl wrote her measurements in a book.

'You have an enviable waist, madam, only twenty-four inches.'

'Are not girls said to have waists of eighteen inches?'

'They are said to.' Beatrice smiled. 'But few have, and fewer keep them for more than a year or two.'

'You are indeed fortunate,' her mother was adding. 'A waist . . .'

Constance jumped as two shots shattered the silence, making the woman drop her tape measure. For an instant everything went black before her eyes.

She was struggling for breath, mesmerised with horror.

'What was that?' the girl asked, her eyes bigger than ever.

'Oh my God!' Constance felt the back of her neck crawling with dread. How could she have wished for this moment to come? She was rooted to the spot in horror until she heard Edwin's scream. It was a mind numbing sound of terror and went on and on, louder and higher.

It made her snatch up her wrap. The screams rose to a crescendo. Constance went flying downstairs with the two women at her heels. A panic-stricken Edwin met them in the hall, his face ashen and wet with tears.

'I've killed Harry,' he shrieked. 'Harry's dead.' He threw himself into her arms. 'Mama, it wasn't my fault.'

'No, dear.' She tried to edge forward to the study door. She could see Ainsley handling one of his pistols with quiet concentration, his finger carefully blocking the touch hole as he tamped the charge down the barrel.

'Father! You said it was safe. You said I could do it. It wasn't my fault.' Edwin's weight pushed against her, hampering her movements. In his frenzy he was uncontrollable.

'It was loaded. I didn't know it was loaded. Harry's dead!'

Constance could see the gun he'd dropped on the floor. Beside it, Harry was lying still, face down on the carpet, with blood oozing through the back of his pale linen jacket.

'Not Harry! Oh my God, not Harry!' She'd imagined this moment a hundred times. She though she'd imagined every possible scenario, but never this! Never imagined anything bad could happen to Harry. She felt a searing loss. Harry, who was so vibrant with youth, so effervescent, everybody's favourite. Harry was dead.

Edwin was in a frenzy, kicking and screaming and pummelling his fists against her. She saw the corsetière's daughter rush to her, heard the crack of her open palm as she slapped Edwin's cheek. Miraculously his hysteria ceased and he was whimpering in her arms. She was aware that most of the servants had come to look on in horror.

'Ainsley?' In the sudden quiet her voice rang out loud and accusing, thick with anger that he should let this happen.

'Sorry, Constance.' His lips had no colour in them. 'Can't believe I could be so damnably careless. Should never have put it away loaded. Should never have allowed the child . . . Should have made sure it was safe. Should never have let it happen to Harry. Not to Harry.'

His face was ashen. While they watched, he lifted the gun, positioned it against his temple and pulled the trigger. The noise blasted through the small room, hurting her ears, making Edwin and the servants shriek with terror. She put her hands over her ears, feeling sick with shock. What Ainsley had done numbed them all, rooted them to the spot.

Constance was crying, screaming, laughing. Of course, Ainsley would blame himself. Impossible for him to believe she'd go near his guns. She hated them, and anyway was incapable of charging one. She was glad Ainsley was dead. Glad, glad, glad, but Harry too?

Seconds later, the floorboards shuddered as Cook crashed over heavily in a dead faint. Still dazed, Constance saw Beatrice Spring recover and go to bend over Harry.

'He's still breathing,' she said in her deep calm voice. 'He's not dead. Help me.' Constance pushed the girl out of the way. She had to see for herself.

'He's bleeding,' the girl said over her. 'We've got to stop it.' Constance was shaking with sobs, trying to turn Harry over. But relief was washing through her.

'He's still breathing!' She was shrieking at her housekeeper to bring the woman out of her trance.

'Lizzie, go and find the gardener. Send him to fetch the doctor,' the housekeeper said faintly.

'Yes.' Constance couldn't think for herself, couldn't do anything.

'I didn't mean to kill him,' Edwin said again. She could feel his body against her own, shaking with terror.

'You haven't,' Beatrice barked at him. 'He might be all right.'

'Such a shock for you, madam. Terrible shock.' Mrs Spring was wringing her hands.

'Some clean towels, try and stem the bleeding,' Beatrice suggested.

'I'll do that. Take Mrs Shearing and Edwin away,' her housekeeper said.

'Come on.' The girl apprentice had her by the hand.

'Come back to your room. You're frozen, you've got so little on.'

Constance was climbing the stairs with Edwin clutching her round her waist. Mrs Spring supported them on one side, her daughter on the other.

'I did it,' Edwin cried, his child's face ravaged by tears and terror.

'No, Edwin. You mustn't blame yourself. It was my fault.' Constance felt she was choking under a tidal wave of guilt. 'All my fault.'

In the bedroom they led her to the bed. They helped her up on to it, made her lie down. Took off her slippers and pulled the eiderdown up to cover them both. Edwin snuggled into her side. She felt icy with horror.

'Of course it wasn't your fault,' Mrs Spring said. 'He shot himself, we all saw him.'

'You don't understand. I shouldn't have let him put a loaded gun away.' Constance knew she was sobbing uncontrollably. 'For a whole week . . . I've lived in dread . . . I knew it would happen, sooner or later.'

'Could you find her some brandy, Beatrice, do you think?' A warm hand held on to hers comfortingly. Beside her Edwin seemed to sleep.

She felt the glass pressing against her lips, the burning fluid in her mouth. It loosened her tongue, relaxed what little restraint she still had. She let it all come flooding out. The nightmare of that loaded gun. It eased the flutter of nerves in her stomach, took away the worry that had weighed on her mind.

She felt calmer when the doctor came upstairs to her. He left a sedative for Edwin on the bedside table, though he was breathing deeply and evenly and his child's face was serene again. He gave her a sedative too.

'Harry has lost a lot of blood and the bullet it still embedded in his shoulder. He's been lucky, it missed his vital organs. He's gone to hospital, but we've every reason to hope he'll be all right. He's young, with a strong constitution.'

'Thank God. And Ainsley?'

'I'm afraid there's no hope there, Mrs Shearing. He put the muzzle to his head.'

Ainsley had always had a macabre streak in his nature. Rather a withdrawn man, who preferred to be alone with his thoughts. He hadn't seen death as final. Merely the moment at which we all move from one world to another. He'd believed the next was much to be preferred. Ainsley had missed his first wife, he'd loved her and spoken to her as though she still lived. It had made Constance's flesh crawl with terror. Now it comforted her. Ainsley wouldn't regret his death, he was with his beloved Dinah again. She need not regret it either. She thanked God she still had Harry.

Rosie looked at Ben's capable hands on the steering wheel of the Rover, and thought how easy it was to take the luxury of a car for granted. It was a bright and sunny Sunday morning, and she'd persuaded him they must visit Flora Pope.

'You don't think Flora will mind my coming with you?' he turned to ask. 'I mean, Mother did sack her on the spur of the moment.'

'Flora isn't one to bear a grudge. Probably she

expected your mother to do it.'

'She hasn't found another job yet?'

'Kitty said not, when she saw her last week.'

'I feel guilty about it. Dad loved her.' He frowned. 'She was a good worker, one of the best.'

'I'm looking forward to seeing her again, though I should have been before now. Most of the other girls have.'

The sharp fresh scent of flowers filled the car. The garden at the farm grew them in abundance at this time of the year, and she had gone out and snipped a whole armful of roses and scabious for Flora which were now on the back seat.

'She may be able to help us. She knew your father better than anyone, Ben. We've got to talk about him.'

'That's why I've come. But if you'd been his love child, he'd have come straight out with it when I told him we were engaged, I'm sure of it. There was something he wanted me to know, but it wasn't too important. He was happy to put it off.'

Rosie tried to smile, she'd heard it all before.

'Flora will be easier to talk to than your grandmother,' she said. 'Ask her a question and she'll give you a straight answer. Always has.'

Ben was nosing the car into Egerton Park. 'Left,' Rosie said. 'Just round this bend, seventh house along.' She got out and lifted the flowers from the back seat.

'Lucky you've been before and know exactly where she lives,' Ben said. Rosie didn't want to think of the visit she'd made to collect Flora's things when she was in hospital.

The front door stood wide open. She led Ben up to the second floor and knocked on a heavy mahogany door.

'Flora has all the rooms on this floor,' she whispered. There had been no attempt to adapt the large Victorian house for multiple tenancy, but to occupy the whole of the top floor gave privacy. 'It's very nice inside.' The girls had thought Flora lucky to live here.

The door opened a few inches and an elderly lady peered out. 'Yes?'

'We've come to see Flora Pope.' Rosie smiled, assuming Flora already had other visitors. She moved the flowers from one arm to the other, hoping the old lady wouldn't stay long. What they had to say to Flora could not be said with other company present.

'Miss Pope doesn't live here any more.' The door was closing again.

'Where's she gone?' Rosie asked hastily. 'Can you tell us? She's a friend of mine and I wouldn't want to lose touch.' The woman was hesitating.

'Do you live here now?' Ben asked. 'Since when?'

'It's a fortnight now. I suppose it'll be all right. She left her new address so I could send any post on. She's moved to Mersey Way. I've a letter for her here, perhaps you could take it with you?'

'We'd be glad to,' Rosie said, and watched her write the address on the envelope. 'Thanks very much.'

'I know where it is,' Ben said, and a few moments later they were getting out of the car again.

'This doesn't look as good. Probably moved here because it was cheaper.' They waited a long time outside the shabby front door. It was opened at last by a man in his shirt sleeves and no collar.

'She's upstairs at the back,' he directed. Rosie felt the hand rail sway under her touch, and the stairs creaked under their weight. On the landing there were several doors to choose from. Ben knocked on the one furthest away.

It shot open. Flora's gutsy laugh was reassuringly normal. 'Hello, come on in.' Her pleasure at seeing them was obvious. It was only when the flurry of her welcome was over that Rosie noticed how much weight she'd lost. Flora said she was coping well, but her flesh seemed to be hanging in empty folds, and her face was pale and drawn.

'You know Ben and I are engaged,' Rosie said. Flora admired the opal before setting the kettle on her gas ring to make them a cup of tea. 'But his mother says we can't marry. She says Edwin is my father too. We've got to know if it's true.'

'Kitty said something about it, the other week.'

'They're talking about us?'

'They're bound to, you know that, Rosie. Didn't they gossip about me and Edwin?' Rosie knew she was right. She couldn't look at the double bed which took up so much of the available space in the shabby room.

'Dad must have talked a lot to you,' Ben said. Since there was only one armchair and one dining chair in the room, Rosie perched on the bed.

'He didn't speak much about his family. Taboo subject for us somehow. We certainly couldn't mention Beatrice's name. I felt she was on my back all the time, but it would have soured things between us if I'd kept complaining about her to Edwin. She made me angry and resentful.' Rosie understood only too well the difficulties Flora had faced.

'Edwin couldn't talk of her either. It was better to push all our irritations to the back of our minds. Not even think of her.'

'Dad admired my mother,' Ben said stiffly. 'He told me so.'

'He admired the way she worked, and the way she made Shearing's Shirts profitable. He said he couldn't have done it himself, but at the same time . . .'

Rosie sipped her tea, remembering how Constance had told her Edwin had been head over heels in love with Beatrice. That she'd tried and failed to talk him out of marrying her.

'Edwin knew when he married her she'd lost someone she truly loved, that he was not her first choice. He told me that when they were first married, he'd loved her more than she loved him.'

'They were married a long time.' Ben was looking thoughtful. 'Over the years, things do change. Living with them, I could see she'd lost patience with him. But she couldn't still be in love with Harry, he's been dead too long.'

'I don't think Harry is dead.' Flora stirred her tea. 'Anyway, it wasn't him she loved so much.'

'What?' Rosie's jerk of surprise made her tea slop into her saucer.

'Why isn't he here then?' Ben asked. 'What happened to him?'

Flora frowned in concentration. 'Let me think. He didn't spent a lot of time at his desk, and even less around the factory. There were all sorts of rumours at the time. Harry lived it up. Harry had glamour.'

'But where is he now?'

Flora's podgy face screwed up again. 'I'm not sure. He was in Paris for a few years after the war. Edwin said it provided what Harry wanted, and it was cheap to live there then. He moved on, to Tangier I think, a few years ago.'

'You don't have his address?' Ben was tense with excitement, sitting bolt upright on his hard chair.

She shook her head. 'Your father had it. He used to send him money. Harry was a remittance man. You might find it amongst his things.'

'Mother went through everything, at home and in the office. She's very efficient like that. If she doesn't want me to find Harry's address, she'll have got rid of it.'

'All this was years before I got to know Edwin.'

'You came to Shearing's as an apprentice, didn't you?' Ben asked. 'What year would that be? I want to get this into perspective.'

'I was fourteen. Mr Slocombe retired as manager shortly afterwards, so it would have been 1912. Edwin came straight from school, he'd been working there for several years. Harry was there too.'

'What was he like?' Rosie asked.

'Handsome, high opinion of himself. All the girls chased him, he was a real ladies' man.'

'Wasn't he married?'

'Yes, but I never saw his wife. A newspaper photograph taken outside the church went round the sewing room, that's all. Harry still encouraged the girls. Your mother was running her corset business in separate premises, but she started coming in regularly when Edwin went to the front. We could hear them arguing. We all tried to catch the gist of what was going on. There were rumours he was taking money out of the business, and bitter, bitter rows.'

'What did Dad think about that?'

'We never discussed it, it concerned his family. This is just what I remember. My own impression of what happened.'

'Yes.' Ben frowned. 'How do you think he felt about Harry?'

'Didn't discuss him either.' Flora shook her head. 'From remarks he made from time to time, I think he had mixed feelings. I think he was resentful because his parents favoured Harry. Life itself favoured Harry – he was so good-looking, so outgoing and popular. Cleverer than Edwin, healthier, tougher, everything. Edwin was resentful too because of what Harry did to the family business. It affected their prosperity for years. As I said, I think he was grateful Beatrice sent him packing.'

'Beatrice was once engaged to Harry,' Rosie said. 'She must have been over that.'

'Well over it. There's a puritanical streak in Beatrice. She feels everybody should work hard and money shouldn't be wasted. Harry didn't share those views. There was someone else she loved more, but I think she wanted revenge on both by then. She bore grudges, always seemed very vengeful towards everybody.'

'My father left Rosie a share in the business,' Ben

said slowly. 'So we have to assume he had good reason. Mother says she's his illegitimate daughter, but I'm not sure.'

Flora was shaking her head. 'I don't know. Edwin never said anything one way or the other.'

'Is it more likely to be Edwin or Harry?' Rosie persisted.

'I'd like to say Harry.'

'I'd love to hear you say Harry.' Rosie smiled sadly.

'But you and Dad, it went back a long way?'

'Fourteen years. I feel devastated. He went so suddenly, and I wasn't able to be with him.'

'I've brought his watch.' Ben was taking it from his pocket. 'He'd want you to have something as a keepsake. You remember it?'

'Of course! I'd love to have it, thank you.' She was clasping it to her.

'He loved you, Ben. He'd say: "Got his head screwed on the right way, that one", or "His heart's in the right place. He'll take care of Shearings, he won't have to rely on someone else to do it for him". I do miss working for you.'

'A terrible thing to sack you like that,' Rosie said.

'I knew she would, from the minute I heard he was dead. She knew about us, you see. You can't hide something like that for fourteen years.'

'I wish I could offer you your job back, Flora.'

She laughed uncertainly. 'Your mother wouldn't stand for it. Anyway, she'd never be off my back.'

'I've heard Rattigan's are expanding.' Ben frowned in concentration. 'Do you know them? They make ladies' outerwear, in Riverbank Road. Apply there,

Flora. I'll ring Tom Rattigan tomorrow and recommend you.'

'That's kind of you, Ben.'

'Dad would want me to. Tom was a friend of his.'

'Thank you. You don't let your mother have everything her way either. She was dead against starting you as an apprentice, Rosie; whether it was because she hadn't chosen you herself or there was some other reason I don't know. I didn't ask and Edwin didn't tell me.'

'I wish you had,' Rosie said. 'But Edwin was always very kind to me.'

'He was to everyone. He'd never have abandoned your mother to the workhouse, Rosie, I'm sure of that. It must have been Harry.'

CHAPTER TWENTY

'Ainsley's dead.' Constance was sobbing with fear. 'He can't taunt me any longer. Ainsley is dead. It ought to be a comfort but it isn't.'

She staggered out of her chair and tugged the heavy velvet curtains across the windows.

'Is the sun too strong for you?' Rosie asked. She felt caught up in Constance's fear. Her mouth was dry.

'The sun? No, it's the seagulls . . .'

The drawing room had lost most of its light with two of the windows curtained closely. Rosie looked out of the remaining one. The gulls screamed and wheeled on the edge of the incoming tide. It was a blustery day with a stiff breeze whipping up white horses on the water and fitful sun glistening on the white foam.

'Ainsley will shoot them if he sees them like this.'

Rosie felt the hairs on the back of her neck lifting in horror. She'd known now for a long time that Constance was haunted by Ainsley's death. That he was not the paragon Ben had thought him. He seemed to terrify Constance, alive or dead.

'Didn't he like gulls?' she made herself ask. They screamed mournfully above the crashing of waves but they were beautiful to look at. Some dazzling white, some grey with darker feathers, all so graceful swooping in the pale luminous sky or bobbing in the swell of the murky Mersey tide. 'Why would he shoot them?'

'To prove to me he can shoot to kill.'

Rosie shuddered. 'To prove to himself perhaps that he still had a good eye.'

'To show me how easily he can, how quick the end.' Rosie saw fear flicker in her face, and shivered with her. It was contagious. 'Ainsley frightens me.'

'But not any more,' Rosie reassured her. 'Ainsley is dead.'

'But I wanted to do it.'

'Do what?'

'Kill him.'

Rosie felt she was choking. Had they not had this conversation before, or something like it? 'But you didn't kill him, Constance.'

'He shot himself.' Her voice was suddenly matter-of-fact.

'There then,' Rosie said, awash with relief again. 'You know it wasn't your fault.'

'Oh yes it was. Beatrice knows it was, she was here.'

'But not when . . .?'

'Yes, when Ainsley shot himself. She saw it all.'

'Then she'd never say it was your fault.'

'She does,' Constance insisted. 'She says it was all my fault, that it would never have happened if I hadn't . . .' Constance gave her that knowing look. 'But she promised not to tell anybody if I gave her money.'

'She'd never do that.' Rosie laughed nervously.

'That would be . . .' She felt light-headed.

Ben had been right when he'd said his grandmother was hiding something.

'It started when she delivered my new corsets a week after Ainsley's funeral . . .'

Rosie felt for her hand. 'Tell me,' she said. 'Tell me everything that happened then.'

Constance looked round the darkened room. She could see Beatrice now as a young girl in her child's dress and button boots with a hat more suited to a middle-aged woman, a broken feather curling round its high crown.

She had taken Mrs Spring and her daughter up to her bedroom while she tried on the corsets. She liked to make sure they fitted properly. If she were not satisfied, they would always alter them.

'Are they comfortable, Mrs Shearing?' the mother had asked.

'Very comfortable and well made.' She had put on the corset covers too. They were beautiful with their cascades of starched frills.

'A perfect fit, if I may say so. Please put on your dress again, Mrs Shearing, so you can see how fashionable they make your figure.'

Constance had returned to Ainsley's dressing room to do so. The girl had helped her do up the hooks and eyes at the back when she returned.

She said: 'For some people, nothing is impossible. You do feel nothing is impossible, don't you, Mrs Shearing?'

Her own mind had been on basques and bustles.

Fashion had seemed a pleasant diversion from the horror of Ainsley's death, and she had neither understood what the girl was getting at nor thought it important.

'I am well pleased with them,' she'd said, surveying her reflection in the cheval looking-glass. 'Kindly leave your bill.' She'd expected them to get up and go then. The girl looked at her insolently.

'You think you've got away with it, don't you? You killed your husband.' There had never been anything childlike about Beatrice's voice, and the menace in it now was unmistakable. 'I was here with you, remember.'

Constance felt herself freeze in dread. She knew she had said too much on that awful day. The shock had made her blather. She had endured the inquest, the funeral, and Francis's accusing gaze. The horror was with her still.

Edwin continued to cling, limpet-like, and would hardly allow her out of his sight, but Harry was recovering. She had told herself the worst was over, but was it?

Constance faced the two women. She had thought of the mother as self-effacing, a skilled and efficient provider of corsetry, but a menial, and certainly not a person to be feared. Her daughter was little more than a child. She found their stand all the more fearsome for that.

'The inquest found that my husband shot himself.' That had seemed disgrace enough. To have shot himself while the balance of his mind was disturbed because he felt responsible for allowing one son, a mere child, to shoot the other. It had been hushed up as much as possible.

'Not everything came out at the inquest. My daughter and I were very careful to say nothing of what you told us to the police. We were mindful of your predicament.'

Constance was shivering. The stark horror was crowding back over her. It seemed Ainsley was reaching out from the grave to get his revenge.

'You told us you had charged the gun.' Beatrice's age-old eyes challenged her. 'Left it loaded for your son to pick up. We had to be very careful what we said because we didn't want anything to happen to you.'

Constance felt cornered, sick with fear. Her nightmare wasn't over. It could be that the worst was yet to come. The girl was looking to her mother, her eyes silently urging her to go on.

'I do not wish to discuss it further,' Constance retorted. 'Please leave your bill and go.'

'Did you husband commit suicide because you had a lover?'

Constance gasped at her effrontery. She could no longer pretend this was a normal fitting. 'He did not.'

'He did not even suspect, did he? You and your lover were very careful. On one visit, I heard talk in your own kitchen that you strolled the Esplanade with him. They were laughing because you sent him to the front door and came up the garden yourself.

'Your boys are very different to look at,' the mother said. 'Was Francis Woodley Edwin's father?'

'He was not! Edwin was born before I ever met

Francis. I shall ring for my parlourmaid to show you
out.'

'Not yet if you please,' the mother said, holding up
her hand.

'Better if no one else hears what we say,' the girl
added. 'The fewer people who know, the better.'

'What do you want of me?' She felt forced into a
corner.

'Just a little help,' the mother said. The girl's
disturbing eyes never left Constance's face.

'It sounds like blackmail.' Constance tried to force
saliva into her mouth.

'Oh no, madam, nothing like that,' the mother said.
'We'd like to put a business proposition to you.'   .

'Yes?'

'You've always been pleased with the corsets we've
made for you?'

'Yes,' she answered reluctantly.

'I've kept your custom for nearly twenty years.
Haven't I given satisfaction?'

'Yes.' She felt even more reluctant.

'Lots of other ladies feel the same way. I deal with
the gentry. I've been fitting and selling high class
corsetry all my life, and the Carstairs Corset Company
has done well from my efforts. My sister is employed
as a machinist and my brother as a cutter. With a little
capital, we could set up on our own. I know I could get
enough orders to keep them busy.'

The silence lengthened. The girl's eyes never left her
face. Constance pursed her lips. She wasn't going to
ask how much they'd need. She wasn't going to make
it easy for them.

'We need two hundred pounds.'

'That's an enormous amount,' she gasped.

'An investment opportunity for you, Mrs Shearing. Your husband was in business, you understand what we're talking about. We'd pay you back, of course.'

'I don't know whether . . .'

'We will need to rent premises, and to buy sewing machines and materials. We think with that amount we could employ another girl. Two hundred is not a lot for a lady like you to find. I'm sure your husband has left you well provided for.'

Constance cast about for some way out of this. She could see none.

'Or we could go back to the police and tell them what we know,' the girl said.

'All right,' she said, desperate to be rid of them. 'All right.'

'Thank you, Mrs Shearing.' The wicked woman was shaking her hand. 'You won't regret this, I promise you.'

She'd been wrong about that, Constance recalled with a shudder. She'd regretted it many times.

'Beatrice frightens me.'

The old lady was twisting her fingers in a grip of iron. Rosie shuddered with her.

'Beatrice frightens me too,' she admitted. 'Most people at the factory are terrified of her.' But if what Constance had just told her was true, she had more reason to fear her than any of her employees.

'Did she really blackmail you?'

She heard Constance's sigh. 'Beatrice is very clever.

Later she denied saying any such thing. She repaid the money in full, calling it an arranged loan from one woman in business to another. She came often to the house to see me. I dreaded her visits, though she talked only of her business. She would come to tell me they were taking on more machinists or about the number of orders they had. She was always offering to make me her latest style of corsets, and I've never had a bill for them since.'

'Perhaps you misunderstood . . . Perhaps you misjudged her.'

'That was what she wanted me to think by then,' Constance retorted. 'You see, Beatrice had seen Harry and was fired with another ambition.'

Rosie was amazed at what she was hearing. She could imagine Beatrice's fury if she knew her mother-in-law was telling her all these details from her past, but Constance had mentioned Harry's name at last and it was about him she really wanted to hear.

'Tell me what he was like,' she said softly.

'I can show you photographs.' Rosie tried to stop her in case it broke her train of thought, but Constance was up on her feet, taking an album from the drawer in a davenport.

Rosie took the calfbound book on her knee and turned the pages. Harry as a chubby child with an engaging grin. A handsome youth with glossy hair. A young man with eyes that expected adulation because he'd always received it.

'We all adored him.' His mother's pale eyes softened with love.

Edwin seemed a rather peaky child, small for his

age, lacking his brother's confidence. Rosie was fascinated as she looked from one to the other and wondered which of these two very different people was her father. She would have said she was more like Edwin in character. Her hands shook at the thought. She even felt a spark of sympathy that Constance had not loved him as she had his brother. She felt nothing for Harry, but then she'd never met him.

'I can see why you all loved him,' Rosie said, staring at a formal group of Constance, in a huge feathered hat, sitting bolt upright with a son either side.

'As a child, he was lovely, full of fun. I'm afraid we all spoiled him, even Ainsley. He was more difficult in his teens. A little wild, too fond of having a good time.'

'He recovered fully from his shoulder wound?'

'Yes. I spoiled him even more after that because I'd so nearly lost him. I needed him after Ainsley died. It was a pity that he wasn't older – I was not used to making decisions.'

'No,' Rosie agreed. Poor Constance. Probably the only decisions she ever made were about domestic details. 'Did you find him a help?'

She shook her head sadly. 'It had already been decided he would go to university before entering the business. Ainsley had hoped for Oxford. I wanted it too, I hoped it would mean Harry would grow up without Ainsley's uncouth habits. But he was no longer interested in school work. I was thankful when he managed to get into Liverpool.'

'Did he do well there?' Rosie prodded.

'No, he never did get a degree, but he spent three

years trying. Or at least, I thought he was trying. He was enjoying himself and doing very little work.'

Rosie turned another page of the album and recoiled with shock. A large photograph showed Harry standing with his arm round Beatrice's shoulders. She was smiling up at him, the relationship between them unmistakable. Rosie got up from her seat and went to a window. The room had grown dark as the evening progressed. She drew back the curtains to see better. 'It is Harry?'

'Yes, Beatrice wanted him to marry her.' Rosie couldn't believe it. 'Harry had a photographer come when they got engaged. Those pictures were taken outside in the garden.'

'But she married Edwin.'

'Beatrice is very clever. I believe she only repaid the loan because she wanted to marry into my family. She had risen socially by starting her own business. I think she saw marriage to Harry as the next move. Her passport to a more comfortable life, a further step up the social scale.'

'What about her business?'

'Oh, that has always thrived. Beatrice is a good businesswoman.'

Rosie slipped the photograph out of its corner fix and turned it over. It was dated July 1904. Despite the high-boned collar of her blouse and her heavy hat, Beatrice looked enchanting. Lustrous intelligent eyes, strong but neat features and a sweet smile.

'She learned how to dress.' She heard the hatred in Constance's voice. 'She'd visited middle-class ladies in their homes and learned to copy their clothes and their manners. Her mother died two or three years after they set up in business. It suited Beatrice very well to manage everything on her own.'

'And Harry loved her?' Rosie could see that it must be so. Beatrice was a good-looking woman today; of course she must have been beautiful in the freshness of youth.

'I thought they would marry. She'd chased him for years, though Harry had lots of girls chasing him. I hoped he'd settle for one of them, anyone but Beatrice. She came to see me regularly, pretending friendship. She frightened me though she was a young and beautiful girl. There was something about her eyes . . .'

'Did she have no other family?'

'She had two younger brothers who were totally dependent on her. She was seventeen when her mother died, and her brothers eight and ten. She brought them up.'

'A responsibility for one so young.'

'Beatrice has always taken her responsibilities seriously.'

'What happened to their father?'

'She said he was a drunk who abused her mother. She'd persuaded her to take the family and leave him. Beatrice didn't know where he was by this time.'

'But she married Edwin not Harry?'

'I think Harry grew tired of her domineering ways. Beatrice was always bossy. He wanted to travel, take a year abroad and enjoy himself, but she was pressing him to start working in the business.

'I agreed with her really, but I took his part.

Financing him for a year so he could roister round Europe was another expensive mistake on my part. I hoped the long separation would break her hold on him, and that Harry would come to his senses. He wanted her to go with him, but I knew Beatrice would never leave her corset business. She'd wanted it too badly to leave it. She waited for him to come home, but he seemed no nearer settling down.'

'Did he never run the shirt factory?'

'Yes, though it would have been better if he had not. Ainsley had had a manager, a Mr Slocombe, who took over after his death. He retired in 1912. He'd already stayed on an extra year because he didn't think Harry was ready to manage the business. He tried to teach him, but Harry had no aptitude. Eventually he was left to run it.

'Beatrice lost patience with him. I don't think she could face marriage to anyone who gave so little heed to business. She expected him to work hard to build things up. Instead he was taking out large sums of capital to have a good time.

'She told me he wouldn't listen to her. That she had pleaded with him not to borrow so much for new premises he didn't need. He wouldn't take her advice and he was making a lot of mistakes.

'I fear Harry grew up expecting to have everything he wanted handed to him on a plate. I believe Beatrice saw what he was like sooner than the rest of us. I was relieved when they broke up. He got engaged again very quickly. I liked Alice much better and was pleased to have him married.'

'And Beatrice turned to Edwin?'

'Not immediately. She found someone she loved more.' Constance stared into space for so long, her face stony with desolation, Rosie was afraid she would tell her no more. But eventually she roused herself and went on.

'I was horrified when I learned Beatrice was planning to marry Edwin instead. He was more the sort of person she was looking for. Prepared to work hard in the business, malleable, not as clever as she was.

'Edwin was in love with her. There was no changing his mind. I was shocked, I can tell you. I tried to talk him out of it, but the fact that she'd been engaged to Harry only increased her attraction for him. He'd always craved what Harry had. I'm sure she manipulated Edwin and made him fall in love with her. She was still building up her business, I think he admired her success.

'Harry, in the meantime, was proving a disaster. In four years he ruined what Ainsley had spent a lifetime building up. I never really understood what happened, but Beatrice turned against him and wanted to call in the police. She said it was fraud – she can be vicious as an enemy. I was worried stiff, begged her to wait till Edwin came home on leave. It was the war, he'd gone to fight.'

'When would this be?' Rosie asked.

'Let me see. The war had been on for some time, and the factory was turning out khaki flannel shirts for the Army. It would be 1915, I suppose, when Beatrice pushed him out.'

Rosie was breathing hard. Then Harry could be her father because she had been born in 1916. And if he had been cast out by his family, he would not have had money to support Grace. Was that why she'd gone to the workhouse?

'Did Harry have a mistress?' Rosie was asking urgently.

Constance's pale eyes looked into hers in embarrassment. 'Harry would never talk to me about that sort of thing – I'm his mother. But he was in trouble with everybody. He was desperate for money, tried to persuade me to give him more. Money was all he wanted to talk about then, but I hadn't any.

'We all had to tighten our belts. Suddenly there was no money for anything. Edwin came home on leave and went back worried stiff. Beatrice said she didn't know which way to turn.' Constance gave her a wry smile. 'They all blamed me for giving in to Harry's extravagant ways, but I'd never been to the factory. I didn't know what he was doing. I trusted him. That was where I went wrong. I trusted Harry.'

Rosie leaned back in her chair. Had Grace trusted him too?

'What a fool I was,' Constance lamented. Rosie almost agreed. Constance had married Ainsley for his money and then let Harry spend it all.

'What happened to Shearing's Shirts?'

'We all had to rely on Beatrice to pull the company round. That was a bitter pill to swallow.'

'And Harry? What happened to him?'

'I never saw him again. Beatrice said he'd gone away, and it was better for him to do that than go to prison.'

'He was killed in the war then?'

'She killed him herself.'

Rosie was suddenly erect in her chair. She could feel sweat breaking out on her forehead. 'No,' she protested. Beatrice was a bully, she didn't care how her victims squirmed, but . . . 'She wouldn't kill him. I can't believe that.'

Constance's pale eyes looked into hers. Rosie saw the nervous tic jump in her cheek and could sense her terror.

'I've done bad things, but Beatrice is evil. I know she killed him.' Her voice was a harsh accusing whisper.

'Where?' Rosie hardly recognised her own terrified croak. 'Where did she do it?'

'In the factory, of course. I'm absolutely certain.'

Talk of the Coronation had been on everyone's lips for months. Preparations had been under way for longer. Ben could remember discussing with his father what Shearing's should do by way of celebration.

Celebration was in the air now. A fun-fair had arrived in town, and he'd heard free tickets were being distributed through the schools. There was to be a mug and a medal for every child. Tea parties were being organised for them.

'No need for us to do anything,' Mother had said. 'With your father only just in his grave, everybody knows we've nothing to celebrate.'

Ben had felt the air of expectancy building up over the last few days. Flags and bunting were appearing everywhere. The streets were hung with them, looking bright, gaudy and cheerful. He'd ordered some to decorate their kitchen at the Albert Hotel, and thought how pleased manufacturers of bunting must be. The manufacturers of souvenir mugs and plates had not been so fortunate. The newspapers were full of stories about how they produced thousands of gross showing the head of Edward VIII before the news of his abdication had broken.

After last year's scandalous revelations about the monarchy, George VI and Queen Elizabeth were very popular, and the girls in the sewing room couldn't get enough news about the little Princesses.

For the day itself, Ben ordered trays of cakes and iced buns from the local baker, and told Mrs Pratt to organise ham sandwiches for everybody at lunchtime.

He'd told the staff they could bring in their own wirelesses if they wanted to, and this morning, had brought in his own and fixed it up so the workers might listen to the broadcast from Westminster Abbey while they worked. They were all keen to know what was going on. All morning the factory had resounded to unaccustomed blasts of music. It brought a holiday air.

At mid-morning he went down to the sewing room. Rosie had told him the samples of her sports shirts were almost ready, and he found her giving them a final press with the iron. She'd chosen to have them made up in cream and blue. He held one against him. It was very different from everything else they made.

'They've turned out wonderfully well. I shall get some for myself.' He could feel Rosie's simmering undercurrent of excitement, due more to the shirts than the Coronation, he thought. He'd feel more pleasure if he could find out what had really happened to his Uncle Harry.

From a machine at the far end of the room, a raucous voice rang out: 'D'you hear that, Gert? The little princesses have matching dresses with bows all the way down the front. You could make those for your Lil's bridesmaids. Wouldn't that be nice?'

'I'll show them to Mother,' he told her. 'Then give them to Charles Avery, to see if he can get some sales.' He draped the samples carefully over his arm. Rosie followed him to the door.

His mother's voice was booming out from the corset room, drowning out the commentary, irritable and untouched by the general high spirits. She came briskly down the corridor, caught sight of him and paused.

'It's like a wake in here this morning. Nobody wants to work. You should never have allowed this. Give them an inch and they'll take a mile. You're too soft with them, Ben.'

'Wish me luck,' he said to Rosie, and followed his mother to her office.

A brass band seemed to be thundering through the building. He could see Eric the van driver marching towards him, banging an imaginary drum. He closed the door to her cubicle behind him. It didn't help.

'For God's sake, I can't think with this racket going on.' He could see Mother wasn't in a good mood.

'Does it matter for one day?'

He couldn't think either. 'Come up to my office,' he said. 'It's quieter up there. I want to talk to you.'

'What are those you've got?' He didn't answer till he

could shut his door on the noise.

'Samples of some new sports shirts. What do you think?' She was spreading them out carefully on his desk.

'The cloth is said to be very healthy, lets the air get to the skin. It's absorbent, comfortable to wear and washes well.' He knew she'd be unbiased in her opinion until she heard they were Rosie's designs. He was afraid that would be another stumbling block. He jerked to his feet and paced to the window.

Irritated, she looked up. 'What is the matter with everyone today? You're like a caged animal.'

'Mother, what happened to Harry? What is the big secret? I need to know.'

She was folding the shirts carefully. 'I understand these are the very latest for hiking? Yes, I like them.'

'Mother! Gran is saying you killed Harry.'

'Don't be silly, dear. Your Gran's mind wanders. You should know better than to take what she says literally.'

'But you sent Harry packing. What did you do to him?'

'I persuaded him to make over his share of the business to your father. Took him to see our solicitor. You should be grateful, Ben. It meant your father had title to two thirds of the business to hand on. Forget Harry, he thought of nobody but himself. What price have you put on these shirts?' Ben took a sheet of paper from his drawer and pushed it towards her. He'd worked out the cost. They'd be able to undercut their rivals.

As he waited for her to absorb this, he noticed

Phyllis Quest had brought up his post. She opened and sorted routine letters, and delivered them round the building. One marked Private and Confidential she'd left sealed in its envelope.

He opened it idly, still watching his mother. It was routine too, containing bank statements for several of the accounts the company ran. He shuffled through them, knowing fairly accurately what funds should be in each. Suddenly the figures were transfixing him. He could feel the blood draining from his face. He felt sick. Their trading account had been drained of funds by one large withdrawal. The cheque number was not theirs.

'What is it?' Beatrice's dark eyes fastened on his face.

He pushed the statement into her hand. Telling himself he mustn't jump to conclusions, he opened the safe, snatched out the company chequebooks. He'd known from the first moment the number was definitely not theirs. It could be a mistake. It had to be a mistake.

His mother's voice was strident in his ears. He had to ignore her. He had to know for sure. He lifted his phone and asked Miss Gibbons to get their bank manager on the line.

He sat with the phone clamped to one ear and his hand against the other till the man answered. Ben quoted the cheque number at him, and the date and the amount, and the account on which it had been drawn. During the time he had to wait, he felt a growing certainty that Oliver had put his hand in the till again.

It was almost an anticlimax to have it confirmed that Oliver had asked for a new chequebook to be issued and had used it. The cheque had been signed by him.

Ben felt stiff with horror. 'We left it too late,' he whispered. 'Left ourselves open.'

They'd withdrawn his authorisation to sign cheques on behalf of Shearing's Shirts the morning after Beatrice had visited the Felthams.

'The money went from our account the day before . . .' He knew exactly how Dad must have felt all those years ago when Harry had done something like this. 'We've got to go to the police, Mother. You can't let him get away with it a second time.'

Her face was putty-coloured. 'No,' she moaned. 'No. The family name will be dragged in the gutter. No, not Oliver!'

'He's taken money we need to pay wages.'

'A family scandal . . . It'll be bad for trade.'

'Taken money we need for bills,' Ben agonised. 'There's one due now for cloth. Our main supplier, we have to pay. We can't risk not getting the same cloth. We should have thrown Oliver out weeks ago. You should never have stopped me.'

'I'm sorry.' Her head was in her hands.

'Being sorry doesn't help. Our liquidity's gone. What am I supposed to use for money?'

'The profit and loss account, there's cash there.'

'Why should Oliver have all our profit? I think we should ring the police now.'

'No, Ben, wait. The corsets can lend . . .'

'Lend isn't good enough, Mother.' He could feel his anger building up. 'You take good care of your own business. You don't even let me near the corset accounts, yet you go right against my judgement on shirts. Dad's judgement too. You knew it was a risk. We were all telling you Oliver would do it again.'

'You've never got on with him.'

'Hell!' He was shaking with rage. 'Who's talking about getting on?'

She seemed to crumple in front of his eyes. Her voice was a faint monotone. 'I'll make good the loss from the corset profits. We can't have Oliver's name dragged through the courts.'

He couldn't bite back the words. 'What if he does it again? From the Felthams?'

She was shaking her head slowly. 'He wouldn't.' There was agony in her voice. 'The trouble is, whatever we do now, he won't be able to face us again.'

Ben felt cold and helpless and drained of feeling. He'd always known Mother loved Oliver best, and in spite of everything she still did.

CHAPTER TWENTY-ONE

The alarm clock jangled in her ears, jerking her out of a deep sleep. Without opening her eyes, Rosie groped along the edge of her bedside table. It didn't help. She had to force her eyes open before she could switch the clock off.

It was a quarter to six. Already a bright shaft of daylight showed between the heavy curtains. In the next bed, Phyllis turned over and settled herself to sleep for another hour. Rosie wished she could do the same.

She'd never found it hard to get out of bed before, even in the dead of winter, but all this week she'd been heavy and lethargic.

She heard Uncle Will's tread on the landing, the creak of the stairs as he went down, and hurriedly she threw off her bedclothes. Reaching for her old clothes, she felt her stomach turn over in protest. She'd not felt too good for the last few days, and the sooner she was out in the fresh air the better.

She hurried downstairs and pulled on a coat. It was a fine morning, still a bit sharp at this hour, but she'd always found morning air invigorating till now. Old

Tom had the cows in and waiting. She hunched her shoulders and pushed her hands deeper into her pockets as she went across to the cowshed.

The trouble was, she decided, she was beginning to feel oppressed by the problem. She and Ben had set themselves the task of finding definite proof that Edwin had not been her father. For weeks now that had been their first priority. Last night Ben had laughed and said he knew more now about his forebears, that they'd unearthed a lot of unsavoury facts kept secret for years, but they were no nearer the proof they sought.

Rosie found it unsettling. The worry was going round her head, day in and day out. It nagged at the back of her mind whether awake or asleep. She felt she was frightening Constance with her questions, but she couldn't give up. No wonder she didn't feel well.

Ben Shearing had seemed out of reach when she'd felt the first tingle of attraction. She'd let herself be persuaded out of her shell, gone on to believe he loved her. She'd felt captivated, enthralled as he'd put the opal on her finger, ready to live happily ever after. She'd believed their only difficulty was to convince his family she'd make a good wife for him.

It had seemed a cruel obscenity to hear Beatrice say Edwin was her father. Every time Rosie thought of that moment, she was filled with anger and frustration.

She found the gossip she heard going on around her difficult to cope with too. She knew the sewing room girls were saying she had been Edwin Shearing's love child. Must be, why else would he leave her a share in his business? She knew they were all pleased for her, though, particularly so because they thought it put Beatrice Shearing's nose out of joint.

As her fingers worked to send streams of milk swishing into the bucket, she rested her forehead against Tinkerbell's warm flank. The pace at morning milking was always brisker than in the evening. She had to change her clothes, have breakfast and get to work afterwards. She was finding it hard to work fast because she was feeling a bit queasy again. She'd felt like this yesterday, and had hardly been able to eat breakfast.

Neither Will nor Tom was as quick as they used to be, so she helped them carry the brimming churns to the dairy. The milk had to be bottled and the float loaded so that Will could start his round as early as possible. He didn't look well either, and sounded breathless.

'This business is getting you down, Rosie. You aren't yourself. You've lost your bounce.'

'We're none of us ourselves, are we, Uncle Will?'

'I can't forget it was the Shearings.' There was anger in his voice. 'Poor Grace, she must have been torn in two.'

Rosie sighed. Edwin's death and the news of her inheritance had increased the tension at home. For her uncle, the old hurt refused to die.

'They were worldly wise compared with our Grace. She wouldn't stand a chance against men like them. They had plenty of money to look after her, it was the least they could have done. You'd better watch yourself with Ben. He's from the same stable, you know.'

'Ben's all right,' she said gently. She could see her

uncle ageing before her eyes and it alarmed her.

'I've been thinking, lass, there must be some way you could get your own back on the Shearings. Maud's right, they've got it coming.'

'Just how am I to do that?' She knew she had reacted too strongly. She understood how he felt, but she was edgy too. 'I mean, what exactly could I do?'

'You could give Ben Shearing his ring back for a start.'

'That's exactly what Beatrice wants. It would be playing into her hands.'

Beatrice might have intended to split them up, but what she'd done had had the opposite effect. It had bound them more closely together. Rosie could no longer see a future without Ben, and knew she'd fight tooth and nail before she gave him up. 'Anyway, I want to marry him.'

'I want to lash out at them,' her uncle said between clenched teeth. 'Hurt them as they hurt our Grace. I'm beginning to hate them. Don't you?'

'You're forgetting,' she said wearily, 'I'm a Shearing too.'

Will saw everything the Shearings did in black and white, but she couldn't do that now she knew them. She loved Ben, and felt a fond pity for Constance. She had liked Edwin, and found Stephen pleasant enough. Oliver was best avoided. Only Beatrice made her boil with resentment and loathing. Rosie was ashamed of the violence of her feelings for her.

'Giving you a share of the business now is no recompense. Years ago, just a few pounds a week to our Grace would have kept you both out of the workhouse.'

With a tired sigh she said: 'I wish somebody could tell me definitely whether it was Edwin or Harry.'

'I used to think Harry was one of the best. Generous to a fault. He'd not have abandoned our Grace. The more I think about it, the more I'm sure of that.'

Rosie turned away, feeling sick again. They were both going round in circles. 'I'm going in.'

'Aye, it's time you did. You're a good girl to come and help.'

She went back to the house and hurried upstairs to wash and change for work. For once Phyllis was already down in the kitchen. Rosie was buttoning her blouse when another thought came to her and she pulled a small diary out of her drawer and turned to the calendar at the front where she'd marked off certain days.

The red ink circles round the dates leapt off the page at her. She was gasping as she sank down on her unmade bed. The room was spinning round her. She was more than a week overdue, and she'd never even given it a thought! The strength was ebbing from her knees. Surely that couldn't be right?

She'd refused to think any such thing could happen to her, though she had been taking Ben to the top of the dutch barn fairly often. He was taking precautions, she knew he was, and yet . . .

She made herself count off the days since the last time, while her heart hammered away inside her. Oh God, there was no mistake. Surely she couldn't be? She was fighting a panic attack, hardly able to get her breath as she paced in the narrow space between the beds and the wardrobe.

'Rosie?' Maud's voice carried from the bottom of the stairs. 'Rosie?' It sobered her like a slap in the face.

'Yes,' she answered cautiously.

'What are you doing up there? Your breakfast's going cold.'

'Coming, Aunt Maud,' she called faintly. The last thing she wanted was food. The very thought of it made her heave, yet she couldn't say so lest Aunt Maud eventually draw her own conclusions. She couldn't think straight, she was numb, but she had to act as though everything was normal.

She zipped up her brown flannel skirt, pushed her arms into her cardigan and went down. She couldn't look any member of her family in the eye. This was going to floor them.

She gulped down half a cup of tea. The scrambled eggs were dry and hard to swallow. Her mind was on fire. She had done exactly what Grace had done, and the same thing had happened. She was going to have a baby. She could feel herself shaking with fright. Would the rest of her life continue to mirror her mother's?

For how long would she be able to pretend that all was well? There were a thousand questions in her mind and she didn't know where to turn for answers. The most pressing was how Ben would take the news.

The morning post brought a letter for Phyllis. She was suddenly shrieking with joy.

'I've been called for interview.' Rosie knew she'd been applying for other jobs for weeks. Now she launched into a long account of the benefits this one would bring if she got it. Rosie was thankful because it drew the family's attention away from her.

She walked to work with her cousin still feeling frozen, hardly able to take in what had happened, and finding the consequences too awful to think about.

'I can't ask Mrs Shearing for a few hours off without telling her what I want them for.' Phyllis was expansive. 'You can tell her I'm not well on Monday, can't you?'

Rosie was too caught up in her own worries. She'd been terribly upset when she'd found out what had happened to Grace, yet she'd dared to do the same, never believing it could happen to her too. What a fool she'd been.

'What's the matter, Rosie? You wouldn't mind telling her I'd had a bilious attack or something in the night?'

She hardly knew what she was agreeing to. 'All right.'

'Thanks, I knew you would. She's terrible to work for. You don't feel the brunt of her tongue as I do.'

In the sewing room Rosie tried to settle into her routine, but she hardly knew what she was doing. The figures in the ledgers wouldn't add up. Ben waved to her as he passed the open door, and she almost ran after him. She'd made up her mind to tell him at lunchtime because he attached great importance to his work and disliked anything preventing him getting on with it.

She started stitching shirt collars. Usually she found it soothing to concentrate on the bobbing needle. This morning, nothing would shut out the dread which was hanging over her in a pall. Suddenly she got to her feet and ran upstairs to Ben's office. When he looked up, she could see his mind had been miles away, engrossed in the figures before him.

'Is something the matter, Rosie?' He was staring at her.

'Yes.' She could hardly get her breath at the thought of putting it into words.

'Sit down. Would you like some tea?'

'No, I couldn't . . .'

'What is it?'

'Not here, Ben.'

Without a word, he started to put his papers away, sliding them into his desk drawer and locking it. 'Come on then.' They'd only been at work for two hours.

'Now?'

'Do you want your coat? Probably not, it's quite a pleasant morning.' He led her straight across the hall.

'I'm taking Rosie out for ten minutes,' he announced at the door of his mother's cubicle. Without waiting for her answer, he was leading her out of the front door.

'Where are we going?' she asked. He tucked her arm through his and they stepped out briskly.

'Just for a little walk. So you can tell me what's bothering you.'

'We could go to the dutch barn,' she gulped. He smiled at her then, a gleam of anticipation in his dark eyes. 'Not for that. I've got something terrible to tell you.'

His smile was gone when she dared to look at him again. 'What is it?'

There was no easy way to break it to him. 'I think I'm pregnant, Ben. What am I gong to do?'

She felt his hand tighten on hers. His step slowed. He was frowning in concentration. 'We,' he corrected. 'What are we going to do?'

She felt a weight lift from her. That had been her worst worry.

'Rosie, I'm sorry!' A moment later he was pulling her round and hugging her in the middle of Bedford Road in broad daylight. Rosie saw an elderly lady raise her eyebrows in disapproval as she stepped off the pavement to give them a wide berth. Then she was tugging Ben on.

On top of the hay, away from prying eyes, they lay down together. Rosie felt his arms go round her and pull her against him. There was no passion in his embrace, it was all comfort.

'Rosie, I'm so sorry it has to be like this.'

'You don't want it?' There was a hard edge to her voice. 'A baby is a big responsibility.'

'I meant, I'm sorry it had to happen this way. It ought to be a wonderful moment, and I've spoiled it for you. I couldn't wait. I've no patience, have I, Rosie? Of course I want a family, but I would have chosen to wait a little longer.'

She let out a choking sob that was half a laugh.

'I love you, Rosie. I'll look after you whatever happens.'

'I'm scared. I can't believe it's happening to me. Is it fate?'

'No, it's my fault. Don't be frightened.'

'I'm afraid that what happened to my mother will . . .'

'No, Rosie, I won't abandon you. I wouldn't hurt you for the world.'

'What are we going to do?'

'I think we should call Mother's bluff. You need . . . We need the security of marriage now, and the sooner the better.'

Rosie sniffed hard. She didn't need Ben to tell her that; it was a screaming need. It brought a trickle of relief that he understood.

'We could go to the Register Office and make arrangements to get married. I think it only needs a few days' notice. What do you say to that?'

'Yes, yes, yes! It will raise eyebrows, though. Everybody will want to know why we're in such a hurry.'

'I'm afraid they're all going to be counting on their fingers when our baby is born.'

'I can live with that if I'm married.' Rosie was smiling as she felt the first spark of excitement at the thought.

'Of course we can. That's what we'll do then?'

'Yes.'

'We'll keep it secret from Mother, so she can't make trouble. We'll have to find a place to live.'

'Hadn't we better do that first?' Rosie pulled away. Suddenly there seemed so many things they would have to do.

'I don't suppose I could stay at the farm, just temporarily till we find somewhere of our own? Will seems to have taken to me.'

'I share a room with Phyllis. There are plenty of other rooms but they haven't been lived in for decades. Aunt Maud wouldn't be welcoming.'

'We'll find somewhere of our own then.'

Rosie felt suddenly cold again. 'What if your mother is right?'

'She isn't, Rosie.'

'But we don't know. What if she is?'

Ben sighed, and tossed his hair off his forehead. 'Our marriage would be declared null and void, I suppose.'

'Before they marry us, don't we have to swear there's no reason . . .? No reason why we shouldn't marry, I mean?'

'I believe so.'

Rosie shivered. 'Ben, it's public knowledge. The whole factory is a hotbed of gossip. Everybody knows I've been left a share of the business. The girls in the sewing room are saying I'm Edwin's daughter.'

He was frowning. 'I don't know if there would be any legal repercussions.'

She groaned. 'It frightens me.' She could feel him shaking in sudden fury.

'I could break Mother's neck for doing this to us! Frightening you, worrying us and spoiling what should be a wonderful time. She made up her mind she didn't want me to marry you. That's all it is, Rosie. Power mania. She wants to control me. Wants to control us all.'

'Your grandmother is taking me to meet Harry's wife on Wednesday afternoon. She'll surely know. Perhaps she'll settle it for us.'

'We'll fix it up after that,' he said. 'Right away. I love you, Rosie. We're going to get married. Don't think of anything else.'

Two days later Rosie still felt like a wet rag. She'd come to work wearing a new floral dirndl skirt and white blouse because she'd arranged to go with Constance to meet Alice Shearing.

When Ben came to the sewing room, early in the afternoon, she was still dithering about what to say to his mother.

'I'll have to tell her. She's in and out of here by the minute. She'll be furious if she finds I've gone without mentioning it.'

'You'll have to get over your shyness with Mother.' He took her arm. 'You've a perfect right to come and go, you're part owner of this business.'

'I haven't got used to that yet.' They were heading across the hall towards Beatrice's partitioned-off office. Ben thumped on the door and threw it open.

'Mother,' he said. Rosie crowded in behind him. 'I'm going to run Rosie to our house to see Gran. She'll be away for an hour or so.'

Rosie met Beatrice's hostile gaze. 'You can't do your job properly if you're never here,' she said coldly.

'I go out for an hour occasionally, and so do you,' Ben said easily.

'If there's a business need,' his mother flared. 'This is social, going to see Constance. And what on earth for, may I ask?'

'She's taking me to meet Alice.'

'Alice? I've told Constance I don't like her going to see Alice.'

'Why not?' Ben asked. 'It's about the only place she does go now.'

'She's got everything she needs at home. I know she's safe if she's there. What's Alice to you?' Her eyes went to Rosie again.

'I want to ask her about Harry.' She saw Beatrice's irritation turn to instant white hot anger.

'Why won't you be told? Edwin was your father.'

Rosie saw something else too. Fear flickered in her dark eyes. To imagine Beatrice Shearing being afraid of anything heartened her. That Beatrice was afraid of something she might find out was a revelation. 'You're just stirring up trouble.'

'I want to hear other people's opinion,' she said. 'No harm in that, is there?'

'Of course there is. You're going round upsetting everybody, raking up the past.'

'Most old ladies like to talk of the past,' Ben said. 'Gran loves it.'

'Alice is my age,' Beatrice said through clenched teeth. 'You're wasting time when you should be here working. We have to know how many shirts have been made today and by whom. You can't rely on those girls not to exaggerate what they've done. We'll never make a profit that way.'

'I'll be back in good time to do all that,' Rosie said with a confidence she didn't feel.

Ben led her out to the car. 'She's right in a way,' Rosie said. 'A good forewoman needs to be on hand all the time.'

'What's more important, the job or this?'

'This,' she sighed. 'We've got to sort it out.'

'Of course we have. Do you want me to come with you?' She did, but wasn't going to say so.

'I'll manage, Ben.' She had to get over this tongue-tied numbness. 'Alice might tell me more if I'm alone. Together we'd seem more of a delegation.'

She had a sort of sixth sense that let her know when people were covering up things they'd rather not talk about. It would function better if she went alone.

'Right,' Ben said, turning the car into the drive of his home. She was surprised he got out too. 'Don't want to find she's already gone.' He smiled. 'You know Gran. She could have forgotten about you, though I did remind her last night.'

The large front door stood open. It was a glorious sunny summer afternoon. A gardener was putting new bedding plants in a border. There was a strong smell of newly cut grass. She thought what an orderly life Ben had, everything so spick and span in his home. But of course, with Beatrice in charge, everything was bound to be spick and span.

She followed him upstairs to Constance's little sitting room. She was dressed ready to go out, already wearing a black straw hat and a stronger than usual aura of eau-de-Cologne. 'I'm expecting the taxi any minute now.'

Rosie kissed her cheek, reminding herself that Constance was probably her grandmother too, yet she didn't feel at ease with her as Ben did.

'I'll go back to my desk then,' he said.

Rosie thumbed through some particulars from a

local estate agent she found on the table. 'Have you seen a house you like yet?'

Below her, through the open window, she could see Ben driving out into the park. The scent of new mown grass was here too, and there were flowers standing on the hearth.

'The rooms seem so poky in new small houses.' Constance was frowning.

Rosie read through one sheet. The house sounded wonderful. She'd love to live in something like that. She wondered what Ben could afford. They hadn't got round to discussing details like that yet.

She heard tyres outside, and the front doorbell ringing urgently. Constance got to her feet in a leisurely fashion. 'That will be our taxi. I'll get my coat.'

With all the doors and windows standing open, Rosie could hear the resonance of a man's voice below in the hall. She got to her feet to hold Constance's coat while she put her arms into the sleeves.

'Will I need this today, do you think?' Constance was titivating in front of a looking glass, tucking a strand of silver hair more firmly under her hat.

'Come in, Mrs Roper,' she called as the footsteps came up the landing. 'Is it my car?'

'No, Mrs Shearing.' Rosie thought the housekeeper's cheeks unusually flushed and could see a man behind her. 'A visitor for you.'

He stood breathing heavily on the threshold, round-shouldered and wearing a dark tweed jacket, rather too heavy for the warmth of the day.

'Hello, Mother,' he said. She watched an incredulous Constance turn slowly.

'Harry, is it you?'

Rosie gasped as though she'd been doused with icy water. She was blinking hard, unable to believe her eyes. She'd believed Harry was dead. Constance had seemed so certain he was, and that Beatrice had killed him. Her head was spinning. Could she believe any of what Constance had told her? Now it all began to look like the fantasy of a lonely old woman.

'Of course it is.' Harry was hugging Constance self-consciously while his eyes looked questioningly into Rosie's.

She knew she was gaping. Her heart was thumping wildly. She felt she was on the brink of learning the truth at last.

'Harry darling! Let me look at you. How much older you seem!'

He looked twenty years older than Edwin had. His hair was crinkly, just like Rosie's own. Shearing hair, but white and thin against a scalp burned brown and dry by strong sun.

'I'd hardly have known you.'

'It's been a long time. You haven't changed much, Mother. Still a handsome woman.'

'You've come home! Oh, how wonderful. Where've you been all this time?'

'Paris. You'd love Paris, Mother. You'd like the Riviera in winter too, but it is expensive. Couldn't afford it on what Edwin sent. I've spent a lot of time in Tangier.'

Rosie knew Constance had forgotten her existence but she could feel Harry's bleary, dissipated eyes examining her. She recoiled from him. Impossible to believe this was the man she'd wanted to be her father.

'Who is this?' he finally asked, no doubt finding her gaze an intrusion.

'I'm Rose Quest,' she said, her mouth still dry with shock. 'Are you my father?' His slack cheeks creased into a wolfish smile.

'Everyone heaps sins on my shoulders, but I don't think I'm guilty of that. It'll be the wrong side of the blanket?'

She wanted to scream at his flippant manner. 'My mother was Grace Quest.'

'Thank goodness for that.' His wolfish grin flashed again. 'Where's Edwin? At work?'

Constance gasped. 'He died, Harry, didn't you know?'

'About two months ago?'

'That's right,' Rosie said.

'You did know then?' Constance breathed.

'No, he stopped paying my allowance then. I didn't have much choice about coming home. I ran out of money. Mother, can you lend me some?' Constance was already opening her handbag.

'Is it safe? For me to come home?' He pushed the notes she gave him into an inside pocket of his jacket. 'Is our ball of flames still around or has the devil called her to hell?' Constance looked at him, her pale eyes blank. 'Beatrice, Mother?'

'She's at work. Still running home and business. Still the iron hand.'

'Oh God!'

'Are you sure you're not my father?' Rosie felt sick again. She felt nothing for this man but distaste.

'Don't try pinning more crimes on me. I know I'm the black sheep of the family but I'll not admit to the sins of others.'

His manner was jocular, she wanted him to be serious. 'I was born in March 1916.'

'No, sorry. My conscience is clean. Would you have liked me to be?'

'No,' she said coldly. But better this dissolute wreck of a man than Edwin. Anyone was better than Edwin.

'What name did you say?' The dark degenerate eyes looked into hers, and he seemed to ponder. 'Grace Quest?'

'Did you know her?'

He took too long to answer. 'No,' he said. 'No.'

It didn't take any sixth sense to know he wasn't telling the truth.

'If you knew her, I'd love to know. I want to hear anything you can tell me. I know so little . . .' She was talking too fast.

'I told you, I don't know her.' His face was blank, he wasn't going to tell her anything. Rosie turned away disappointed as she heard the front doorbell ring again.

'That must be the taxi now,' she said.

'Were you going out, Mother?'

'Yes, we were going to see Alice.'

'Alice? My wife?'

'Yes, I go every Wednesday for tea and a game of bridge.'

'Good lord!'

'Do you want to come with us?'

'No, can't face her as well, not today. There's no

point anyway. I haven't heard anything from Alice since I left. You knew we'd split up, of course? Haven't seen her since your virago threw me out.'

'Then I shan't go either.' Constance started to remove her coat. Harry was on his feet immediately to help her get it off.

Mrs Roper was at the door again. 'Shall I send the taxi away, Mrs Shearing?'

'No,' Rosie got to her feet. 'If you don't want to use it, I will. I'll tell him to come next week as usual, shall I? That you don't want him today?'

'Yes, dear, and phone Alice and tell her I'm not coming will you?'

'Yes,' Rosie said. 'I'll do that. Goodbye, Constance. Goodbye . . .'

'Harry,' he prompted. 'Harry Shearing. And I'm not your father.'

As she crossed the landing to the head of the stairs, she heard him say to Constance: 'What a strange girl.'

As she paused by the telephone in the hall, she was shaking with shock and frustration, tears of disappointment stinging her eyes. Ben had assured her so many times, had been so confident it was Harry. He'd convinced her.

She'd imagined Harry to be very different. Another version of Edwin, but more handsome, a man with style and wit. Instead she'd felt sickened by him. He was a remittance man who had battened on his brother all his life. Not a person she wanted as a father. She couldn't bear to think of herself as descended from a man like that.

She told herself he'd been trying to hide something.

He'd known her mother's name, she was sure. His denial had been too smooth and too definite. There was a lot at stake. Perhaps she shouldn't accept his word for it?

There was nothing to stop her from going to see Alice on her own. It would save her looking up the phone number. She dithered a few moments longer, and then told herself she had to go.

If Alice and Harry had broken up before he went away, there could have been another woman. She shivered. Surely Grace would not have been attracted to a man like Harry? He might have looked better twenty years ago, must have had some charm then since everybody seemed to have loved him, but even so . . .

As the taxi took her through unfamiliar streets, Rosie was worried about what she was going to say to this complete stranger. She could think of no way she could ask politely if there had been another woman in her husband's life at the appropriate time. But she had to do it, she had to know without a shadow of a doubt. Only if Alice said no would she believe Harry.

She hadn't asked where Alice lived because Constance had been going to take her, and the taxi driver must know because he went every week. It surprised her to find the vehicle slowing down in a street of modest redbrick terraced houses. The cab pulled up in front of a door.

'Is this it?' She knew it must be, the front door was already opening and a well-built woman wearing a brown dress with a lace jabot came out. Rosie could see her looking uncertainly from the cab to her.

She got out and said: 'Constance asked me to let you know she wouldn't be coming today. I'm Rosie Quest.'

'Isn't she well?' The woman seemed concerned.

'Yes, it's not that, something's happened. I'd like a word with you. Can I come in for a moment?' She followed Alice up the narrow hall, squeezing past a tea trolley set with fine china cups. In the narrow kitchen, a parlourmaid was cutting dainty sandwiches. She was sent away. Alice damped a clean tea towel under the tap and covered what she'd cut. The whole place seemed to exude respectability.

'I take in paying guests, old ladies. I'm sorry, this is the only private place. I'm full to overflowing. Looking for larger premises to expand.'

'This will be fine.' Rosie felt embarrassed. 'Did Constance tell you she was going to bring me to see you?'

'You're the girl who thinks Harry could be her father?'

'Yes.' There was nowhere to sit down. Rosie leaned against a kitchen cabinet.

'You'll get nothing from Harry. I wouldn't bother if I were you.'

'He's come home. Constance was all ready to come here when he turned up.'

'What?' Easy to see she was astonished. Alice's brown eyes were wide with shock. 'Harry's come home? After all this time?' Now there was a wary look in her eyes. She turned suddenly and began folding tea towels and moving plates, tidying up a kitchen that was already spick and span.

'Yes, today. A few minutes ago.'

'You're sure it was Harry?'

'Quite sure.'

'Then you could have asked him yourself.'

'I did, he denied it. But I want to be sure.' Rosie felt desperate, she didn't care if it showed. It might persuade this stranger to help her. Haltingly she told Alice why. All Shearing's employees knew, one more person didn't seem to matter.

'You'd be right not to believe anything Harry tells you. Unless . . . Has he changed? What's he like now?'

Carefully choosing her words, Rosie tried to paint as polite a picture as possible of a man gone to seed.

'I don't want to see him. Not ever again. Surely he doesn't want to come here?'

'No.' Rosie tried to recall his words. 'No, I don't think it's likely.'

'I hope he doesn't.' Alice took a deep breath. 'You see, when I moved here, I pretended he was dead. Easier to say I was a widow than that my husband had gone off with another woman. I can't get over that he's back.'

'Is it possible that he knew my mother? Her name was Grace Quest.'

'Quest?' Alice was frowning. 'It sounds familiar somehow. I just can't think of anything, except he's back. Harry's come back. Yes, I do remember now. I get my milk from Quest's. The name's on the float.'

'My mother's brother,' Rosie said, disappointed. 'He was asking . . .'

'Yes. Look, I was born in March 1916. So it's the year before I'm interested in.'

'1915? A bad year for us. We split up then.'

Rosie felt a glimmer of hope. 'Did he have a girl friend?'

'He had lots. Girls thought him fun. They loved his capacity for drink and dance, carousing and indulgence. He loved parties.'

'Didn't he have anyone special?'

'Oh, yes, Marietta something, he was very serious about her. She was on the stage, a singer in the music hall. He saw the show at the Argyll and went backstage and invited the whole cast to a party. Most of them came, they filled the house. Would she be your mother?' Rosie shook her head.

'Harry was a spendthrift, a gambler, and he sponged off everyone. That's really why I left him. He always had to be the centre of attraction. Only seemed to come alive when he was surrounded with people. He wanted life to be one long party.'

Rosie nodded, that fitted the impression she'd had of him.

'He was twenty-four when we married, but he'd never grown up.'

'What year would that be?'

'Before the war, 1906. I thought the incessant partying should stop, that he'd get down to earning a living. I came from a hard-working family. When I married Harry, they gave us enough money to buy a small house.

'What we could have bought wasn't good enough for him, so we rented something much grander. Within a year he'd spent all my money, and I was so besotted with him I let him do it. He was a rotten husband. My family called him a wastrel and he was.

'It took me a few years to find out what he was really like, and to accept it. I found him impossible to live with, so I left him. Just walked out.

'He was in trouble with his own family by then. They were ashamed of him, always trouble over money and women. He'd been taking money from the business for years. Almost bankrupted poor Constance. Neither she nor Edwin knew what he'd been doing. It was all hushed up, of course.

'Beatrice was tougher than Edwin. She sorted Harry out and sent him away. I was glad. I didn't have to worry about him after that. Well, not till now.'

Rosie sighed. This was getting her nowhere.

'Emmeline might remember more. Do you know of Emmeline? Her husband was very friendly with the Shearings for years, though she ran off and left him. Same as me really, except she had someone to go to. Sad to see what she's come to now. In a wheelchair. She'll be in the sitting room if you'd like to talk to her.'

Rosie looked at her watch. What was the use? 'I ought to be getting back.' It was all taking so much longer than she'd expected. 'You kept in touch with Constance all these years?'

'I felt sorry for her. She was so filled with fears about Beatrice. I asked her here so she could talk them through. She thought the sun shone out of Harry, the only one who was sorry to see him go.'

'She still does. I think he'll have a home with her.'

'Not if Beatrice has her way,' she said tartly.

Rosie held her tongue, better not say too much. Alice would find out sooner or later that Constance had the house on the market.

'So Harry was telling the truth?' She felt sick with foreboding.

'He'd have made a rotten father. The very last man you'd want. He'd be sponging off you now.'

But anyone was better than Edwin because now their problem was insurmountable. Rosie didn't know how she managed to thank Alice and get herself outside again. Thank goodness she'd asked the taxi to wait. She collapsed on the back seat.

It was impossible for her and Ben to marry. She had to face that. The happy future she'd so looked forward to could never be.

CHAPTER TWENTY-TWO

Back in the sewing room Rosie began feverishly to count the stack of shirts completed that day. All were in the fashionable new style with longer pointed collars.

To make matters worse, she was in a rush because there wasn't much time left before the girls went home, and each one had to have her output checked and logged. She could see her fingers shaking, and was so agitated she wasn't counting properly. Kitty, her false teeth slipping and whistling, was trying to make her listen. Trying to tell her about something else. She couldn't take that in either.

Rosie stopped and told herself fiercely she had to calm down. She went to the cloakroom, splashed cold water on her face, and drank half a tumblerful. Then made herself take deep breaths. She wouldn't think of the future, she would go back and count shirts. She had to get the right figures down in her book. It wouldn't matter if she were late leaving for once.

When she went back Kitty pushed a sheet of paper in her hand. It had columns of figures on it.

'I did the totting up for you, Rosie, I was afraid you

wouldn't get back in time.' She'd forgotten Kitty had sometimes deputised for Flora.

'Thanks, Kitty. Good of you to think of it.' Then she was blinking back a rush of gratitude. Kitty had already logged each machinist's output, and counted the finished shirts for her. She only had to put the figures in the book.

Rosie was beginning to feel better till she heard the tattoo of heels on the bare wood floor and knew Beatrice was coming to find fault.

'Really, Rose, this won't do. You've been out most of the afternoon. You've let all these finished shirts pile up here while Ethel is standing idle in the packing room.'

'I'm sorry, Mrs Shearing.' The apology was automatic. She knew the shirts had been left so she could check the count if she wanted to.

Kitty had begun to pile them into the waggon. Rosie put more on top as she pushed it towards the packing room where the shirts would be pressed, have celluloid stiffeners put in the collars and be packed in cellophane bags.

'It isn't good enough. We can't make a profit if the workers are standing idle.'

'Ethel is on piecework too.'

'Don't answer me back.'

Rosie still had a sour taste in her mouth but she was thinking again. Beatrice had come into the sewing room with the express purpose of upsetting her. They all knew Ethel would come shouting for shirts if she ran out of work. Rosie wanted to kick back at her, and for once knew how to do it.

'Harry's come home,' she said. 'It kept me away longer than I expected.' She was watching for the effect of her words. It was starling. All the colour left Beatrice's face, leaving it drained.

'Harry?'

'Yes, Harry, your brother-in-law.' Beatrice was staring, transfixed with horror.

'What's he come back for?'

'It seems his allowance hasn't been paid since your husband died.' Beatrice's face flushed with fiery colour at that. Rosie wondered if she'd known Edwin was sending him money. She couldn't resist adding: 'Constance was delighted to see him. She thinks it will be like old times to have him back.'

She felt she'd scored a victory when, without another word, Beatrice's heels beat a sharp retreat to her office.

It was only when she was hunched over the ledger, copying in Kitty's figures, that Rosie began to feel less satisfied. Of course Beatrice would be displeased to have Harry return. Both Constance and Alice had told her Beatrice had thrown him out when she'd discovered he'd been fraudulently taking company funds. He'd confirmed it himself, and his manner had told Rosie he wasn't looking forward to the meeting either. Of course Beatrice wouldn't want another confrontation with him.

Rosie's fingers were white where they gripped her pen. Beatrice had disliked her from the moment she'd started as an apprentice. She'd regularly found fault with all she did, played on her natural nervousness till it had deepened to a festering dread.

Now Beatrice could make her boil with resentment and loathing. It was Beatrice who had said Edwin was her father, who was preventing her from marrying Ben. Beatrice who was causing the trouble. Rosie was almost afraid of the violence of her feelings.

But her puny display of strength had changed nothing. She felt at that moment she'd welcome a real set to with Beatrice.

With ten minutes to go before home time, Rosie put the ledger away and went upstairs to Ben's office. His head came up from a file as she closed the door carefully behind her.

'Harry's come home. He's not my father. I've asked him.'

Ben was blinking at her as though understanding came only slowly. 'Harry? He's not dead then?'

She shook her head. 'He's come home because he hasn't received his allowance since your father died. He's definitely not my father, Ben.'

He was holding her tight against him then, crushing her in his arms. She could still feel herself shaking.

'Where's he been all these years? Gran thought he was dead. Nobody ever mentioned his name – not even Dad, his own brother.'

'Harry stole from them. Almost ruined the family business. They wanted to forget him. Probably had a big row over it.'

'But why didn't I know he was still alive?'

'You were only two or three years old. You wouldn't remember.'

'No. I was sure Mother believed him dead too.'

'Wishful thinking on her part then,' Rosie said.

'He's back and I've asked him. Your mother's right about one thing – Edwin must be my father.' That had been banging away at the back of her mind all afternoon, reducing her to pulp.

'No,' Ben said.

'If it isn't Harry, it must be Edwin. There's no two ways about it. Not with Constance recognising a family likeness and Edwin remembering me in his will. There's a Shearing streak in me. It has to be from Edwin.'

'He would have told me.'

She could see Ben digging his heels in. There was a mulish look on his face. He couldn't and wouldn't accept that. 'Mother has some devious reason of her own for saying so.'

'But we can't get married, Ben. Brothers and sisters can't get married.'

'We aren't brother and sister. Nor half-brother and sister either.' Ben's mouth was set in a stubborn line. 'Don't even think it.'

Rosie felt she'd been through this a dozen times, and they weren't making any progress. 'We have to. What are we going to do?'

'We'll get married where nobody knows us. Emigrate to Canada, or America if you like. We'll just disappear. Mother will never find us.'

She felt astounded. 'You'd do that for me?'

'I'd do it for myself too. Though it's a pity about the business. We'll have to abandon our interest in that. Steve and Oliver couldn't afford to buy us out. Impossible to ask Mother, and if we tried to sell our shares to Gran, it would look as though we were

taking advantage. We'll just have to forget them.'
He smiled wryly. 'I'm an accountant, I can earn a
living anywhere.'

'But you're wrapped up in the business, totally
engrossed in it,' she said. 'You think so much of the
family connection. It's the breath of life to you.'

He said nothing, staring beyond her, wrapped in his
own thoughts.

She felt she had to draw back. 'I thought you'd
choose the business.'

'I don't want to choose at all.' For a moment he
looked agonised. 'But it looks as though I can't have
both.'

'You're hooked on it, Ben. Admit it, the family
fascinates you.'

'I thought it was what I wanted.' Rosie held her
breath. He smiled at her.

'I don't see myself as an ambitious man. I've no
great talent. The best I can do is head the family
business, make is successful. But I love you, Rosie. I
want you too.'

'It's not an easy choice.'

'It's easy enough. I can't live without you. I'd choose
you every time.'

'You must love me very much.'

He laughed. 'Haven't I convinced you yet?'

'I suppose I'm afraid you'll regret it later.'

'I won't.' He pulled her closer. 'We need to re-think
this. Come home with me. You're all shaken up. I don't
want you to go off on your own when you're like this.'

'Uncle Will expects me home to help with milking.
He'll worry.'

'He won't mind for once. Send a message with Phyllis. If you run down now, you'll catch her before she goes. I'll ring Mrs Roper and tell her there'll be another for dinner. If Harry's there, one more won't make much difference to her. Come on, Rosie, we need to decide our next move.'

'Won't I need to change?' She knew she was putting obstacles in the way. She was wearing her new dirndl skirt. 'What about your mother. Hadn't you better ask her?' But she'd had Beatrice on the run herself half an hour ago.

'Sometimes it's better to take Mother by surprise.'

She ran down to catch Phyllis then, and have a wash in the cloakroom. Things had taken a turn for the worse and she felt overwhelmed. All the way to Ben's home they mulled over what they could do.

'Come on up to my room,' he said as they went into the hall. 'I want to change into something more comfortable.' Already he was taking off the jacket of his suit.

Rosie hesitated. 'Your gran would think it improper. I can't come to your bedroom with you.'

He laughed. 'She'll be more than shocked when she knows what we *have* done. You'll find her in the drawing room then. Gran will be having a glass of sherry now.'

Rosie went to the door which was already ajar. Her hand went to push it wider when she heard Gran say: 'I'll need some help, Harry.'

His voice replied: 'Of course you will, Mother. I'll do all I can.'

Rosie drew back, afraid she might be interrupting a

personal conversation. Above her, she saw Ben watching from the landing. She signalled she'd wait for him in the small sitting room.

A large high-backed sofa had been pulled up in front of the hearth. She'd seen Ben and Stephen sprawl with their feet up on its loose cretonne covers. She put hers up now and leaned back against the deep corner cushions. No fire had been lit today and the empty grate was hidden behind a petit point firescreen.

She wondered whether Constance had embroidered it herself. She was leaning forward for a closer look, trying to see how it had been fastened into its mahogany frame, when she heard the door open again. There was no mistaking the sound as two people came in, and the door closed with a confidential click. She was about to sit up and make her presence known when Beatrice's voice, pitched deliberately low, grated harshly: 'I told you never to come back here. You're not welcome, Harry.'

Rosie caught her breath, and suddenly her heart was pounding.

'I can see that, my dear Bea. I've not come at a convenient time for you.'

'After stealing what you did, you should have had the sense to stay where you were safe.'

'If you're going to call me a thief, then so are . . .'

'Shut up, Harry. If you've come to make trouble . . .'

'I haven't, but I can't live on fresh air.'

'Edwin had no business to send money to you.' Her voice was thick with exasperation.

'I had to find out why my allowance stopped. So suddenly, with no warning.'

Rosie was rigid with alarm. The last thing she'd intended was to listen to Beatrice and Harry having a row about their personal affairs.

'Well, now you know, I want you gone. You had no business to tell Mrs Roper you'd be here for dinner, or to ask for a room to be made ready for you. You'll have to leave first thing in the morning. I can't have you here upsetting Constance.'

'Upsetting you, you mean. Mother is delighted to see me.'

Rosie felt panic-stricken, unable to make up her mind whether it was more embarrassing to stay hidden or to reveal her presence. She'd already delayed too long and heard too much.

'Get out of my house, Harry. I'm not going to put up with you.'

'I'll have to have money, a regular allowance.'

'You're not expecting me to give you money?' She gave a mirthless laugh. 'You should be thinking of paying back what you took. You'll not get a penny more out of me.'

'Oh, I think I will, Beatrice.' His voice was lower, with a touch of menace. 'It's twenty years since you blackmailed me into leaving. The boot's on the other foot now.'

'Hardly blackmail, Harry.'

'A clear case of blackmail, Beatrice. You had me in a cleft stick, but the police won't be interested in what I did twenty years ago. They'll ask why you've condoned it since, and I'll tell them it was because I

agreed to your terms. And Mother's been telling me
you used the same method on her. That's why you
want me gone, isn't it?'

'Don't be silly.'

'I know you have some hold on Mother, that you've
frightened her for years.'

'Nonsense.'

'Dear Bea, how you've cheated and manipulated us
all for your own ends! You wanted power, didn't you?
Power to control us Shearings.'

'I've worked hard for you. Your business would
have gone bankrupt but for me. I did it, Harry, not
Edwin. None of you was capable.'

'You're forgetting, we know each other very well. I
know how determined you were to worm your way
into this family. Have you forgotten you set your cap
at me? Proposed marriage and slept with me. Tut tut,
Beatrice. In those days you were willing to do anything
to become Mrs Harry Shearing. Thank God I saw
through you in time.' He laughed. 'I count that a
providential escape. Love never entered into it for
you, did it?'

'Get out of my house.' She was almost spitting at
him.

Rosie could hear her own heart pounding; it seemed
loud enough to be audible to them. She closed her
eyes, covered her mouth with both hands. She was in a
terrible position.

'You wanted our money, Beatrice. Money is what
you really love, it brings its own power. You pretended to enjoy my parties, but you thought them a
waste of time and hard cash. I saw through you, and

you've hated me for it ever since. I know exactly what you are.'

Rosie sat transfixed. Perhaps after all Ben was right – Beatrice did have some devious reason of her own for saying Edwin was her father? She remembered then that Ben would come looking for her any minute and she would be caught listening to all this. Hastily, she swung her feet to the ground and stood up.

Beatrice was facing her. There was no mistaking the shock she felt. Her mouth dropped open and the colour drained from her cheeks. Harry had his back to her, and carried on.

'You've committed more sins than I have. But you're cleverer, Bea, you've managed to keep yours hidden. Now you're afraid we're all going to compare notes and find out you've cheated us.'

Rosie forced herself to stretch and pretend a yawn.

'What a way to be woken. I was just having a nap while Ben changes.' Her voice sounded squeaky and artificial.

Now they were both staring at her in stunned silence. She gulped, knowing she'd failed to make her excuse ring true. They both knew she'd been listening.

Harry recovered first. 'Ah, yes, young Rosie. Is she the reason you want me out of here?'

Beatrice's face was tight with tension but he seemed relaxed, his hands in his pockets. She watched him look from her to Beatrice.

'I'm going to do what you've been doing all your life. It's worked for you, you got exactly what you wanted. No reason why it shouldn't work for me. If, Bea, you're prepared to do business, I might be persuaded to leave you in peace.'

'That's outrageous.'

'Rosie's already checked up that I'm not her father. Soon she'll think of other questions you wouldn't want me to answer.'

The door flew open and Ben came in, wearing a grey pullover and slacks, with his hair freshly slicked back.

'Oh, good, I thought you'd be sitting here on your own, Rosie.'

Harry smiled smugly. 'Better make up your mind quickly, Bea, or it will be too late. Now this is . . .?' He turned to Ben.

'I've made up my mind,' she choked. 'Keep your mouth shut, Harry.'

'What is it you don't want me to know?' Rosie demanded furiously. 'There's something you're trying to hide.'

'That's our business.' Harry threw back his head and laughed. 'Time for a drink before dinner. Would you be Ben or Stephen?'

'What's all this about?'

'Young Rosie will put you in the picture.'

On Sunday morning, Ben woke with an uneasy weight on his mind. The two airmail envelopes sealed and ready to post were propped against his clock. They brought his worry into focus.

When he'd talked to Rosie about emigrating to America he'd deliberately made it sound simple and straightforward. Rosie was worried enough and he had to do the best he could for her. He hadn't mentioned the difficulty of finding money for the scheme. He'd not been working long enough to save any, and they needed to go soon. There was nobody he dare ask for a loan.

Yesterday, he'd seen two jobs for which he felt suitably qualified advertised in a professional journal. One was in Canada and the other in South Africa. He'd not felt much enthusiasm for either, but applied for both.

'It doesn't matter where we go, providing it's a long way away,' he'd said to Rosie. 'If I had a job to go to, it would be so much easier.' He had to be able to support them both. He owed Rosie that much.

Not that she seemed very concerned about money. If he mentioned it, she'd smile, as she had a couple of days ago, and say as though to reassure him: 'There's always the money in Grace's account.' She seemed to think it was as good as in her own pocket already.

'Goodness knows when you'll be allowed to get your hands on that,' he'd retorted, remembering that Oliver had been trying to achieve it for some months. He led the way into Oliver's old office and they found the file in his cabinet.

'Her estate ought to be easy enough to sort out,' he'd grumbled. 'It's eighteen years since her death. When I compare the speed at which accountants are expected to act and the laggard ways of the legal profession . . .'

With Rosie looking over his shoulder, he spent ten minutes mulling over Oliver's correspondence and trying to understand the procedure. Settlement seemed as far away as ever.

'I have a friend who'll know more about this.

Someone I knew at school, he's a solicitor now.' He picked up his phone and asked him to push it through as quickly as possible.

Ben felt full of foreboding for the future. How could he have been so stupid as to let this happen to Rosie? It seemed the forethought he could muster at his desk did not extend to his personal life.

And even at his desk, he'd not done as well as he'd hoped. Family considerations had made him alter decisions he took at work. Mother had pleaded with him not to go to the police. Not to make trouble between Oliver and Lydia by trying to confront his brother. Not to warn Arthur Feltham to expect trouble.

'He'll be careful now, not to queer his pitch,' she had said.

'Eventually temptation will prove too great.'

'He's getting a higher salary from them.'

'It won't be enough. Whatever it is, it won't be enough for Oliver.'

'He wouldn't be such a fool.'

'He's the biggest fool out,' Ben said.

'Then it will be his own doing, not mine. I can't bring myself to . . .'

Ben groaned and turned over in bed. Should he get up? The hands of his clock pointed to six-thirty. He couldn't lie here agonising, but it was too early to get up on a Sunday morning. He felt down to the rug beside his bed where he'd piled the old account books. He'd forget the present and carry on with his appraisal of the company's past performance.

It had got so late the other night, and he'd been so

engrossed in the furore Harry was creating, that he'd skimmed on too quickly, wanting to know the worst. There was much he hadn't absorbed yet about the war years. His hand closed again on the records for the year 1915, a great bundle of files and books tied together. He pulled them up on his counterpane.

They made depressing reading. The company was weaker than it had ever been during the early years.

His mother had apparently pulled it back from the brink then, but could she do it again? Because now, it seemed to Ben, the business had come full circle. Oliver had pulled it down to another low. But his mother no longer seemed such a pillar of strength, was less decisive. Ben was afraid she wouldn't be able to manage what she had in her youth. It meant, if he were to go, the family firm would probably go under. He hated to think Shearing's Shirts might no longer exist.

He tried to concentrate on the figures for 1915. They were not so gripping the second time round. He flipped through other documents in the bundle.

Suddenly he was alert and sitting up. He found himself skimming through a contract between Shearing's Shirts and a Mr Clive Woodley who had loaned their business five thousand pounds for five years at an interest rate of three percent a year. It was said to be for the purpose of paying off bank loans.

Certainly some of the money had gone to reduce them. But money had been needed more urgently to finance the purchase of materials and pay the wage bill, both of which needed ever-increasing amounts. Some had gone on easing the cash flow there.

Clive Woodley had been paid his interest for the

first half of the year but not for the second. Frowning, Ben reached for the 1916 books and opened them. Florentine endpapers, neatly kept, the ink less faded now. Some documents were typed. There were more copies of Government contracts. Before the end of the year, his father was heading the company.

Ben wondered who Clive Woodley had been as he retied the accounts for that year. He abandoned every other consideration and went searching forwards. Interest was never paid on that loan again. Neither was there any sign of its having been repaid.

He was surprised and wondered what had happened to it, making a mental note to search further forward still when he brought home the returns for future years.

He got dressed in a hurry. He'd spent too long perusing company accounts, trying to picture how things had been for his father all those years ago. He'd told his grandmother he and Rosie would take her out to look at houses.

Ben realised he need not have rushed. His grandmother was still eating her breakfast and it took her a long time to get ready to go out. He'd made appointments for them to view three houses and felt added irritation because they'd be late picking Rosie up.

He left Grandma searching her dressing-table drawers for her dressing cape and went to collect Rosie first. She was ready, but in the morning sun the blue shadows under her eyes were all too obvious. It drove home to him how much of a strain she was finding things.

'I'm fine,' she told him, and smiled. 'I've got over

the morning sickness now.' But she didn't have the bounce she'd once had. He stopped to post his letters, telling her all about them.

Back home, it was Rosie who brought Grandma out to the car while he found a car rug and collected her coat and handbag. They were twenty minutes late arriving at the first house.

'I don't like the look of it from the outside.' Grandma said as soon as he pulled the car into the kerb. 'It's very small.'

'Grandma, you don't need a big house now. It has three bedrooms.'

'The road is busy. Rather too noisy.' Ben had picked on Bebington because he'd thought it a quiet residential district. It was not too far away, so she could still visit Alice and attend the same church. The inside didn't please her either. The second was a bungalow.

'A much quieter road,' Rosie said as she helped Constance out of the car. 'I like this, and it would be better for you to have no stairs.'

'I can manage stairs perfectly well,' Constance retorted. She took a long time, peering minutely into every room. 'There's only one bathroom?' she enquired of the owners.

'It tells you that in the particulars, Gran,' Ben said hastily, waving them in front of her.

'I'd have to share it with Mrs Roper.'

'Yes,' he agreed.

'We'd be on top of each other in a little house like this, and the garden isn't up to much. No, I don't think it would do.' Ben got her back to the car.

They were drawing up outside the third when Rose

said delightedly, 'This is lovely. You couldn't help but like this.'

It pulled at his heart strings to see her excited like this. If things had been more normal, they would have been house hunting for themselves.

'Very pink bricks,' Gran complained. 'I'm not sure that I like . . .'

'It's a modern house,' Ben said firmly. 'It's what you need, easy to run. Much warmer for you.' It took her longer to get out on the pavement. Rosie went to help. It was obvious Gran was tiring now.

'The other houses are crowding in very close.'

'You don't need a big garden, it makes more work. You never sit out in the one at home.'

'But I must have some space to call my own.' Her eyes were full of doubt.

'It has a very handsome front door,' Rosie said as they waited for their ring on the bell to be answered. Ben wondered if he was doing the right thing in encouraging her to think of living alone. Suddenly she didn't seem capable, and Mrs Roper was not much younger; she wouldn't be able to look after the two of them for very long. They were being shown round the ground floor.

'A comfortable sitting room,' Rosie enthused. 'French doors to the garden.'

'And very private at the back,' Ben added, unable to look at Rosie. Her face had lit up. He knew this was what she'd like for herself.

'An easy garden to look after,' the vendor told them. 'An easy house. I wish I didn't have to move, but my company's transferring me down to London.'

He was showing them the central heating boiler. 'Who will look after this?' Gran asked him.

Ben said: 'It doesn't need looking after. We'll explain how it works.'

Her lips were pursing. 'Is this the dining room?'

'Yes,' he agreed.

'It's a bit poky.' She lowered her voice to a stage whisper, but Ben was quite sure the owner heard.

'Oh, I don't know, the dining room at home is far too big,' he said hastily. 'I like this.'

'Just right.' Rosie smiled. Her eyes, dark with longing, were darting in all directions, trying to see and memorise every corner. Ben liked the way the sun streamed into the sitting room, loved the relaxed and friendly feel to the whole house. If they'd been looking for a place for themselves, this would be it. He thought he would be able to afford the mortgage on it. Constance took a long time getting up the stairs.

'Steeper than I'm used to.' She was breathing heavily on the landing, and shaking her head in disbelief at the size of the bedrooms.

'You don't need anything bigger than this,' he told her. 'You'd be very comfortable here.'

He couldn't look at Rosie again. Marriage and a home of her own were now urgent. He had made it so. It was unkind to trail her round houses she knew she couldn't have. It must surely be hard for her to listen to Gran finding fault with them all. He was failing them both.

He'd got Gran out on the path and away from the owners before she said: 'All the rooms are too small. I don't care for it.'

He was afraid his mother had been right. Gran had left it too late to think of living by herself. Too late even to make up her mind for herself. This was her way of putting off the decision. He drove home knowing he'd added to his worries and solved nothing.

CHAPTER TWENTY-THREE

On Saturday, after seeing everybody out of the factory and locking it up for the weekend, Beatrice drove home alone in the Rover. Ahead of her, she could see Ben driving the Ford.

Once she had savoured the weekends. She'd found it pleasant to exchange the scurry of week days at the factory for the peace of home, and the time to think and do those jobs needing more concentration. But now, with Harry back, home was anything but peaceful. His eyes had a way of challenging her across the table at every meal.

She let herself into the hall and hung up her coat. She heard his deep throaty laugh through the drawing-room door. That alone was enough to unsettle her. The dining room was empty when she looked in, but the table was set. On Saturdays they usually had lunch as soon as they were all home. Mrs Roper came puffing up from the kitchen, wiping her hands on her apron.

'The estate agent's bringing people to see the house at one o'clock. Do you want me to keep lunch until they've been?'

Beatrice felt a flash of irritation. 'Coming at a meal time? Who gave them permission to do that? It wasn't Harry?'

The woman cleared her throat. 'Yes, I believe it was.' Beatrice flinched. Harry knew how to rub her up the wrong way. She'd been a fool to give him money. It made her squirm to think of it now.

'It's none of his business. He has nothing to do with the house.' She was in the drawing room to confront him before she could stop herself.

'If you want to sell the house, there's no point in putting prospective purchasers off,' he said rudely. That brought her up short. She didn't want to sell the house, but she couldn't spell that out in front of the whole family.

'They're coming for a second look,' Stephen said. 'They must be interested.' It annoyed her further to see they were drinking beer. Her eyes went round the room.

'Really, Constance, sherry at lunchtime too? It's only too easy to overindulge. I hope you won't make yourself ill.'

'A glass of sherry won't do her any harm.' Again Harry's irritating laugh. 'A little of what she fancies at her age, isn't it, Mother?'

Beatrice felt growing apprehension. Harry knew too much and his mind was clear. Unlike Constance he couldn't be convinced otherwise. Mrs Roper cleared her throat in the doorway.

'Shall I serve lunch now, madam?' Beatrice was about to snap: 'Of course. Why should we worry about buyers?'

'I think we'd better wait ten minutes,' Constance said gently from her armchair. 'I'd prefer to. It'll feel like feeding time at the zoo if they come when we're eating.'

'Make sure they see the dining room first,' Beatrice instructed Mrs Roper before collapsing on a chair.

Once, Constance would never have dared argue about household arrangements. Being Edwin's wife had given Beatrice a secure anchorage. Edwin had loved her enough to defy his mother's wishes and marry her. By the time he'd got over that, she'd secured her future. His extramarital affairs had strengthened her hold over him, and he'd allowed her to do what she wanted in both his business and his home.

Yet within a few weeks of his death, Constance was signalling that the old order had changed. Even so, Beatrice couldn't believe she'd sell the house. Edwin had said she loved it, that they mustn't sell it while she was alive. Mustn't even try to persuade her to sell. Without him, she felt uneasy. The power she'd so carefully built up over the years was beginning to crumble.

'Would you like a glass of sherry?' Harry's manner was insolent. He was refilling Constance's glass.

'No, thank you.'

'By the way, I think you'd better order more drinks, Beatrice. I can't find any more whisky, and the beer is almost finished.'

'Can't you buy your own?' She was bristling with bad temper.

'You know the best places to buy everything, Bea.'

That he seemed relaxed goaded her further. 'You like to see to everything yourself. Oh, by the way, I'm not keen on the brand you got for Edwin, I prefer Bell's myself.'

She saw Stephen's eyebrows rise at the enormity of this, and exploded: 'Get your own, Harry. I don't propose to.'

There was an uncomfortable silence until Stephen said, 'Looks as though you might have a buyer for the house, Gran.'

He stretched out in his chair and put his hands behind his head. Beatrice knew he was trying to soothe her by deflecting her attention from Harry, but that annoyed her more. She hadn't believed the house could ever be sold. It was outrageous that Constance should think of selling the roof over her head. It would make her homeless.

Edwin would never have allowed it. He had loved her, she was the mother of his children. He owed her for getting the business out of trouble, and Edwin never forgot what he owed. He'd treated everybody fairly.

'You'll have to decide where you're going, Constance, before you can agree to anything.' Beatrice hoped that would unsettle her. She'd been so sure she couldn't make decisions at her age.

Ben must be encouraging her.

He had a way of looking at his own mother as though he knew more than he should. A way of pitting his will against hers and winning. An inner strength that Edwin had never had.

'Are there any houses here you'd like to see, Gran?'

He was shuffling through the pile of particulars which was being added to with every post. 'Could you take her out this afternoon, Stephen? She needs to see some of these.'

'Really, Gran.' Stephen was looking at Constance earnestly. 'Don't you honestly think you've left it a bit late to live by yourself?'

For a moment, Beatrice allowed herself to believe Stephen was on her side, that he wasn't lost to her. She rushed to support his argument.

'Of course you have, Constance. You've always been content to sit back and have everything done for you. You'll not be able to run a household now. Find help with the cleaning, pay the bills. You'll find it too much for you.'

'What I was going to suggest, Gran,' Stephen's eyes flashed a warning in his mother's direction, 'was asking Alice to take you in.'

Beatrice watched Constance's pale blue eyes go from Harry to Stephen, and knew all was not lost.

'Live in Elmhurst Road?' Constance's voice rang with indignation. 'Me?'

Ben was leaning forward in his chair, relief in every line of his body. 'It's a wonderful idea, Gran. You'd be much better off with Alice. She runs a comfortable home, you said so yourself.'

'Not for me.'

'But you're fond of Alice. You've been going there for tea every week for years. You could play bridge whenever you wanted.'

'She couldn't take me, she has every room filled.'

'You could ask for the next vacancy. Just think, you

wouldn't have to worry about anything once you were there. She'd coddle you.'

'I couldn't possibly live in Elmhurst Road.' Constance had the mulish look on her face Beatrice knew so well. They'd never get her there. Probably wouldn't leave this house until she went feet first in her coffin. Ben leapt to his feet and went to the window.

'You're a terrible snob, Gran, that's your trouble. That's why you won't consider any of the houses I've taken you to see either. You say they're too small.'

'They are.'

'You want your house to be imposing, in a private park at the end of a drive. It's the last thing you need, Gran, but it's what you want.'

'It must have bedrooms for you and Stephen, and a guest room for visitors like Harry.'

'You can count me out,' Ben said stolidly. It made Beatrice shiver with foreboding. It sounded as though he meant to go ahead with his wedding plans after all. She felt herself break out into a sweat again; she had to hold on to Ben.

'Me too,' Stephen said. 'Somebody I know at the bank has a flat he wants me to share. I'm thinking of trying it.'

Ben swung round. 'What about you, Uncle Harry? Now you've come home you'll need somewhere to live. Are you happy to live with Gran? Permanently, I mean.'

'Well, I . . . I have a permanent home in Tangier. I don't think England . . . I'll probably be going back.'

Beatrice thought she saw the chance to strike at

Harry's weak spot. Discussing his domestic arrangements in front of his mother would surely embarrass him. It was one of the reasons he'd agreed to leave the country all those years ago. She'd have found it harder to dislodge him from the business if he hadn't been caught up in problems with women.

'Of course, Harry, I didn't expect you to stay.' She smiled sourly at him. 'You have that common-law wife to go back to. What was her name, the woman you picked up from the music hall? Something terribly theatrical – Marietta Mannering, wasn't it?'

'That's her stage name, as you very well know.' Harry's grating laugh came again.

'Her stage name? That sounds very grand,' Ben said, his face alight with interest. 'There's so much about my family I didn't know.'

'She travelled round the less important music halls singing, didn't she?' Beatrice couldn't resist saying, though she knew it would be dangerous to get Harry's back up too much.

'She's a dancer too.'

'Don't tell me she's still at it? Are there music halls in Tangier?'

'She sings in nightclubs and bars, she's had to carry on working. She couldn't expect me to support her on what Edwin sent.'

'Edwin was far too generous,' she flared at him. 'You wouldn't have got that if I'd known about it.'

'It was Harry's share of the profit,' Ben said amicably. 'A dividend sent twice a year. It wasn't coming out of Dad's own pocket.'

'How do you know that?' Ben had surprised her

more than once with what he managed to pick up. It made her uneasy.

'Well, from the old accounts.'

'I didn't say you could read those. I should never have allowed you to use your father's office.'

'Dad suggested I read them. He encouraged me to, said I'd learn a lot. Anyway, why shouldn't I?' Ben had an odd expression in his eyes. Beatrice wished she'd held her tongue.

'I would have understood, Harry,' Constance said.

'It would have been social suicide to stay here, and Beatrice didn't want me to go on working in the business.'

'I did write to you, but you never answered.'

'No, Mother, but I sent Edwin a Christmas card every year, just to let you all know I was still alive. He did tell you?'

'Never anything about . . .'

'What's her real name?' Stephen asked eagerly.

'Edith Smith, but she's more generally known as Mrs Shearing these days,' he said easily.

'What's that?' Constance demanded. 'You're not living with another woman?'

'Mother! You wouldn't have expected me to be celibate all these years?'

'Really, Harry! You do shock me. I thought it was trouble in the business. Though Edwin did try to suggest the reason you disappeared was some dalliance . . .'

'You'd be surprised how respectable we appear now. A middle-aged couple known to have been together for years.'

'What will Alice think?' Constance was scandalised.

'She'll have given up thinking about it. It all happened in 1915, Mother. People were pretty strait-laced in those days, but I've been living with Edith for over twenty years. Time brings respectability. She's been more of a wife to me than Alice ever was.'

Beatrice felt fear prickling at the back of her mind. Harry was right, time had weakened her hand. She'd forced him out of the business by threatening to reveal his fraudulent removal of company funds, and out of his home because he was involved with another woman. Yet now he was quite relaxed about discussing his mistress in front of his mother. Today she couldn't turn either into a scandal.

'I mean, just look at our ex-King and Wallis Simpson. Who's going to take any interest in my affairs of the heart after that? They've just got married. Everything has come right for them. It's in the paper this morning.'

'I read about it.' Constance looked tight-lipped. 'Shocking for a man in his position. In my day . . . But at least they have got married. You have not.'

'What about lunch?' Stephen asked. 'I'm hungry, and I want to go out.'

Beatrice tutted with annoyance to find half an hour had passed. 'These people are late, no consideration. I knew we should not have waited. Stephen, tell Mrs Roper to put lunch on the table at once.'

Ben ate his stew slowly, pondering on how much he'd learned while waiting for lunch. He'd watched some bitter exchanges between his mother and Harry. She'd put in the knife once or twice but he'd seen fear on her face too. But fear of what? She was nervous, on edge, and acting totally out of character. And why should she object to his studying the old accounts? It didn't make sense.

He helped himself to more carrots and told himself everything Mother did made sense. It was just that he couldn't see it yet.

And as for Harry – he'd shown hatred for Beatrice, and a red hot need for revenge. But he'd been careful not to spell it out so that Ben and Stephen would understand. Rosie was certain there was a secret Harry and Beatrice were deliberately keeping from them.

'What made you decide to leave the business, Harry?' he asked.

'That would be telling.' The knowing glance towards his mother revealed more.

'Where was my father when all this went on?'

'Fighting for King and Country.' Harry forked stew into his mouth. Ben was not surprised by that. Though his father had rarely spoken of the war, he'd imparted a first hand knowledge of the trenches.

'I did him a good turn by leaving then,' Harry maintained. 'I had to go and fight and he got the job of running the factory. It was protected work.'

'He had a leg wound,' Beatrice said sullenly. 'Invalided out.'

'So you joined the Army, Uncle Harry?'

'No, the Royal Flying Corps. I figured it would be more fun flying over the trenches than being stuck in them.'

'Was it?'

'Never got the chance to find out. They said I was too old to fly. I got a desk job.'

Ben studied his mother seated at the end of the table. So she'd had to cope with Harry's incompetence on her own, as well as take care of two children and run her own business. Dad had been away at the front.

She'd put Harry out eventually, but he could see anxiety on her face now. It was something very new to see Mother scared of anything. It was obvious she was frightened of Harry. Frightened he might spill more family secrets.

Rosie was convinced Harry was blackmailing his mother. He'd thought that a bit far fetched when she'd told him, but it would explain why he kept silent. There had to be some secret, and the person black-mailed had to have an interest in keeping it hidden. Harry knew more, he was certain. And there were areas in the accounts that remained unexplained . . .

Mrs Roper was bringing in rice pudding and the kitchen girl was taking away their empty plates when he asked: 'Who was Clive Woodley?'

He saw his mother blench and knew he'd touched a nerve. At the same time Gran gave such an alarmed jerk of the hand she knocked over her tumbler. Water spread over the cloth creating a diversion. Mrs Roper rushed dishes to the sideboard, towels had to be found to mop it up. Harry looked so smug Ben was sure he knew all about Clive Woodley.

In the middle of the mêlée the front doorbell rang, Ben heard the commotion and tramp of feet in the hall, and knew the estate agent was showing buyers round.

'Coming now!' He couldn't mistake his mother's agitation. 'Mrs Roper, if they want to see this room, they'll have to wait till we've finished.'

'Yes, madam.'

Ben waited till the door had closed and the voices moved away. 'Who was this Clive Woodley then?'

'Just a friend of your father's.' Beatrice's voice sounded tight and strained.

Ben guessed he'd meant more to her than that. The old accounts had told him more. He said: 'He put money into our business, and it's never been repaid.'

'He died. Killed in the war.' Now she sounded breathless.

'Lucky for us.' Harry reached for the pudding bowl to help himself to more.

'No interest has been paid on it either,' Ben went on. 'The capital should have been repaid to his estate, with the interest earned.'

'I think I'll go for my rest.' Constance was getting to her feet.

'Mother, you won't be able to go to bed till the would-be buyers have seen your rooms,' Harry reminded her.

'Oh dear, I feel quite light-headed.'

'You put the house on the market,' Beatrice snapped. 'Why complain about the consequences?'

'Gran!' Stephen exclaimed. It was Ben who caught her as she slumped off her chair in a dead faint.

Will Quest felt a little out of breath. He'd walked the herd back to their pasture near Lever Causeway, an added chore he didn't need. Perhaps he'd set out too briskly. It seemed a long drag back to the farm before breakfast.

The smell of hay was strong as he came back up the lane. Sharp and grassy, the scent of summer, it brought memories flooding back. Strange to see hay cut down in his own hay meadows, and not feel the usual rush of nerves. Especially on an overcast morning like this.

Normally, he'd have been working like a madman at this time of the year, hoping desperately the rain would hold off till the hay was in the barn.

He'd known farmers grow wonderful crops of grass, and pick the wrong moment to cut. There was no more dismal sight than heavy rain falling on a cut crop that should be drying. He'd done it himself, and known the loss it could bring and the desperate lack of fodder for the herd before winter was over. He'd never known a hay harvest like this before. It gave him an empty feeling.

The agent had offered to buy the hay as a standing crop. Will had been grateful, believing his offer was an act of kindness.

'You're not going to do that?' Maud had demanded.

'We won't need it. The herd will be gone before October.'

'And doesn't he know it! He's not offering enough,' she'd grumbled. 'You could earn more by making it yourself and selling it as hay. A standing crop indeed!'

It had been laborious work these last few years, hitching the old mower behind Flash. The ancient machine he had for turning hay was worse. Both had broken down and wasted so much of their time; both were a year older and rustier. Like everything else he owned, they were worn out.

Strange to see all the latest machinery here now, making such light work of it. No other Quest had ever stood aside and seen this happen. Some of the crop had already been carried, but it had not gone to Will's barn.

He shivered. The hay was not his concern any more; he felt his life slipping away. He was finished. How could he be relieved yet depressed at the same time?

He went on towards the house and saw the postman coming in from Gordon Drive. He waited to get the morning mail: a bill from the vet, a circular about cattle food, and an official-looking letter. When he opened the kitchen door, the house was filled with the scent of crisping bacon.

'Where've you been till now?' Maud wanted to know, looking round. 'We had to start without you. Rosie's got to get to work.'

'That's all right,' he said, opening his letter.

'You promised you would, Rosie,' Phyllis was saying in exasperated tones.

'Promised what?' he asked.

'Are you ready for breakfast, Uncle Will?' Rosie got up from the table to get his bacon from the oven.

'I'll just wash my hands.' He abandoned his letter and noticed Phyllis was wearing her old dressing gown, and her glossy brown hair was screwed in a row of metal curlers.

'What's the matter with you this morning?'

'I told you, I'm going for an interview. I can't stand

Beatrice Shearing any longer. Rosie promised to make my excuses for me.'

'Did I?' She was eating quickly. She'd changed out of her milking clothes. 'I don't like telling her lies.'

'I can't tell her the truth, can I? What if I don't get it? She'd have me out on my ear if she thought I was looking for another job.'

'What if you do? She'll know then I told lies for you. You couldn't get another job without an interview.'

'I think you should help her, Rosie.' Her aunt frowned.

'Do me a favour for once,' Phyllis pleaded. 'Tell her I had a bilious attack in the night. Tell her I have diarrhoea too. She'll be glad then I haven't come in to give it to her and everyone else.'

'All right.' Rosie looked up, and Will thought the blue shadows under her eyes were more marked this morning.

'Eh, lass, you're the one who looks ill.' He hadn't noticed when she'd come out to help with the milking. Beside her, Phyllis's cheeks looked rounded and healthy. Odd, because it was Rosie who usually had the better colour.

'I'm all right,' she said, so quickly that he wondered if something was upsetting her.

His bacon was hard and the yolk of his egg set, not the way he liked them. He reached for the letter and opened it beside his plate. The note paper jerked in his hand when he saw it was headed: 'Estate – Miss Grace Mary Quest, deceased.'

'What is it?' Maud asked peevishly.

'Grace's estate has been settled at last. Good news for you, Rosie.'

Three pairs of eyes met his. Maud's cutlery clattered down on her plate. Her hand twitched the letter nearer so she could read it.

'It's you he's asking to call at his office. He means you to have the money.'

'Yes, Maud, Grace didn't leave a will, and because she wasn't married . . .'

'Legally it's yours, Will. You have the greater claim.'

'Of course it is.' Phyllis ranged herself with her mother, combative, bristling for a fight to the finish. 'There's no legal reason to give it to Rosie. No need at all now she's got a share of Shearing's. She'll never want for much, even without this.'

Will stole a glance at Rosie. Her eyes were wide, shocked and upset, her face paler than ever. She was pretending an interest in her breakfast.

'We're the ones in need,' Maud went on. 'You giving up the farm like this. You're no age to retire.'

'You don't have to give it to me, Uncle Will.' Rosie's voice was gentle with understanding.

'I said I would,' he grunted. But four hundred pounds seemed a fortune now, and Maud was right – Rosie did have her share in Shearing's.

'After all, Rosie,' Phyllis said with a flash of spite, 'you've got everything else your mother left. That should be Dad's too, by rights. He's already given you plenty.'

'You don't have to give her all the money,' Maud said, her mouth dragging down even more at the corners. 'It's cost us to bring her up. Only fair we should be recompensed for that.'

'I'd have had to pay for more help about the farm if it hadn't been for Rosie. Tom and I wouldn't have been able to manage on our own.'

'But the law says . . .'

'It's what Grace would have wanted. We'll be all right. To hear you, Maud, you'd think we were on our beam ends. We'll be quite comfortable in our old age. It's all working out. I'm going to keep the orchard and three acres. Enough for one cow. Don't imagine you'll not have all the milk you need.'

'I'm not bothered about milk. It would be a relief to buy it in a bottle like everybody else, instead of listening to the fuss you'll make about having to milk a cow.' She was glaring at him.

'And I'll be able to grow my own vegetables just like I do now.' He'd wanted something to do, not be forced to sit in the kitchen every day, getting under Maud's feet.

'Sounds like you're telling me we won't need much to live on.'

'There'll be plenty, Maud. You'll not want.'

'We need the money more than Rosie does. She's on easy street now. Look at poor Phyllis, saving and scrimping to marry.'

'Phyllis has decided she doesn't want to marry that fellow, hasn't she?'

'Only because he has no money, and neither have I,' she wailed.

'Look at us,' Maud snapped. 'You're talking about scrimping and growing vegetables. I know we'll be as poor as church mice.'

'No.'

'Well, give Rosie something if you must, but there's no sense in giving it all to her. She's part of the Shearing family.'

'I don't want any of it.' Rosie crashed her cup back on its saucer.

'You don't know how lucky you are.' He heard the envy in Phyllis's voice. 'It's all come to you without any effort on your part.'

Rosie was looking positively ill. 'It hasn't,' she was protesting. 'There's all this trouble about my being related to Ben—'

'Rosie, everything's changed for you. You don't know how lucky you are. You've got a share of Shearing's business whatever happens. What more do you want?'

'I'd rather marry Ben,' she said flatly. 'That's what I want.'

'He'd be quite a prize as a husband, but I'd not say no to having him as a brother. It's put you on easy street, and it's all happened so quickly.'

'Too quickly,' she said with feeling.

'Don't be silly, how can it be too quick? What fun is there in saving up? Waiting years before anything can happen? You'll have money of your own. You can do what you like.'

'It makes no sense to give her more,' Maud said. Will saw her lead grey eyes watching Rosie warily. She was afraid Rosie would make a big fuss. After all, he'd promised the money to her. But Rosie wouldn't, he knew her well enough for that. If he wanted to keep the money, Rosie wouldn't fight for it.

'I'm going to work,' she said, getting up from the table. She wouldn't look at him, and she didn't look happy.

'Diarrhoea,' Phyllis said. 'Don't forget to tell the old cow that. And I'm still feeling sick.'

'Good luck with the job,' Rosie replied quietly.

Will felt he was letting her down. He'd talked big about giving all Grace's money to her, but now it had come to the point he wanted to hold back and keep some for himself. He was a greedy old man. Selfish too.

He knew he had to make up his mind fast. He'd failed in almost everything he'd tried to do. He wouldn't be able to live with himself if he gave in to his selfish instincts over this.

'Grace would have wanted you to have it, Rosie. You shall.'

'You don't have to. I know it's legally yours to keep.'

'I want you to have it all.'

'Are you sure? It's a lot of money.'

'Of course I'm sure, lass.'

She smiled then, a pale wan smile. 'It'll be a blessing, a comfort. With money like that behind me, I'll never have to go to the workhouse. Not like my mother.'

That left him frowning, sitting over his hard bacon after she'd gone.

CHAPTER TWENTY-FOUR

Constance had felt ill since she'd fainted at the table on Saturday. She'd lain on her bed for the best part of three days, feeling drained of energy. Yesterday evening, Ben's girl had come to sit with her. She'd brought newly picked raspberries with her from the farm, and they'd eaten them together.

Constance couldn't look at her face without seeing Hilda, yet oddly her manner reminded her of someone else. She knew she was saying far too much to her.

Rosie's resemblance to Ainsley's sister had cata-pulted her back to the days when she used to come visiting, but she'd never confided in Hilda as she had in Rosie. There was something about her quiet manner that made Constance open up and relive the most painful moments of the past.

'You must be very pleased to have Harry home again,' she'd said.

'No.' Constance had been so vehement, she'd felt compelled to explain further. 'Harry's changed. Everything's changed.' Before she realised what she was doing, she was letting it all pour out.

'Not like the time he came home from hospital with

533

a healing bullet wound. Then it seemed a miracle he'd survived, and a wonderful consolation.'

She'd been so lonely with Francis gone. She'd had only Harry to fill her days.

'Once he meant everything to me. He was all I had. All I asked of life was that he should be happy. I wanted to guide him, make sure he didn't make the mistakes I made.

'We were happy for a time, but Beatrice was never far away.' Beatrice was the one flaw.

'I think she fancies me . . .' She could see Harry now, laughing down at her, putting an end to her peace of mind for ever.

Constance shuddered, pulling the eiderdown closer about her shoulders. Once she'd realised he found Beatrice attractive, she'd been filled with a growing dread. Beatrice was pretty, she didn't look the bitch she was. Harry was nineteen years old and tireless in his search for pleasure. Up to that moment she'd encouraged it.

'Harry brought her to family meals, ogling her across the table. Beatrice treated me with disdain, and encouraged him to do the same.' More than anything else, she'd resented the way Beatrice took her son from her.

Constance knew they went to his bedroom. She could hear giggles and scuffles and was left in no doubt as to what was going on behind the closed door. It had shocked her so much she'd dared to face him with it.

'What will the servants think?' she'd had to ask. 'What about your brother? He's only a child.'

She'd told him what sort of a person Beatrice Spring

was, and what she wanted from him. It made no difference: Beatrice grew more beautiful as she grew older. All the years he was at university, the affair went on. Then Harry wanted to travel in Europe and Constance had sent him off with her blessing and a full purse, hoping the separation would cool his affection. He was twenty-two when he bought Beatrice a diamond and announced that they were engaged. She had been cock-a-hoop with triumph.

It had taken her a long time to realise there was a wild streak in Harry she couldn't control. Longer still to find he couldn't control it either.

'But Harry came to his senses at last, and gave Beatrice her comeuppance.' How she'd rejoiced at that. Before long, he'd taken up with Alice North, a girl from a good family of whom his mother could approve. It had been another slap in the eye for Beatrice when they'd married.

Constance hoped she'd seen the last of Beatrice when Harry said she had another man friend. She'd have liked to see her burn in hell, but was glad of anything that kept her away from Rock Park and the Shearings.

'Of course I saw less of Harry once he was married, but it was his happiness I wanted. I missed him all the same.'

'What about Edwin?' Rosie's green eyes searched into her face.

'Beatrice got her claws in him within a few years, and it seemed like a further turn of the screw. I told him exactly what she was like, but he didn't believe any of it. "I love her," he said. Stupid boy. He married her so quickly. He wanted to bring her to live with me.'

She'd stood out against it for a long time, but he'd said the business was not earning enough to allow them a place of their own, so she'd capitulated. The grandchildren came fairly quickly.

'Ben was a lovely baby.'

'Lovely now.'

'Beatrice was careful always to seem polite and pleasant when Edwin was around. She was quite different when we were alone.

'The war came and he volunteered for the front, I looked on the bright side. At least Harry would have to stay and run the business.

'Harry continued to come to lunch every Sunday, bringing Alice, but now Edwin wasn't here Beatrice didn't try to hide her feelings. She seemed to despise us all.

'She's always wanted to run everything her way. She pushes herself. Imposes her will on others.' It had taken Constance a long time to see she was doing it to Harry. Telling him how he should run Shearing's Shirts.

' "Don't dare do that," I shouted at her over the lunch table in front of them all. "Shearing's Shirts has nothing to do with you. Leave our business alone."

' "Somebody had better take care of it, Constance," she said. "He'll bankrupt you if I don't stop him."

' "Don't be silly," I told her. "Keep your nose out of our affairs."

' "If you'd ever taken the slightest interest in the business you'd know I was right. I don't suppose you've even noticed how your income has been diminishing over the last few years? I don't care about your share, Constance, but I feel a need to look after Edwin's interests, and his children's." '

Constance sighed. 'That was the last time I saw Harry. On Wednesday Beatrice announced that he'd gone and wouldn't be coming to lunch again.'

Wednesday was Constance's day for going to see Alice. It would do her good to get away from the house for a few hours. She had been late getting out of bed, and it had taken her the best part of an hour to dress, far longer than usual, but at last she was ready.

It was almost lunchtime, hardly worth settling down with her book. She paused at the open window in her adjoining sitting room to watch the gardener digging up bedding plants that had flowered, and heeling in new ones to flower in the autumn.

Another movement below caught her eye, and she leaned forward to find herself looking down on Harry's bare head. Hands in trouser pockets, he was hanging about waiting for his lunch too. Constance was reminded her lunch would be served in the dining room. Beatrice had ruled years ago that she must eat in the dining room if there was company. Today, she would have preferred the peace of her own room. She would have asked to have her table moved closer to the window, so she could watch the birds as she ate.

Having Harry back in the house was not the blessing she'd thought it would be. He was a stranger. After twenty years without any contact, what else could he be?

Constance craned forward further. His sandy hair had faded now, the thinning strands flickered in the breeze. She could smell the cigarette he was lighting. The Harry she'd loved so much had had thick hair and handsome laughing eyes. He'd come back middle-aged, looking dissolute and rather seedy. Not a man she would want to introduce as her son. He hardly seemed a gentleman.

She couldn't forget that Harry had let her down. It still hurt to think her beloved son had gone away for twenty years with no word of goodbye. She'd felt so close to him, done so much for him, and it had taken years to accept he wouldn't even answer her letters. He'd stolen from the family and made them all dependent on Beatrice. He'd caused her to feel guilt, and to grieve, and she found it very hard to forgive him now.

She had welcomed him back as an ally against Beatrice, but he was doing nothing about helping her find another house. He was no help at all in the present crisis. He had refused to stay and support her. Constance felt doubly rejected.

She went slowly downstairs. The phone began to ring before she reached the bottom. She didn't hurry her step, she never answered it, nobody expected her to.

She heard the girl's quick steps on the kitchen stairs and saw the flare of her uniform skirt as she ran across the hall. Constance was turning into the drawing room when the girl said: 'It's for you, Mrs Shearing.'

She was surprised. No one ever telephoned her. She couldn't hear very well on the phone. The girl was holding the instrument out to her.

'Who is it?'

'The estate agent wants to speak to you, madam.'

She took the instrument. 'Hello.'

'Mrs Shearing? I'm delighted to tell you we've had an offer for your house.'

She was gasping for air. It had come too quickly! She wasn't ready. She realised then that she was holding the instrument away from her, that the voice was crackling on. She put it to her ear again.

'Hello, are you there?'

'Yes.'

'As I said, a good offer. So close to the asking price, I'd recommend you to accept.' It took her too long to answer. 'Hello, Mrs Shearing?'

'I'll have to . . . think it over,' she managed.

'Of course. I'll put the offer in writing. You should get it by the first post tomorrow.'

Constance felt shaky. She put the phone down and stood over it, wanting to ask Ben what she should do.

Mrs Roper was setting the dining table. Constance had to ask her to dial his number.

'An offer?' His voice was reassuringly calm. 'How much?'

She didn't know. 'Don't worry, Gran. It'll all be in the letter tomorrow.' It made her feel such a fool. 'There's no need to do anything till we get that. You make up your mind whether you really want to move. We'll talk about it tonight.'

Constance saw her hand shake as she put the phone down. She was wound up like a watch spring. Ever since she'd set the wheels in motion, she'd felt she was being torn in two over the sale of the house. The thought of getting rid of Beatrice, of putting her out and making her find her own accommodation, had been so sweet a revenge it had blinded her to the effect it would have on herself.

Now the thought of living alone loomed over her like a black cloud, but she was determined to go through with it. It would be worth it to get rid of Beatrice and deal her some of her own medicine. But Constance had to admit she was frightened at the prospect.

Ben felt drained as he drove home from Ivy Farm. The weeks were passing fast and he was making no headway. He'd had to watch Rosie putting on a brave face for his benefit, but tonight it had slipped. In an emotional outburst she'd wept against his shoulder, and he'd known he was failing her.

They'd gone to the dutch barn again, and he'd comforted her with love. It seemed love was all he had to offer, and it was no longer enough. When Rosie had recovered, he felt despondent.

'This is what got us in the mess in the first place,' he said. 'I should have been more careful.'

'Too late to worry about that now.' She was always practical. 'We've got to sort this out – what are we going to do?' He didn't know, but it was now imperative that they do something.

Ben nosed the car into the drive and put on the handbrake. Then, with an exasperated sigh, he remembered his mother's recent instruction.

'If you use the cars, you must garage them at night.

It shouldn't be too much to ask you to take reasonable care of them.'

He drove round the circular flower bed and into the garage. Stephen had left it open for him, the Ford was already there. Ben was halfway up the front steps when he changed his mind. He was too full of anxieties to sleep, and it was early enough to walk down to the Royal Rock.

In the bar, with a glass of beer on the table in front of him, he took out the letter he'd received that morning which had brought about the most recent crisis. They'd both been pinning their hopes on his being able to get a job abroad. He read it through again. In response to his application for a job in Alberta, it invited him to the Canadian Immigration office in Liverpool for an interview and medical examination.

When he'd first read that he'd felt the heady prospect of success. It evaporated as he'd read the terms of employment enclosed within. He would be required to travel out alone, and temporary bachelor accommodation would be provided. A passage for his wife would be forthcoming after a satisfactory six-month probationary period. It was a major setback to his plans.

It also raised a host of other problems. To qualify Rosie for the free passage, they'd have to be married before he went.

He'd made up his mind immediately – he was not prepared to go without her. He couldn't leave her here to have the baby alone. Possibly he could raise enough for her fare but she'd still have to go through Immigration formalities.

He gulped at his beer. How naïve he'd been to think they could leave the country without trace. Immigration meant forms to be filled in, addresses given. His mother would know they'd gone together, she'd be able to track them down. They would not be able to disappear this way. They might just as well marry here and brazen it out. He'd always been in favour of doing that, but Rosie was afraid they would fall foul of the law, with terrible consequences.

The factory was still seething with the story that she was his half-sister. It was too good a tale to be forgotten. At one stroke it embarrassed his mother and gave Rosie a share of the business. Popular opinion equated that with her having come up on the pools. Ben wished he knew what to do for the best.

'Can I get you another?' Harry was standing over him, sliding his own glass of brandy on to the table.

'Er . . . yes. Yes, please. Half of mild.'

'Not bad news, I hope?' Ben suddenly realised Harry was nodding towards his letter. 'You've been frowning over it for a long time.'

'No,' he said hastily, stuffing it in his pocket. 'No.'

'That's all right then,' Harry said easily, sitting down next to him. 'I've been meaning to have a quiet word about your grandmother.'

'Yes?' Ben guessed what was coming.

'I don't think she should be selling the house. It's a big step at her age, finding something different. A new life.'

'You don't help much,' Ben said. It rankled that Harry was free all day and did nothing, while he and

Stephen had to fit house hunting with Gran in at weekends.

'She'd be better staying with Beatrice.'

'Whose side are you on?'

'What do you mean? Who's taking sides?'

'I thought you were at war with Mother. She doesn't want it sold. Gran does.'

'The line of least resistance, my boy.'

Ben stared at the full glass in front of him. 'That isn't why you're both keeping your mouths shut about Clive Woodley. Who was he?'

He'd had to press Mother before she'd said Clive had been a friend of his father's who had been killed in the war. She said she couldn't remember anything else about him. Ben was convinced she knew a lot more.

This was another hold-up to his plans. Poor Rosie had worked hard at digging into his family history, and a real hornet's nest it was proving to be. He'd been certain Gran would tell her who her father had been, or that Rosie would find definite pointers in the old lady's outpourings, but everything seemed to confirm their worst fears.

'Uncle Harry,' Ben said, 'you know exactly who Clive Woodley was. So does Mother. Why won't you tell me? What's the big secret?'

'Not mine to tell. Personal to your mother, not fair to open my mouth.'

Ben almost laughed. Would have done if he hadn't been in such dire straits. 'You don't give a damn about being fair to her! Harry, you're grabbing every opportunity to strike back, you *want* to hurt her. Come on, tell me.'

All Harry's attention was on catching the barman's eye. He succeeded and indicated his glass. 'Have another?'

'No, thanks. What I want to know is the truth about Clive Woodley.'

'Leave it, Ben.'

'You aren't going to tell me?'

'No.'

'Then I might as well go home and go to bed. Got to take Gran house hunting tomorrow.' Since she'd agreed to the sale of the house, finding somewhere else for her had also become an urgent matter.

As he walked home along the Esplanade, he pondered on Harry's refusal. He was clearly sparring with Beatrice, the whole family felt their enmity. They were barely civil to each other. It was logical to assume he'd take a dig at her where he could. If there was something she didn't want made public knowledge, Ben would have expected Harry to shout it from the roof tops. Clive Woodley had obviously played an important role in his family's history. He'd put money into the business. Yet nobody would talk about him.

He didn't sleep well, but tossed and turned for hours and then fell into a heavy sleep towards morning. He was late getting up, and still felt fuddled at breakfast. Harry seemed unusually lively.

'I've decided to return to Tangier,' he announced. Ben saw his mother look up. Her face registered relief. 'Perhaps next week, now we've settled our business. You'll have to let me know your new address, Beatrice, I don't want to lose touch again.'

She almost snarled, 'I have no idea where I shall live.'

'You'll keep me posted on that, won't you, Ben? Everybody moving from here. I ought to wait till I see you fixed up.'

Sunday breakfast was a leisurely affair. The men of the family usually sat over the teapot with the Sunday papers. Gran didn't come down but preferred a breakfast tray in bed. Ben went up to see her. He wanted to make sure she hadn't forgotten they were going out.

She was still in bed, with a frilly pink nightcap on her head and wearing a fluffy bedjacket in matching pink. She looked fragile.

'Gran, it's time you were getting up. I've asked the estate agent to make appointments. I'm taking you to see two bungalows and two flats.'

'I told him I wanted something bigger. I hope these are more my sort of thing.'

They weren't. Ben thought it important Gran didn't over-reach herself financially. Until now, she had provided accommodation for the family, but they had provided everything else for her. He had to make sure she had sufficient income to live on if she was going solo, and she'd have no idea what it was likely to cost.

'Gran, how much money do you have?' Her pale blue eyes met his with a fey look.

'Wouldn't you like to know?'

He stifled a smile. 'I'm not just being nosy, I don't want you to spend too much on your house.'

'I'm selling this one,' she said in exasperated tones. 'I can afford something bigger than those you've shown me.'

'Not necessarily. There isn't much demand for big old houses like this any more. Not in this district. You might have to pay more.'

'For those little boxes? Nonsense.' She was reaching over to her bedside table. 'Look, the agent sent me these.' She was pushing more house particulars on him. 'All more sensibly sized. These are what I need to see.'

'What do you want with five bedrooms, Gran? And an acre of garden? These houses are as big as this one, they'll be no easier to run. And can you afford these prices?'

'None of your business.'

Ben sighed, he was afraid it was. He felt responsible. He was encouraging her to think she could live alone. But she'd never manage it. Everybody agreed she needed a nursemaid, but nobody else wanted to help.

'How much do you have in the bank?'

'A lady never discusses money, Ben. Or religion, or politics.'

'It's the accountant in me, Gran.' It was an effort to stay calm. 'I don't want you to get into difficulties.'

'I know what I'm doing.'

Ben was afraid that wasn't true. He closed his eyes in silent supplication. He had to know! But he had neither time nor energy to spar with her. He'd have to take a quick peek at her bank books on his way out through her sitting room. He knew where she kept them. He'd seen her push them away.

He was also afraid today's expedition was doomed from the start. She wasn't going to like what he was taking her to see.

'I want you to think very seriously about these four places,' he told her. 'No stairs in any of them. Now then, how soon can you be dressed and ready?'

'I can't start with you sitting on my bed.'

'I'll go then.' By the time he'd reached her door another problem had surfaced in his mind. He turned: 'Gran, who was Clive Woodley?'

She'd fainted when he'd first mentioned the name. He had to assume it meant a lot to her too. Her pale eyes held that fey look again.

'Your mother's young man. She meant to marry him, but he was killed in the trenches.'

Ben straightened up in surprise. Why should Mother make a big secret of that? Why should Harry?

'Just think, if he'd not been killed, Edwin wouldn't . . . You'd have had a different mother. Beatrice would never have come to live in my house.'

He knew he was staring at her. 'Come on, Gran. Get up now.' He was careful to close the door firmly. It was a solid old house and noise didn't travel easily, but he opened her bureau in the adjoining room as quietly as he could. The bank books were where he'd expected to find them. She had more than he'd expected too. Perhaps she could afford to spend a little more than this house would bring, and still have enough to live on. Maybe she knew what she was doing after all? It made him feel guilty that he had looked.

Ben went back to the dining room, poured himself another cup of tea. He pulled a newspaper in front of him, but couldn't concentrate on the written word. His thoughts were running riot. There must be more to know about Clive Woodley than she'd told him.

After they'd picked up Rosie they viewed a flat and then a bungalow. In Ben's opinion either would be suitable. Gran would have to decide whether the trouble and expense of keeping a gardener for the bungalow was greater than the irritation she expected to feel at hearing other people above and below her in the flat. He decided he must pin her down to one of the four properties they were going to see today.

'All those stairs up to the fat,' she grumbled.

Ben sighed. He and Stephen had covered most of the Wirral in their search for a place that would please Gran.

'I think perhaps I liked the bungalow better, but the flat is in a nicer area.'

'Lovely views of the Dee.' Rosie was trying to sound enthusiastic. Her face was noticeably paler this morning, she had deep mauve shadows beneath her eyes. 'You'd feel at home with a river view, wouldn't you?'

'Not if the wind gusts off it as it does at home. So draughty.'

They had been looking in ever-increasing circles which meant Alice would no longer be a few minutes' drive away. Gran would need her social contacts more if she lived alone. Oxton would have suited her better, and Stephen had been quite keen on a flat they'd seen there. Ben felt as though he was chasing his tail.

He was heading towards Chester because the next bungalow was out in that direction. Impossibly far from Birkenhead really. Gran moved in the seat beside him.

'Now, Ben, where are you taking us for lunch?'
He'd given no thought to that yet.

'It's going to be a surprise.'

He turned into the country lanes, then wished he
had not. There were hotels in Heswall and on the main
Chester Road. It would have been easier to find
somewhere to eat there.

'It's lovely country,' Rosie said from the back seat.
'Good farming land. Uncle Will would love it.' Ben
slowed down, he could see crossroads ahead.

'Ben!' Rosie's voice was suddenly more urgent.
'That sign said "To Hendlesham Hall". Isn't that
where . . .?'

He braked hard, then put the car into reverse. Sure
enough the signpost read Hendlesham. Below that was
another advertising Hendlesham Hall Hotel.

'Was it turned into a hotel, Gran? Do you recognise
this place?'

Beside him, Gran's head moved doubtfully under
her large black hat. Ben turned the car in the direction
the sign indicated. A mile further along they went
through a sleepy village; he turned a corner and saw
the house away to his right, standing on a little rise.

'Is this where you lived as a child?'

Gran was staring at it perplexed, he couldn't believe
she wouldn't recognise it. The car park was in front.
He pulled into it.

She was shaking her head. 'No, this isn't it.'

'No car park in your day, of course.' He tried to
visualise it with gardens stretching away in front. Gran
was climbing out stiffly as he turned to look at the
house. It was much smaller than he'd envisaged from

549

her description. Very old, built of Cheshire sandstone, attractive.

'No.' Gran had straightened up against the car, her eyes puzzled as they wandered over the house. 'My home was much bigger, altogether grander, and yet . . .'

'Let's see if we can get lunch here,' he said, heading towards the front steps. It cheered him to see lunch and dinner menus in a glass case to one side of the open front door.

'But I do believe this is it.' Gran hovered on the threshold. 'This is the hall, just as I remember it.' Ben led her inside, marvelling at the change in her. Suddenly she was interested and alert, as though she'd shed two decades.

'And this is the dining room.' She veered off to her left. It was about thirty feet long and opened on to a terrace. He was impressed in spite of himself. As a family dining room it must have been magnificent.

'Very elegant,' Rosie murmured, her green eyes wide with interest. The small tables were draped with starched white cloths. Only two were occupied although the lunch hour was well advanced. A waiter settled them at a table near a window looking out on well-kept lawns.

'Perhaps the oak panelling is a little sombre,' said Ben. It made the room dark.

'I remember the sycamore trees,' Constance said excitedly. 'This is a lovely surprise, Ben. A wonderful surprise.' The head waiter advanced with three menus. 'This room is exactly how I remember it, though of course we had one big table. The sideboard is still in the same place.'

As the man was looking at her rather strangely, Ben felt he had to offer some explanation.

'This was my grandmother's home as a child. After we've eaten, would it be possible for her to see round the hotel?'

'Of course, sir, I'm sure the owner would be interested to speak to you. You'll know the history of the place. I'll ask him to come and have a word.'

Ben thought the meal heavy on style but low on flavour and value for money. It didn't matter, Gran was more interested in her surroundings. Her pale blue eyes were shining as she gazed about her, taking in every detail. He'd never seen her sit so upright in her chair.

The owner came after their coffee had been served. Had it been a hotel for long? Gran wanted to know, hardly able to contain herself.

'About six years. The Army used it as a hospital in the war and it stood empty for over a decade after that. A shame really. It was in a very poor state of repair when we bought it.'

'So changed outside,' she said. 'I didn't recognise it till I got to the door.'

'Yes, we had to demolish two wings. One from each side of the main façade. They were found to be in a dangerous state when we came to do the place up. Dry rot. You'll know, of course, they were added a hundred years after this part was built.'

'That explains why you didn't recognise the house from outside, Gran. It's much smaller now than it was when you lived here.'

'Yes, dear, I'm perfectly capable of understanding what the man says, and I did tell you it was smaller.'

'A good deal smaller,' the owner agreed. 'We thought we'd have a decent hotel when we bought the place, but it's left us with too few bedrooms. The only solution would be to build a separate bedroom block in the garden.'

'That wouldn't do. It was always a lovely garden.' Constance frowned. 'How many acres do you have here now?'

'The gardens extend to over two acres, madam.'

'Practically nothing left,' she mourned. 'Not when you have to have a car park.'

'We've had problems with planning permission, and what with one thing and another, it would be too expensive. We've decided to sell. It's on the market at the moment. We're too far from the main roads to get much passing trade for the restaurant, you see.'

'How many bedrooms are there here now?' Gran demanded.

'We have seven, plus of course our own family accommodation. As it is, it isn't too large to be a private house again.'

'What a splendid idea! Do let us look round.' Constance was on her feet and moving to the door at twice her normal speed. Ben tried to dismiss the impression he was getting. Surely she wasn't thinking of buying it? She turned to smile at him. She had that fey look in her pale eyes again.

'I would so love to live here once more. It would be like coming full circle, back to my roots.'

He found he was sweating. 'Gran, it's an enormous

house. The upkeep would be too expensive.'

'We've almost rebuilt it.' The owner rubbed his hands. He was now treating Gran as a possible purchaser. 'Re-roofed, re-wired for power and electricity, new heating. There's nothing else needed, certainly no further expense. All the beautiful panelling retained. Because it's all new, the upkeep is modest for a house like this.'

'Ah, yes, the drawing room.' Gran stood in the doorway. 'Such a sensible-sized room.'

Ben looked up its forty feet and quailed. 'It's far too big for you. And all these other rooms . . .'

'The library? Which way is that, along here? Now that really is a big room.'

'I think the library might have been demolished. Was it in the west wing?'

Ben could see Gran trying to think. 'Yes, it would have been. What a pity.'

He closed his eyes. 'It's too big, Gran. It's bigger than the house in Rock Park. Far bigger.'

'I always said so. Isn't Hendlesham a much nicer house? You didn't believe me, Ben. How providential it happens to be on the market when I'm looking for something to buy.'

Rosie was pulling at his arm, trying to attract his attention. Trying to detach him from the others. He watched Gran bustling after the owner on her way to see the kitchens.

'It's a ridiculous idea,' he couldn't help gasping to Rosie. 'She's out of her mind. This isn't at all the sort of place she needs.'

'Think of Alice,' she was hissing at him, an excited

flush on her pale cheeks. 'She's looking for bigger and better premises for her old ladies. She wants to expand. Perhaps she and Gran could buy this between them, perhaps that's the answer? Your gran could have two or three rooms to herself, all the bridge she's ever wanted to play, and Alice on the premises to take care of everything.'

He stood staring down at her. Rosie's green eyes were sparkling. The lamp under which she was standing shed light on her hair, burnishing it till her curls were coppery.

'Rosie, you're wonderful!' He wanted to hug her. It seemed the perfect answer to Gran's problem. 'Why didn't I think of it?'

'You would have – eventually.'

CHAPTER TWENTY-FIVE

Beatrice stretched her neck, trying to relieve the ache between her shoulders. She'd been sitting too long at her desk.

She felt uneasy, unable to lose herself in the job today, yet all was well here. Around her she could hear the familiar sounds of the factory: Miss Gibbons typing in the adjoining office, the whirr of sewing machines in the background, and the chatter of voices. Of course, if they were working as hard as they should, they wouldn't have time to chatter like magpies.

From out in the hall she heard a second typewriter strike up a staccato beat. Phyllis Quest. She felt another wave of irritation. Damn the girl! Giving in her notice. Announcing she'd got another job.

The Quests were all the same. She'd come bleating to Edwin as an inexperienced college leaver, and as soon as they'd knocked the rawness off, and taught her to make herself useful, she was off to Cammel Laird. Well, she wouldn't find them better employers. Good riddance to her.

She'd been cross with Ben yesterday when he'd said he'd already given her a reference. He should have the sense to leave things like that to her. She'd have fixed the little madam.

'It's a bother, finding another girl. Breaking her in.'

'I don't think we should replace her, not just yet,' he had said. 'Miss Gibbons could work at her desk in the hall and see to reception at the same time.'

'Miss Gibbons is my secretary.'

'With Dad and Oliver gone, there'll be less typing.'

'I can't have her leaving my work in her typewriter in full view of everyone while she does reception duties.'

'Then the corsets will have to pay three-quarters of her salary, not just half as at present,' he'd told her. 'I must keep overheads down on shirts.'

Restlessly Beatrice got to her feet and went to the window. What was the matter with her?

It was Harry, of course. She had to get rid of Harry. It made her nervous to have him in the house. He was still hanging on, though he'd said he was going. In this time of flux he was waiting for one of the family to buy another house. He wasn't going to risk losing touch. She was afraid he'd tell Ben the truth. Ben had a way of worming things out of people.

She went downstairs again, giving Phyllis Quest a glacial stare as she went past her desk. She went to the rooms she called her own, where the corsets were being made. In all the years she'd been running this business single-handed, she'd never had a major crisis. Company funds had never gone missing. She'd never made a big mistake. It had gone along steadily, year in and year out. She hadn't made a fortune, but it had kept her in comfort. It brought her huge satisfaction to know she was wealthier in her own right than all the Shearings put together.

Edwin had ignored her corsets, counting the money she made from them as her own. She'd paid a proportion of the costs of the Albert Hotel, but that was all. She made no secret that she was making a profit but her husband didn't even see her accounts, never requiring any contribution to household bills or asking what she did with her money.

Ben was the only one in the family who had ever taken the slightest interest. She knew he'd studied business management before coming to the firm, but hadn't attached much importance to that. She hadn't treated his suggestions as important at first. Not until she'd thought them through.

She'd decided then he could be right about suspender belts and satin brassieres. She'd designed the suspender belts herself, and made up two different designs in both satin and twill. She'd started making satin brassieres using their current patterns. Now they were turning them out as fast as they could, and Ben was talking about new styles.

He'd nagged her about making roll-ons too, and success with the suspender belts had encouraged her to try them. Now they were using both one-way and two-way stretch.

She'd had to buy new machines to handle elastic, but the girls were having no problems with them. The first garments had been snapped up by retailers. Repeat orders were flooding in. Ben was urging her to buy more of the new machines and hire additional machinists.

The trouble was, she wasn't sure he knew what he was doing. He wanted to fly before he could walk. He hadn't proved himself yet; could turn out to be like the rest of the family: better at spending money than making it.

'You've got to keep up with the latest fashions in this business,' he'd told her, as though she were a new apprentice just learning the ropes. 'You've got to give the public what they want.

'It's no good being afraid of investing in new machinery if it's needed. Either you make your business grow or it'll contract. It won't stand still for long. Market forces will make it slide.'

He was right about the two-way stretch roll-ons being blissfully comfortable. Ben was being proved right about too many things. It was sapping Beatrice's confidence. Why had she not thought of these things herself?

A week later, Ben felt he was coming to grips with one of his problems.

Alice's manner had been guarded when they'd taken her to see Hendlesham Hall for the first time.

'It's a wonderful house, of course. Roomy but not unmanageable. Having been run as a hotel it lends itself to my business, but . . .' Her face had been wary.

'The cost needn't stop you.' He'd explained that the sale of the Rock Park house was going through and Gran was prepared to put the money she received from it into Hendlesham Hall. That she could, by drawing on her capital, cover half the cost of Hendlesham.

'I know I shall be happy here,' Gran had pleaded. 'I want to end my days where I started.' At that moment her end did not seem close. She was a different woman since she'd made up her mind what she wanted.

He could see they'd sparked Alice's interest. 'I've been wanting to move to a bigger house for a long time. Something in a better area. But I hadn't envisaged anything quite as grand as this.'

'We'd have an agreement drawn up by a solicitor so you both know exactly where you stand.'

'I'm certainly tempted.' Alice was frowning. 'It would be an ideal house for my purpose.'

'Good address,' he told her. 'You'd get wealthy widows clamouring to come and live here.'

'It's all freshly refurbished,' Rosie pointed out. 'No further expense needed.'

'Except for furniture and fittings,' she said.

'The furniture from Rock Park could come,' Gran said.

'There's quite a lot,' Ben added. 'Large pieces, very suitable for the big rooms.'

'There's more stuff in the attics,' Constance said. 'I've put all sorts of things up there through the years.'

'You could move your present ladies straight in.'

'They'd have to be prepared to pay more, but to be honest that isn't the problem.' Alice's face was still troubled. 'I'm still married to Harry, you see. Legally I'm his wife.'

'Yes?'

'Because of that, I haven't felt able to move house. He bled almost every penny out of me before he left. I've inherited capital from my parents since then, and saved a little from my income. If I go into this venture with Constance, Harry is bound to know and at any time in the future could legally claim a share.'

'Why don't you divorce him?' Ben asked. 'It shouldn't be difficult since he deserted you over twenty years ago.'

'I'd love to. I've thought of doing it so many times, but that would mean our financial affairs would have to be legally settled.'

'So what's wrong with that? Isn't it what you want?'

'Well, Harry was going through my money so fast, I finally insisted we bought a house of our own. I was afraid we'd end up with nothing in our old age. Harry hated Elmhurst Road, hated the mortgage too, but it's in our joint names. He's the sort to claim his share of anything.

'I've paid the mortgage off now, but I believe he has a legal claim to half the present value. To buy Hendlesham I'd have to sell the house and I couldn't without his agreement. I've felt in a cleft stick for years. I can't afford legal proceedings.'

'I don't know too much about the workings of the law,' Ben said. 'It seems very unfair if you've paid the mortgage all these years.'

'The down payment was mine too.'

'I have a friend who's a practising solicitor. I could take you to see him. See if he can suggest a way round it.'

'If he could, it would be wonderful,' Alice said.

'I'll phone him now. Perhaps we can see him tomorrow.'

Two days later, Alice was as enthusiastic as Gran

about buying Hendlesham. Ben was reasonably confident it could all be worked out. If so, it would be a weight off his mind.

Later that evening Rosie held his hand against her abdomen. 'Feel it? The baby's moving now.'

It moved against his hand, a miracle. The baby was real and it was growing. It helped to concentrate his mind.

'Rosie, we can't go on like this. We ought to get married. We haven't managed to find out anything more about your father. I think we should risk it. Go to the register office and fix it up for next week. I'll rent a house to start with, get a few sticks of furniture, and we'll move in straight away. Come on, what do you say?'

He felt her shiver with anticipation. 'What about your mother, what will she do?'

'I don't know. If she isn't telling the truth, there's nothing she *can* do. It will call her bluff.'

'But if she's right? If it's true Edwin was my father?'

'He wasn't.'

'Everything we've found out seems to show he was.'

'Look what Wallis Simpson and the King did last year. Everything's worked out fine for them. They're married now. They had to face world publicity. Our marriage would be nothing compared with that.'

'They'll say we committed incest.'

'Rosie, it doesn't feel like incest. It can't be. I know it isn't.'

'We don't know. We're going round in circles,' she said hopelessly.

★ ★ ★

Rosie set Aunt Maud's sewing machine rattling down the last seam. She was making herself another skirt from flower-printed cotton. The dirndl skirt had been the height of fashion all summer, and they were quick and easy to run up. She'd made this one fuller with extra gathers, and a bigger waist band to fit loosely. She knew her figure was thickening, and was desperate to hide the fact.

She could hardly believe Sunday morning had come round again. The weeks were passing with frightening rapidity. She couldn't bring herself to think more than a few days ahead. She wanted time to stop.

Rosie glanced at the kitchen clock. There was just enough time left to sew a button on, then she could wear it today. Ben had said he would come for her about ten.

'Gran wants me to go up in the attic and see what's there. It'll all have to be cleared out before the house is sold. Do you feel up to helping with that?'

'Of course.' She wanted to spend all the time she could with him. She liked attics and rooting through bric-à-brac. As she ran upstairs to change, she thought again of Ben's plans for the rest of the day. She was to stay for lunch.

'Alice is coming too, but you're not to breathe a word. I want to take Harry by surprise. I've just told Mrs Roper I'll be bringing two guests.'

Rosie knew he'd got his solicitor friend to draw up an agreement for Alice. 'A sort of peppercorn claim against her property, one pound in full and final settlement. All we have to do is to get Harry to sign it, and she's in the clear.'

Rosie put on a clean blouse and the new dirndl skirt and went out to Gordon Drive. The Rover was just coming round the corner.

'New skirt looks very nice,' said Ben. Rosie nodded, pleased, but all she asked of it was to make her bump unnoticeable.

'I've told Mother I'm bringing you to lunch. I think we should tell her today. I'm in a mood to get everything straightened out. We've wasted enough time.'

'Ben! You're not going to mention the baby in front of everybody?'

'Perhaps. We'll tell them we're going to get married straight away, and take it from there.'

Rosie closed her eyes. 'She'll say terrible things to us, and blame me. Let's wait a bit longer.'

'All right, not about the baby, just the other. We've got to settle it, we can't go on like this. If we can straighten things out for Alice, Gran will be happy and I won't have her to worry about.'

Sunday at the farm seemed like any other day, milking and bottling still had to be done, but at Ben's home it had a leisurely air. As Rosie followed him up the hall she heard the rustle of newspapers from the dining room. Ben paused at the open door.

'You still here, Mother?' he said in surprise. Rosie saw three Sunday newspapers being lowered to the uncleared breakfast table. 'I've brought Rosie to help clear out the attic. Do you feel like giving us a hand, Stephen?'

'Not this morning, I want to go out.'

'Who gave you permission to root about in the

563

attic?' Beatrice was bristling with sudden irritation.

'Grandma did. She wants it cleared now the house is sold. It'll have to be before we all move out.'

'I'll do it,' Beatrice said. Rosie thought she didn't look herself this morning. She was paler, and showing her age more. 'I'll see to all that.'

'Gran wants me to do it. Rosie and I are making a start now.'

'You mustn't throw out anything until I've checked it. We can send things we don't want to the salerooms.'

'All right, Mother.' Rosie felt his hand on her arm, moving her away. 'There'll be the dust of ages in the attic, got to cover your new skirt.' She followed him down to the big kitchen on the floor beneath. A large joint of beef stood ready in its roasting dish on top of the cooker.

'An overall and a couple of dusters, please, Mrs Roper,' said Ben. She was busy rolling out pastry on the large table. Another girl left the chopping of french beans at the sink to find Rosie an overall and helped guide her arms into the sleeves. She followed Ben upstairs again.

'I've been up already this morning. Just as well. It took me ages to find the keys and get the light to work.'

On the top landing, Rosie was dismayed to see Beatrice had already hooked down the folding stairs to the attics and had gone up ahead.

'There's a lot of stuff here, Ben. You'll have to make lists. Sort it all into piles.'

'I know, Mother. I've brought a pad and pencil. We'll list any useful furniture for Gran.'

'She won't want anything from up here! A small modern house won't take much furniture. She's being silly if she thinks she can take a fraction of the furniture downstairs.'

Rosie saw Ben freeze and she held her breath. It seemed neither he nor Constance had yet told her about Hendlesham.

He said easily: 'We'll see to it, Mother. Better if you get on with more important things. Is there anything you want?'

'How will I know till I see it?'

'Right, then I'll pile everything I'm planning to take to the tip here on the landing.'

'Yes, I must check what you're throwing out.' Rosie smiled with relief as Beatrice disappeared down the steps.

Ben said quietly, 'Gran's afraid it could still fall through. Three lists then, and three separate piles. One for her, one for things we want, and a third for stuff worth sending to the saleroom.'

'Gosh, it's an enormous attic.' She looked up at the underside of the roof. There were great beams crossing it, just as in the dutch barn at home.

'Covers the whole house.' It was gloomy although the day outside was bright. There were several small skylights let into the slates but the glass was made opaque with dust and cobwebs. 'Nobody comes up from one year's end to the next.'

Rosie looked at the dusty clutter all round her. Stepladders, an old crystal set, an even older typewriter.

'It's going to be a job to clear all this. Oh, there's a rocking horse here.' She slapped its wooden rump and dust flew from it. 'Was it yours?'

'Yes, and Stephen's afterwards. Spent many hours playing on that. I'll ask Gran if we can take it. Lots of other stuff that will come in useful too.'

'A nursery fireguard here,' she said. 'A high chair and cot.'

'We can use all those. Let's stack them over here,' he said. 'Get some organisation going.'

'You know, I feel more settled already, just looking at things and hearing you say we'll use them.' Rosie scribbled on the pad.

'I'm glad we've decided we don't have to go to Canada.'

'A dressmaker's dummy and an old sewing machine. I'd love to have them! This is a gold mine. Do you think your gran will want them?'

'Doubt it.' Ben carried a disintegrating wicker chair down to the landing. Took another trip with a broken sun canopy and some old deck chairs.

'There's a playpen here. Odd to think you might have used it.'

'I bet I did. After lunch, we'll go out and see if we can find somewhere to rent for ourselves. We'll both feel better if we can get that fixed up.'

Rosie couldn't have agreed more. 'I wonder if that house we both liked in Bebington is sold?' It was comforting even to think they would have a place of their own. 'This box is full of curtains. Will your gran want them?'

'We'll ask her. No, didn't they say carpets and curtains were included?'

'I could make them fit the place we get.'

'There's a large box of crockery here, a dinner and tea service. Might be useful for Hendlesham.' He dragged it to the collection building up near the stairwell. 'Gran should be pleased with this. Loads of ornaments, and trunks of sheets and blankets. Not much furniture though. Most of it is still in use downstairs. There was never any need to replace it.'

'Who's this?' Rosie had found a large painting in a heavy gilt frame, propped facing the wall. She could swing it round just far enough to see it was of a woman in a red dress and had been deliberately defaced. Ben came to help her move it.

'Mrs Dinah Shearing,' he read. 'Who could she be?'

'I know,' she whispered, staring in horror at the portrait. The eyes had been gouged out, the face slashed with a knife. 'She was Ainsley's first wife.' She took a deep breath. 'Your gran told me he used to talk to her after she died.'

'Who could have done this to her picture?'

Rosie moistened her lips. 'Your gran?'

Ben was staring down at it. 'She must really have hated her.'

'Or been frightened by her.'

He shrugged. 'It's no good to anyone now. I might as well take it to the dump.'

'Cover it, Ben. Here, this old curtain is faded. It'll upset her if she sees it again.'

Rosie was sorting through another box of curtains, separating those too old and shabby to be of further use, when she heard Beatrice tutting with impatience on the landing below.

'The silly bitch! Fancy ruining a painting like this. A

first-class Victorian artist too.'

Ben went down. 'I'm going to take it to the tip.'

'Not the frame. That's still worth a pound or two. Help me take the picture out.'

'Why did she do it?' he asked.

'She's no sense. Frightened of her own shadow. There's nothing else of value here. It might as well go. I'll send Stephen up to help you carry it out to the car. Use the Ford, Ben, it's all very dusty. No point in messing up the Rover.'

'Rosie,' he called up when his mother had gone, 'I'll take this stuff to the tip and then it'll be time to pick up Alice. Do you want to come with me?'

She had just opened a large trunk. 'It's exciting not knowing what I'm likely to unearth next. Books and hats and shoes . . .'

'Mostly junk, I'm afraid. You carry on, I'll not be very long.'

Rosie sat back on her heels when he'd gone. Burrowing amongst the cast-offs of the Shearings reminded her of looking through Grace's belongings. But for her there was nothing personal about these. She pushed the pile of dresses back in the box.

There was a trunk next to it. Old-fashioned and heavy by today's standards, battered and well travelled. One corner had been damaged beyond repair. She prised the lid up. A sketch book lay on top. She flicked the pages over and was instantly captivated. It was filled with pencil sketches and water-colours.

Suddenly, her heart was racing, her attention caught by a pale water-colour of an instantly familiar house.

Even in the poor light, she recognised Ivy Farm. If she had had any doubt, on the opposite page was a view of the yard, with the cow-shed door open and cows tied up inside.

Rosie turned another page and found herself looking at a portrait of a soldier in uniform. As she made out the name 'Clive Woodley' painted at the bottom, her stomach was churning. Ben had told her how curious he'd been about this man, and how Harry had refused to tell him anything about him. She took the sketch book directly under the bare electric bulb but the light was still too dim to appreciate the fine detail and subdued tones.

It was time she went down. Ben would be back any minute now. She ran down to the bathroom on the floor below, threw her overall across a chair and rinsed her hands. It was only when she took the book to the landing window that she saw the name 'Grace Quest' on the first page. Suddenly her knees were shaking. She was overcome. At last she had positive proof that Grace had had close links with the Shearing family.

She was excited because this was more of Grace's own work that she hadn't yet seen; she wanted to give the paintings her complete concentration.

Rosie turned again to the portrait of the soldier. Had this man been her father? It had been painted with confidence. She had the feeling Grace had known him well. Was it wishful thinking to see love in every brush stroke? He was handsome, someone she would be proud to call father. She didn't dare hope.

She was turning over the pages quickly, breathless with the importance of her find; looking to see if there was a portrait of Edwin or some other member of the Shearing family. There was not.

Another thought came to her. She turned it over in her mind, growing more certain by the second that she had stumbled on the truth. Seconds later she was running downstairs with the sketch book clasped to her chest. Ben had said his family would be collecting in the drawing room but she guessed Beatrice would still be at her desk. She flew up the hall to the heavy mahogany door of the study, rapped imperiously and opened it without waiting for permission.

Beatrice was full of affront at the intrusion. Rosie pushed the book in front of her. It was open at Clive Woodley's portrait.

'What's this, Rose?' Beatrice wrinkled her nose in distaste.

'Mrs Shearing, I have come across my mother's sketch books in your attic. Was this man my father?'

Beatrice's mouth tightened in impatience. After one glance, she was pushing the portrait away.

'How many times do I have to tell you? Do you think I like admitting my husband had an affair with another woman?'

'I don't believe you!' Rosie's heart pounded so hard it felt as though it would burst her ribs. 'Ben has never believed you.'

'Edwin would not have left you a share of his business if he had not been your father. Why should he if you were nothing to him?'

'If I were Clive Woodley's daughter, and the capital he'd invested in the business was still owing to him, then Edwin would feel he had a debt that must be repaid. That's why he gave me a share. He was a fair-minded man.'

'You're being stupid.' Nothing in Beatrice's reaction told her she'd hit on the truth. 'Searching for answers where there aren't any. You have to accept what I'm telling you. It's unpalatable to me, too, that my husband fathered you.'

It shocked Rosie to see her face so malevolent. She had always known Beatrice disliked her, now she clearly hated her.

'Common civility should stop you raising this question over and over. You must see I find it very hurtful.'

Rosie felt her confidence seeping away.

'Whatever your expectations of my son were, you must see they're impossible now. You're just causing trouble by persisting. Leave Ben alone.' Rosie had snatched up the book and was backing out. 'I'm telling you, leave him alone!'

At the door she paused, wanting to tell Beatrice they planned to marry soon. The words wouldn't come. Her courage failed and she took to her heels, but not before she thought she saw fear flicker across Beatrice's face.

Rosie tore upstairs to the top landing, not knowing what to do with herself. She was standing at the window with her forehead pressed against the glass, fighting back tears, when she saw the Ford drive up to the front door. She only just had herself under control, but Ben wanted her to be there when he brought Alice in.

She took a deep breath and, still clutching the sketch book to her, went down to the drawing room. Bright sun was streaming through the windows. Harry was stretched out indolently with a glass of beer at his elbow. Constance was sitting primly with a glass of sherry in her hand.

'I've found—' Rosie began, then realised the old lady's attention was on the newcomers at the door.

Ben ushered Alice in, uncertainty in every line of her big body. She was wearing a smart brown costume with cream frills showing at her throat.

'Why, Alice! I didn't realise.' Constance went forward to greet her, kissing her cheek.

'I've brought her to lunch with us,' Ben said, as though it was a normal social occasion. He was already guiding her over to Harry who was struggling to stand up, looking anything but pleased to see his wife.

'It is Alice?' Nervously he offered his hand. He was shorter than his wife.

'She wanted to meet you while you were here. I thought this would be a good opportunity.' Ben sounded matter-of-fact but Rosie could see he was nervous. They were all nervous.

'What for?'

'Harry, I'd like a divorce.' Her voice was crisp and unemotional.

'Yes – well, why not? I don't see that it'll make much difference to me. I mean, I live abroad, we haven't met since . . .'

'Exactly,' she said.

'You're planning to get married again?'

'No, nothing like that. I'd just like to feel free of you.'

He shrugged. 'If you'll see to what's necessary?'

572

'I'll see to everything. As a first step I'd like you to sign this agreement.' She opened a handbag the size of a portmanteau and took out a document.

'What sort of agreement?' Rosie could see him prickling with suspicion.

'To settle our financial affairs.'

'We don't have any financial affairs, Alice. Haven't had for the last twenty years. It's no good trying to claim maintenance after all this time.'

'This agreement guarantees I'll never be able to claim anything. It's a full and final peppercorn settlement of one pound against your assets. Once an amount is agreed, it's fixed for all time. No good my asking for more later.' Harry was perusing the document anxiously.

'And of course it's reciprocal,' she said. 'You are expected to sign the same agreement regarding any claim you might have against me.'

'It's just a formality then?'

'Yes.'

Rosie watched him take the fountain pen Ben offered and sign both documents. Ben witnessed both signatures.

Moments later, Alice slid the documents back in her handbag with a satisfied smile. 'I take it you won't contest the divorce?'

Harry put both palms up in a gesture of mock obeisance. 'What difference does it make in real terms, Alice?'

'It'll take away your excuse for not remarrying.'

'I'm not sure I need one. Once was enough for me.'

Ben was beaming at them all. 'That clears things up

for you, Gran. You and Alice will be able to go ahead now.'

'I'm so excited at the thought.' Alice laughed. 'Is this some of the furniture you'll be bringing?'

'Yes.' Constance was beaming too. 'Will it do? You must see the rest before you go.'

'It'll suit the place, Constance. It's all large and rather grand. I'm sure you'll be very pleased when you see it there.'

'What's all this about?' Harry was looking from one to the other.

'I can hardly believe my luck,' Constance laughed. 'I'm going back to live at Hendlesham Hall.'

Ben was pulling an armchair forward for Alice. 'What about a glass of sherry now the business is completed?'

'It isn't,' said Rosie, opening the sketch book. 'Ben, look what I found in the attic. These water-colours were done by my mother.' She found the portrait of the soldier and held it up.

'Did you know Clive Woodley?' she asked Harry.

'No,' he said shortly.

'Of course you did.' It was Alice who answered. 'We all knew Clive Woodley, and you knew him better than I did. Quite a good likeness, isn't it, Constance?' She came over to examine the portrait more closely.

'Who was he?' Ben asked fiercely. 'What was his connection with us?' Alice was looking at Constance.

'Gran!' Ben said fiercely. 'Rosie is asking about Clive Woodley.'

Constance looked stricken, her face paper white. 'You're always badgering me, asking questions all the time. Beatrice said I could be sent to prison for what I did, and the less I said about any of it the better. She said I must keep my mouth shut. I know none of it would have happened if it hadn't been for me . . .'

Rosie felt stricken with guilt. 'We didn't mean . . .' She went and put an arm round Constance's heaving shoulders.

'Come on, Gran, we have to know,' Ben insisted.

Her lace handkerchief fluttered to her mouth. 'It was all my fault, you see. He was Francis's son. Beatrice said I must push it to the back of my mind and forget about it.'

'But Clive?'

'My fault he came here at all. I insisted. It meant I could see more of his father. Then after . . . After Ainsley died, Francis tried to stop him coming, but by then the boys were growing up and he and Edwin were friends. He still came here, didn't he, Harry?'

'I suppose he did.'

'Harry!' Ben turned on him. 'What is this? A conspiracy of silence? You lied, you knew him well. What's it all about?'

Harry took a deep breath and let the air whistle through his teeth. 'Beatrice was never like us. Her first ambition was to marry well. First she tried me, but I didn't like her bossy ways. Then she turned her attention to Clive. He meant a lot more to her than I ever did.'

'She was besotted with him,' Alice agreed.

Constance blew her nose and dabbed at her eyes with the lace- trimmed handkerchief. 'Clive and Edwin met up again in the Army. He even put money into our business. It was all my fault.' She was weeping again.

'No, it wasn't,' Rosie assured her. 'Don't let Ben upset you, but it's important to me to know. Was Clive Woodley my father?' Constance's eyes seemed to roll to the back of her head. 'Are you all right?'

'I feel a little fuzzy. My smelling salts, dear. On the mantelpiece in my sitting room upstairs.'

'I'll get them.' As she sped to the stairs, Stephen let the front door bang behind him.

'Hello,' he called. 'Where's the fire?'

As she reached the landing, she looked up and saw the light switch off in the attic two flights higher. She was aware of Beatrice coming down. Constance's rooms were on this floor. She went in her sitting room and found the small blue glass bottle containing smelling salts.

When she came out, Beatrice had come down to the same floor. She was clutching a large cardboard package. Stephen stopped her before she reached her own room.

'Mother, why shouldn't I go next week? What's the point in my hanging on here now the house is sold? I'd have thought you'd have been glad to see the back of me.'

Rosie saw Beatrice's arms tighten round the box with a guilty jerk when she saw her. There was fear as well as malice in her eyes. She guessed Beatrice had brought the cardboard box down from the attic and did not wish her to know about it.

'You haven't said whether I can have some bed linen for my flat,' Stephen went on. 'The bed's there and the pillows, but I need sheets and blankets.'

'There's plenty of bedding in the attic,' Rosie said as she passed.

She held the salts under Constance's nose, and caught a whiff of the sal volatile herself. As it brought the colour back to the old lady's cheeks, she thought she remembered seeing the box Beatrice had held under the sketch-book in the trunk upstairs. Did it hold more things that had belonged to Grace? Rosie's head was thumping. That would explain Beatrice's guilt and fear. She was coming in now, her face like thunder.

'I've brought Alice here for lunch,' Ben said easily.

'Why didn't you tell me?'

'I couldn't help it,' Constance whispered. 'I couldn't help telling them.'

'You knew Clive Woodley, didn't you, Mother?'

'You loved him, didn't you, Beatrice?' Alice put in. 'Wasn't he the love of your life?'

Rosie felt the atmosphere in the room suddenly crackle with tension. They were all on the edge of their seats now.

'Possibly the only man you ever did love.'

It wasn't love Rosie saw on Beatrice's face, but hate. Quivering, pulsating, twisting her handsome features into an ugly mask.

Alice attacked again. 'Unfortunately he didn't love you, did he, Beatrice? You managed to get yourself engaged to him but he broke it off.'

'You turned him against me!' They all saw the ferocity with which Beatrice swung on Constance, loathing on her face. 'It was all your fault.'

'Clive asked me about you.' Constance raised her

577

ravaged face. 'Said I seemed wary when you were near. I told him I had reason to be. I only told him the truth, but it opened his eyes. Nothing, Beatrice, has given me greater pleasure, before or since.'

'You deliberately poisoned him against me?' There was real fear on Beatrice's face now.

Rosie felt her own confidence growing, but Alice hadn't finished yet.

'Like Harry, he changed his mind about marrying you. You hated Harry for that, didn't you? You hated me because he preferred me, but you never loved Harry. Your hatred for Clive was ten times greater – especially when, like Harry, he married someone else very soon afterwards.'

'He did!' Rosie squealed. 'Who?'

'Emmeline Weller. I wanted to introduce you when you came to Elmhurst Road asking about Harry.'

'But I thought Clive Woodley – I hoped . . . my mother. She painted this portrait of him. Didn't she love him?'

'All this happened years before he met Grace,' Harry joined in at last. 'When would it be, Mother? About 1910, I suppose. He was embroiled in an unhappy marriage with Emmeline, and she ran away with another man. It was after all that he met your mother.'

'Then he was my father?' Rosie demanded. 'Clive Woodley was my father?'

'I believe he could have been,' Alice said. 'Much more likely than Edwin. I know you asked me, the day Harry came home, but my mind was on him. All this happened so long ago, and they were not my happiest years. I've tried to forget them. I don't think I ever knew your mother's name.'

'Harry?'

'Yes.' He shrugged. 'No point in denying it now. The cat's well and truly out of the bag.'

'Why didn't you tell me when I asked you weeks ago?' Ben asked in disgust. 'You could have put an end to all our worries then.'

'Because you knew Beatrice would pay you to keep your mouth shut,' Rosie guessed.

'It suited him better to keep quiet,' Beatrice put in spitefully.

'My only source of income,' he said. 'A man's got to live.'

It was Ben's turn now. 'If the business performs well enough, you're still entitled to your share of the profit. You must know I'd treat you in the way Dad did, though there won't be much this year. If it isn't enough, you could find a job.'

He turned on his mother. 'Whatever made you say that Dad . . .? It was cruel and totally pointless. It put Rosie and me through hell. And why, for heaven's sake? What was the point of it?'

She took a step back, breathing heavily.

'Why else would Edwin leave a share of his business to her? What other conclusion could I come to? I was sure, Ben.'

'You knew all the time,' Rosie choked out. 'Yet not ten minutes ago you assured me I was wrong. Why did you do it? What were you trying to do? You've always hated me, haven't you? Was that it?'

'A woman scorned.' Harry laughed mirthlessly. 'She

loved Clive but he wanted nothing to do with her. It wasn't long before she wanted revenge. You were his love child, Rosie, of course she hated you.'

She couldn't take her eyes from Beatrice who seemed to be shrinking into herself. She said: 'You don't know the difference between love and hate. Do you hate Ben, too?'

'Of course not. He's my son, my own flesh and blood. I love him.'

'You say you love Ben, but you go out of your way to hurt him.'

'No, I want the best for him.'

'But you wanted to stop him marrying me. Why do you think I'd be no good for him?'

'Power is what Beatrice is hanging on to,' Harry said. 'It's what she's always wanted. Rosie, you were seen to have more power over Ben than she had. You gave him the reason to refuse the girl she wanted as his wife.'

'I would have anyway,' Ben grunted.

Harry drained the beer in his glass. 'Your empire's breaking up, Beatrice. No longer will we all toe the line and do what you want. You wanted power at any price, but it was based on cheating and lies.'

'You manipulated the whole family and we let you do it,' Constance sniffed. 'More fools us.'

Mrs Roper tapped on the door and came in. 'Can I put the lunch on the table, Mrs Shearing? I'm afraid it will spoil if it's kept waiting much longer.'

Beatrice's eyes were closed.

'Yes, please,' Constance said. 'It's high time we had lunch.'

Rosie stared out across the river. The tide was fully in now. She felt a huge sense of relief, an unburdening. Her father had been Clive Woodley. He was related to Ben, but it was a distant link. There was nothing to prevent their being married. Beatrice had put her and Ben through months of unnecessary anguish, but it was behind them now.

The nightmare was over.

CHAPTER TWENTY-SIX

Ben was carving the beef. 'I'm afraid it's a little overdone. Is this enough for you, Rosie?'

'Plenty, thank you.'

Rosie kept meeting his eyes across the table. The smile wouldn't leave his face.

'Rosie and I will be getting married just as soon as we can. We've wasted more than enough time because of what you said, Mother.'

'I've said I'm sorry I misled you. I was misled myself about Edwin.'

'I'm surprised you could think that of Dad.' Stephen was frowning. 'Surely you knew, one way or the other?'

'I thought I did, Stephen.'

Rosie thought of Flora Pope. What was more reasonable than to suppose Edwin had had an earlier lapse? She herself had believed he was her father.

'Rosie, we'll go out this afternoon and look for a house of our own.' Ben was euphoric, eating quickly, caught up in a burst of energy. 'Though we should get on with the attic.'

'Leave the attic,' Beatrice said between clenched

teeth. 'Plenty of time for that. Go and find yourself a house. Take the Rover.'

Rosie struggled with her beef. It seemed a complete change of heart on Beatrice's part. She wondered why.

'The rats are leaving the sinking ship, Beatrice.' Harry too seemed full of energy, but his was more malicious. 'Your run of good luck is over. Not that things always went your way . . .

'You might not believe it now, Rosie, but once Beatrice set her cap at me. Proposed too, didn't you, Bea?'

'I might have known you'd try to get your own back,' she snarled. 'Is that why you're raking all this up?'

'I thought you were clever, but you weren't clever enough. You let me see that what you were really after was financial security. You thought marrying into the Shearing family would give you that.'

Alice's laugh boomed out. 'Financial security! Beatrice, I did you a favour. He'd have been no good to you. Look at him now.'

Harry laughed too. It sounded a little wild. 'Alice is no longer enamoured of me.'

'Neither is Beatrice! You're a wreck, Harry, it'll feel good to cut myself free of you. I should have done it years ago.'

'Beatrice got over me when she found Clive Woodley had inherited money from his father. His wasn't tied up in an ailing business, and anyway she liked him better. You thought then, Bea, you could have love and money, but he saw through you too, didn't he?'

'Let it drop. Can't we have our lunch in peace?' she asked tartly.

'You felt more bitterness for Clive because you really loved him.' Harry was not going to be stopped easily. 'You hated Emmeline because she had what you wanted. Probably you prayed their marriage wouldn't last.'

'It didn't.'

'That pleased you. I can still see your face now when we heard Emmeline had run off with someone else. You were over the moon. But you didn't like Grace any better. From the start you wanted to kick her in the teeth. Well, you managed it, didn't you, Bea? And you managed to keep Clive's money in the business. We none of us have a lot to thank you for.'

'I don't have to listen to this.' Her lips were set in a straight line. 'Stop it, Harry.'

'Then you switched your attention to Edwin. You got what you wanted there – marriage. But I doubt you were happy or made Edwin happy.'

'We've all had enough. Leave me alone, can't you?'

Rosie felt there were questions still unanswered. Harry had admitted he'd been blackmailing Beatrice, but about what? She had deliberately lied about Edwin being Rosie's father, and she'd hated being found out, but Rosie was left wondering whether she had more to hide.

There must be more. Harry was goading her, had her on a knife edge. Beatrice was afraid he was going to reveal more, Rosie was sure of it. Then she remembered the large cardboard box and Beatrice's obvious guilt.

She was burning with curiosity. Beatrice had more right to anything in the attic than she had, and would say it was none of her business what she took down to her own room. It would enrage her to be asked. Yet if Rosie did not, all her life she would be wondering whether the contents of that box were in some way connected with her. Her heart was thumping again, she was chewing and chewing on the beef, moving it round her mouth. Rosie made herself swallow, then forced the words out.

'What else did you find in the attic, Mrs Shearing? In the cardboard box?'

She'd broken an uneasy silence. The curiosity she felt was in her voice. Everybody was looking at Beatrice now. The colour drained from her cheeks.

'Nothing. Nothing much.' She laughed nervously. 'Some old hats I used to wear years ago.'

Rosie was quite certain she was lying. The box had held something heavier than hats. She saw Beatrice standing on the landing, supporting it on her hip as she spoke to Stephen.

She said, trying to make herself sound innocently satisfied: 'There's lots of old clothes up there. So much work and more material in them than modern clothes.'

Her mind was on fire again. She knew she'd have to look inside that box before she could rest. She felt overwhelmed with curiosity, and certain the contents concerned her. Dare she go to Beatrice's bedroom and look? She felt almost faint at the thought. Would she even get the opportunity?

Rosie knew she must make the opportunity. She had to or she'd always wonder about it. Butterflies danced

586

in her stomach. She couldn't clear her plate, but the meal was coming to an end.

Alice was talking about her plans for Hendlesham. Rosie heard only half of them.

Ben said: 'Alice, Rosie and I have been turning things out of the attic and we've put some things on one side for you and Gran. You must look through them and see if they'll be of use at Hendlesham.'

All the time, Rosie was turning the other problem over in her mind. She had to do it. At last they were all pushing their chairs back and standing up, going back to the drawing room for coffee.

She hung back. Ben waited for her. She knew Beatrice was watching them. She had to do it now. In the hall, he put an arm round her waist to guide her forward.

'I won't be a moment,' she murmured, and headed straight for the downstairs cloakroom. She kept the door open an inch and watched till the drawing-room door clicked shut and she was sure Beatrice was safely inside. Then she hared up to the next floor as quietly as she could. She knew which was Beatrice's room. With her heart in her throat she opened the door. She would just peep into the box, and if it did contain hats, go straight down again.

She was gripped with sudden panic. She couldn't see the box anywhere. The white candlewick bedspread danced before her eyes. The fluffy mules seemed out of character for Beatrice. It was a big room, almost masculine. She had an impression of austere simplicity. Had she been mistaken? But no, the box was on the floor beside the wardrobe. She tiptoed over. The floor creaked beneath her weight, making her freeze for a moment. She lifted the lid.

There were no hats in it. The blood was singing in Rosie's ears. A bible and a bundle of letters were the first things she saw. The letters were addressed to Major C.A. Woodley in a girlish hand. Rosie was fighting for breath, overcome with her find and knowing she was right, right, right. Beatrice had meant to keep these things from her.

She was sure she'd found letters from her mother to her father. She rammed the lid back, scooping the box up. For the first time she noticed it had come through the post. It was addressed to Miss Grace Quest. The Hoop Lane address had been heavily scored out, and Rock Park replaced it. She must move it somewhere where Beatrice would not see it.

Ben's room was the safest place she could think of. She sped up to the next floor. She'd never been in his room either, but she had seen it from the door. She pushed the box under his bed, tugged at the counterpane to try and hide it from view. It wouldn't come low enough. She pushed the box up to the bedhead and further into the middle. That was better.

As she turned, she recognised the water-colour she'd given Ben. Now in a handsome frame, the view from the dutch barn was hanging where he'd see it as soon as he opened his eyes in the morning.

Seconds later she was scudding downstairs again as silently as she could. A maid was crossing the hall and saw her, but said nothing. To go prying round bedrooms was an unforgivable thing for a guest to do, but Rosie knew she'd been right to do it.

At the drawing-room door she tried to compose herself. It was impossible. She went in and Ben put a cup into her hand. She was shaking so much, coffee slopped into the saucer. He looked at her in surprise.

'Are you all right?'

'Later,' she whispered. He'd noticed, but Beatrice must not. She couldn't cope with questions just yet. Her mind was racing and she was desperate to read those letters. She sat down and tried to concentrate on what was happening here.

Beatrice was sitting facing her, her face ashen, visibly smouldering with resentment and jealousy. Rosie knew she would explode with fury if she found out what she'd done.

Stephen was describing the flat he was going to share with a bank colleague, and his mother was looking even more sour. Constance was glowing with victory, and showing just how happy she was to be moving to Hendlesham. Even Harry was going back to Tangier to the woman he loved. They were all escaping her domineering ways, and Beatrice didn't like it.

But more than anything else, Beatrice hated the thought of Ben marrying Rosie. She'd done her best to prevent it, but she'd failed. To know she could now marry Ben soothed Rosie more than anything.

Harry's lined face was beaming round at them all. He was glorying in Beatrice's loss of power. Rosie felt the same pleasure. They had all suffered too much from her tongue in the past not to feel glad at this reversal. Only Ben seemed free from the general feeling of triumph. He was engrossed in Alice's enthusiastic plans for Hendlesham. Rosie was taking in only half of them. Suddenly she was conscious of a general move to leave.

'Are you coming to help?' Ben was asking her. It took a moment to realise they were going up to the attic to bring down the things they had put on one side for Hendlesham. Stephen was leading the way, saying he wanted to sort out some bedding for himself. Rosie put her cup down hurriedly. She couldn't stay here with Beatrice.

As soon as they were out of earshot, she hissed at Ben: 'Got to speak to you.'

She ran quickly up ahead to his bedroom, and he followed. They left Constance well behind. Alice and Stephen were helping her upstairs, one on either side.

'I saw your mother take a box from the attic,' she whispered breathlessly. 'She hid it in her bedroom and I've stolen it. It's addressed to Grace. There are letters to Clive Woodley inside. I've got to have another look.'

'What?' His face showed shock that his mother would do such a thing, then he was squeezing her hand.

. 'You look now, Rosie. I'll see to Alice and Gran.' She could see the other three coming up to the landing as he quietly closed the door.

Rosie threw herself down on her knees and felt under the bed for the box. She tossed the lid aside. Her heart was thumping like an engine.

It felt wonderful to handle the contents. There was a bundle of letters, kept together with an elastic band; several other letters, unsecured and still in their envelopes; a calf-covered bible with the name Clive

Anthony Woodley written on the fly leaf; a fountain pen, watch, and, find of finds, a diary.

Rosie sat back on her heels. She understood now. This box had been sent home from the front. It contained the personal effects that Clive Woodley had had with him in camp. Uncle Will had received the belongings of his brother George this way, and valued them highly. These things had belonged to her father.

She found a photograph in a folding leather frame. She'd not seen it before, but surely this must be her mother? Rosie lifted the box to the table near the window. The sun was streaming in, the light hard and bright. No doubt about it, Grace's face smiled up at her from the browning photograph. Her father must have kept this near him. Her stomach was churning. Hope and eagerness made her fingers shake.

The first letter she picked up was addressed to Miss Grace Quest in Hoop Lane. The envelope had never been opened. Tears were blurring her sight. Grace must already have been in the workhouse when the parcel arrived. She began to read:

Dear Miss Quest,
It is with great regret I have to tell you that Major Woodley was killed in action, on 28 December 1915.

Rosie gasped. She had found her father at last. She could be certain now. This must be proof, why else would it be addressed to Grace? Her eye went to the bottom of the letter. It had been signed by his commanding officer, a Colonel Alfred Winterbottom. She skimmed on through the sentences.

A very courageous man. Gave his life for our country. A sad personal loss to me, he was a good friend. Proud to have known him.

Rosie brushed a tear from her eye. She would return to this letter later. She couldn't do it justice now, but she was glad Grace hadn't received it. Why hadn't she?

She went back to the first page. It hadn't been written till 12 January. How long would it have taken to reach England after that? Poor Grace. She understood now. Her father had been killed before she was born.

There was a thick bundle of letters addressed to Clive Woodley. She pulled one out. The writing was small and girlish. Tears were filling her eyes as she started to read:

Darling Clive,
You must not worry about me. I'm far more concerned about you than I am about myself. I'm keeping very well, in rude health in fact. A typical farmer's daughter.

But I do so want you back. Fear is the most dreadful thing, and I'm afraid for you. Every day the newspapers carry lists of those killed, and they are frighteningly long. So many people in the town are wearing black armbands.

I am comforted by the thought you have named me as your next-of-kin, so that I will be informed if the unthinkable happens.

To have it happen and not to know would be dreadful, because I tell myself that no news is good news. I pray every night and twenty times a day for you to be kept safe and come back to me.

I'm getting the money you send regularly, so money is no longer a worry, but I do miss you so. It's you I want.

I've already been to see the midwife who lives not far from here. I promise, I won't just stay here alone until the time comes to send for her. I'm still hoping you'll be back home by March for the birth, but if not I plan to ask Will for help. I'm sure he'll want to do all he can.

Thank you for writing to Beatrice on my behalf. You have reassured me about her. Perhaps I misjudged her when I called her hard. I know you were fond of her once. Though not so fond as all that, or you would have gone ahead and married her since she'd asked you to and had the marriage service, the reception and honeymoon all organised!

However, I don't think it'll be necessary for me to appeal to Beatrice to help when the baby is due. Will won't be sent to the front. I was silly to tell you I was scared of going to her. I still don't relish asking her for anything, but I will if I have to. Now that you've told me about investing the money your father left you in Edwin's business, I shall not feel I'm a burden to them. Beatrice will surely want to help if only to repay your generosity.

Do not regret helping Edwin. You say you'd feel happier if you hadn't tied up your capital. That if you had money in the bank, it would be easier for you to provide for me and the baby. I shall be all right. It's you we should be worrying about.

I pray that you get a minor wound or illness that will get you away from the front. Even better if it would bring you back home to me. Especially in time for the baby.

I know you're brave, Clive, and would want me to be brave too. I do try.

There was another letter addressed to him that also appeared not to have been opened except by the censor. She pulled out the sheets of paper, and started to read.

Dear Clive,

I know you try to write to me every day, even if it's only a few lines. It's nineteen days since I heard from you, and I am so fearful.

Rosie was choking with pity and anguish. She could barely take it in. She was being torn in two. She wanted to put her head down and cry for Grace.

She would savour the contents of this box later. At last she'd found answers to the questions that had plagued her. A diary was a wonderful find. She would know at last what had been in her father's mind. She flicked through pages covered with small writing in brown ink. It was an account of what he'd gone through on the Somme. Of life in the trenches and being under fire with death all around him. Her eye stopped on a page filled with different matters.

I must survive this. Grace so desperately needs me at home. I feel so powerless, so useless. I must get back to her. Do something to help her.

I feel I'm living through six nightmares at once. I could ask for compassionate leave to go home and marry Grace, except that I'm still married to Emmeline.

She would agree to a divorce, I'm sure, if only I knew where she was and could ask her. What a mess I've landed Grace in. I can't believe now I could be so irresponsible.

I wish I had not tied up all my capital in Edwin's business. Of course I wanted to help him last year, but now Grace's need is much more important to me. Even worse, Edwin is here and as worried about things at home as I am. I wish we did not have to rely on Beatrice's good nature.

He has promised to write to her explaining Grace's predicament. He will tell her to provide money and support too – though I fear Grace will get precious little help from her, and find giving birth to my child out of wedlock very unpleasant.

The fact that I love Grace won't endear her to Beatrice. She was frighteningly vengeful when I tried to break off the relationship though I did it as gently as I knew how. Beatrice and I are as different as chalk from cheese. I could not have survived a month with her. Yet she was convinced

I was what she needed, and nothing I could say would change her mind.

What sort of man am I, so impatient for love that I do this to Grace?

Rosie overflowed with love and pity. Her mother's luck had been well and truly out. She understood now. Her father had been sending money to her. It had stopped when he died. When it ran out she'd had to go to the workhouse.

Grace had asked Maud for help and been refused. Rosie knew now her mother must have gone to Beatrice too. Grace had known Beatrice was short on kindness and generosity, but she'd had an obligation to Clive Woodley.

This must be what Beatrice was so desperate to keep from her. It was clear Harry knew she'd gone against the wishes of both Clive and Edwin.

Beatrice had wanted Grace to go to the workhouse. Beatrice had wanted Rosie to be born there and carry the stigma for life. It had been an act of revenge on her part.

Rosie was filled with anger at the unjust way Grace had been treated. Everybody had refused her help when she needed it most. Galvanised with fury, she swept her tears away and went tearing down to the study to have it out with Beatrice. One glance inside was enough to see that the room was empty and the desk bare. That Beatrice wasn't back at work surprised her. She went instead to the drawing room.

Beatrice was where she'd left her. Eyes like black

sloes locked straight on to Rosie's as she opened the door. Her gaze was instantly malevolent.

For the first time in her life Rosie faced Beatrice without fear. She was so filled with rage she had no room for other feelings.

'You're a liar, Beatrice Shearing. A liar and a cheat.' She was beside herself, her voice thick with contempt. She saw shock register on Beatrice's face.

Harry was dozing and had slipped down in the big chair until he lay splayed out horizontally, his limbs like a rag doll's.

'I've just found out what you were trying to hide. You were the reason I was born in the workhouse! You managed to push my mother into a position where she had no other choice.'

Beatrice was like a spitting cat. 'Your mother should have had more sense than to get herself pregnant before she got the wedding ring on her finger.'

Harry was grunting. She'd woken him up. He was pulling himself into a sitting position.

'How could you be so heartless? Clive and Edwin both asked you to take care of her.'

Harry was blinking, sufficiently awake now to join in. 'I told you what I thought, didn't I, Bea? What you did to Grace was unforgivable. You knew she had a right to money from the business. You knew she had no one else to turn to.'

'I didn't,' she protested, but Rosie knew she was blustering.

'You were there, Harry,' she said. 'You must know what happened.'

He was yawning, scratching his ear. 'She's paying

me to keep my mouth shut about this, aren't you, Bea?'

'Keep it shut then. There's no need to say anything.' Rosie didn't miss the desperation in Beatrice's face, nor the contempt in Harry's eyes as he glanced at her.

'It's too late. The rest of the story's leaking out, Bea. All your faults and failings laid bare at last.' He got up and jangled the change in his trouser pockets. 'You had us in your power, didn't you? You enjoyed watching us like a cat watching mice, knowing we couldn't escape. But we have escaped now, haven't we?'

Rosie heard Ben come into the room. 'Tell me about my mother,' she demanded of Harry. 'What exactly happened?'

'It was Christmas. The season of goodwill, 1915. Edwin was away at the front. Beatrice was trying to nudge me out of the business.'

'You were taking money out,' she rasped at him. 'You'd made big mistakes. Run up an overdraft the business couldn't maintain. There was precious little money left for any of us, although we were working overtime. We ought to have been raking money in. It's a kindness to say it was due to your "mismanagement" that we weren't.'

Harry went to stand behind Beatrice's chair. 'Go on, say it, Bea. Tell them I'm a thief. You threw it in my face often enough then.'

'All right, you had your hand in the till!'

'And how about you? You weren't above taking money that rightfully should have gone to Constance. I know that happened more than once.' Harry's lined face creased into a leer.

'Beatrice and I had had a couple of years at each other's throats. She was wearing me down. She was so proud of keeping Shearing's Shirts solvent, she's never told anybody how she did it. But I know, don't I, Bea?'

'You were running the business down. You'd fallen out with Alice as well as me.'

'I was at a low ebb,' he agreed. 'I bought Alice a bracelet for Christmas, rubies and diamonds. Beatrice went at me for taking the money.'

'It had come out of the business, not your own pocket.' Her eyes blazed. 'And Alice knew too.'

'She certainly did. She asked me if it was a softener, a sap for my conscience. Said she'd no money left for essentials, and wished she'd never set eyes on me. Said her life would be a bowl of cherries if I went. I was able to help her there. We never saw each other again till today.

'As I said, Rosie, I was at a pretty low ebb, two women out for my blood. Grace Quest chose that day of all days to come asking for our help. She was shown up to my office, wanted me to plead her case with Beatrice.'

'She was afraid of her,' Rosie said sadly.

'Weren't we all?' he said. 'I left Grace in my office and went down to talk to Beatrice. She was in high dudgeon. I can remember exactly what she said.

' "We can't spare money for her. Not a penny."

'I said: "She needs it. Only like giving her the interest early."

' "She's having a child and she isn't even married. It's not our concern," was Beatrice's reply.

' "We can't afford any more hangers on," she told me. "You waste money, Harry. You've no money sense at all – none of you Shearings has. Grace Quest won't get a penny from us. Let her stew in her own juice. Let Clive Woodley stew in hell. He's got his just deserts. So has she."

'You were jealous, weren't you, Bea? You knew Clive had asked Edwin to look after Grace. But you and I were controlling the cash, and you were succeeding in pushing me out. You refused to give Grace anything.'

'I can never forgive you for that,' Rosie told her. 'Or for pretending to despise me for being born in the workhouse, when all the time it was your fault we were there.'

She turned on Harry. 'And you could have insisted. Even if ordinary human kindness didn't dictate that you help, you knew Shearing's had an obligation.'

'I tried.'

'Not hard enough. You were taking money to buy a diamond bracelet to placate Alice. What did you do for Grace? That money might have been enough to prevent what happened to us. Any decent person in your position would have done more.'

'It just wasn't possible at the time.'

'You were too wrapped up in your own problems to think of anyone else.' Her head was throbbing. 'Tell me, how did we manage to get out of the workhouse?'

'Edwin came home. He got you out, guaranteed an income for Grace when he realised what had happened.'

'My mother had guts. After all that, she was trying

to earn a living with her paint brush. She had more strength in her little finger than you have in your whole body, Harry.'

He threw back his head and laughed. 'Whoever said women were the weaker sex? Just look at young Rosie now. You've met your match here, Bea.'

She leapt to her feet and ran to the door, but Rosie put an arm to bar her way. She was beside herself and hardly knew she was shouting.

'You really must loathe me. You've never given up trying to harm me. Of course you couldn't let me know the real reason Edwin left me a share of the business. Everybody, here and at the factory, would have despised you for that. So instead you pretended he was my father. You deliberately lied to twist the circumstances so that I'd be hurt again. You didn't want me and Ben to marry, did you?'

Rosie was only half aware of him slipping an arm round her shoulders. 'And you've just tried to hide my mother's letters from me now,' she accused. 'You've gone too far, Beatrice. Playing at God and making decisions for others.

'I wouldn't have believed anyone capable of such heartlessness. Well, it's done you no good. We all know what you are now.'

'Leave her, Rosie. We've better things to do with our time.' Ben was pulling her away.

She watched, feeling flushed with success as Beatrice fled upstairs. Beatrice would never dominate her again. She didn't look as thought she'd dominate anyone again.

'I'm not heading for the same disaster as Grace,' she

croaked. 'Not a mirror image after all.'

'Rosie, I kept telling you that.'

Scalding tears were running down her face as Ben helped her into her coat and led her down the front steps to the car. He pushed a folded handkerchief into her hand, opened the car door for her.

'What made me so proud of my family?' he mused. 'They've done terrible things.'

He started the engine and nosed the car out of the drive. 'I admired my mother for what she achieved. I admired Ainsley, and look what he did to Gran. And as for Harry . . .'

'Your father was a fair man.'

'And I'll try to be.'

'You already are, Ben. At least something good has come of it. We know now there's absolutely no reason why we shouldn't marry.'

'Other good things have come from it too, Rosie.'

'What?' she demanded. She still felt harrowed by what she'd said to Beatrice. Shaken and saddened by the revelations about Grace.

'It's changed you. Because you've had to confront my mother, you've got over your fear of her. Because you had to seek information from Constance, you've mastered your shyness.'

'I think it's called growing up.' She smiled. 'And it's made me recognise your worth, and your love.'

'Come on then,' he said. 'We'd better start looking for a house so we can get on with our life. The Shearing family may not have deserved its reputation in the past, but in future we must see that it does.'